The
DILEMMA

USA Today and *Wall Street Journal* bestselling author Meagan Brandy writes New Adult romance novels with a twist. She is a candy-crazed, jukebox junkie who tends to speak in lyrics. Born and raised in California, she is a married mother of three crazy boys who keep her bouncing from one sports field to another, depending on the season, and she wouldn't have it any other way. Starbucks is her best friend and words are her sanity.

The Deal Dilemma

MEAGAN
BRANDY

This edition first published in Great Britain in 2023 by Orion Fiction,
an imprint of The Orion Publishing Group Ltd.,
Carmelite House, 50 Victoria Embankment
London EC4Y 0DZ

An Hachette UK Company

A CIP catalogue record for this book
is available from the British Library.

ISBN (Paperback) 978 1 3987 1950 7
ISBN (eBook) 978 1 3987 1951 4

The Orion Publishing Group Ltd
Carmelite House
50 Victoria Embankment
London, EC4Y 0DZ

An Hachette UK company

Typeset by Born Group
Printed and bound in Great Britain by Clays Ltd, Elcograf S.p.A.

www.orionbooks.co.uk

To the one who hurts in ways others can only assume to understand, your worth is not measured in your mistakes, your love is not useless, and your life has more value than you know.

Chapter 1
Davis

"I don't have much time, Baby Franco, so let's hear it."

My lips pinch at the nickname, something he's called me since I was twelve, the blatant reminder that I, above all freaking else, am the baby of my family—his chosen family, that is until he washed his hands of us, unlike the faded nightclub stamp smeared along his knuckles.

It's whatever. He showed, didn't he?

Sure, he threw himself in the chair across from me, without so much as a one-armed hug, and buried his face in his phone before bothering to look at me, but again, he *is* here, which is more than I can say for the last several years.

Who's counting, right?

It went from seeing him every single day—as one does when their bedroom is directly across from your own—to every other, to once a month, then twice a year, and as of yesterday, he broke an entirely new record for us. It's been almost three years to the day since the two of us have been in the same place, at the same time, and even then, it was for no more than a wave through a dusty Mazda window, which, considering his apartment is less than a ten-minute drive from my own, is telling.

And, apparently, it's not long enough for him if the annoyed sigh pushing past his cherry-ChapStick-covered lips clues me into anything. I'll wait him out, though, because I need his undivided attention in order to ask what I brought him here to ask, so I sit back, waiting for the moody man to look up.

Several more moments, a couple seat shifts, and a flash of a frown later, he finally does. Dark, hazel eyes rimmed in gold meet mine and the hint of irritation rising in my throat simmers.

My gaze softens, a small smile pulling at my lips at the direct sight of my brother's best friend.

Best friend turned foster brother turned ex best friend, that is.

As if his thoughts mirror mine, as if I'm nothing but a reminder of the friendship he lost, Crew winces, flicking his attention away.

"When was the last time you woke up this early?" I tease, glancing at his disheveled hair and last night's hoodie.

A ghost of a grin tugs at the corner of his mouth, but he doesn't quite let it loose. "Been a while." A single beat passes, a second sigh leaving him as he leans forward, arms crossed flat on the tabletop.

Crew's eyes skim over my upper half in a long, slow pursuit, and with each passing second, the deeper the creases along his forehead become. "Your hair's different."

"Oh." Subconsciously, I reach up, running my fingers through the soft caramel-colored strands. "Yeah, I thought it would be fun to go a little darker."

"And shorter."

I nod, squashing my hands between my thighs to keep from touching it again. I had forgotten what I'd changed about myself since the last time he saw me. Chopping my long dirty-blonde hair and going brunette had been a random, rash decision, but I love it. It's short, hanging just above my collarbone, sleek and spunky. My hair never held curls anyway, so now it's ten times easier to jump up and head out the door, not like I ever spent too much time trying to do much more than that, but still. My life had become a monotonous merry-go-round—a boring circle I wanted out of—with new hair, I at least saw something new in the mirror each day.

I also stopped wearing—

"And no more contacts?" It's as if he reads my mind.

An anxious laugh escapes, and I uncross one leg, recrossing them the opposite way beneath the café table.

"My dad has to take me off his insurance when he retires this summer, so I finally gave in and had laser eye surgery."

"You're afraid of needles. And doctors."

My mouth opens and closes, his sharp memory a surprise, and I give a small shrug.

"It was . . . embarrassingly terrifying but needle-free, and I can't really afford to pay out of pocket right now, so it was kind of the only option."

And I was suitably sedated, plus or minus a Xanax or two.

His brows pull in close, and he gives a slow nod.

For a moment, he simply stares, seemingly lost in thought, but his grumpy little glare comes back, and he looks at his phone again.

If there's one thing about Crew Taylor that drives me mad, it's his ability to live in the in-between, where you show no sign of being happy or glad, mad or sad, serious or playful.

You name it, and his signals are crossed. He can go from calm, cool, and collected to ripping a dude out of a chair with no warning and serving up a fresh fistful. You never know how he feels until the moment he's ready for you to.

He and my brother were opposite in that way.

Memphis wore his emotions proudly. If he was upset, he wanted you to know. Happy, he was eager to share why. On more than one occasion, I witnessed him walk up to a total stranger and ask if they were okay, simply offering them someone to talk with. He would say he felt they needed it, and so there he was, an ear for anyone who needed one. Of course, it worked both ways.

The source of Memphis's anger was made unmistakably clear, but it was Crew who would step in when that happened. It was part of the reason he and Crew fit so well as friends: what one lacked, the other made up for in spades.

Not to say they weren't similar; they were. Their likes and dislikes were matched, be it games or food, clothes or hairstyles.

Both were silly and shameless, outspoken, and athletic, so much so, they'd bet on who could get a random girl's number at the fairs or school football games.

Baseball was their game of choice, so they ate up all the attention they could snag under the Friday night lights.

There was so much bait tossed their way; it's a shock they didn't puke.

Pretty sure I gagged a time or two.

But there was always a different kind of shadow that hovered over Crew, and sometimes, he couldn't quite step out from under it.

"I don't have a lot of time," Crew complains with a quick flick of his gaze.

"You don't have work until seven."

His head snaps upright as my lips smack closed, my eyes bulging, but only for a second.

I'm about to apologize when his familiar chuckle warms the air, and this time, while it only holds for a split second, his grin slips free, the small scar along his chin becoming more defined, revealing a new one just left of the other.

Yeah, he's textbook "take me to bed," as the headline would read if you opened a book cataloging men and the thoughts they induce on sight.

He'd be the first photo featured.

His skin is forever tan, body trim yet toned, though looking at him in his hoodie, his shoulders seem to span wider than before. His dark-brown hair is still short on the sides, a pile of lazy waves on top.

Just how I like it.

Crew leans back, crossing his arms. "Been checking up on me, huh?"

"I'd say old habits die hard, but I'm not old, and I don't see this one dying."

His eyes hold mine. "Tell me why you asked me to come here, Sweets."

Sweets.

Man, I haven't heard that one in a long time. Little does he know not much has changed. I still have a solid stash of snacks—all of the sugary nature—in my bag as we speak. That's what he called me before, "Baby Franco," and after, on the rarest occasions, of course. Like when he was drunk and goofy.

Like when he—

The lift of his dark brow snaps me out of my thoughts, and I remember why I called him here.

Not that I forgot. I obsessed over it. *Stressed* over it.

Ate three pounds of chocolate and got sick over it . . .

Each time I tried to talk myself out of calling him, it worked. I mean, it had been a long time since we talked.

So, I texted him instead.

"Right, so . . ." I sit up in my chair, folding my hands and laying them on the table, holding his eyes with mine. I square my shoulders, give a curt nod, and grin.

"I want you to take my virginity."

Chapter 2
Davis

Okay, so I anticipated some shock, a chuckle or two, and definitely expected to see the look-away grin thing he does—where he really wants to smile at what I say but doesn't want me to know he's smiling.

What I did not expect was his face to remain so incredibly blank. Like, *blank* blank.

I'm talking if a wax figure of Crew Taylor existed, I'd swear someone froze time, kidnapped the real Crew, and placed the art version of him in front of me. He's that still. That freaking stuck.

"So . . ." I drag out when I take several sips of hot tea and wax Crew doesn't so much as lower those long lashes. "I wrote out the pros and cons, and when that started to go in an entirely different direction—don't ask—I decided . . ." I dig into my book bag, pulling out the clear protective-sleeve-covered paper inside it.

"You wrote an essay." He speaks so monotone I have to wonder if he meant to say those words in his head, but then, with measured movements, his fingertips come down on the table, slowly pressing, stretching, and gliding along the painted iron. "You wrote an essay?"

I nod.

"About why you and me should have sex?"

"Yes," I say instantly, but then shake my head. "I mean no."

He frowns. "Yes or no?"

"Yes *and* no." I sit forward, set the plastic slip down, and tap it with my pointer finger. "It's a persuasive essay detailing all the reasons why *you* should have sex with *me*." I sit back, folding my hands in my lap.

It's simple, really brief, precise, and only took me a few days.

We won't talk about the many months of planning and pep talks leading to this moment.

Crew's gaze sharpens. "You do realize it takes two people to have sex, right?"

"Right, but—"

"No buts." He leans forward, his eyes locked on mine. "*Sex* is not one sided."

"Will you stop saying sex over and over again?"

His eyes widen as his head tugs back. "You want to *have* sex, but you can't handle hearing the word?"

"I can handle it fine. It's science. I am *great* at science." *Did he forget who he's talking to*? "But the girl to your left looks over every time you say it."

"Fuck me." He runs his large hands down his face, and his attention falls back on me, with a heavy, set glare. "*Sex*," he says even louder than before. "Should not be looked at as science, just like it's not one person fucking the other. It's about both people. Who they are, how they know each other, what both want, like, and how they like it."

"Well . . ." My face flames and I know my skin is wildly flushed. His eyes dart to my cheekbones, inadvertently confirming what I did not need confirmed. "I know you; you know how we know each other, and the rest you can fill me in on. It's not rocket science. There is a proper practice for everything, and I'm more than sure if sex were an exam, you'd ace it. You could probably lead a lecture on it."

"Stop," he snaps.

I scowl. "Stop what?"

"Doing that."

"Doing what?"

His jaw clenches, and when this happens, nothing good can come of it.

Like that one time we went to Six Flags and the probability of getting a sunburn was literally not even a question and so me and Drew, Crew's superhot, younger than him, but older than me, brother took turns putting it on each other. Crew, being prone to punching, gave his brother a fat lip while mine ripped his wristband off. Poor guy had to go get back in line, and by the time he made it inside again, we were long gone.

Okay, that was mild. He and Drew boxed all the time, but still! Lock-jawed Crew means he's annoyed, and when he's annoyed, you can only sit back and wait for whatever happens next.

Typically, it's a slightly stressful shit show.

Suddenly, he jerks to his feet, tucking his phone back in his pocket. "I don't know why I'm listening to this shit. Go to class, Baby Franco." He shoves the paper back at me. "And get rid of this fucking thing."

"You didn't even read it."

An incredulous laugh leaves him, and he tosses cash on the table, even though he didn't order a dang thing. "I don't need to read it."

He starts leaving, so I quickly snatch up my bag, the paper he left behind, and follow him.

"So, you agree, then?" I ask once we're outside the little patio area.

"What, no!" He jerks to a stop, spinning to face me. "I do not agree. You shouldn't agree, either. You're not doing this."

"I am twenty-one and a virgin. That is like . . . that's like graduating high school having never kissed anyone before."

He blinks, crossing his arms over his chest.

Tucking the extremely convincing, if I do say so myself, essay under my arm, I reach into my bag once more. "I hoped I was wrong, but I pretty much knew I wasn't."

Crew lifts a dark brow, so I lift one right back.

I tear out the *second* clear sleeve with another paper. "Which is why I *also* wrote this."

"Davis—"

"You know when I would sneak into your room at night to play *Clue*, and you would swear I always found a way to cheat, so I would win?"

His eyes narrow, and my grin grows.

"I never cheated. I simply outsmarted you, but this, it kind of feels like cheating, because I know it ensures I win."

His brows are nearly touching now. "You are out of your mind if you think I will have anything to do with this." He creeps closer. "And you're downright dumb if you think I'll allow anyone else to either."

"You've always claimed I was kind of crazy." Shoving the paper in his chest, I shrug, and then I head to class, knowing at some point, Crew will call.

Until then, I'll keep getting waxed.

I'm nothing if not prepared.

Chapter 3
Davis

Stubborn, I swear. It's not like I asked him to give me a baby.

Ohh, that's a perfect idea for my "unmarried at thirty-five" backup plan!

Wait, focus. One use of his anatomy at a time, and *time* is precious, something Crew apparently doesn't seem to grasp.

It's been nine days since I asked him to help me with my little problem. By the third, when I hadn't heard a word, I half expected an angry voice mail from my dad, but nooo. Mister Cool Cat Crew didn't even bother to snitch me out. He used to tell on me to Memphis all the time and then Memphis would play dad, even though we had a perfectly strict one of those already. It was annoying.

It's funny how the things that drive you batty about a person are the things you miss most.

Day five made everything clear. He was pretending I didn't ask him to give me the *D*.

But I did. And he knows I did.

So, by the sixth day, I decided to remind him by sending him a cherry emoji, following it up with the explosion one, and a pair of begging hands.

He *did* respond, but only with a single, four-letter word I hate, being it's been his go-to when it comes to me since forever.

Ugh!

So yeah, it's the ninth day, and I'm pissed, so I pull up the message thread, glaring at the word "stop," and I swear it grows big and bold and mocking.

And blurry, but that could be the half bottle of grocery store wine I've consumed.

Wedging the bottle between my legs, I jolt when the chill meets my thighs, and text the maddening man again.

Me: In case you have forgotten, I always sucked at the silent game my mom tried to trick us into playing on road trips.

Me: I don't like silence.

Me: It makes me want to scream.

Me: So maybe I'll keep being annoying and texting one line at a time.

Me: Over and over until you respond.

Me: It could work.

I go to text another random spew of nonsense, but before I can, those three little dots appear in the thread, and I grin. A grin that falls flat five seconds later.

Crew: I'm at work. Stop.

There's that word again!

Me: Say you agree.

Five minutes go by, and I groan, take a swig from the bottle, and send another message.

Me: Don't make me beg. I am not above begging. I will literally get on my knees, Crew.

Crew: Swear to god, girl. Quit, or I'll call your dad.

My mouth gapes. See! "Ass!"

Me: Okay, sure. Tell him his sweet, perfectly virginal daughter is asking his second son to deflower her in exchange for a 1939 Chevy half ton!

Annoyed, I hop off the edge of the bed and begin pacing the room. What if he *is* calling my dad? At this very moment?

Oh my god, what if Crew *does* tell him I offered him what was supposed to be my brother's prized possession in exchange for something so . . . trivial. I mean, I know virginity is important to a lot of people. Some want to wait until they're married, and that's fantastic. Commendable, really. Yay them.

I, however, am not one of those people. I'm only a virgin because the opportunity to rid myself of the title has never been naked before me or I probably would have grabbed hold—hopefully requiring *both* hands—but again, I've yet to get the chance.

It's probably because I like to stay busy. Always. I work and go to school and guys are . . . difficult. To be fair, most of the men I talk to are hungover customers, looking for the perfect meal to settle their queasy stomachs. That or their polar opposite and instead of liquor, they get book drunk, thinking they're smarter than me, and speak as if they're fresh off page five of *Communication Essentials for Dummies.*

To be fair: they're also not Crew.

I squeal when my phone rings, peeking at the screen out of the corner of one eye. The utter relief that washes over me when it's not my dad's smiling face greeting me, but the sneaky side profile shot I took and programmed for Crew is embarrassing.

Maybe it's the alcohol, but I end up staring at the screen rather than answering, and then it stops. Seconds later, his text comes through, and I growl.

This man is impossible, but liquor can help with that.

Picking up the pink-colored wine, I take another swig.

Crew

I swear to fucking God, if I wasn't working, I'd need a damn drink, times ten. Had I lacked self-control, I'd have busted out a bottle the morning she begged me to meet her, saying the last fucking thing I'd ever expected to leave those lips.

It's like she's gone mad.

For real mad.

I don't even know why I'm entertaining this conversation. Should turn my fucking phone off already.

Should but don't.

Instead of calling me back, she sends another message.

Davis: You should really say yes. You won't like the alternative.

What the hell is she talking about?

Glaring at my screen, I pretend I didn't already give her the only possible fucking answer.

Me: What happens if I say no?

Davis: Are you saying no?

Me: Sweets.

Davis: Salts.

A scoffed laugh escapes me, and I kick off the wall, glancing toward the end of the alleyway when drunken laughter reaches me.

I sigh when my phone vibrates in my hand.

Davis: If you won't take my virginity, I'll find someone else who will.

"What the fuck?" Frustration heats my chest, my fingers flying over the keys.

Me: You can't go shopping for dick in a bookstore.

Davis: No . . . but you can in a bar.

"Oh, hell no." I whip around, heading for the sidewalk instead of turning to the back exit I came out of. My phone is at my ear in seconds, but all I get is her voice mail.

"Hi, you reached Davis, I'm either in class or effectively ignoring your call."

"Swear to you, Baby Franco, you do something dumb, I'll—" I cut myself off, hanging up with a huff.

I was going to say whoop that ass, but considering what she's asking, she'd probably assume that meant I was agreeing to her "offer," as she called it.

An offer.

"Relieve her of her virginal status" as she so callously put it in the damn contract she typed up, "in exchange" for her brother's rebuilt 1939, dusty-red Chevy half ton. The one we spent two summers fixing up alongside his father and grandfather before he passed. The one Memphis spent a year saving for the final part to get it on the road, but never had the chance to get it installed.

Mad. She's gone fucking mad.

Memphis isn't around anymore to give me a hand in what we liked to call "don't be dumb, Davis," not that I'd hit him up if he were, and I'd never call her pops, even though I threatened to. He doesn't need the stress and spilling something like this to him might send the old man into a heart attack. He went through enough with his son to have to worry his daughter has lost her damn mind, and only weeks before her college graduation.

It's not like I'd want help with this anyway. No way I'd listen to what someone else thought was right, wrong, or too much. She's too fucking much, and I didn't go through all the shit I did, stay away all this fucking time, to allow her to pull this.

There's no fucking way.

You'd have to quit ignoring her to stop her.

Grinding my teeth, I curve around the small line outside the bar, patting the bouncer on the shoulder as I walk by. "Last name Franco doesn't pass the door."

"You got it, boss."

Shoving my way through the entrance, I slip behind the bar.

Drew nods his chin from the other side, but I shake my head and get back to picking up my employees' slack.

She might have hinted at knowing where I work when I did my best to keep it from her, but Matt won't let her past the door. No way she'll Uber her ass all the way down here, and she's too chicken to go out alone, so that scratches the bars by campus.

Her little plot twist will have to wait another night.

Minute by minute, the place grows fuller, and before I know it, I'm drowning in orders, passing out free shots just to get the area clear for all the others waiting to get up here to order.

One minute I'm pouring vodka on the rocks, and the next, I look up, locking onto a pair of eyes that shine like malt whiskey.

Davis smiles wide, pushing a twenty-dollar bill across the wooden bar top. "Drink please, something extra sweet."

Fuck.

Chapter 4
Davis

Rag in one hand, liquor bottle in the other, Crew stands perfectly still, his eyes icy sharp and pinned on me.

This look used to scare me. It's dark, dangerous, and daring you to make a move while promising no matter what you choose, it's the wrong one.

When angry Crew comes out to play, everyone loses.

I learned that in junior high when I snuck two bottles of Corona from the ice chest I was tasked to clean out after a trip. Jimmy Hanson, a kid from down the street, came over, and we rode to the park, hid behind the bathrooms to "indulge" in a flavor I could only describe as warm piss. Not that we had a chance to stomach more than what was held in the neck. Crew found us too fast, and all hell broke loose.

Jimmy's nose didn't fare too well.

And then Jimmy's older brother Johnny came to the house ready for a fight.

His nose didn't look so hot in the end either, and my bike tires were right there with him.

That was the first time my mom grounded Crew. Discipline was new to him, being his parents didn't parent *at all*, but my hot, older neighbor crush turned foster brother took it in stride. Mostly.

He did sneak out the window once, but only so he could chaperone my eighth-grade dance alongside Memphis. Pretty sure my dad was in on that one, though.

Why else would the alarms on the windowsills mysteriously be off that night?

The second time he was grounded was when he boxed the kid across the street's older brother for fun . . . and a crisp hundred-dollar bill. He used his winnings to pay for his baseball uniform before my dad had a chance to cover the fees for him. Pretty sure my dad only pretended to ground him that time.

Crew never did well with handouts, always working to earn his keep and fighting for that sense of independence.

Sometimes literally.

Maybe if I weren't slightly intoxicated—heavy on the slightly—I'd still fear the wrath of Crew Taylor, but for some reason, I find the sharp angles of his forever-frustrated facial expressions quite entertaining.

He's pissed, but I warned him good and well.

If you really think about it, it's his fault I'm here.

It's not until a girl with dark hair stretches her arm across his chest to try and reach whatever it is he's blocked that he shows any sign of life.

Familiar with his surroundings, he lowers the bottle back into its place without so much as a glance, drapes the cloth over his shoulder, and leans forward on his forearm, bringing us eye level.

He pushes my twenty back toward me. "Go home. Now."

I tap my lip as if contemplating his command, but I don't get a chance to say a word.

"Davis." He says my name like a warning. A hot, growly one. "Go. I will call you tomorrow."

"Why? So you can deny me in the daylight?" I grab hold of the chair beside me, attempting to hoist myself into it, without looking away as he had with the bottle, but I slip a little, forcing me to focus on the task at hand. Giggling at myself, I hoist my body up and turn to him once more.

He stares, shock drawing a line between his brows. "Are you drunk?"

"This is a bar, is it not?"

"You just walked in."

"Maybe I drank earlier. Maybe I didn't."

"You're going home." He yanks the rag off his shoulder and tosses it to the counter.

"I just got here!"

"*I* don't give a shit." Crew begins curving around the edge we're near, so he can get to the same side I'm on, but even as he passes person after person, he keeps his eyes connected to mine with each and every step.

He's almost to me now, his lips pressed in a firm, angry line.

"Well, fuck me! Is that my future wife?!"

Crew stops midstep, and my attention snaps toward the voice, to the blur of bronzed skin flying around the opposite side of where I am.

"Drew!" My smile is wide. "You're here, and you're . . . wow." My gaze falls to his strong neck, up and over his strong shoulders, all to drag back down to the deep cuts visible through his army-green shirt. Damn.

"You're like . . . *wow*, wow."

Hands lock into the armrest of my barstool right then, and my shoulders are nudged a hair. My neck stretches to glance behind me, finding Crew pressed at my back. He's so close I have to lean forward an inch to see his face. The way he stares down his nose like a disappointed father has me ready to roll my eyes, but my knee is nudged, so I turn back to his brother.

"My god, Drew. What did you do in Yosemite, wrestle bears and eat them for dinner?"

Drew's smirk is playfully insufferable as he leans down, wrapping his arms around me until I'm lifted off the seat. "You look good too, wifey." He kisses my cheek.

"Back behind the bar," Crew barks, his palms coming down on my shoulders, pressing my ass back into the black leather.

Drew's dimples grow more defined, and he lifts his hands. "Don't shoot. I was only hugging the girl." He looks to me quickly. "I'll find you later and fill you in on them bears, huh?" he teases, tossing me a wink as he gets back to work.

I sigh, watching him go.

The genes in that family, I swear.

Swift and sudden, my chair is spun, causing my hands to shoot out and latch on to the faux leather for dear life.

Crew is there, bending to my level, his musky, minty man smell all up in my soused senses.

He glares, and it's as glorious as ever.

"If I didn't fire someone yesterday and have another person call out tonight, we would be out the door already," he promises. "If I don't start pouring drinks, this place is gonna get crazy. If it gets crazy, I'll have to whoop some ass. If I have to whoop ass, yours will be one of them. Got me?" My chest flushes, and he continues, "Sit. Do not move. And wait."

Ugh!

I'm about to argue, but then a pretty pink drink is lifted over my shoulder, a large candy straw with an umbrella sticking out of it.

Crew groans, and I spin so I'm facing the bar again, smiling at Drew as he passes it to me.

"Extra sweet, just for you."

"Why, thank you, kind sir." I accept, and off he goes, but not before flipping his gaze to the brute at my back.

Pulling the sweet straw between my lips, I flick my eyes to Crew.

Jaw clenched, he gets back to work, his eyes bouncing my way every few minutes, but as soon as my drink is long gone, the sour candy nothing but remnants along my lips, I forget to pay attention to whether or not he is and hit the dance floor.

I can't say for sure when I went from slithering snake to super sloth, but it definitely happened. My body is heavy, my feet unsteady, and as I turn, I'm ten seconds from taking a tumble, but a steady hand comes to my rescue.

My eyes manage to meet the man's in front of me, and two-point-five seconds later, the security the blond beast's stature provided—who saved me from face-planting—is long gone. The next thing I know, I'm transported back to summer camp before eighth grade, when I busted my head and Crew thought I was dying. He swept me up in his arms and carried me all the way to the office. Except there are no big, bright butterflies in mismatched frames on these walls, instead messy files and notepads lie randomly on a rickety, chipped bookcase.

Crew tosses me on a tiny cot in the corner and points his long, strong finger my way.

"We're twenty fucking minutes from closing." He speaks through gritted teeth. "Think you can keep your ass where it is until then?"

Sure, he phrased it as a question, but it was so not a question, and he's already on his way out the door when he says it. I manage to give a half nod before he slams it with his exit.

With an exasperated huff and blurry vision, I push to my feet.

And then I snoop around what must be his office.

Crew

The crowd doesn't linger too long after last call, leaving no more than a handful of stragglers to arrange rides for, but in a frustrating twist of events, I'm standing here wishing there were a dozen. Two fucking dozen. Anything to keep me from having to go back into that office and lift a limp Davis into my arms so I can get her into the bed she belongs in . . . which is no-fucking-body's but her own.

A fact she doesn't seem to understand.

Four days. I glared at her little "offer," printed on baby-blue paper, I might fucking add, for four days before I finally read it over, only to find the sneaky little thing had a copy of the essay I shoved back at her hidden behind it. Read them both, put them back, and did it again the next day.

And again the day after that.

Each time was worse, bringing with it guilt I can't place.

One of the many fucking problems I'm having is knowing Davis Franco is no liar. She's not conniving or manipulative, both rare, desirable qualities. Both annoying as fuck in this specific circumstance, as it means she's not only certain I'm the man to do what she wants done, but dead serious. She knows what she's asking for, and she's ready to do what needs to be done to make it happen.

As if giving her body away isn't worth more than a hunk of fucking metal, sentimental value or not. A perfectly pristine, limited-edition hunk of metal, yeah, but that changes nothing. Her body's worth more and she should know this.

Her mama would lose her shit if she knew what her baby girl was up to.

I'm about to lose mine, almost did tonight.

The bloodstain on my shoulder from a certain blond bitch who dared to touch her did nothing to ease my irritation.

She's lucky I didn't—

"Are you restocking those bottles or testing their durability?"

My head whips left, and I glare at Paula, the only server I can depend on.

"Spoiler alert? They're not shatterproof. Clay has the scars to prove it." She chuckles as if her busting a bottle over her boyfriend's head ain't no thing. "Not much to do in here. I'm on for another hour, and Drew's getting the last of the drunkies into their Ubers as we speak." She jerks her head toward the back. "Go, take the girl home, but hurry back, so you can tell me who she is."

When my frown deepens, she laughs louder, tossing the used rags in a basket and carrying them around the corner.

Sighing, I set the crate of liquor on the countertop and head for my office, shocked as shit when Davis isn't out cold but leaning against the desk chair, staring at the bookcase against the back wall.

She turns when the door creaks behind me, stumbling over her own feet, but I dart forward, catching her upper arm before she can trip.

Bloodshot and half-closed copper eyes meet mine. Davis giggles, smashing her lips to one side as she stares up at me.

"Crew Taylor," she whispers. "Who knew you could be so . . ."

"So what?" I prompt, moving my hands to her hips, steadying her.

"So . . . unorganized."

I scoff, shuffling back a few inches to put some space between us.

Davis waves a drunken hand at the files she's stacked two times too high on the small wooden desk.

"I found coupons"—she points to the garbage can—"that expired in January. It's May."

"Surprised your vision's clear enough to read the dates."

She grins wider. "That makes two of us."

I'm tempted to smile at the brat. "Time to go home, Baby Franco."

"K, but fair warning, if I try to move, I *might* fall. Or puke. I had seventy-seven percent of a bottle of wine to the dome, and I left nothing from the drink Drew gave me. I even licked the rim."

"Seventy-seven percent, huh?" I pull the string on the light a couple times to turn the fan on.

"Possibly seventy-nine."

"Sounds about right." I guide her through the door, and sure enough, she trips over nothing, causing her to laugh and fall against the wall.

Her head rolls along the wood until her gaze finds mine and she lifts her arms like a child. "Commander Crew to the rescue?"

Shaking my head, I bend, cradling her in my arms, instantly regretting it when the silky pads of her fingertips come up, tapping along the skin just above my collar.

"How come you don't want to help me?" she begins to slur. "Your choice of words on this subject is bullshit."

Davis's head snaps up, and she tries to glare, but since she's so trashed, she only manages to look cross-eyed at me. "Oh, come on. Like people haven't offered you less, and you haven't accepted with ease. At least you get something out of this."

"Stop," I snap, cutting off her bullshit as I round the corner, taking the four short steps down to the main floor with quicker movements than I should with her in my arms.

Accept with ease, she said.

Yeah, fucking right.

"Come on, Crew," she whines, undeterred. "You don't even have to like it."

For fuck's sake.

"Just slide in and—" She cuts herself off, a loud, popping sound pushing past her lips.

I jerk to a stop, glaring down at her, but she tugs herself up, looking up and over my shoulder when my brother's loud-ass laughter fills the space.

"Hey, Drew." She smiles.

"Hey, gorgeous," he teases, his eyes sliding to mine in question.

"Go away."

"No, wait!" Davis wiggles, but I don't let her go, so she tips her head all the way back, looking at him upside down while I keep moving for the door. "What do you think, Drew? Shouldn't he help me if he's capable of helping?"

"I say give the girl whatever it is she's asking for." He chuckles, and I'm about to slap him upside his head.

He has no idea what she's asking for.

"Aw," she practically fucking coos. "See, you're the sweet one. That's why I used to pretend you were my boyfriend."

She did what?

Davis jolts then. "Oh my god! You could totally—"

"Okay." I shift, tossing her over my shoulder, and get the hell out.

Enough of that shit.

Is she about to throw her crazy my brother's way? My brother, who would probably jump straight to it, taking what she claims she's ready to give as if he was worthy of it.

He's not.

I'm sure as fuck not.

Why's she doing this?

"Swear to God, if I could whoop your ass, girl," I mumble as I buckle her into my front seat.

"Hmm?" she hums, attempting to get her lids to open.

"Nothing. Go to sleep." I slam the door, taking a few deep breaths before climbing in on the driver's side.

If I didn't help her dad move her into her apartment three summers ago, I'd have no idea where I was going. I haven't been back inside since that day, the bullshit her brother dragged me into forcing my fucking hand in ways she couldn't imagine, but I remember well which one it is.

Might have passed by a couple times on my way wherever.

She doesn't stir once on the drive, so I figure she's sleeping, but as I turn off the engine at the curb of her place, she sits up, smearing black shit all over her face as she rubs at her sleepy eyes. I help her to the door, trying to keep quiet once inside so we don't wake her roommate if she's home.

"Same room?"

Davis nods. "Wait, wait."

I freeze.

"The wine bottle, it's on the counter. Throw it away in the dumpster outside? It can't be in the house."

My lips form a tight line, and I can almost hear her unspoken thought . . . *just in case*. But I nod and she closes her eyes.

"Thanks."

She's feeling like shit now. Her brows are caved, and she groans as I lower her to the bed. She manages to get her shoes kicked off and her blanket pulled over her on her own, even if she is lying on top of the other half of it.

In the kitchen, I search for a water bottle, but she has none, so I fill a cup from the sink and take it to her.

She's already breathing softly, but I bend down, giving her a little shake and her lids peel open. She smiles at the cup and pushes onto her elbow.

"Such a do-gooder," she slurs, taking a small drink before lying back down and closing her eyes again. "But won't do me gooder than someone else will."

I can't stop the small chuckle that escapes, and her lips twitch.

Davis sighs, my name leaving her lips in a soft, longing whisper.

Moving her hair from her face, I push out a deep breath, slowly rising to my feet.

The girl has no idea how far I've gone to protect her.

From the world and from me.

"Missed you too, Sweets," I murmur.

And then I get the fuck out of there.

Chapter 5
Davis

My alarm went off at eight this morning, but after several uses of the beloved snooze button, it was nearly nine by the time I whined my way into the shower. Of course, the extra bit of craptastic sleep left me with a whole three minutes to get ready and rush out the door.

The diner is kitty-corner to my apartment complex, so I jaywalk my way to work most days, unless I have to haul ass from school and don't have time to drop my car off first. Thankfully, all that is almost over.

The end of May is in sight.

Lucky for me, my manager gets one look, takes pity on my poor, hungover soul, and tells me to go home. I've never been much for arguing, so I oblige, doing the math in my head on how much I'll need to save of last shift's tips to cover the loss today.

Car after car zooms past, but before I can dredge up the strength to dash across the road, I decide home will have to wait. So I start toward one of my favorite places on earth.

7-Eleven.

Normally, I get a medium Slurpee, but today, I break out the big guns, going for the thirty-two-ounce full of every single flavor outside of piña colada, and snag the biggest-framed glasses I could find.

Right as I drop onto my preferred grassy patch at the park by my complex, my phone rings, Crew's side snapshot lighting up the screen.

I really need to update that photo.

Accepting his call, I quickly swap it to FaceTime.

Several seconds of silence pass and I assume he isn't interested in a visual conversation. Then the screen is filled with him. The man is still in bed, face half covered with a blue blanket, left arm draped above his head.

Tired hazel eyes blink, quickly narrowing. "Up and out already?"

"It's practically noon."

"It's not even ten."

"I said practically."

He licks his lips, eyeing me. "I thought for sure you were still drooling all over your pillow."

My mouth gapes. "I do not drool."

"We shared a tent for years, kid. You drool."

"Whatever, *old man*."

His grin is a gorgeous mix of entertained and exhausted, unfortunately, as quickly as it comes, he cuts it, and he turns away from the screen. "Where are you?" he asks without looking back.

Straw between my teeth, I press a few buttons on my phone, and his gaze returns with a slight squint.

"It's ridiculous you can send someone your exact location like that."

"My dad thinks it's the best invention since Pop-Tarts."

"He still obsessed with those things?"

"Oh yeah. He calls me every time he comes across a new wacky kind. He found root beer flavored ones once."

"That sounds like shit."

I grin. "Knew you'd say that."

Crew stares a moment before slowly pushing into a sitting position.

My attention is instantly drawn to the bronzy bare skin of his solid and powerful chest, which is now impressively decorated with several shades of black ink. "Um, excuse me, did you have a secret relationship with Kat Von D you're not allowed to talk about, that why you've been MIA nearly the entire time I've lived here?"

His eyes fly up, narrowing, but then quick enough, he realizes what I'm referring to, and suddenly, I'm staring at a black screen. "Don't move."

He hangs up.

Being I had zero plans to move until my temples stopped pounding, I play golden retriever and obey his command.

Crew

I spot her instantly. She's lying flat on the grass, a giant pair of bright-yellow shades covering half her face. If it weren't for the protective hold she has on the massive Slurpee, I'd swear she was out.

Completely fucking oblivious, as usual.

I take the last three steps toward her, pausing with my shoes a foot from her head.

"I could murder you right now and you'd have never seen me coming."

Her eyes open behind the cheaply tinted glasses.

"What are you doing?"

"Waiting for my headache to morph into a sugar rush, so I can move without feeling like Travis Barker is giving me a personal show from inside my brain."

I lift a brow. "That bad?"

"The baddest. I'm talking Memphis the morning after Sarah Hall broke up with him, senior year, and you snuck from my dad's liquor cabinet to help."

Her eyes fall the moment she says it, and a long breath pushes past my lips.

I'm not the one who stole that bottle, but there's no reason to tell her so, not that it matters anymore.

A moment later, she pats the slightly overgrown grass, so I drop beside her.

"If I get bit by a gang of red ants—"

"I'll rub you down with ointment like I did last time," she interrupts, the smile on her lips heard, but I glance over to catch it anyway.

That was a long time ago. She was maybe twelve, and Memphis was too grossed out by the welts that spread along my legs and torso to touch them, but Davis wasn't, so she dropped to her knees as fast as I could get the ointment out of my bag. I remember how much her little hands shook that day. She was trying to be quick to soothe the sting, but it was more than that. She was terrified of the allergic reaction, kept asking if I could breathe and made me recap the entire morning to keep me talking. Her mom had introduced her to an old movie called *My Girl* that week, so Sweets was feelin' extra uneasy.

But we're not kids anymore, so if she dropped to her knees and started rubbing her hands all over me while looking up with sweet, scared eyes like that day . . .

Nope.

Does she really think I would fuck her for the fuck of it?

There's no fucking way.

She's lying straight, her head pointed at the cloudy sky, eyes closed, so I stare at her a moment. At the soft curve of her cheeks, a little narrower and more defined than before, and long, dark lashes that seem to have gotten longer, brushing against them.

No fucking way.

"I can feel you thinking. Watching me." Her voice is soft, almost sad, and she takes a deep breath. "Just say it, Crew. It's okay."

Drawing one leg up, I stare at the slight shake of the tree's limbs around us. "What is it you think I'm here to say?"

"That you can't or won't *make me a woman,*" she teases herself, but an annoyed huff follows. "You don't have to bring morals and values into this, you know? It can be simple."

"As simple as a business deal, right?"

She peeks at me from the corner of her glasses, and I pull her "offer" out of my pocket, holding it out between us. She nibbles at her lip.

"This is kind of fucked up." I nod toward the folded paper. "You're trying to back me into a corner."

"I know," she admits in a whisper. "But I only raised Thor's hammer *after* you gave me the *here goes delusional Davis* look."

"You had it ready, Davis. An essay and this. Why?"

"Because I know you," she mutters. "And I knew you'd need something worth your while to . . . touch me."

Damn. That's—

Damn close to what I expected you to say.

Clearing my throat, I push to my feet and shove the paper toward her, but she scrambles to hers just as fast, cradling her head in her hand with a wince.

"Crew, wait. I didn't mean, I don't know what I meant."

"Yeah, you do, Baby Franco." Pulling the little orange and white packet from my pocket, I pass it to her. "Take these. They'll help with the hangover. You'll be good before lunch."

I walk off, but Davis darts forward, jumping in front of me.

"I'm sorry." She pushes the glasses up on her head, her features pinched with panic. "Crew, I'm sorry, okay?"

Holding in my sigh, I look into her bloodshot eyes.

Still can't stand the thought of me being mad at you, Sweets?

Reaching out, I push her hair from her face, tucking it behind her ear, and her frown deepens.

"If you think you're worthless than or equal to a fucking car, then your virginity is the least of your problems."

"You have no idea." Her response is quick, quiet, and possibly unintentional.

Unexpected from my end, and for whatever reason, the irritation whirling in my gut twists.

"You'd really sell Memph's truck if I don't do this? Your grandpa left it for him."

Guilt washes over her, and she tries to lower her head, but I don't allow it, holding her still with my knuckle under her chin. "You're not supposed to ask me that."

"Come on, Baby Franco, tell me."

With a sad smile, she shakes her head. "It's not his anymore, Crew."

"Keep going."

The sorrow in her smile fades, her lips quirking a bit higher at my ability to read her. She gives me a long look, quietly admitting, "If anyone should have it, it's you. You know that. You put in more work on that truck than anyone."

My chest inflates with a full breath, and I drop my hand, glancing to the side. "This isn't like when you asked me to kiss you when we came back home that summer. You understand that, right?"

"Well . . ."

My head snaps up at her sugary, coaxing tone, and I frown at her gleeful expression.

"Davis."

She's grinning now and draws her shoulders up to her ears in a long, slow-released shrug. "I mean, it kind of is."

I jerk back. "No, it's not."

"Come on, Crew. I had two whole friends, and both had boyfriends going into my senior year, and I was too chicken to talk to their boyfriends' friends because I knew a kiss would follow at some point and I hadn't kissed anyone yet. Not that you agreed when I asked anyway."

"This is completely fucking different."

"It's basically the exact same thing."

"Girl, I swear, you're making me wanna—"

She's laughing now, and for whatever reason, I cut myself off with a low huffed chuckle. It quickly becomes a sigh, and hers follows.

She's always been one to light the fire, just to see what happens. Especially with me.

Almost as if she does it on purpose.

Brat probably does.

My phone goes off with an incoming text, so I look at the screen.

Paula: SOS. Breaker blew again.

Me: Fuck. What's that the third time this month now?

Paula: Fourth, and Jose didn't show again, so I can't get into the basement.

Fucking great.

Me: On my way.

"I have to go," I tell her, shoving my phone back in my pocket.

Giant yellow glasses greet me when I look up again, and Davis nods, having expected as much.

"Look."

Look what? I have no fucking clue what I want to say to her right now.

She's nutty is one thought, but I've known that for years. It's part of her charm. It's also not worth mentioning. Davis is fully aware her little mind works in wild ways that others don't.

"Go, Crew." She attempts a smile, but it's tight.

I go, ignoring how each step takes a whole lot of fucking effort.

It's hours later when I'm back lying in bed, staring at the cracks in the corner of my ceiling, when my phone beeps with a notification. Drew is live on Instagram.

Baited by curiosity, I click the link and watch him bullshit with the few dozen people who hopped on, but then he shifts in his seat, tilting his phone to his right.

Davis sits beside him with a smile, and I fly into a sitting position.

"What the fuck?"

At his instruction, she waves at the screen, and in the beat of a second, her cheeks grow a familiar shade of red. In an attempt to cover the blush, she lifts what looks to be a Shirley Temple in cheers and draws it to her glossy lips. Drew does the same, and I recognize the space around them.

The glasses they're using.

The seats they're sitting on.

They're in the fucking bar.

Instantly, her words from last night come barreling back.

That's why I used to pretend you were my boyfriend . . . you could totally help . . .

My fingers tighten around the phone, and I force my feet still.

Drew props his phone on something as he scoots closer to Davis and challenges her to a game of thumb war.

Her slender shoulders straighten, and she smiles, offering him her hand.

The bastard presses his lips to her knuckles, and my eyes fly to hers, waiting for her reaction.

She gives none, not even her famous shy, subconscious look down.

They play their little game, laughing and starting over an annoying number of times, tempting me to disconnect. I don't and finally her hand is free of his.

Drew focuses on the viewers then and begins answering questions people ask while Davis drags her finger through the condensation building along her glass.

My brother's talking, but I'm not listening. I'm watching her. The way she moves, laughs, speaks.

The way she's watching him, curious and slightly amused.

I shrink the live feed, so I can still watch while texting her.

Me: Did you mean what you said last night?

She pulls her phone from her little purse, a small smile crossing her lips as her fingers fly across the screen.

Davis: You know me. I need specifics.

Of course you do, Sweets.

Me: You said if I won't take your virginity, you'll find someone else who will.

Me: You mean that?

I look at her face, to the bitten-back smirk threatening to cross it.

Oh, you think this is funny, do you?

Davis lifts her chin a bit, and I know before it comes through the answer is yes.

Davis: Yes, but I want it to be you.

"Fuck." My eyes clench closed, a harsh breath pushing past my nostrils.

Didn't expect the second half of that.

Fuck, fuck.

In the next instant, my phone is ringing, and it's her name flashing across the screen. My attention flies to the live video feed, and I frown when it's only Drew in view.

I don't answer but pull my shoes on and grab my keys. Sending her one more message on my way out the door, I turn off my phone, leaving her to decipher its meaning.

Me: I'm coming over.

Chapter 6
Davis

I've been pacing my kitchen for ten minutes now.

Crew said he was coming over, so I yanked Drew out of the bar and had him drive me home since he insisted on picking me up, but I walked in fifteen minutes ago, and still no sign of Crew.

He should be here by now.

His apartment isn't that far from mine, so if he left right when he said he would, then he should have knocked no less than—

I jump as my doorbell sings to me; it doesn't even get to the final note before I'm yanking the door from its frame.

Crew stands there, dominating the small space so much more than I remember. I swear he's even taller than he was last time he stood on my front porch.

Twenty-five looks good on him.

So did the other twenty-four.

"Um . . . hi." I swallow.

Crew raises a brow. "Is your doorbell the theme song to *Victorious*?"

"My dad still thinks I'm twelve . . . so."

He nods, a frown falling over his face, but he makes no move to enter my apartment, so I grip him by the hem of his shirt, pull him inside, and lock the door behind us.

Three or four steadying breaths later, I turn to find him watching me, clear intent calling on the darker shades of his eyes.

Several beats of silence pass and then he blinks.

"Ready?" Crew peels his jacket off, and honestly, he should charge for that.

It's quite intoxicating, as is the way he runs a hand through his unruly hair. The way he shifts. Breathes.

Exists.

Wait. Did he say . . .

"Ready?" I ask.

Crew doesn't respond. He stares.

One at a time, he yanks his shoes off his feet, dropping them to the linoleum with a thud. "Should I take you on the couch, or is your roommate home?"

"Oh." My muscles freeze, but my core, it heats. Boils. "Um."

Crew undoes his belt, his eyes sharp and steady, determined. He tears the thick piece of leather from its loops and sets it on the kitchen table with a loud cling, cling, clack.

My core clenches, a tickle zipping up my spine.

"Are you going to use that?" I wonder.

Long, strong fingers clamp around my wrist and my eyes fly to the contact, to the space between our bodies. To where my hand decided to reach for the opening of his jeans without permission.

His fingers flex against me and my gaze snaps to his.

Crew scowls and gives a subconscious shake of his head, and then those hazel eyes widen with surprise.

"Holy shit," he mumbles, but I'm pretty sure he's speaking to himself.

The realization on his face activates my own, and for once, I'm the one to frown first.

"You have no intention of dicking me down tonight."

Crew flies back, putting no less than ten feet between us, and when he faces me again, a furious fire stares back. "No. I don't."

"You were testing me."

"Not testing."

"Assessing. Studying. Hypothesizing. Call it as you please. You wanted to see if I'd go through with this."

He runs his tongue along his lower lip, eyes narrowing. "Didn't think you had it in you."

"Did you miss the part where I basically begged you to let me pimp you out *to myself*?"

The vein in his neck pulses, and he shakes his head. "It's not going to happen, Baby Franco."

"Why not? It's a fantastic deal! You get a truck, something you can keep for a lifetime in exchange for five minutes of your time."

He scoffs. "Five minutes is pathetic."

"Good to know. I'll make sure to mention that to whoever signs on the dotted line."

"Swear to God, girl."

"There's a church around the corner for that." I blindly reach for the handle behind me, tugging the door open.

He widens his stance, his jaw flexing. "If I didn't call you tonight, would you have begged Drew to fuck you?"

"How did you know I was with Drew?"

"Answer the question, Davis."

"You're being annoying," I tell him, but when he doesn't so much as blink, I answer his stupid question. "I had no plans to screw your brother tonight, no, but I hear it happens naturally sometimes."

Crew shakes his head, his big-ass arms crossing over his broad-ass chest. "Why not let that happen?"

My head tugs back. "You want me to ask Drew to take my virginity?"

"Fuck no."

"Then what are you saying?"

He growls, pushing closer until he's directly before me. "I'm *saying* why not wait for it to happen naturally. Why not wait until you find someone you actually want, who wants you back, and let it happen like that?"

Okay, ouch.

My chest pinkens, and I look down, but he hates when I do that, so before his knuckles can lift my chin, I reach out and catch his fingers in mine, holding them between us.

"I get it," I whisper, slowly looking up into his dark, scornful eyes. "Honest, I do, but I don't want that. That's just a whole new level of anxiety for me."

"What do you mean?" he wonders, the muscles in his palm relaxing.

"If I answer that, it will be a whole new level of *embarrassing* for me."

Crew's still for a moment, and then the corner of his lips quirk up a bit.

"Oh, this must be good, Baby Franco." His words are forced, as is the half grin, both completely for my benefit, but that's the beauty of it. Of him. "'Cause you didn't so much as blush when you told me to slide inside you and 'pop' your—"

"Oh god!" I cut him off, my hand releasing his and joining the other to shield my face. "I totally said that. Sound effects and all."

His body jostles as if to laugh, but no sound escapes.

Stretching my fingers apart, I peek at him through the small gap. His amusement hasn't fully faded, so I allow my arms to fall.

"Are you hungry?" I blurt out instead. "I have frozen pizzas?"

He looks away, and I'm sure he's about to leave, but then he looks back, something I can't quite reach hidden in his eyes. "What kind?"

My smile spreads, and I skip to the freezer.

This is good.

A start.

Now to find a way to get him to deflower me . . .

Crew

"Are all those pizzas in there yours?" I joke, finishing off my water. "Your mom would have a fit if she knew you were eating frozen shit every day."

Davis leans forward, snagging a pineapple off the lone piece left and tossing it in her mouth. "I do pizza and movie night with my friend Jess next door at least once a week, but I bailed last time when I woke up with a jackhammer attached to my temples."

"That's what you get for letting Drew serve you after seventy-seven percent of a wine bottle."

"Yeah." She grins to herself. "That didn't go well with the froufrou vodka drink he gave me. It was delicious, but my body was really pissed at what I did to it."

"About that body of yours and what you want me to do to it." I shift, facing her fully from the opposite side of the couch. "Why are you so serious about us fucking?"

She knocks back what's left in her orange soda can as if she's shotgunning a beer and looks to me. "Is it necessary to discuss this in dirty terms?"

"Is it necessary to fuck under dirty terms?"

"Oh my god."

"Yeah, women say that when it's good."

"Okay!" She throws her hands up, adjusting as I had, so she's facing me. "I get it. Got it. You want me to get to the point, blah blah blah. On it."

Davis takes a long breath, and finally, her almond-shaped eyes meet mine.

"What if I find someone, fall into this epic love, like *The Notebook* kind of shit, and everything is perfect and then we have sex and he hates it? Or what if *I* hate it?" She scoots forward. "Holy crap, what if it's catastrophically awful and—"

My laughter is unexpected and has her mouth closing, a small smile pulling at her lips.

"Okay, rare, epic love aside." She folds her hands in her lap, her shoulders falling. "Is it really that horrible of an idea?"

An instant sourness coats my throat, but before I can say anything, she rushes to continue.

"Okay sure." She tips her head back and forth. "One day, you'll look my future husband in the eye and think, 'I fucked your wife,' because that is just *so* you, but who cares? I'll be thinking the same thing every time you introduce a new girlfriend."

"Oh, so you get a husband, and I don't get a wife?"

"Oh please, Casanova." She draws her feet up onto the cushion, laying her chin on her knees. "You'd have to allow yourself to love someone to have a wife, and before you say you do love someone, my family doesn't count."

She's not being mean; in fact, the entire conversation is slightly playful, even though I'm damn sure she's serious. She's an oddball like that, but still. That last part stings.

Truth always does, even if it's only the half of it.

She and I stare at one another a moment, and then I move to the edge of the cushion, leaning forward with my elbows on my thighs. "I get what you're saying, and I know you well enough to know nothing I say will convince you *not one* of those things will happen, so I won't bother."

Her eyes narrow spiritedly as we both knew this was my way of saying exactly that.

"What if . . ." Fuck me, I should shut up now. "What if I say yes"—her eyes light up, but I lift my hands, halting whatever it is she planned to follow with and finish—"but instead, I help you find someone else."

I brace for her horror. For her shouts of refusal.

But Davis fucking Franco does neither of those things.

She squeals, loudly, and then she jumps up on her feet, staring down at me with a giant, full fucking smile on her puffy, full fucking lips. "Are you serious?"

I frown, and the nod I give is forced when it should come easy.

"So you'll be my wingman?" she asks.

I bite back a grimace. It's on the tip of my tongue to say no, but is that not what I offered? To "assist" her in finding a man worth her time.

Worth a spot in her memory.

Worth being inside her?

A cough fights its way free, but I swallow it down.

You can control this shit, my man.

It's with that thought in mind, I nod. "Yeah. Like a wingman."

She claps her hands, lowering herself onto the coffee table in front of me.

Right in front of me.

I'm talking knee to fucking knee, face to face.

"Okay, what exactly do we do?" Her brown eyes sparkle, her teeth sinking into the corner of her bottom lip.

I'm tempted to free it.

"What do you mean?"

"I mean, are you going to give me tasks or a list or homework or something and grade me on it? What's the grading scale? Are we talking a letter grade or a percentage or what should I work toward? And what do you think is a good baseline to start, like how do I know if I'm getting better or ready or whatever? Oh, and do you think you should show me some moves before I play jelly on toast and spread—"

"Whoa, back up." I gape at her, at the wild excitement buzzing across every inch of her satiny skin. "What the hell are you talking about?"

"The lessons."

"What lessons?"

"You said you'd help me, remember?" Her eyes widen as if her shitty explanation should make perfect sense.

It doesn't.

"It was less than sixty seconds ago, so yeah, I remember."

"Then you should be following." She pauses, cocking her head with a single, swift blink. "If I'm going to go get a guy to have sex with me, I need to know how to first *get* a guy. I'm pretty sure that's simply stated."

"No, it's not. Not at all."

"Well, now you know."

Leaning even closer, I bring us eye level, and her knees knock mine in a stubborn attempt at dominance I'll never give her.

"Are you really sitting here acting like you don't know what to do to get a man's attention?"

"Did you somehow miss the entire reason I wrote a two-thousand-word, double-spaced essay trying to convince you to have sex with me?" Her features pull, her tone a mix of sass and frustration. "If I knew how to rope a guy in on my own, I wouldn't be standing here pathetically happy to have a less than eager man help me convince another man to have sex with me."

"You have to fuck them right back, you know?" I spat.

"You know what I mean, Crew Taylor." She glares, crossing her arms over her chest in a pout.

My eyes follow the movement, and I frown at the swell of her breasts, at the soft sweep of skin that curves down, disappearing beneath the yellow tank top she's wearing.

"This is a bad idea." I push to stand, slipping past her.

Moments after I'm on my feet, she leaps up, jumping over the back of the couch to block my path.

"Davis. Move."

"You cannot back out now. I need your help."

"Bring your next date home and it's a done deal. Problem fucking solved." I press my lips together firmly. She's driving me fucking mad.

"Yeah, sure, I'll just take out my little black book and magically find someone to take me out to fuck."

"It's called Tinder, sweetheart. You'll bleed in a click of a fucking button."

"Ew."

"That's what you want, is it not? To be fucked for fun?"

"And potentially be on the next episode of *Body Cam*? No, thank you."

My jaw clenches, and I want to fucking scream at her, but I hold back, and she shakes her head.

"Crew," she breaks off. "I've never dated before."

"Bullshit," I snap, stepping into her. "You've always been up front. Don't start lying to me now."

"I'm not lying to you," she snaps right back. "When I say never, I literally mean *never*. As in not once. I'm as clueless as a church-born nun."

"I don't believe that." My eyes flick to her lips, to her sleek, slender neck with a candy necklace tightly wound around it, the ice cream pendant I gave her for her birthday years ago hanging beneath it, to the inviting indent of her creamy collarbone, and the arc of her soft, silky breasts. My eyes settle on the deep dip of her waist. "Not for a fucking second."

"It's the truth." Her hands find her hips and she straightens. "I've gone to the movies and dinner and other places with friends or in groups over the years, where I maybe gave my attention to one person for the night, but that's it. I've never gone out with someone, one on one, with the potential of naughtiness following. I might as well be wearing a chastity belt 'cause I'm beginning to believe every guy sees one when he looks at me anyway."

"Not a chance."

"Then what makes me so undickable?"

"Stop," I rush, dragging my hands over my face. "I need a fucking drink for this shit."

"Okay, you're obviously getting stressed out, so let's take a breath and regroup, start simple. With the basics."

Almost afraid to ask, I turn to look at her. "Basics?"

"Yes." She steps backward, holds her hands out and does a slow spin. "Okay, go."

I blink. "What?"

"You know, tell me what you see. It's always best to start with the root of the problem. If we do that, we should be able to break it down in a way that makes sense, analyze all components, and put it back together more effectively. So, look at me, and tell me what's wrong with what you see."

"You're not some class project, Davis." My voice is rough. Hard.

She says it so matter of fact, so emotionless, I want to grip her and shake her. Yell at her.

Davis flicks her eyes to the ceiling. "Oh my god, come on." She laughs. "It's called problem-solving. You agreed to help solve my problem."

"No, I agreed to find someone who will."

"It's the same thing, Crew! Same outcome. I got you, you get guy, I *do* guy, and right after the big fat equal sign of the equation, in gorgeously golden ink, it'll read 'hymenless.'"

"Fucking Christ." I drop my head back, a low growl working its way up my throat.

She's fucking with me. Has to be.

"Let's not play games, okay?" she suggests. "It gets us nowhere to tiptoe around. It's not like you're being mean by answering. I'm literally asking you a direct question. That's it. Promise, I can handle it."

Angry, I turn my body so it's facing hers again, crowding her in. Her hands fall to her sides with my approach, her neck cracking up to keep our gazes connected.

"First of all, there's nothing wrong with you. Second, I don't know a single man, pun in-fucking-tended, who wouldn't fuck you if given what *I guarantee* is the pleasure of doing so, so do not stand here and pretend if you wanted to have sex right now, you couldn't walk into any damn bar in this town, leave with a man in mere minutes, and wake up without what you're trying so hard to be rid of."

Not that I'll let you.

With that, I jerk away, taking two steps at a time until my hand's wrapped around the doorknob, but right as I yank it open, she shouts at my back.

"I'm afraid!"

I tell myself to keep moving, to slam the fucking door and get the hell out because the shit she's saying, what she's said, it's too much. Instead, I look back at her.

"There, I said it. I'm scared, okay?" Her shoulders slump with defeat, and she glances off. "Crew, I've . . . never done anything with a man. Or a woman, for that matter, but seriously I . . ." Hesitantly and clearly embarrassed, she finally meets my gaze.

"I have kissed two people in my life and we both know who one of them was. I've never touched a man, never seen below the trunks of one, other than in a movie or two, so, yeah." She nods, her arms crossing as her cheeks grow bright red. "Maybe it would be as simple as throwing myself at a stranger at a bar, but I'm afraid. I don't want to be, and I don't know why, but I am."

Davis begins pacing the short space between the couch and kitchen table, and all I can do is stare. From the jerky steps she takes to the way she chews her nails. She's a ball of anxiousness.

"It's annoying and I don't get it." She shakes her head, working through things out loud. "Nothing's ever happened to me before, and I don't know anyone who's been assaulted or anything like that so it's not that. I'm on birth control for girly reasons, so it's not fear of pregnancy." She pauses. "Maybe it's because all I ever did was focus on school. *Guys'll get you grounded, grades'll get you to graduation,*" she mimics her dad's voice as best as possible, rushing into her next words without a break. "Maybe I didn't put myself out there enough to allow myself to get comfortable with a man's attention. I mean, I did spend all of high school following you and Memphis around, and you guys were too psycho to let me out of your sights, so I stood no chance then." She stops suddenly, leaning her back against the wall.

A long, dramatic sigh escapes her, and she gives a feeble shrug.

There's so much I could say right now, but my lips remain sealed.

"You have always been confident, Crew, charismatic and mysterious almost. Effortlessly attractive and an expert flirt." She shakes her head. "I'm not. There isn't an intriguing or interesting thing about me. I've had study groups and class projects with assigned partners dozens of times, more than half of those being male partners, and never once did any of them ever try to so much as cop a feel or steal a kiss. Not once did any of them ever ask me out for lunch after or anywhere at any time, if it wasn't directly related to getting our work done. I just need your help to . . ." She pauses, swallowing, and when she speaks again, it's a low, broken whisper, "God, I don't even know what I need help with because I don't know what's wrong with me."

I don't know why, and I know I'll question myself later, but later is later, and now is fucking now.

I go to her, grab her by the hand, and tug her to me.

At first, she smiles, that tight-lipped, sad side smile, the one she gave me when I finally looked up at her that day at the café, after years of staying away. But that smile smooths out, as does the tension in her gaze, replaced by something deeper, darker, when I lift that hand up. I press the tips of her fingers to the edge of my throat, just beside my Adam's apple, right over the beat of my pulse. It kicks up then, and I step in more.

My left palm closes around the dip of her waist while my right snags a strand of her silky, copper-colored hair as I lean in, closer and closer, until I can whisper in her ear, but I don't just yet.

I wait, dipping my chin a bit as I breathe, slow and long, through my mouth, allowing my warm breath to tickle along the exposed skin of her neck.

Only when her fingers curl into the arm of the couch I've got her against, do I speak.

"I can promise you, Sweets, there isn't a damn thing wrong with you. Quite the opposite, in fact." I give that strand a tug, and her huffed little breath brushes my collarbone. "See, men can be real dumb creatures. Sometimes, if we're feeling inferior and think we're not equipped with the tools needed to win over the woman we want, the one that catches our attention the second she's spotted, then we simply choose not to try."

My thumb sneaks beneath the hem of her shirt and I draw slow, skimming circles along her hip.

She gives a short, sweet gasp, and I lick my lips.

"I've watched guy after guy look at you the way you're craving to be looked at, Davis. They see you, want you . . ."

"Don't lie to me, Crew." Her voice nothing more than a raspy whisper.

"No reason to, Sweets. It's the truth. I've seen it with my own eyes." I turn my face into hers a bit, yesterday's shave grazing the curve of her cheekbone.

The slightest of shivers works its way through her body, and her hands come up to clutch my biceps.

"They used to look at you and see this bombshell with long legs and lush lips . . . then everyone else grew, caught up and passed you, but you were done getting taller. You went from a long, lean dream to a short, sweet little thing, but one thing that has never changed is the pull you possess. Men want you, but they know without daring to swing, a strike is coming, because how could a woman like you, who is so adorably fucking clueless of her own appeal, possibly feel the same?"

"Crew." Her fingertips dig into my skin.

I shuffle closer, dipping my head into her neck a bit. "I feel you shivering, your muscles tightening. Feel my own body heating . . . hardening. So, there you go, proof there ain't a damn thing wrong with you, Davis Franco." I hold a moment, slowly pulling back to meet her dark, dilated eyes. I release her, stepping out of her grasp, out of her reach. "We'll call this lesson one. Remember it."

This time when I move for the door, she doesn't stop me, and thank fuck for that.

Pinning her against it would be a shit idea.

Chapter 7
Davis

I jolt at the overly aggressive knock that could only mean one thing. Crew Taylor is at my door.

The same Crew Taylor who hypnotized me not nine-ish hours ago.

Seriously, he must have because of all the times I've dreamed of touching him, I would never dare, and I clutched him like I could. Like it was allowed.

I held on to him like he did me, tight, and skin to heated skin.

I obsessed over it all night, the why, the how, and the what the hell led us to that moment, but in the end, the answer was simple.

Crew is unpredictable. As kids, we all sort of sat back and waited to see what he'd do or say next. One day, he might say he hates wheat bread and the next, he was subbing out the white for it on his club sandwiches. Can't stand a girl, and then out they'd come from behind the bleachers. Friends with a guy, and then punches him without sharing why. He keeps you guessing, and I've always enjoyed that about him.

Okay, that's an outright lie. Sometimes it's incredibly annoying, but whatever. Girls love a good mystery, so it's probably why they all seem to love him.

That and the perfect skin, the muscles and the thousand other things I could tick off, but who has time for internal list making when the man consuming my mind is at my door, waiting for me to let him inside.

"You sure you want to come in, work more voodoo magic on me, 'cause I'll warn you, I'm feeling a little empowered right now."

He raises a dark brow. "Is that right?"

"It is."

I shuffle out of the way, and he steps in, closing the door behind him.

"Do I want to know?"

"I doubt it." I quickly move back to the stove, stabbing a small dough ball and nudge it off the butter knife with a fork, easing it straight into the small pot of boiling grease. "But basically, knowing I can put my hands on you *and* feel your hands on me without combusting, does a lot for the mind."

In my peripheral, Crew's head snaps my way, and when I look at him, his eyes are narrowed.

"Don't worry," I assure him. "I'm on board with the role you've chosen, but you're like top tier, so if a man of your godliness can enjoy any part of me, even a tiny bit, then there's hope somewhere."

His frown seems to deepen, but a sigh shortly follows, and he comes to stand beside me, wordlessly rolling one of the fried donut balls in the bowl of sugar. "I can't believe you still make these things."

"Every Sunday."

"So same as always."

I love that he remembers the small stuff. "The cinnamon and sugar ones make the perfect breakfast and after-dinner dessert. Without mom's treats in reach, these are a lifesaver after a craptastic day."

Crew nods, and we finish off the last few batches in silence, easing into the cleanup as if we still do this together each week when the last time he made donuts with me was the summer before my senior year when he and Memphis came home for a visit.

The last visit they ever made.

Crew kissed me and never came back . . .

That was almost five years ago, yet he still takes the lead on the hot oil because I'm "clumsier than my mom after her Booze and Books Club," or so he would always say.

"I don't spill at work," I tell him suddenly, and then I think about it. "Well, I don't spill *much* at work. I can't exactly serve a tray of drinks, thank the bank for the hostesses, but still . . . I've only spilled directly on a customer a couple times."

I peek at Crew, and while his profile shows a slight quirk of his lips, he doesn't say anything when I sort of think he might want to, but again, who knows with him.

"At the café the other day," he begins after a few quiet moments, "you said you made a pros and cons list."

The metal tray full of homemade donut balls slips from my fingers, hitting the edge of the countertop I was trying to move it to, and I jerk forward, saving a good handful with my shirt-covered stomach.

"Oh shit." Crew flies over, quickly nudging the treats back onto the tray and easing it down on the counter.

Looking to him, I admit to the obvious. "Okay, so I'm as spill prone as ever."

Crew's expression speaks for him, a loud ass "you think" printed across his face, before bending to clean up the mess I made on the floor.

Careful as possible, I peel my top off and shake it out over the sink to avoid inadvertently inviting a trail of ants to move in.

"There goes tomorrow's dessert."

"There's a solid three dozen left unscathed. Even you can't eat all these in a day."

We face each other at the same time, and instantly, his attention snaps to my chest. "What are you doing?"

"It has food all over it." Duh. "And while I am almost certain I can easily eat three dozen in a day's time, they aren't all for me. I made a dozen for Jess as a *sorry I bailed on you* gift, and I was planning on tracking you down today and giving you a batch for old times' sake, but now you'll just have to share mine."

I wait for a smile, but his lips only press together more.

"How is it you're afraid to hook up with a dude, but not afraid to stand half-naked in front of one?"

"One, I am not half-naked."

His eyes snap to mine. "You're only wearing shorts and a bra."

"It's sports bra and Spanx Sunday."

"You're not wearing a sports bra."

"Yes, I—" I look down to find my basic black bra. "Oh." I shrug. "Well, whatever. You've seen plenty of naked people, so the sight of me in a bra shouldn't even faze you."

"Mm-hmm," he deadpans. "So this whole never getting dirty with a man thing has nothing to do with your body?"

I jolt, feeling the sudden need to cover up.

"Should it?" I ease away. "I sort of thought my body was satisfactory enough, but if you think I need to—"

"No." He flies forward, taking my hands and lowering them to my side with an urgent expression. "That is not what I meant. *At all*. Your body is . . ." He pauses, his head remaining still while his eyes look lower. "You have nothing to worry about there."

"Are you sure, because your questions sort of suggest otherwise?"

"Trust me. I'm sure." He holds still, then slowly releases my wrists. "I guess I thought maybe that was part of it. I'm just trying to figure this shit out."

"What is there to figure?"

"Honestly, Davis, I'm shocked as shit," he says suddenly, his hands finding his hips. "I would have thought you lost your virginity a long time ago, and not for any reason other than the things related to what I told you last night. Men want you. Men stare at you. I'm sure as fuck not mad about it, but it blows my mind no one pushed until you grabbed hold. And to be real with you, I'm beginning to think some have, but it went right over your head." He shakes his own, his attention briefly flicking along my exposed skin. "You have no idea what you do to a man."

My chest heats, and there's nothing I can do to stop it from spreading, or from Crew instantly spotting—*following*—the path it burns up my neck.

I knew he meant what he said last night, Crew would simply not speak rather than ramble on about things that weren't true. I knew this when I told him not to lie but knowing and hearing him talk about me in such a way was . . . a lot. I was nervous, anxious, *excited. Basically a hot flippin' mess.*

He stretches tall. "I want to see the pros and cons list."

Horndog meet cold shower.

A panicky laugh leaves me, and I round the kitchen, the long way. The way that takes me away from him. "I was kidding."

He starts to step from around the small island, so I move as fast as I can, without running, and shut myself in my room.

Giant steps echo down the hall, and I squeeze my eyes closed.

"No you weren't," he accuses.

"I was."

"Davis."

"Oh my god! Fine!" I tear a shirt from the hanger, pulling it over my head, the second he pushes the door open as expected. "Yes, I did, but you cannot see it."

He crowds my doorway, forced to tip his shoulders to the side in order to slip through.

He walks straight up to me, and I freeze, my eyes locked on his as he reaches out, guiding his hand around my neck.

A million thoughts run through my head, the first, loudest and most irrational being, *dear god, please say he changed his mind and we're getting naked right here, right now,* but then he simply frees my hair from the collar, and his hand falls to his side.

So anticlimactic.

Crew scowls. "Why not?"

"Because I said."

"So let me get this straight." He crosses those big arms of his. "You're willing to lie on your back and open up for me, but sharing your tick list is a no-go?"

Okay, wow. He said that.

And my, my, the visual that comes with it . . .

Crew

Davis's cheeks grow an even deeper pink, and I'm tempted to push more.

"Look, if we're doing this, shouldn't I understand every aspect of why and how it makes you feel or something?"

"I do not think that's necessary, no." Her nose lifts into the air. "That would be like getting a new job, sitting down with the person who hired you, and asking them why they chose to be manager."

"If that manager was asking for something real fucking personal from their employee, I'd say it's very necessary." A small frown creases along her forehead. "Come on, Baby Franco. I know no man has touched you, I know you want to be touched, and you straight up asked for my cock. How are we not passed the holding-back stage after all that?"

"Are you trying to make my skin catch fire?"

I ignore her and keep going. "According to you, you're not thinking, asking, or looking for anything outside of the fact that you don't want to be a virgin anymore. I get that, now tell me why."

She chews on that lower lip of hers and turns to her nightstand, straightening items already straight to give herself something to focus on. "There's not some deep thought process or reason, Crew, and maybe that's the worst part, I don't know." She pauses, and when she turns to me, it's with a soft sigh and timid smile.

"I'm twenty-one years old, graduating college in a couple weeks, and I haven't done or experienced half of the things the people my age have, but I'm not dumb. I don't have some naive notion to be like everyone else, and there's no peer pressure involved. My mind isn't stuck in high school repeating 'all the girls are doing something and so I want to do it too.' It's nothing like that. It's just . . ."

"Just what?"

She takes a deep breath and squares her shoulders, all to pull them in close. Her gaze turns toward the empty hall and stays there. "This might sound really bad, shitty or trashy, I don't know, but the honest truth is I *want* to have sex. I want to know what it feels like and not to feed some deluded sense of curiosity, but because I want to experience it. I want the excitement that comes from lust. I want the rush. I want the sense of closeness with a man. I want to drown in need, shake with desire.

"And this isn't about being homesick or pitifully lonely. It's like I said, there's not a deep-rooted reason other than I want to. I've waited long enough. I'm ready to look into the eyes of a man while he makes me come undone, and I want to know how to do the same to him."

I don't realize I'm stuck where I'm standing, silently staring at her, until she looks over. The second our eyes meet, unease clouds her features, and she looks away.

The strange thing is I hear her, understand everything she's saying. I've felt those same desires, still do here and there, so it's not all the things she admitted causing my chest to feel a little tight, or my limbs a little heavy. All right, it kind of is.

Lonely. She said she's lonely.

How long has she felt like that?

Why does she feel like that?

Why do I feel like that?

I have a gang of friends who ask for my time, and I work with a lot of people. My brother moved home a while ago, and yeah, we don't always see eye to eye, hardly ever do in fact, but he's here and we hang. Sometimes. I don't have a woman of my own, but I choose it to be that way. A normal day for me is getting up, going to work, and going to bed. Shit, sometimes

I'm so busy busting my ass trying to get ahead that I forget to eat and I'm stuck with beer nuts for the night. This last year was spent trying to get back on my feet, getting debts paid off and accounts into good standing. I haven't paused long enough to think about life outside of the bar.

Not until she showed up in it and I carried her ass out.

I didn't even know she drank.

Does she drink alone?

Spend all her time alone?

Growing up, it was always me and Memphis . . . and Davis. She never did have her own little crew. To know she's never dated means she's spent *all* her nights alone, but what about the rest of her time?

Work and school are important to her, so I'm sure those things keep her pretty busy, but what about after that? She did mention pizza night with her friend Jess, but there have to be more people in her life than those who have to be, and the one girl who lives in her complex. Right? She has a roommate; do they not go out together? I'm pretty sure there was a picture on the fridge of her and a couple girls at a concert, looked new enough.

Maybe one was Jess, and the other was Jess's friend?

"Why are you still here, Davis?" I say suddenly, and I almost want to take it back.

I really want to take it back when she winces, her eyes cutting to the carpet. She's quiet a long moment, and then she peeks up at me, her chin still pointed to her chest as she whispers, "Why are you still here, Crew?"

And isn't that the fucking question.

Southern California isn't our home.

It's not the place we planned to stay forever.

I followed Memphis out here, and his baby sister did the same.

Now he's gone, and look at us, two people who once knew more about each other than friends should, asking questions we should—and maybe did—already know the answers to.

But Memphis was home to us, until he wasn't; he was the link between us, until he wasn't, so how the hell are we supposed to leave this town now?

Apparently, the answer is we can't, so instead, we live with the loneliness the night brings, knowing when we wake up . . . not a damn thing will be different.

I dare say it's all Memphis's fault.

Chapter 8
Davis

Monday comes and goes, as does Tuesday, without a word from Crew, and while I didn't expect him to drop everything for mission "deflower Davis," some part of me must've assumed he would've reached out by now. Why else would I be pouting into a bowl of moose tracks ice cream?

Call me eager or impatient, or maybe just needy, but I'm going to need him to agree to some kind of schedule. Then I can bust out an Excel sheet, add in everything there is to add, and come up with a reasonable deadline.

He knows I like order, so maybe he's doing this to mess with me?

Or maybe he just has a life, Davis.

Ugh.

I annoy myself.

School and work might rule my existence for the most part, but that's cake compared to running a bar. I bet he's in there long before they open, getting things ready, and even longer after dealing with the chaos of the night. Not to mention making the schedule, keeping tabs on his employees, inventory, restocking, and who the heck knows what else. Not me, but I see some of the stuff my manager does and it's a lot.

Plus, he has to find time to sleep somewhere. He basically works swing *and* graveyard shifts.

It's whatever, and it's those two words I play on repeat in my mind. It works until Wednesday rolls around and all my classes are done. That's when I throw the whole "whatever" thing out the window, but rather than blow up his phone and wait for a response, I decide to not so casually be in the neighborhood. *His* neighborhood, that is, and with a giant plateful of homemade peanut butter cookies that may or may not be his favorite.

Like my apartment complex, parking here is atrocious, and the closest thing to his building is not close at all, so I sneak my mini-Mitsubishi into one of the assigned carports, since I don't plan to be here long. I figure popping in and dropping off a treat is a great way to remind him I exist and he made a deal. You know, in the off chance he forgot.

Like I said . . . *needy*.

His apartment is upstairs, so I use the forced moment of exercise to squat with each step up. Three-quarters of the way, I grab the railing for support, since my legs are quickly jiggling like Jell-O. There's an ugly upside-down beaver-looking statue beside his door, the tail sticking out to the side and holding an aloe vera plant that could use some water, so I make a mental note to mention so and knock on the door.

And then I knock again.

Why I continue to knock after several minutes of waiting, I don't know, but it's not to no avail, as after the third and maybe a half, a groggy voice groans from the other side.

I perk up, holding the bag in front of me with a smile.

The door is yanked from the frame, but I'm not met with the deep dark eyes of a miraculous male, but instead a short, skinny, green-haired girl I most definitely woke up. If the wild-child hair and smeared makeup didn't clue me in, the see-through crop top that wouldn't stretch past my shoulders and a teeny, tiny strip of cloth covering her vag would have done it. Maybe.

"Are you going to tell me why you're here or are you just going to stare at my underwear? Because if it's the second one, I could turn around and show you the back. There's a little jewel that hangs just between the cheeks."

Only then do I remember where I am, and that a woman—an extremely attractive, even in a state of disarray woman—answered Crew's door. Without pants.

And underwear equipped with jewelry, apparently.

I didn't even know such a thing existed.

"Okay, backside it is then." She begins to spin, and I snap out of it.

"No!" I shout as quickly as I can, and she pauses, her annoyed stare meeting mine once more. "I'm sorry. I came by to say hi to Crew." Lame, Davis. "But I'll give him a call later."

My words indicate I'm out of here, yet my feet don't move, and she cocks her head, looking me over.

"You're looking for Crew?" She eyes me.

I nod, attempting to secretly slide the bagful of cookies behind my back, but she sees it, a judgy, slightly strained gleam slipping into her eyes. One leading me to believe she's thinking something along the lines of "poor, pathetic, *plain* girl."

Maybe I'm the one thinking that?

"When's the last time you saw Crew?" she questions.

I'm tempted to lie. What if he doesn't want her to know where he was this weekend? Maybe she doesn't know he's been anywhere?

Maybe she's his girlfriend and will want to fight if I tell her the truth?

"Sunday." Truth is always best.

She nods, holds up a finger, and closes the door in my face.

On the other side, several bangs sound, and I half expect Crew to be the one who yanks the door open this time, but not a single part expected the gorgeous girl to come back. Just as naked as before, she shoves an old shoebox into my chest.

"Tell this *Crew* to take his ass to the post office already. The next thing I get of his, I'm shredding and using as a shit pad in my hamster's cage."

"Uh . . . okay?"

She slams the door.

I look up at the number hanging above it, double-checking it's the right one, it is, and peeking into the shoebox on my way back to my car confirms as much.

Placing it in the passenger seat, I drop back against my own.

'This Crew,' she said.

So she doesn't know him.

So Crew moved.

When?

Why?

Where?

I consider calling and asking him all these questions, but instead, tear into the cookie bag on the drive home, officially claiming his surprise treats as my own.

What's worse? I'm almost as relieved to discover he no longer lives where the feisty green-haired girl is sleeping half-naked as I am annoyed I was unaware he didn't.

Almost.

My favorite class is my humanities one. In part, because Mrs. Anna, as she insists on being called, is hilarious, but mostly because it's a totally random class I'm only taking to satisfy the elective credit needed for graduation.

I'm not sure what you are supposed to do or learn in a humanities class, but we pretty much search for and stare at ancient artwork all day, coming up with a sophisticated outlook or perception of why it was created and what it could signify.

Basically, we use our imagination to stimulate our professors, and I'm all for it. It's sort of cleansing to complete a task that literally has nothing to do with anything outside of challenging our own intellect. Unfortunately for me, today, I'm only able to pop in before class begins to turn in my assignment, and then I'm rushing toward the student parking lot—after asking permission to do so, of course. Mrs. Anna just laughed and waved me on.

Rachel, my boss at the diner, works with my schedule pretty well, but every now and then, she's forced to add me at times employment paperwork notes I'm unavailable. She knows when she does it, I've been here since winter break my freshman year and to convince her to give a student the job—something she hates to do—I had to agree to keep my schedule as is. If I tried to change it, it would be grounds for termination.

I agreed, and honestly, it makes my life easier, but like I said, sometimes I'm her only option, so if I can make it in, I do.

The relief on her face as I push through the door this fine Thursday says it all; she's damn happy I pulled it off this afternoon.

Tying my apron behind my back, I quickly jump behind the counter, using the tablet bolted there to clock in. "Okay, fill me in. What do we got?"

"One fryer is down. Sarah had to leave to pick up a sick kid, and Marla is two seconds from losing her mind if she doesn't get a break."

"Lunch, Rachel." Marla swoops by, snagging a batch of chili cheese fries and a pile of napkins. "I need to take my lunch."

"Right. Lunch." Rachel looks at me mid-count of the money. "Got it?"

"Got it. Work Sarah's section today, cover Marla's for the next thirty, and convince people they would rather have fresh fruit than fries."

"Attagirl, I'm going to call Stephanie to see if she can come in an hour early tonight, and I'll be back on the floor."

"And I'm clocked out!" Marla whisper-shouts, disappearing through the double doors behind Rachel.

So, I get right to work.

I need the distraction anyway.

Anything to keep from wondering why there's a pile of unopened mail with Crew's name on it on the floorboard of my car . . . and where I can score myself a jewelry-like G-string.

Chapter 9
Crew

She's hustling around like a pro, hitting table after table, never once having to be called back for forgetting whatever it is these needy fuckers ask for. So much so, she's snuck around the counter twice now to stealthily swipe away the hint of sweat building where the loose strands of her mini ponytail are pushed behind her ear.

I've been tucked in a corner booth on the opposite side of where she's working for about an hour now, and not once has she stopped moving, but she doesn't seem to mind. I've followed her every move, waiting to see her make a face when she turns away from a hungover punk, or overworked trucker, but if she is annoyed or irritated, she doesn't show it.

She smiles sweetly, nods agreeably, and seems to know what everyone needs before they have a chance to ask for it.

She's the picture-perfect employee from where I'm sitting, and in the fifty-something minutes I've been here, I got what I needed.

Tossing a ten on the table for taking up the space, I nod at the redheaded woman who brought me a water and drop into the booth just wiped down in Davis's section.

She's back to making her rounds this way in seconds and stops beside the table I now am at a minute later. Order slip in hand with the pen pressed to it, she smiles at the thing.

"Thanks for waiting. Can I get you something to drink? A soda or maybe a shake?"

"Which is your favorite?"

"Oh, I love the—" She looks at me, mentally trained to look away so fast, she has to do a double take. "Oh shit."

Her eyes widen, and she peeks around her.

I bite back a grin. "It's safe to say no one heard."

"Uh-huh. Where've you been?"

I raise a single brow. "Been waiting on me, or what?"

"Obviously." She juts a hip out, creating an even deeper curve at her middle. "Do you really think I'm the type of person who, in the middle of something as we are in the middle of, would simply *not* obsess over every little thing, every single day?"

"I'm a little surprised you just threw that out there."

"Are you?" She's full of sass and sarcasm. It's cute on her. "Because you've known me since forever, so I feel like you should've expected this."

I did, but I'm not about to tell her that. "You could've called."

The girl gapes at me and leans her hip the opposite way. "Do you not understand what happens when someone obsesses over something? You know what, never mind." She eyes me, and it's clear she wants to say something but decides against it. She presses that pen back on that little paper and arches a brow. "What can I get for you, kind sir?"

Leaning forward, I tug on the edge of her apron playfully. "You're about to take the dude with the hat a basket of fries, right?"

A small scowl covers her face, but she nods.

"Don't take the ketchup."

"Why?" Her head pulls back slightly. "If I don't take it over with the basket, I'm going to end up making two trips."

"Take him the basket, set it down in front of him, and look him in the eye when you ask if there's anything else he needs."

Davis blinks at me, completely lost. "But I already know what he needs because he asked for ketchup on his burger. Logic says he'll then want it for his fries."

"I have watched you for the last hour, Baby Franco, and you had no idea because your little eyes never wander around this damn place, so you have no idea who is looking at you and when." Opening my fist without taking it off the table, I point toward the ball cap dude. "That guy? He's turned his head your way more than once. It has nothing to do with waiting for a refill or to order or anything else I'm sure you're lining up in your head right now to throw back at me because you're so damn prone to arguing."

"I am not prone to arguing!" she hiss-whispers. "I happen to think full circle, which means every possible scenario pops into my head and I play the process of elimination game to get them out."

"You're arguing about arguing instead of listening to what I'm telling you. Quiet, and listen. Walk over there, do what you gotta do, and look him in the eye when you do it."

I pull my phone out, aimlessly scrolling through it to get her to walk away, and she does, but I don't miss the slight shake of her wrist or the tight press of her lips as she makes her way back to the jockstrap at table four.

It's hard not to laugh when her chest rises with a deep breath as she leans forward a bit to set the fries down, but she doesn't have time to straighten her spine before the guy's eyes pop up to meet hers. She didn't even have to wait.

I can't hear from here, but he nods, she smiles, and the conversation is taking a little longer than asking for fucking ketchup.

I stare, and finally, she goes to walk away but stutter-steps twice, and I rub my hand over my mouth to hide my smile.

Condiments in one hand, straw in the other, she sneaks a small glance in my direction as she quickly sets both down in front of him. She doesn't look him in the eye this time, and within seconds, she's sliding into the seat across from me.

Her mouth forms an *O* but it takes her a good second to push the words out. "What just happened?"

"You tell me." I watch her closely, and she smiles into her hand.

"I don't know. He started asking me for the stupid ketchup as he looked up, but then he totally lost his train of thought.

He did the whole chuckle thing you do, you know, how you sometimes stop and start to laugh in the middle of a sentence?" she says, then quickly continues, "And then he remembered what he was asking, and asked again, so I was like, yeah sure, but then I got nervous and forgot to look away." Suddenly, she glares at me. "Wait. Was he being flirty?"

"Did you feel like he was being flirty?"

"Well, he kind of gave me one of those sexy side-grins I love, and his eyes did that flick down, flick up thing after, so I don't know . . . yes?"

Sexy side-grins?

Her eyes widen, and she pushes off the table, her back against the cushion. "Hold the ship. He totally wanted me to notice him checking me out. He *was* being flirty." She looks off, as if stunned by the realization. "Weird," she whispers then, but when I shift in the seat, her gaze darts right back. "Where you going?"

"Home."

The hint of triumph in her gaze is gone, replaced by the nervous nibbling of her lip as creases begin to frame her eyes.

"What?"

"Nothing."

My eyes narrow at her quick response. "Davis."

She shoots from the seat. "No, nothing. I have to get back at it anyway."

I glare, trying to read the sudden change in her demeanor. "Right."

She stands there, watching as I slip from the booth, meeting my gaze when I step in front of her.

"You busy later?"

She gives a little shake of her head.

"Do you think you can stop by the bar around four? It doesn't open until six, but we should talk."

"I feel like you didn't understand what I was trying to say earlier. I am not good with guessing games or half answers or seriously confusing Crew-isms."

At that, my lips switch. "I think you'll survive a couple more hours."

Her nose scrunches and I get the feeling she's holding back a little stomp.

I hold her gaze for a few moments, then intentionally flick it above her head to the dude in the black hat, who happens to be staring this way, but I don't leave my eyes there long enough to know if he jerks away when caught. I give my attention back to her.

"It's about our little deal." I shift in closer. "How is that for making it clear?"

I wait for the flush I know is coming, and it does, slipping up and above the high collar of her T-shirt and meeting the hollow of her cheeks.

"I'll see you in a bit, yeah?"

"Yeah." She nods, clearing her throat. "See you."

With that, I turn and walk away, slipping out the door without another glance back, but I don't have to look to know the guy is staring at her, noticing the red on her cheeks, and fully aware something I said put it there.

As ridiculous as it is, there's something about a woman's possible unavailability that attracts a man more.

It's shitty, but it's true.

So now, the guy will do one of two things. He'll either find a way to ask what he wants to know and make his move after he gets his answer . . . Or he'll do what I told her most men do when it comes to Davis Franco.

Take the *L.*

But I wouldn't be walking out of this place if I thought he had the balls to do the first.

Even if he did, she wouldn't bite.

Not when her teeth are set on sinking into me . . .

Davis

Rachel kept me to the very last second, but I still managed to make it home before two thirty, leaving me with an hour and a half of a gap to spare.

I've been known to make treats in less time, so I whip up a new, fresh batch of peanut butter cookies. My plan was to sneak them up to his office before he got there, but even arriving twenty minutes early, I was too late.

Crew's leaning against the large stone door with his phone to his ear as I climb out of my car.

He holds a finger up to his lips, so I make a zipping motion with mine.

I'm not sure if his eye roll is for me or the person pissing him off on the phone when he says, "I don't care about the why, Jose, are you making it in for your shift tonight or not?"

The squishy sound of the Ziplock in my grasp draws his attention, and olive eyes bounce from it to meet mine.

"That's what you said last time." Crew speaks into his phone but stares at me as he kicks off the wall. He opens his mouth.

I freeze for a second, and a single brow lifts before me, so with slow *is this or isn't this what he's trying to tell me* movements, I peel open the plastic, reaching inside.

Checking now would be gross, but I'm pretty sure my palms begin to sweat as I lift the fluffy, still-warm cookie to his moistened, thick lips.

Crew leans forward and takes nearly the entire thing into his mouth, the corner of his tongue sneaking out to help it along. He chews quickly, but his mouth is still half full when he adds, "Guess we'll see," before stuffing the phone in his pocket, his gaze never once leaving mine.

"Those mine?"

"You mean you haven't heard?" I hold the clear plastic to my waistline, giving a little sideways pose. "Ziplocs are the new fanny packs."

Crew nods in playful mockery, snagging the bag before I realize he's reached out. "Maybe the comeback of the fanny pack isn't the worst relaunch after all." He digs in for another.

Nudging his shoulder with mine, I follow him to the door, slipping under his arm when he holds it open for me. The heavy metal slams with a loud smack behind us, making me jump. Short and shadowed in darkness, the area allows no outside light, and suddenly, I'm aware of the hard, wide chest pressing closer to my back.

"Thank you, Sweets. I like that you remember."

His words, they're so soft, almost as if he chose to wait until we were hidden in this small space to speak them.

"Of course, I do." I don't know why I whisper, but that's what comes out, so I follow in a rush. "I mean, you only begged for these every day for an entire summer."

"I didn't have to beg, and you know it. You like making things for me."

My lips pull to one side, but I try and hide the smile in my voice. "Maybe . . . maybe I only did it to prime you, so you'd help buy me beer until I turned twenty-one."

"How'd that work out for you?"

I chuckle and the lights flick on up ahead, so I start walking forward. "Meh, you said yes once, so not a total loss."

Crew scoffs as he slips past me. "Yeah, once out of too many is what you call a success."

"Hey, I was the wonder woman that night, came to the rescue of several girls in my class, considering none of it was for me."

He shakes his head and curves around the bar, quickly pouring two glasses of water. He sets one down in front of the stool I climb up on and downs half of the other before I've wrapped my fingers around my own.

"Seriously, thank you." He taps on the cookie bag, going in for another. "I've missed your sweets."

"You're welcome." I smile, willing my stomach to stop swirling at his omission.

Crew stares for several moments, quietly chewing before finishing off his glass and setting it somewhere behind the bar. And then he stares some more, all calm, cool, and collected, giving me nothing to go on.

"Are you going to make me guess or what are we doing here?"

His lips form a tight line, and he presses his forearms against the counter. "Impatient. Some things never change."

"Oh please." I give a dramatic eye roll. "Don't act like you don't know me or I don't know you."

"We're not around each other every day anymore, Davis. There are a lot of things about you I don't know, and plenty about me *you* don't know."

He leans forward in challenge, and I meet him with one of my own, fully prepared to prove him oh so wrong, but then I remember the other day, and the girl behind the front door I knew to be his. Clearly, it isn't anymore, and while I didn't go through his mail, I did peek at the envelope at the very bottom of the shoebox. The date on it was from November. It's almost June.

Crew's right. I don't know everything about him anymore, and maybe I haven't for longer than I realized. Sure, it's been three years since I've seen him—not that him helping my dad move me into my apartment counts—but it's been a lot longer than that since we shared a home, shared lives.

He and Memphis left for college my sophomore year of high school, and while they visited it wasn't enough, and then after the summer before my senior year, it wasn't at all.

Sadly, it was the same when I got here. My presence didn't magically bring him back to me, if anything, the distance felt greater. We went from neighbors across a pond to oceans away from one another, or at least that's how it felt.

But while I may not know him like I wish I did, like I used to and want to, and feel this deep, irrational need to, there's not a whole lot about me left unsaid, the one and only thing I can think being my sad sex life and its lack of existence. I cleared that up quick, didn't I?

"You said you wanted to chat about our deal," I press.

"What happened with that guy today?"

My brows snap together. "What guy?"

A huffed laugh escapes him, and he licks his lips. "Anyone else and I would've sworn they were playing dumb, but not you." It's on the tip of my tongue to ask what he means, but he continues before I can. "The guy from the diner this morning. The one with the hat. The one who forgot what he was saying."

"Ohhh. Right." *That guy*. "What about him?"

Crew stares some more, and I'm about ready to throw my water in his face to force him to form some sort of readable expression, but then he sighs. "Nothing. Forget about the guy. I thought about this deal we made, and if there are things you want or need—"

"Lessons for, help with, assistance in?" I jump in, eager to hear what he's been thinking.

Creases form along his forehead, but he nods. "Yeah."

"There are things. There are a *lot* of things, lessons, for me to learn."

He blinks hard. "Right. That's what I'm getting at. You're going to have to tell me what those are. Some will be obvious or might become obvious, but others not so much."

"So we'll need to collaborate more?"

I'm not sure Crew could look any more irritated than he does right now, what with the instant sharpness of his gaze and pissy twist of his lips.

"What?"

A harsh breath pushes past his nostrils and he shakes his head. "Nothing. This is your show, but I will have questions."

"I like questions."

A shadow of a grin crosses his lips, but he licks it away. "I know and I expect you to answer all of mine, no matter what. Can you do that?"

I nod so hard my ponytail comes loose.

He pushes on. "Without hiding things you're too embarrassed or afraid or whatever else to share?"

"I'm not embarrassed."

"When was the last time you made yourself come?"

"Oh my god!"

Crew smiles wide, a low laugh leaving him as he leans forward once more. "What's wrong . . . embarrassed?"

"Remember when I was eight, and you asked if I wanted to see the giant worm you found in my backyard, but when I nodded, you dangled a two-foot snake in front of my face? That's what happened here. Expected one thing, got another, nothing else, so if that was a real question and one intended to get a rise out of me, ask it again, and I'll tell you."

He watches me closely, his knee bouncing a bit, but when he says nothing, I continue.

"Yes, I will answer your questions without shame, and you will be working on finding me a guy, correct?"

The glare comes quick. "That's final stage, Baby Franco. Far the fuck away from right now."

"So, we're doing this thing all the way through?"

In true Crew fashion, his agreement is a heavy rumble deep in his chest.

A quick squeal leaves me, and I clap my hands together, wiggling my fingers at the edge of my lips. His eyes jerk back to mine when my palms slap against the wooden bar top with a loud smack.

"Okay. Now let's talk about the deadline."

"Deadline," he deadpans, slowly crossing his arms over his chest. "What *deadline*?"

"All projects have a due date, Mr. Taylor."

"You're not a project, Baby Franco."

"Call this little partner pact whatever you wish." Leaning my elbows on the wooden surface, I loosely entwine my fingers, resting my chin where my knuckles meet. "But I expect to be properly probed thirty days from today."

Chapter 10

Davis

It's safe to say I freaked Crew out with my little "properly probed" spiel. He didn't have much to say before I left that day, and here we are, another four days dry, taking my thirty-day deadline down to a scarce twenty-six. Not that I'm worried. He knows a lot of people and I'm sure it won't be too hard for him to convince someone to claim my *V* as their own, not that I'm giving up on him giving in and claiming the job for himself.

To pass the time, I made a list of all the things I need his help with, and it's a bit longer than expected, but again, I'm not worried. He's some sort of woman magnet, so I know he'll catch me up to speed on how to be the kind of woman capable of gaining the attention of a man like him.

My classes seem to drag, my days even more so, since everyone is gearing up for the end of the school year. With finals approaching, my courses have morphed into nothing but study hall sessions for people who fell behind to catch up on things for a lower grade. I have nothing left undone, so I used the time to review for said finals, leaving me with more free time outside of class. Rachel was eager to fill in the gaps for me and no way am I going to turn down the extra cash. I fully intend to take a trip after graduation, one wholly funded by tips.

Thirty minutes into today's last-minute shift, none other than Black Hat Guy walks in, requesting a seat in my section.

Calling on the last lesson, I step up to his table, looking directly at him.

He leans back in the booth, one long, lean arm lying out across it. "Hi again."

"You have blue eyes."

His lips curve up. "Since I was born, yeah. You have brown eyes."

"Yeah, I do, basic like a boss."

A chuckle escapes him, and his smile seems to hold, so I give myself a metaphorical pat on the back.

Pad and pen in hand, I grin. "What can I get you?"

There is a wickedness that weaves into his eyes, even I can't miss, and he leans forward, the octave in his tone lowering. "Surprise me."

Oh, he is so flirting!

Yay me!

Wait. What do I do now?

Keep flirting? Make a dirty joke? Say something interesting?

I smile and walk away.

And then I have Martha deliver his plate . . . followed by his check, being sure I made myself scarce until he was long gone.

Yeah, ignoring him is probably not the right decision, but it's Crew's fault! He's slacking in his instructions, and I'm prepared to tell him so. As if he's a mind reader, my phone beeps with an incoming text.

Crew: working today?

Me: clocked out ten minutes ago. Just walked in my front door, mentally preparing to call and yell at you. Why?

Crew: you can yell at me on the way to a barbeque. Wear whatever you would to something like that. I'll pick you up at four.

Glancing at my clock, I see it's a little after two, so I call Jess for a quick, homemade caramel Frappuccino date.

A few hours later, Crew's knock comes, and I open to find him dressed in a gray T-shirt, doing its best to suffocate his biceps.

He steps inside, his gaze passively washing over me. "You got a swimsuit?"

"Yes."

"Grab it, let me see." Crew turns, dropping onto the couch without another word.

Okay then. I beeline toward my room, digging around in not one but two messy drawers, finding each piece in a different spot, and carrying them back into the living room.

He looks over as I stop beside him and throws himself back in annoyance. "Not in your hand. Put it on."

"Why?" I hold up the top, then toss it over my shoulder, doing the same with the bottoms. "It's the same thing."

"It's not, but if you're worried about something showing, I can wait while you handle that."

My mouth opens and closes. "What?"

His eyes snap to my lower half then come right back up.

"Yeah . . ." I trail off with a shake of my head. "Still don't understand Crew-isms. Sorry."

A harsh breath pushes past his nostrils, and he scoots to the edge of the seat. "If I pull down your mom jeans, are you going to have braids sticking out of your granny panties?"

"I do not wear granny panties, thank you very much."

"Braids or no braids?"

"Ugh!" I drop my head back, quickly refocusing on the man in front of me. "Sure, since you're unwilling to strip me naked and lay me down to find out on your own, I'll tell you, I am fully and completely groomed. Bare to the touch and smoother than any pickup line you could muster."

His head jerks forward then, pressing his lips into a firm line. "Good. Forget trying it on." He shoots to his feet. "Let's just go."

"You sure I won't embarrass you in my outfit? I'll have you know they're called boyfriend jeans, and they're trendy."

"Then they must be meant for girls who already have boyfriends and intended to deflect the rest of the male species."

I gape at him. "You said wear what I would normally wear

to a barbecue. This is what I would wear to a barbecue, jeans and a cute top. So what is the issue?"

Crew steps into my space, stealing all my air and claiming it as his own as he barks down at me. "The problem, little girl, is you look like a kindergarten teacher who raided her mom's closet and swore off men, but then stand here looking me in the fucking eye while you paint a pretty fucking picture of your pussy like a twenty-one-year-old woman who's trying to get fucked." He drags in a quick breath. "You make no fucking sense, and you piss me off."

I take a step back, studying him closely, noting the slight tic at his temple and the sharpness of his jaw. His muscles are tense and the vein in his neck throbs.

He does this, rants and raves when something's not quite right, been that way since forever. Pushes when feeling pulled in two.

"What's wrong?"

His eyes snap to mine, narrowing. "What? Nothing, let's go."

He goes to walk away, but I reach out, catching his pinkie and ring finger, and he glances back.

"What's wrong?"

For a long moment, he doesn't say anything, so long in fact, I'm convinced he won't, but as I'm about to let go, his shoulders sag, and he fully faces me.

"I'm being a dick."

"You're being a *super*dick." I tip my head. "You know they have little capes for cocks, right? With one little clip, we can call you Captain Cock."

A laugh spurts from him, and his lips hook up the slightest bit. "Pretty sure Captain America doesn't have a cape."

"Hey, this is my fan fiction. Get your own."

Another soft chuckle escapes him, and his gaze roams along my face.

"Come on," I say softly. "What's wrong?"

Glancing toward the sliding glass door, he sighs. "It's dumb shit with the bar."

"Did someone call in again?"

"No, there's some electrical issue we have to work out, and we will, but forget all that. Let's get out of here." Twisting his wrist, so he can grab hold of my hand, he leads me toward the door. "I'm starving, and the food's going to be good. My buddy's wife used to work for some catering business, so she's always making cool shit."

"You had me at food." Climbing inside the car, I buckle myself, waiting until he's behind the wheel and we're pulling out to ask, "So what happened to the Mazda? You swore you'd never give up on that thing."

Crew's lips form a tight line, creases building along his temples. "Totaled."

My brows jump, waiting for an explanation.

Is that how he got the second scar on his chin? Or the hint of the one peeking from under the sleeve covering his right bicep?

He says nothing else on the matter, and I swallow the disappointment.

He doesn't have to share with you everything you've missed, Davis.

I swallow, asking something a little more relevant. "So you're pretty close with this person?"

Small creases frame the edge of Crew's face, but he nods. "His name's Willie. He used to work at the bar, but he saved up some money and opened a little brewery. It's small and only makes enough to sell back to the bar he started at, but it's his. He's a good guy."

"Weird."

He cuts a quick look my way. "What is?"

"You're old enough to have married friends now."

"Girl, you're not much younger than me."

"And *finally,* the man admits it."

Crew grins but tries to hide it.

"So, you met Willie working at the bar?"

"No, I met him when I visited the bar for the first time. I was dancing with some girl, and the next thing I know, I woke flat on my back, Willie standing over me with an ice pack." He shakes his head, turning left at the stoplight. "Come to find out, he was the son of the bitch who punched me."

"I take it the girl you were dancing with was his wife?"

"Nope. His baby sister."

"That will do it, too."

"Yes, it will," he mumbles, and then we're turning into a small court.

The houses around are small, modest homes, a little older, but clean and welcoming.

Shoving my bathing suit into my small purse, I hustle after Crew, almost having to break out into a run to keep up with his mammoth strides.

He goes to open the door, but I slap his hand away from the knob before he can grip it fully, and he looks at me with a frown.

"Okay, now I'm nervous. Do I really look like a man repellent? I don't want to embarrass you in front of your friends. To be honest, I didn't even think you had friends, so now that I know you do, I really don't—"

My mouth clamps shut when Crew pushes forward to grip my chin.

"I said I was being an ass."

"But my pants—"

"Hug your ass nicely and shape your hips just right. Yeah, the legs are baggy, but know what that does?"

I shake my head, and his eyes move between mine.

"It makes a man wonder what's hidden beneath them."

"What if they're mediocre at best?"

Creases form along his brow. "I've seen your legs, Davis."

K, but what does that mean?

Without warning, Crew opens the door and pulls me through it.

Not one foot inside and I'm met with a tall, tan, *shirtless* man with eyes the color of cotton candy, the blue kind from the fair. His smile's crooked and deepens by the second, his tongue slipping out to tease along his upper lip and . . .

"My, oh my," I mutter. "It's a fuckboy in the flesh."

My hand is jerked, my head snapping toward Crew, who glares hard, but it's the laugh from the man a few feet away that steals the show.

It's deep and rich and—

Fuckboy's staring at me.

Now he's walking toward me!

Oh my god, he's smirking, and it's delicious and dirty and—

I can't do this.

Holy shit, I can't do this.

Can't be the butter in the spiciest of feasts, I'll spread too easy, melt too fast.

I'll be a puddle for him to lick up and that wasn't the deal. Crew gets to pick, and something tells me this guy is *not* the one.

The gorgeous creature stops right in front of me, opens his mouth to speak *to me*, and my pulse threatens my consciousness, so I do the only logical thing I can think of.

I spin.

And then I crush my lips to Crew's.

Chapter 11
Davis

Oh my god, I'm kissing Crew.

Oh my *god*, his lips are as lush and as pillowy as they look, all soft and full, but with a hint of toughened skin, giving the slightest bit of a graze. Goose bumps spread along my arms, and chills follow.

What the hell am I doing?

"What the hell are you doing?" he whispers, his breath fanning along my face.

My eyes snap open and I tug back, but only by a hair.

"Holy shit. I'm sorry."

My hands latch on to his biceps, and his frown deepens, but he dips his chin as if to ask if I'm okay.

But as he silently asks, the reality of the situation hits.

First, it's that I kissed Crew Taylor, and he didn't kiss me back.

Second, there's no noise in the background behind me. The room's gone silent, when it was full of banter and movement two minutes before. My blood warms, my palms flying to my cheeks, and sure enough, they're hot to the touch.

Sighing, I drop my forehead to Crew's chest.

"Are you mad?"

"I might be."

"I panicked."

"Yeah, I got that."

Yeah, he's mad. His tone leaks with irritation, frustration. Condemnation.

"Everyone is staring, aren't they?"

His chest rises with a deep breath, and so I lift mine, meeting his eyes. "Only Julius."

"Wow, even his name is—"

"Stop," Crew snaps.

My lips smack closed, and I nod, lowering my hands to my side as I take a deep breath.

Slowly, I turn to the *should be the lead in a porno* male with an awkward wave and tight smile. "Uh . . . hi."

"Hi." He doesn't miss a beat, his gaze flicking to the broody man beside me and back. He takes a slow step closer and offers me his hand, so I give him mine.

He squeezes and little imaginative hearts dance in front of my eyes. "I'm Julius."

"I'm a virgin."

His eyes go wide.

Mine go wider.

And then he laughs and I'm certain I'm about to catch fire.

"Oh my god." I tear my hand away, and I must try to retreat because, next thing I know, I'm bumping into Crew and his hand latches on to my hip, forcing me not to run.

"A virgin, huh?" He couldn't possibly grin wider, and I sort of want to die, but I'm glad I don't when I get to watch the path his hand takes as it rises, gliding along his tattooed chest. "Haven't met one of those in a while."

"I'm working on it."

"For fuck's sake," is huffed near my ear.

I go to look over my shoulder, but then Julius speaks again.

"Are you now?" He crosses his arms. "This guy helping you out with that?"

I scoff. "You should have seen his face when I—"

Crew's fingers dig into my hip bone in warning, his fingers hot and tight against my skin, and my words die in my throat, my every muscle curling into the next as all sorts of spicy images flash in my mind.

I swallow, and Julius's grin manages to spread wider.

"Julius, down boy," an unfamiliar male voice teases.

Beyond Julius, my gaze finds the new incomer, and oh god.

"No . . ."

"Yeah," a sweeter, softer voice sings.

Not a moment later, a petite woman is at my side. She's young with white-blonde hair, big brown eyes, and a very pregnant belly. She can't be much older than me, if at all.

The woman playfully scowls at Crew, literally pries his hands from my hips, and wraps her arm through mine, dragging me away.

"Yeah," she teases playfully as she guides me out the back door. "I hit the husband jackpot."

"You didn't think so when they tested you!"

"Hey, Xavier. Fuck off." She smiles sweetly, and Xavier, as she called him, comes into view.

He's also shirtless and perched on the edge of the pool, beer bottle dangling from his fingers. He winks my way, quickly going back to his conversation with the girl beside him.

"That's X, Will's younger brother. As soon as the other two found out Willie told me he loved me, Julius snuck into my bed. He tried to get me under the sheets, so I walked over and smashed the four-inch wedge I was wearing into his balls. He thought he could fool me, but I know every inch of my man." She smiles proudly as she releases me and taps her palm to one of the ice chests pushed against the wall. "Whatever you'd like is yours, but if you take the last one, grab a new case from the garage and refill."

"My name's Davis," I say lamely, but she simply grins.

"I know." She grips the back of a wicker chair, glancing toward the living room. "With a husband as hot as mine and brothers-in-law I love, do you really think I'd allow a single woman to walk through my door without knowing who she is and why she's here?"

"If my husband looked like that, I might make a 'no women allowed' rule."

"Exactly." She wiggles her brows. "Remember that if you and Crew go far."

"Oh god. No. Oh no." My head shakes wildly. "We're not dating. See, I panicked inside when Hot Twin One came at me, and it was the only thing I could think of at the time. Not that I haven't thought about it before, but I *definitely* wouldn't have done it if my brain cells were circuiting properly."

The woman laughs. "Relax. I was kidding. I have to go check on the food, but please, unwind, hop in the pool, eat whatever you can find, and if you need me, ask for Layla." With that, she winks and walks away.

I decide I like Layla.

Feeling far more comfortable than before, I breathe a sigh of relief and accept her offer for something cold to drink. I take the first thing on the top and pop it open, unconcerned with what it is. The chilled aluminum meets my bottom lip right as Crew appears, making me jump, the contents of the can splashing over me.

"Holy shit, it's cold." I bend, pulling the material from my skin.

Crew's eyes fall to the wet spot, quickly snapping back to mine. "You need to relax."

"And you need to warn a girl when she's about to walk into a Magic Mike audition," I hiss.

Frown deepening, he presses forward. "How do you expect to fuck a man if you can't even handle attention from one?"

"You can't push me straight to the top of the male scale. You've got to start me off slow, and I'm pretty sure I peak at a low six. *That man*?" I hook my thumb over my shoulder. "Is next-level shit."

His jaw tics, and I wait for it. "And *that man* thinks you're fucking adorable."

Okay, not what I was expecting him to say.

That makes no sense. "But . . . I acted like a crazy person."

"His ex would sleep on his front porch when they would fight, so he couldn't leave without talking to her." Twin number two steps up beside Crew, his grin as ridiculous as his brother's. "Crazy is kind of his thing."

The corners of my mouth lift. "Willie, I presume?"

"Aww, he told you about me?" Willie presses a hand over his heart, stumbling when Crew shoves him in the arm. Willie smiles and gone is the teasing glint in the man's eyes. All that's left is a sweet, sincere fondness for the boy I grew up with.

"Yeah, girl, I'm Willie." He grabs my hand, cupping it with his own, a moment before letting go and snagging a fresh beer for himself. "Nice to meet you, Davis. Surprised you don't know my brother and some of his boys already. He plays baseball for Avix."

That explains the sugary swag and lean, muscular builds.

"I haven't been to a game since—" I pause, cutting a quick look at Crew. Since the night of their first game their freshman year at Avix, the only one Crew played before he was kicked out of college. "You know, I didn't make it to a single one since I started here."

"If you can't make it before the end of this season, don't bother with next. Two of their best players graduate with you this year, so these punks will probably fuck up my fantasy league for next season anyway."

"Dick!" someone shouts from the left.

Willie grins, his comment clearly made to purposely tease those around us. "Well, hey, glad you came, the more here to celebrate, the merrier."

"Celebrate?"

"He didn't tell you?" Willie smacks Crew in the chest. "This man's the only person who knows the power of my seed. We're going to pull the string on these popper things and see if I get myself a poker table or if Layla's getting a massage chair."

"She's pregnant. She wins."

"Honey, she's been winning. Trust me. Twice most days, all right, but daddy needs a new card table, so he can win enough to buy her that damn chair." Willie chuckles, and I pretend to follow.

"He means he makes her come twice a day."

My head snaps to Crew, and I glare. "I know."

"Sure, you did."

My stupid cheeks threaten to heat, so I spin away from Crew, blocking him as best I can while still facing Willie. "So this is a gender-reveal party?"

He shrugs. "I guess. We barbeque often, at one house or another, usually once a week, but yeah, we're adding that to the fun today."

"You want a boy?"

"Nope." His eyes seem to drift on their own accord and I follow his line of sight to the platinum-blonde woman bobbing to the music in front of the food table, one hand cupping her belly, the other holding a half-eaten slice of watermelon.

He wants a mini-Layla.

Aaand I'm back to melting.

He walks away, and once again, I'm left beside Crew, but this time, he doesn't speak. He quietly drinks from his water bottle, so I do the same.

It's no more than an hour later that I find myself laughing hysterically at something a guy named Neo says and doubling over when another named Matt acts out the scene Neo shared.

Apparently, Matt works at the bar Crew manages, and he came equipped with a shitload of stories to tell.

It's closer to six now, the sun's still beating heavily above us, so I quietly leave the group conversation in search of something to drink. Deciding on good ole H_2O, I walk over to the fan plugged in on the patio.

Lifting my hair, I let the slightly cooler air blow along my neck for a few minutes.

My eyes travel the yard, from the grassy area on one side to the pool and lawn chairs on the other, noting how people casually go from one group to the next, some even shouting across the space to get whoever's attention it is they're after. There's a sense of comfort among them all, making it appear they've known each other for years. Maybe they have.

A blond guy standing next to a girl Layla introduced as Toni catches my eye, saluting me with a wink before looking back to her, and that snags twin number one's attention. Julius looks over, grinning around the neck of his beer bottle, and he doesn't look away.

"You might be in a T-shirt and jeans with polka dot shoes, but you've got a bathing suit dangling from your bag, and those little flowery strings alone are keeping the single men here locked onto your every move."

I look at Crew, but he continues facing forward.

He takes a small sip from what looks like lemonade and continues, "They're waiting for the moment you disappear, and hoping when you come back, it's all you've got on."

My stomach dips with an unfamiliar sensation, a mix of nervous excitement sprinkled with something a lot like cool confidence, but I don't allow it to spread.

I swallow. "So why tease me earlier?"

Crew's quiet a moment before he says, "I'd tell you if I knew."

He meets my eyes, and then he's gone.

A little over an hour later and everyone has migrated toward the water.

I've been sitting along the edge in the shallow end for about fifteen minutes, laughing at the poorly played game of volleyball happening in the center, when Julius lowers himself beside me.

"So . . ." He dangles his feet as I am, nudging me with his solid shoulder.

"Yeah," I drag out with a sigh. "Awkward, and I vibe sometimes."

"Hey, it was pretty memorable, and is that not the point?" That grin of his grows into a smirk.

I eye him as I take a small sip from my freshly popped soda can. "What makes you think I want you to remember me?"

"See, that's the beauty of it, Davis the Virgin." He leaps down then, submerging his body in the water before popping back up. He brings his hands up, wiping them over his face, and then runs them through his hair, purposely flicking the cool water along my thighs. "It's the ones who don't try for the attention who end up earning it."

"Well, if you would be so kind and point yours in another direction, that would be great."

"And why would I do that?"

"Because there is no way a girl like me could handle an ego like yours. You're a Polo model gone rogue, and I'm more on level with the dude from the insurance commercials."

He barks a laugh, gaining the attention of a few of his friends swimming nearby. Crew flicks his eyes from Julius to me but moves them back to Willie just as fast.

"See. Shit like that . . ." Julius darts forward, and before I realize what's coming, I'm already lifted and lowered into the water.

I gasp as the chilled water swashes over my heated middle, my gaze settling on his.

He's shorter than Crew by a few inches, so I don't have to stretch my neck as far up with him directly in front of me. Water droplets roll down the tattoos covering his bronzed skin, and while I do my best not to follow the path they take, my best is a solid *C* minus.

"It's shit like that," he repeats in a tantalizing tease. "That guarantees I won't forget the sweet, not quite shy . . . virgin."

I smack him in the chest, and he laughs good-heartedly, slowly backing away.

"I'm pretty sure it's the virgin thing."

"I'm pretty sure you're right." He winks, disappearing under the water, and takes off to the other side.

Shaking my head, I breathe a little sigh, a small smile on my lips. I know he's kidding. While the whole virgin thing was probably a shock, mainly because of the way I casually confused it for my name, he's not mocking me. He is simply a big fat flirt, and honestly, I'm proud I can recognize the difference.

I'd say lesson number two has been mastered.

Thank you, Mr. Taylor.

I push off the side, dunk under the water, and do a few laps. If swimming underwater from one end to the other counts as "laps." I never did learn how to swim overhand, but I see no need for that. Out of breath, I move to the little bench seat on the curved edge near the middle.

Giving my hair a quick shake out with my fingers, I flip the top over and lean back on my palms, so the sun can beat down on my face.

It can't be but a few minutes later, when the water sloshes around me, and I don't have to open my eyes to know who sat down.

"I knew he'd make his way to you eventually," he claims.

Opening one eye, I glance at Crew.

His attention is pointed at the game of keep-away he abandoned. "What did he have to say?"

"He wanted to make sure I wasn't dying from embarrassment."

"And that requires touching you?"

"I get the feeling he's a touchy-feely guy." I look across the water to where Julius mirrors Willie's position, hanging off the edge of Layla's raft. "I really—"

Crew's sharp scoff cuts me off, and I face him just in time to catch the shake of his head.

"What?"

"You don't know him enough to like him, Davis."

"Have you never heard of love at first sight?"

His head swivels my way so fast, I would bet his vision needs a moment to catch up, but when he spots the hidden grin on my lips, his glare goes from pissy to puzzled.

"Kidding. Obviously." My smile breaks free. "All I was going to say was I really *appreciate* you bringing me today. I don't hang out with people outside of school, so this has been fun."

Crew's brows crash, and he looks off, attempting to hide the way he clears his throat. "I'm glad you're having fun."

"Uh-huh, so long as I'm not having *too* much fun, right?" I tease, dropping myself back into the water.

Crew's eyes come to mine and a small grin crosses his lips, but he erases it, as usual.

I wait until he looks off and then swim in closer, pressing the bottom of my foot against the pebbled wall. Grabbing both his legs, I yank as hard as I can, and thanks to the water, I'm able to pull his big-ass body straight in.

He sinks, coming back up with a splash, his sunglasses floating off around him. "Oh, you think you're cute."

I swim away, yelping and holding my breath when he tugs me back, and I go down, but he's got us back to the edge in seconds. In a flash, I'm tossed over his shoulder and he's stepping out, right onto the diving board.

"Crew Taylor, I will castrate you!" I shout. "I know exactly how to do it without cutting too deep!" I tug at his black tank top.

"Rip it and pay," he warns.

"Why are you wearing this in the water anyway?!"

His friends whoop and holler around us, and Crew laughs, smacking my ass so loud it echoes, then into the air we go.

I scream as we crash into the pool, and when we come up, we're both laughing.

This time, he doesn't cut his short.

With my lips tucked beneath the surface, I grin, enjoying the way he smiles back.

I miss this Crew.

The one who didn't hide himself from me.

It's sad how we grew apart the last few years.

It's even sadder knowing he wanted it that way.

By eight, all guests are gone, and Layla needs to get off her feet so she asks if I want to join her in the house. Being it would have left me with Crew, the twins, and brother number three, her invite is lifesaving.

We sit at the makeshift bar, but every few minutes, she looks at the mess, so I found a way to convince her to let me do the dirty work.

Once the kitchen is spotless, she walks me to the back of the house to show me the baby's nursery.

"Willie painted the walls, and then all the boys came over one day, put the furniture together, hung the shelves, and all I had to do was point out what I wanted where. We managed to get it all done in a weekend." Layla smiles at the space, running her fingers over the soft-pink shams she and I slid onto the rod not five minutes ago.

Willie is getting his girl.

"It's really beautiful, Layla."

"Thanks. We told Crew we could scoot the crib over and he could put his mattress down or even crash on the couch until everything gets squared away with the electric issue at the bar, but he wouldn't go for it. He'd rather put himself in a bad spot by getting a hotel. The man is always worried about wearing out his welcome, which will never happen around here."

Wait, what?

Squared away at the bar . . .

It hits me then. The cot in the tiny, closet-sized office in the back of the bar, the pile of mail sitting on my bedroom dresser, the near-naked woman who opened the door that's no longer his.

Crew's living at the bar on the springy foldable cot crappier than a hotel rollaway. Now the bar is closed, hopefully for no longer than a couple days, but still. A few days is a few days he'll be without a home.

Layla looks at me, and I realize I've yet to say anything, so I draw on a small smile and nod.

"Yeah, he's sort of always been that way. My mom would ask him to stay for dinner every single day, but she would say 'it's like pulling teeth to get him to accept without a fight.'" I don't tell her how the nights we couldn't convince him, he would go to bed hungry because there was nobody to make him meals at home.

There was nothing for him to make himself either.

"After a while, she stopped asking and pulled her mom voice out. Basically, he wasn't allowed to go home until he cleared his plate." And then his parents signed their rights over to mine. Unwanted by his family at fourteen years old, Crew legally joined mine. His mom and dad disappeared with Drew, not long after that.

That was the only time I saw Crew cry.

Layla's low laugh has me blinking back into reality, and I watch as she lovingly rubs her belly.

She may know that about Crew already, but if she doesn't, it's not my place to tell, though the sorrowful smile covering her lips in the next moment indicates she knows a little bit of something. Whether that something has to do with Crew's upbringing or knowledge of my brother, I don't know.

"Ready?" Crew pops his head in the room.

Masking the runaway thoughts in my mind, I nod, saying a quick thank you and goodbye to Layla on my way out.

The ride home is an odd mix of relaxed and uneasy.

I've never been anxious around Crew. And while I do enjoy the nonsense of it, I've never felt a need to fill in the silence with random conversation, but before I *knew* Crew, and as he flat out said, I don't anymore. Not fully.

Not as well as his new friends do.

A heavy sense of grief washes over me and I look to my lap, rolling the stray strings where the rips in my jeans are.

He was Memphis's Crew before.

My Crew.

He's not anymore.

Now, he's theirs.

It makes me wonder. If I hadn't reached out to him, would he have eventually reached out to me?

I'm beginning to think not.

"Are you headed home from here?" The moment I ask, I wish I could take it back, especially when Crew's lie rolls off his tongue without pause.

"Yep."

I nod back, even though he's focused on the road ahead, but the closer we get to my apartment, the more the situation nags at me.

So, once he's pulled up in the space beside my car, I turn to him, blindly pulling on the handle.

"Come in a minute?" Before he has a chance to say no, I add, "I have something of yours I've been meaning to give you."

Unable to taper down his curiosity, he turns off the car and follows me to the door.

Inside, I move straight to my bedroom, heading back into the living room in seconds. Stepping up to Crew, I place the box against his chest, forcing him to grab hold or let it fall. His questioning frown bounces from it to me, but I quickly swivel into the kitchen, grabbing what I'm after in the first drawer to the left.

Being the box is still closed in his palms when I turn to face him, I have no doubt he's about to get far more confused, but it won't take him long to figure out.

"Here." I drop the key on top of the shoebox, and he glares from it to me. "My roommate moved out last summer, so the room next to mine is as empty as it was the day you helped move me in."

"Davis . . ." His face falls.

"Stay, Crew. The room is as good as yours now." Offering a small smile, I give an encouraging nod as I begin to back away.

"Where you going?" His question is a quick demand, yet his tone holds a heaviness he can't—and no doubt tried—to hide.

"I have to be up early so . . ."

He shows no sign of breaking eye contact, and even once I do, something tells me he stays frozen in the spot I left him long after I close my bedroom door behind me.

Chapter 12
Davis

Last night I did something I never do, something my dad would ream me out over, but it felt necessary. I slept with my headphones on, "putting myself in a potentially dangerous situation," as he always said, because I knew if I didn't, I would obsess over everything I heard, trying to decipher whether Crew took my offer for what it was.

A not-so-subtle confirmation that I am aware he lied to me in the truck, not that he had any reason to look for one. He had no idea I knew he moved, let alone he was living at the bar he worked at.

Is he there because he wants to be?

Has to be?

Likes to be?

Doubtful. Crew might not have come from a safe, heartening place, but he was brought into one with my family, and while the adjustment was extreme, he came to crave the calm a quiet night under a warm, clean comforter provided.

I go about my normal morning routine, making my bed and laying out my clothes for the day on top, before heading to the shower.

The apartment is silent when I step into the hall, as it was when I woke with my earbuds wrapped up beside me, so there's nothing off the bat that indicates he's here, and I refuse to look inside the bedroom.

Besides, the door's closed.

So I climb into the shower, take my time under the spray,

and when I get out, there's still no sign of the man. Returning to my room, I dress, brush out my wet hair and twist a small section on the left, adding a hot-pink, double-cherry hair clip and head into the kitchen.

As I'm squeezing the Hershey's strawberry syrup into my glass of milk, a door in the hall is torn open and heavy footsteps pound against the floor.

Crew stalks into the kitchen like a bat out of hell.

I catch the excess drizzle from the tip of the bottle with the pad of my middle finger and swipe it along my tongue, while using a straw as a stirrer. I look up at him, and his glare comes out to play.

"Want some?" I offer.

"Are you fucking kidding me?"

Well, okay then. He's had time to process.

I don't bother speaking. He's sure to continue, and it only takes two-point-five seconds of silence for him to get to it.

"You have been living here *by yourself* for a year and you didn't fucking tell me? Does your dad know? I'm betting he doesn't, because if he knew, then I would know. He would've done what *you* should have done and told me. Why the hell didn't you tell me?"

He drags in a quick breath, crossing his arms over his chest, as I draw the straw between my lips, watching as an array of emotions flicker across his face.

"Davis," he snaps.

Tearing a napkin from the holder, I fold and set my drink on it. "I have a final in about an hour, a four-hour shift at the diner after, and this evening, I'm celebrating acing said final with pizza night at Jess's, so I'm going to get going." I move around the corner and his eyes follow. "The room is yours if you want it, for as long as you want it."

"Davis," he calls at my back, but my keys are already in my hand, and I'm out the door.

I'm half surprised he doesn't follow and force me to talk to him, but I have a feeling he knows if he does, I can direct his questions right back at him.

We both know he's not interested in answering, so for the first time, possibly ever, I have a leg up.

Knowing Crew, though, that will only last so long.

It's almost midnight by the time I'm shoving my key in the hole that seems to have shrunk since the last time I used it; the dang thing doesn't seem to want to fit. The key grows heavy and slips between my fingers, bouncing off my purse and clanging against the doorframe and my Willy Wonka doormat.

"Ugh!" I bend down, using the knob as support, and just as I'm at full bend, the knob is turned, the door tugged open, taking me with it.

"Ah!" I fall sideways, right into warm, waiting hands.

My eyes snap up, connecting with a pair of deep, marble ones.

I smile at Crew. "You stayed."

Small creases form along his temple as he helps me stand, his arm shooting around my middle when I trip over his foot. My chest crashes into his with one single yank, and those creases deepen.

"Aww, you're like a worried dad, waiting up and stuff."

"You're drunk," he notes softly.

"Mmm." I tip my head back and forth. "I'm a hair past buzzed, at best."

"Only a hair, huh?" His attention moves to my hair then, and he lifts a knuckle, freeing the strands sticking to my ChapStick-covered lips. His gaze holds on the cherry hair clip, before returning to my eyes. "Better?"

I nod.

"This what you normally wear to pizza night?" He flicks the waist of my yoga pants, as his eyes focus on the falling strap of my baggy tank.

I shrug.

He frowns at my outfit. "Wouldn't even call those pajamas."

"Frozen pizzas, remember? We never leave the apartment, and it's literally right next to mine. Shocked you didn't hear us laughing through the wall."

Crew shifts, gripping the wide collar of my top, his knuckles scarred from one too many fights in his life, creating a roughness that softly scratches over my skin as he lifts the thin material back onto my shoulder.

Heat floods my veins, my body growing heavier.

"If a guy grabs me like this, what's it mean?"

Crew's frown is quick, and he tenses slightly. "What?"

"You know, if I'm out with someone, and they haul me into them, all caveman, like you just did. What's it mean?"

His teeth clench. "Someone grab you like this before?"

"I wish."

A beat passes, his lips forming a tight line as he stares, and then he jerks closer, drawing a short gasp from me.

"If you're out with a man and he holds you like this." His grip tightens. "It means he wants to be close to you, to feel you. It means he wants to touch you and for you to touch him back."

"Touch him how?"

He gives a slow shake of his head. "Davis—"

He cuts off when my palms come up, pressing over his pecs. I expand my fingers, closing my eyes as I picture it, me in the strong arms of a man who wants me there—I imagine it's Crew who wants me there. My hands drift down to his sternum and back up until the pads of my fingers meet the heated skin of a firmly corded neck, discovering a tiny scar at the nape of it. I soothe the spot with my fingertips, slowly dragging them toward his throat.

A grin pulls at my lips, and my lids peel open, locking with his. "Like that?"

Thick veins flex against my fingertips, his gaze piercing, voice low and raspy. "Why are you smiling?"

"Because that was fun and I kind of feel accomplished now, like I took a pop quiz and made it my bitch."

"Jesus," he whispers, shaking his head with a low, huffed chuckle as he slowly releases me and moves toward the kitchen.

My kitchen.

Our kitchen?

"So, are we back to old times?" I close my hands over the back of a chair, kicking my shoes off. "Me and you under the same roof?"

Crew nods, setting a glass of water in front of me with a stern gleam in his gaze.

I drink it without argument, and with each slow swallow, a heaviness settles over the man before me. One last swallow and I set the glass back down.

"I'm pissed at you, Davis." He looks away, running his tongue along his lips. "How fucked up is that?"

"Pretty fucked up."

His head snaps my way, and he settles slightly when he's met with my small smile.

"You mad at me, too?" he asks.

"You know I'm not." My tone is soft. "A little sad I'm not a part of your life anymore, but not mad you chose not to tell me."

"Stop." He shakes his head. "That's not true."

"No, really, I'm not mad. How fair would it be if I were?"

He pins me with a pointed look. "That's not what I'm talking about."

I shrug.

Crew regards me, something I can't quite read, shadowed behind his eyes.

Unsure of what else to say, I circle around to the couch, and Crew follows, but remains standing when I flop onto the cushion.

Okay, maybe I'm a hair past buzzed.

"You know," I drawl teasingly. "This is pretty ideal. I basically have a live-in tutor now. I'd have killed for one of those my freshman year, when I didn't do my research and signed up for Mr. Moreno's English class. Talk about a tough grader." I narrow my gaze on Crew. "Are you going to be super tough? Make me do things over and over until I'm, I don't know, immune to blushing or something?"

It takes a moment of his staring for him to respond, and when he does, his tone is lighter. "I doubt we could ever get you past that."

"Really? You think I'll forever be plagued with sharing my inner 'he's so fine' and 'that did not just happen?'"

He settles into the spot beside me. "I hope so."

I frown. "What, why?"

His lips pull up, and he peeks at me from the corner of his eye. "I like it when you blush."

I fake gag, and this time, he laughs louder.

Both of us grow quiet, understanding passing between us.

I'm a little hurt, he's a little hurt, but we both made the choice not to inform the other person of our situations and the reasons why are ours alone. You would think the distance and time apart would make the lack of sharing irrelevant or expected, but it isn't. Maybe it's because we're connected on a deeper level.

Maybe it's because I want to know him and for him to know me better than anyone else.

For me, I was trying to respect the distance he made clear he needed for himself, so why say a word when he could still find me if he wanted to? Had we been talking every day, like before, he'd have known the moment I knew, but we weren't.

Plus, he would have so told my dad, and he's right: the parentals have no idea.

My dad's far too paranoid for that. Being a sergeant at a men's prison will do that to a man.

Why Crew didn't tell me about his situation is as obvious as it is depressing—he simply didn't want to, not that it crossed his mind to begin with. And that's okay. Sad, but okay.

He used to call me for no reason, so for him to not call when there was one further confirmed he was settling into a life I wasn't wanted in. Or so it felt.

I know if I needed him, even if ten years of no communication passed, I could still call, and he'd come. I can depend on no one like I can him, cut from his circle or not.

Perching my elbow on the back of the couch, I rest my head on my palm, a small smile on my lips. "When the bar reopens, will you go back to staying there?"

"When you finish school in a few weeks, are you moving out of here?"

"No."

Crew shakes his head, his voice low. "Then, no, I won't be."

"So, we're officially roommates again, only, this time, I won't have to sneak into your room for movie nights when my brother and parents go to bed?"

"Looks like it." He holds my gaze. "Think you can handle me?"

"I literally bribed you for the opportunity to try."

His brows snap together so fast, my laughter cannot be tamed.

"Hey, you have to be careful of your choice of words or things might get a little tricky around here."

He scoffs, running his palms down his face. "Yeah, no shit."

Relaxed, I start browsing through Netflix, settling on a murder documentary, and instead of getting up and walking out, Crew leans back.

We sit in silence, but about fifteen minutes in, something comes to mind, so I press pause and turn to Crew.

"Not to be a cockblocker or anything, but your cock is officially blocked in this house. I can't listen to someone else get boned down when you refuse to play me like a puppet."

"For fuck's sake," he mumbles, then shoves to his feet and hurries down the hall.

"Oh my god, you don't have to pout about it!"

"Good night, Davis!"

Could be a better one . . .

Chapter 13
Crew

My back smacks into the doorjamb, and I shove Willie's way. "I said left, dick."

"My bad." His grin peeks beyond the mattress a second, and he adjusts, so we're able to ease inside my new room. "Down in one, two—"

I let go, and he's forced to refocus his weight.

"Fucker." He shakes his head, lowering it to the floor.

Picking up the bottom edge, we push it onto the metal frame.

"So." Willie puts his hands on his hips. "This is the new spot, huh?"

I don't answer, tossing my sheets and comforter onto the memory foam mattress. "You sure this is the one Layla said to get?"

"Same one we got, yeah."

"And your big ass doesn't sink to the bottom?" I push on it, my hand melting into the soft material.

"Nah, it's made to hug you, so you forget you're a lonely, sexless son of a bitch."

My head snaps toward Willie, and he grins.

"What? It's true." His eyes spark, and he walks backward from the room. "Speaking of the fuckless."

"She's not home, and if she were, I'd smack the shit out of you for saying that out loud."

"Wonder what color comforter she has. I'm betting pretty pink or lovely lavender? Extra fluffy."

I scoff, and his gaze narrows.

"You son of a bitch. You already looked," he accuses.

My smirk is small as I reach for her door handle, opening it no more than a crack for him to peek inside.

A low whistle leaves him. "A surprising little virgin." He pushes closer. "What is that? Gold satin?"

I close the door, forcing him to step back. "Rose gold satin. Black satin sheets."

"Get it, girl." He smiles, following me into the kitchen. "It looks expensive. You sure she doesn't have a sugar daddy sending her things?"

"She kissed me because Julius staring at her made her nervous. I think it's safe to say, there's no sugar daddy."

"Julius is a good-looking motherfucker," he teases, laughing at himself as he speaks of his identical twin. "Sugar daddy's can be fugly *and* virtual. Maybe that's her type, the ones who steer clear and are just below good-looking. You know, like you."

My middle finger is all he gets in response.

Sugar daddy.

Come the fuck on.

And no way she talks to guys online. She'd never, I warned her ass about that before Memphis and I moved out. She knows I'd have her ass for that.

Right?

Willie's laugh is loud and barking, and when my eyes slide to him, he's staring right at me. "Man, you're too fucking easy when it comes to her."

"Fuck's that mean? I'm no different than any other time."

Willie smiles, pulling his phone to his ear when I didn't even hear it ring. "Hey, baby. I'm at Crew's."

I flip him off again and step back into my room to make my bed while he's on his call.

Like Davis, my sheets are black, but a cooling cotton in tune with your body temperature.

Never heard of them before, but that's what you get when you send money with your buddy's wife. She did good, though, and I like the deep-blue down comforter she bought with it.

I used it at the bar, but twin sheets didn't even fit the cot in my office, the thing was that small, so Layla went and snagged these for me today while we picked up the mattress in Willie's truck.

Tonight, I plan to get a full fucking night's sleep, and I'm dying for it to be on a real bed for once. The last two nights don't count since I spent the first one cussing out Davis in my head until I fell asleep, and the second, when I lay down, I realized it wasn't even a mattress I was lying on, but more like something you'd lay down on the bottom of a ground tent to make camping less miserable.

It's hard to believe she's slept here alone for a year.

Growing up, she was afraid to be home alone, afraid to sleep with the lights off or her door closed, that's why she found her way into my room so often.

Or so I told myself.

She's grown now, asshole.

So fucking grown . . .

"All right, let's get this bitch into the dumpster. Layla wants nachos from across the street."

Eyeing the wall that connects my room to hers, I nod and push to my feet. "Yeah, let's go."

Behind the wheel of his Ram, Willie looks to me as he puts the thing in gear. "Me and Layla made a bet. I gave you a month."

"A month?"

"Before you go caveman on the girl."

"You know it's not the fucking time. You should listen to your wife. She's smarter than you."

"She gave you a week."

My head snaps his way, and he laughs like a maniac.

"Just drive, dickhead."

He does.

He drives right across the street, and the first thing I see through the window of the diner is Davis Franco . . . smiling at a familiar black-hat-wearing asshole.

I turn mine backward on my head and walk inside.

Davis

Black Hat Guy's eyes fall to my nametag, then quickly pop up to mine. "Were you named after the university?"

"No, my parents were huge football fans growing up, so they named me after their favorite team's owner." I stick my pen into my apron, drawing out a straw and lowering it onto the tabletop.

"Nice, which team?"

"Raiders."

Before I can turn toward the voice, heavy arms snake around my middle, and I'm drawn into a warm, solid body. Soft brown hair teases along my jaw as wet, full lips press at the skin of my neck, sending a shiver shock through me. As fast as they plant, they rise to my ear.

"You didn't tell me he's been coming back," Crew whispers his disapproval. "Not okay with that."

Shifting slightly, I meet his eyes, but I'm immediately called to the brim of his hat. His *Raiders* hat, flipped backward on his head, nothing but short, shaven hair showing from beneath it.

He straightens to his full height, my body no longer cocooned in a fascinating mix of pillowy hardness but braced against him.

His lips leave my ear, so I peek up at him, but his attention's locked on Black Hat Guy.

Crew releases me and slips away, walking backward until he can fall into the empty booth two spaces over and across. One by one, he raps his knuckles on the table before him, his gaze finally flicking to mine.

His smirk is instant, ill behaved, and when he cocks his head, my feet deem it a demand, one they're clearly eager to follow, leading me right to him.

"Burger will be right up." I excuse myself, and seven steps later, I'm in front of Crew. "That was unexpected."

Back half leaning where the seat meets the wall, Crew has one arm thrown over the seat, the other stretched long across the table. He is the picture of carefree, but there's a darkness in his gaze, proving otherwise.

"Did you come for lunch? The meatball sub's on special."

"How many times has he been back?"

My brows tug in the center. "What?"

Crew leans forward, his chin nearly level with my stomach, his eyes pointed up and focused on me through a thick layer of long, dark lashes. "How many times . . . has he come back in here?"

His words are delivered slow and low, very Crew-like, but they roll right over my head as I fixate on his. A thought sparks, a naughty one, and my expression must show it as his gaze narrows in question.

"What are you thinking right now?" he presses.

"I'm not sure you want to know."

"You said you'd answer when asked." His neck stretches the teeniest bit. "Answer me, Sweets."

"If you insist." I step in until the table is smashing into my right thigh, bringing myself as close as I can, without dropping beside him, so I can keep my voice as low as possible. Don't need Mr. and Mrs. Joe eavesdropping from their spot across the way.

"I'm pretty sure this is about where you'd reach if you were on your knees in front of me," I whisper, then straighten and hold a finger up to the girl trying to gain my attention a skip over. Hurriedly pulling my pen from my pouch, I press it to my order pad. Did you want to try the sub or no?"

Silence.

My eyes lift to Crew.

He's yet to move an inch, his attention frozen on my face. My eyes. I'm not even sure he's blinking.

"Crew."

His frown deepens, though he shows no other sign of life.

"Miss!"

Ugh.

"Look at the menu. I'll be right back." I go to walk away, but Crew's reflexes are on another level.

His large fingers lock around my wrist so fast, I'm forced to jerk to a stop, my head snapping back in his direction.

Eyes on me, he glides his closed fist across the table, nudging the silverware right over the side, and it falls to the floor with a clatter. Crew scoots to the end of the seat, gently nudging me backward as he slips his body free, pressing a single knee to the floor.

Blindly, he stretches his long arms, scooping the fork, spoon, and napkin into his palm. He straightens then, his left knee still pressed firmly to the cheap linoleum, his chin leveling out. Only then do his eyes leave mine, now pointed directly forward, but only for a split second. Long enough to push a harsh, intentional breath out, one that seeps beyond the cotton of my clothes, teasing over my ribs.

Slowly, he rises to his feet, the next words leaving him a low rumble. "I'd have to hook your leg up high for that to work. Maybe put you in heels." And then he sits back down and says, "Three nachos. One steak, two chicken."

My mouth opens, closes, and then I nod.

"One chicken, two steak, got it."

Unsteady, both mind and feet, I run through my tables on autopilot, all the while picturing my thigh braced on Crew's stout shoulders, my favorite, glittery heels, I've never worn but had to have, resting along the muscles in his back.

He'd have to grab me by the ass cheeks to hold me still, and I bet he'd squeeze, knead.

Yeah, he seems like the type to enjoy a good handful and I've got a couple.

Why won't he just take one for the team? And by team, I mean me.

"Davis?"

My head jerks up, and I realize I've come to Black Hat Guy's table.

Look at that, I've already set his meal down.

"Ketchup?" I guess.

The guy chuckles, adjusting his frame in his seat, so he appears taller. "I didn't think you heard me."

He was talking?

"Sorry." A low laugh leaves me. "My mind is—" in the gutter. Crew deep. "Anyway . . . what?"

A cup slams against a tabletop with a loud clank, and all eyes dart toward the sound. Toward Crew.

He's slouched over, head lazily hanging forward. Eyes on me.

"Is he your boyfriend?"

"I wish," I mumble.

It's quick, instant. Accidental.

Crew looks away, but the shake of his shoulders tells me he heard, and he's entertained.

I, on the other hand, ripen like the finest of tomatoes.

Black Hat Guy is looking at Crew but faces forward as I turn back around, shocking me when a large smile spreads across his face, and you know what? It looks good on him. It's not crooked, and it doesn't reveal any scars or dimples, but it is nice. Straight.

"Good to know." Black Hat Guy—*okay I really need to ask his name, or at the very least, peek at it on his card when he pays*—winks and scoots his food closer. "Think I could get that ketchup?"

"Ketchup, coming right up."

I spin on my heels, and Crew's chin lowers to his chest as I pass, but that doesn't stop me from shoving his head with my open palm as I walk by.

This time, his laughter echoes.

It's an annoyingly glorious sound.

Chapter 14
Crew

"Girl, let's go!" I pull the door open, listening for my car's engine to fire up when I press the button on the key fob. "If you're not out here in three minutes, I'm leaving!"

A package catches my eye as I go to let the door close behind me, so I take it back inside, setting it on the table, right as Davis slips from her room.

"Sorry! I couldn't find my other sandal. I had to get on all fours and pull a serious yoga move to reach it—oh! Is that mine?" She smiles, rushing over.

Her hair is down and sleek straight, small braids on each side pinned in place by Laffy Taffy hair clips, the same shade of teal as her tank top. Her shorts are high on her waist and high *up* her thighs. She looks good. Sweet.

Sexy.

"Your shorts are too short."

Her eyes flick up to mine.

"Where you going again?"

"Some street fair thing. Crafts and food and what not. Jess's little cousin's dance team is in the parade, so it should be fun." She shrugs, picking up the package. "One more minute?"

"Hurry up. I'm grabbing my wallet, and we're out."

She squeals, dashing back to her room, and quickly closes the door, so I head into mine, digging through the laundry for the jeans I took off last night.

I find them in the bathroom, and the second I come out, Davis does too.

She smiles, slings her purse over her shoulder and heads out the door. "Come on, slowpoke!" she teases.

My eyes fall to her outfit.

Same teal shirt, same too-short shorts.

Huh.

The car door opens and closes, letting me know she's inside it, so I push her bedroom door open, picking up the plastic wrapping that she threw on her bed.

My brows fly up, and I flip it over, viewing the example photo on the other side.

Round and full, a bare ass stares back, nothing but a string disappearing down the crack, but it's what's above that, that catches my attention.

The stretchy strings of the strappy lace are sewn in the shape of a diamond, the bottom point resting right at the crack of the ass and hanging from the top center is a dangling diamond.

Panties.

My eyes slice to the floor, scouring from left to right, and sure enough, a purple pair lies bunched at the foot of the bed.

She came back in here to change her panties.

She's wearing panties meant to be played with.

Meant to be twisted around a tight fist and tugged on, nipped on.

Sucked on.

My dick twitches in my jeans, and I glare at it.

Don't fucking start, my man. We've been through this. You can't have her. Not now.

The devil on my shoulder smirks, whispering words I want to hear.

No one else can either.

"Yo, we need more of that wine!" Drew shouts, hustling to pour out a row of shots, then moving on to the next drink.

Paula sighs, stretching to snag some napkins and tosses them on her tray. "If I don't get table four their Tom Collins, those frat boys are going to cause a stir."

"I got it." Tossing my towel in the bucket, I slip away, rushing to the basement for another crate of wine. How we ended up with two bachelorette parties and a nifty-fifty party on the same night, I have no fucking clue.

It's good for business but having half the staff I need on a night like this is the opposite, so I call my boys for a bailout.

"What's up, fuckhead?" Willie answers the first ring.

"Any chance your brothers are over?"

"Yup. Layla made meatloaf."

"Bring me some and pour some drinks?"

"Be there in fifteen."

Thank fuck.

Upstairs, I don't even have a chance to put the bottles away before we're opening and refilling glasses. At least we're getting through this shit. I've been sitting on it for weeks now.

As promised Willie, Julius, and Xavier tear through the crowd, and like I knew it would, it draws every female that wasn't already hovering around the bar, right fucking to it.

Yeah, the Sanchez brothers' presence made us even busier, but they're quick with charm and quicker with the shake-off, so it works.

We grind through the orders with ease, bumping and nudging each other all the way through, and finally, a little after ten, we're on good timing. Taking orders and pushing them out before the next person steps up ready to put theirs in.

"Goddamn, son." Willie nods, looking around. "You're getting more and more students than ever. Surprised they're Ubering this way with two bars down the road from the school."

"It's almost the end of the semester. They're in party mode and there's more shit to do around here," X says.

"True."

Drew walks up, chugging down a glass of water. "Think I can sneak away for a smoke?"

Cutting my eyes to the clock, I nod. "Go out back and don't be letting anyone in through there."

He salutes me with a smirk, slipping past.

My phone vibrates in my pocket, and I pull it out to find a text from Davis.

Davis: Any chance you have a free table?

Hot pink-ass jewelry.

I frown, shaking off my thoughts.

Me: No. It's a madhouse in here.

The last thing I need is for her to walk in here with those tiny shorts.

Holding my phone in my palm, I wait for a response, but it doesn't come quick enough, so it's stuffed back in my pocket, looking to the group who just slid up to the bar.

"Another round of Crown?"

They laugh and nod, and I get to pouring.

Drew comes back in, stepping up beside me, and slips the limes over the rims while I cash them out.

"You didn't tell me my wifey was coming tonight."

My head snaps his way, and I follow his line of sight to the edge of the crowd Davis has just pushed through.

She pauses, looking back, and I wait for her friend to step around the guy who shoved his way through behind her, but she faces forward then.

Walks forward, the tall, lean blond at her side.

"Or that she was bringing a date."

Date?

I frown, my eyes locked on her approaching form.

Willie slides up then. "Uh-oh."

Julius is next. "Well, well, Davis the Virgin has herself a friend."

She reaches the bar with a smile, says hello to all *my* boys, and likely looks to me, but I can't be sure. My attention is locked on the person smiling at her side.

"This is my friend, Jess," she says, and something in me boils.

Jess.

This is *Jess?*

Jess isn't short for Jessica.

Jess is simply fucking *Jess.*

Her friend.

Her *male* friend.

Her tall, trim, preppy-looking fucker of a *friend.*

Hot pink-ass jewelry . . .

A wall slams over me, and I glare at the SOB who sticks his hand out to me. Slowly, my head turns, my eyes locking on hers.

You fucking serious, Sweets?

Davis

Is he serious?

He's just going to stand there and stare with crazy eyes?

"Willie."

I look over, catching the quick wink Willie tosses my way as he offers Jess his hand.

Jess visibly relaxes, accepting the handshake. "Nice to meet you."

Relief washes over me, and I smile, glancing from Jess to Willie.

"Thanks for bringing Davis." Willie nods as he leans forward. "You can go now."

My head snaps his way, expecting a grin to curve his lips, but Willie simply stares, one arm bent on the bar top, the other stretched out wide, palm flat against it.

What the hell?!

"Such a joker." I force a chuckle, gripping Jess's arm and tugging him backward with a big-fat fake smile. "We're going to try and find a table so—"

"Sit here."

My eyes snap to Crew's.

"*Right* here." There's a warning in his gaze, one that flicks from my face to my hand on Jess and back.

I wish I had a pie to smash in his perfect face. A hot one.

Willie nods from his right.

Julius appears on his left.

And not a second later, Drew wedges his way in, presses his forearms to the bar top, and stares.

They *all* stare.

A sudden anxious laugh breaks from my throat before I can stop it because . . .

Seriously, what the hell is happening?

"You know what, I have an early day tomorrow." Jess turns to me, his smile soft. "I'm going to head home, but if you want to ride back with me now, you can."

I open my mouth to speak, but then an arm wraps around my shoulder, and I look over to find the third and final brother.

"She's in real good hands here." Xavier grins wide. "But hey, maybe she'll call you later or you know, not."

My tongue is officially swallowed, and just like that, Jess nods as he takes a few steps away.

"Thanks for today," I rush out. "And I *will* call you later."

Jess grins then, his eyes flicking toward the bar before he leaves.

The arm on my shoulder is shoved off and mine is gripped between long, firm fingers.

Before I know what's happening, Crew is steering me off the floor with swift strides, curling us around the bar and up the short set of stairs leading to the office.

Two feet in, he whips around to face me, but I snap first.

"What is your issue?"

"That's Jess?"

Eyes wide with mockery, I nod. *Duh.*

His jaw tics. "The Jess you went to the street fair with today, the one you make desserts for, have a weekly dinner with . . . drank with the other night?"

"I only have one friend named Jess, so yeah." I shake my head.

What is his problem?

Crew glares. "He's a dude."

My mouth opens and closes.

"Yeah . . ." I drag out. "I'm aware."

"You came home buzzed and hard up, horny as hell."

"I was not!"

"You started asking about how and why a man holds you, then ran your hands all over my body. You were so desperate for something." His tone is hard. Short.

"I was not desperate!"

He pushes into my space. "Your straps were down your shoulders when you came in. He push them there?"

"Oh my god! No!"

"Do not lie to me, Baby Franco." He speaks low, lethally calm.

"Why would I lie, and again, what is your issue?!"

Crew scoffs, running his hand down his face as he jerks back with a low growl. "You're unbelievable, swear to God."

He looks at me, an incredulous expression tightening his features. "Is all this bullshit about you needing help and what-the-fuck-not your way of trying to become brave enough to climb on that motherfucker's cock?"

I blink. Hard. And then I shout, *"What?!"*

"You spend all your time at work and school . . . and with that yacht-club-looking dipshit. Admit it, he's the person you want to learn how to fuck for."

"You are so off the mark, it's not even funny!"

"Then why put on the slutty panties today?"

My mouth drops open, anger rushing through me. "How do you know what panties I'm wearing?"

He rolls his eyes.

Rolls. His. Eyes. As if my question is dumb or irrelevant.

I push my chest into his, glaring up at him. "Jess is my friend."

"Men cannot be friends with you, Davis. There's no fucking way. And women don't wear shiny new toys for men they don't want to fuck."

"Oh, okay. So, then what, huh?" I snap. "If he and I can't be friends, I should just offer him the spot in my bed and see what happens?"

Crew growls. Literally *growls* and presses me into the wall. "Watch your mouth, little girl."

"Hey, it was your idea," I sass back. "If you're not going to take our arrangement seriously, I'll—"

"You'll do what?" He speaks through clenched teeth, lowering his head so we're nearly eye level. "You will do nothing. It's like you said, we made a deal." He jabs a finger in his chest. "I decide who, when, maybe even where. Me. Not you or anyone else. You got me?"

I lift my chin in defiance and a deep rumble works its way up his throat.

"I said. Do. You. Got. Me?"

"Yes! I got you. You're in charge of the cherry, pop it at your pleasure!"

He scoffs, stepping back from me, but only by inches, so with as much added force as I can muster, I knock my shoulder into his with my exit, but again, he's annoyingly steady on his feet. No part of him budges.

I get a solid, single foot past him when a harsh curse leaves me.

In true Crew fashion, he allows me no farther, gripping my wrist suddenly, then tugging and tucking me back into his chest.

Lips press firmly against my ear, as he speaks in a low, needy rasp, "I lied, Sweets."

Thrown off, I frown, my heart thumping erratically as I wait for more.

"The panties, they're not slutty. They're fire." His palms lower, latching around my waist for a quick, short squeeze. "And I have no fucking doubt they look even better on." And then he's gone.

Me?

I'm a broken faucet, drip, drip, dripping away.

Melting internally after he acted like an ass. A bossy, controlling ass.

What's that say about me?

Sighing, I lean against the wall, toying with the ice cream pendant necklace locked around my neck.

Yeah, I'm busting out Betty the Boy Toy tonight, and turning the dial to ten.

A thought hits me then, and I wonder if Crew will go for it.

It's doubtful, but all a girl can do is ask, right?

Right.

So, several hours later, when we're walking into our apartment, I set my bag down and turn to Crew.

"You said to tell you if there's something I want or need."

His attention snaps my way, his movements slowing as he sets his keys on the table. "I did."

"Right, so . . . will you watch me touch myself?"

Chapter 15
Crew

I did not hear her right. There's no fucking way I heard her right.

My head cocks to the side, heat brimming beneath my skin. "What?"

"I need to, you know . . ."

"Come?"

She nods, a pretty pink polishing her cheeks. "I want you to watch."

Fuck me, I heard her right.

Watch her come.

Watch her fucking come?

There's no way. I'd lose my shit. Grab her and take her to my room. Toss her on the bed.

I'd spread her legs and then her lips, her pussy lips. Push inside her in a slow, measured move. I'd fuck her senseless, stealing her moans and claiming her mouth.

The mouth she put on me when she got nervous.

It's fuller now than it was when she was seventeen. Softer. Ready for more.

Ready for me?

My tongue was two seconds from shoving between the folds, from tasting her—when we were younger and when she pressed her lips to mine at Willies.

Just one taste. That's all I wanted.

Lie to yourself some more, dumbass.

"Please," she whispers. "I have all these thoughts and images in my head."

What kind of thoughts? Images of what?

Who?

Fire flares in my groin.

"But maybe if you're watching," she continues, "It could be like it's not me doing the work, maybe even be more intense."

It will be. So much more.

I'd coax you through, tell you what to do, ask you how it feels and what you want to do next.

"It could be a lesson, maybe?" She grips for straws.

I swallow, forcing my head to shake. "I'd call that some advanced shit."

"I've taken advanced classes all my life," she argues.

"We ain't there yet."

"Figured not, but it was worth a shot . . . and you did say 'ain't there *yet*,' so that's promising."

My mouth waters.

My eyes tail her into the kitchen. She pulls open a drawer, grabs something and closes it with her hip. She walks by, rolling something in her palm, and the heavy *click-clack* can only be one thing. Batteries.

My muscles flex, tightening and loosening over and over.

She reaches her door, peering at me over her shoulder. "Night, Crew." She closes herself inside, and my dick is well aware of what she's about to do.

Squeezing my eyes closed, I try to erase the images of her blushing and breathless.

Try and fail.

I lock myself in my own room, realizing as I do, the sound of the bolt turning never came from Davis's door.

She left hers unlocked.

Just in case I change my mind?

Slow and cautious, I peel my shirt from my body, unwilling to allow even the sound of shifting cotton to break through the air, and press my back against the wall. The wall we share.

My eyes close, my ears perked and waiting to find out if it's solid or hollow, if it is hollow, will I hear her?

Is she loud when she plays?

When she comes?

Yeah, I think she is . . . if she knows how to do things right. She would be for me.

The thought has me gritting my teeth.

No, motherfucker. Don't even fucking start.

The moment I think it, she does. Or at least that's when her moans break through.

Soft and fucking sugary, just like her. Just like I imagine her body and the taste of her would be. My cock swells instantly, straining against my jeans, so I quietly flick them open, and dip my hand inside. My large hand wraps around myself, and I give my base a good squeeze, tugging once. Twice. Three times.

My head falls back with a silent knock, my lips parting as I picture hers doing the same thing. Her eyes closed in pleasure, tongue poking out to wet her dry, plump lips, teeth sinking into her fuller bottom one the way mine does.

Her moans grow into desperate little whimpers, and I pump myself harder, faster, my hips working with my hand, anxious for release.

I picture Davis in the center of her silky sheets, head bowed back into the pillows.

Her legs fall farther open, begging for more, her back arching, pleased when she gets exactly what she asks for. I would give her all she fucking wanted.

I groan, grinding my teeth, sweat building along the nape of my neck.

She reaches for me, and I dive down, clamping her lips the way they are meant to be claimed, owned.

Fucking devoured.

My cock swells, heat building low in my groin, and it doubles when her gasp pierces the air.

My head still pressed back, I roll along the wall until my body is spun completely, my forehead pressed to the cool, white-painted wood. My palm slaps against it, my fist forming as my muscles lock, my head falling back.

"Crew."

My chest rumbles, low and deep.

She said my fucking name.

My body clenches, my orgasm on the brink. Right fucking there.

I press my ear to the wall.

"God, yes, Crew . . ."

And there it is.

Cum spills from my cock, and I jerk harder. Squeezing.

Sweets . . .

Davis

With pancakes stacked two times too high, and maple sausage ready to be draped in syrup, I knock on Crew's door.

It's his prize for delivering an epic ending . . . even if it was simply his voice on replay inside my head that sealed the deal. Sure, he's unaware he's the inspiration behind my masturbation, but still. Breakfast has been earned. Punishment for last night at the bar has also been put into effect, though, which is why there are no strawberries and whipped cream to be found.

I knock again. "If you don't answer, I'm taking the bottom stack, and I know how much you love the overly buttered ones!"

No groan, no shout, nothing follows.

Hesitant, I turn the knob and peek inside, frowning when I'm met with a bed in disarray, but missing a giant male body.

I check the bathroom, and when it's as empty as it was when I left it, I look outside.

Crew's car is gone.

Huh.

With a shrug, I text Jess.

Me: I've got a pile of steaming pancakes I could use a hand eating. Come over for breakfast?

He replies as I lower into the seat.

Jess: Damn, I would, but I'm already on my way to the library. Study tonight?

Me: All my assignments are in. I don't have to be on campus unless I want to be until finals in two weeks.

Jess: Nice! Call you later?

Me: bye

I look to the giant stack of yumminess, large enough to feed a small army, and dig in. I'm on the second pancake when my shoulders begin to sag, and the silence becomes too loud. Almost mocking.

It's worse when I pause to play around on Instagram and come across Drew's story. It's a picture of him biting into a giant breakfast burrito, and in the background sits Layla and Willie. And next to him is Crew, a plate of his own before him.

They're at Layla and Willie's house.

A small smile curves my lips, happy Crew has found himself a group of friends he can trust. If he didn't, he wouldn't give them the time of day. He's withdrawn like that.

With that happiness, though, comes a teeny hint of longing.

I miss before and everything it entailed.

Saturday brunch with my family, Crew being the fifth member of it, with Drew in tow too on occasion. Sunday's making donuts and quick dips in the cool bay waters. Weekly baseball practices and traveling for tournaments. Walking around selling beef jerky sticks to raise money, so Crew could play in said tournaments.

He never would allow my parents to cover him, and my dad would have done it in a heartbeat. He loves Crew as his own, even when he had to step into the fatherly role that made it a little less obvious. It's like I said before, reprimand was new to him, so I imagine it was easy to sometimes confuse discipline with dislike.

Maybe that's why he distanced himself from us after Memphis's accident.

I had thought about it many times, assuming he didn't feel right about being so easily loved by a man who suffered physical and mental pain loving his own son, but it could have been the opposite.

Maybe it was both.

A sudden wave of homesickness washes over me, so I pick up the phone and call my mom.

When she doesn't answer, I try my dad.

He doesn't pick up either, and I remember they joined a tennis club on impulse.

Maybe they're with their new friends having brunch. Either way, they'll call me the second they realize I tried them. They always do.

After clearing the table, I straighten the pillows on the couch and take out the garbage, mindlessly searching for something else to do, but I'm not a keeper of many things so my house pretty much stays clean and clutter-free, the most common mess being piles of papers and school supplies.

I've yet to experience a point in my life when I didn't have something to study for, or a class or a shift at work to get to. I'm not so sure I like the whole "clear schedule thing," especially now that I have a taste of what having someone I truly want to spend my time with is like.

It all reminds me I've been flying solo out here, something I never quite had the time to consider before now.

It's with that thought I grab my keys, head out the door, and make my way across the street.

Maybe Rachel needs me at the diner today.

Maybe she'll let me work a double.

Crew

"So, what happened, Davis had to work?" Layla asks, collecting our plates and dropping them in the sink.

Davis had to come, and when she did, it was with my name on her lips.

"Yeah. She had work." Pretty sure that's a lie. With school, she doesn't work mornings and when I quietly snuck from my room this morning, she was still closed inside hers.

"Heard she was out with a good-looking pretty boy last night?" Layla crosses her arms over her swollen belly.

"Course you did. Your husband has a big mouth." I think about what she said a second, adding. "And shitty taste in men. He wasn't good-looking. He looked like a douchey motherfucker."

"A tall, blue-eyed, chiseled-jawed, white-picket-fence-wanting, Polo-wearing douchey motherfucker." Willie waltzes in with a grin.

My glares slices to him.

"Admit it, the dude had Barbie Dreamhouse written all over him."

"I admit you're a dumbass."

Layla laughs, cupping her stomach. "So this is the friend that lives next door to her?"

"Yes, the Jess that is not short for Jessica." Her husband thinks he's fucking hilarious.

"I'm out of here." I stand, turning toward the door.

"Love you, Crew."

"Fuck off, Julius."

Climbing in my truck, I pull out my phone, checking to see if Davis's location tracker still works. It does, and when it shows me that she's at the diner, I breathe an annoying sigh of relief.

With any luck, by the time I get home, Davis will be asleep.

I can't look at her, not when I pictured her lips wrapped around my cock while I fisted her hair between my fingers and tugged to test her reaction. Not when I imagined she loved it and took me deeper. Sucked harder. Longer.

My dick hardens, straining against my jeans at the thought.

Pressing my palm over my zipper, I close my eyes, hers flashing behind the lids when they do. I lick my lips, and I snap out of it.

Throwing my car in drive, I pull away, trying to come up with a plan to keep my shit together. To keep my feet on the right side of the line.

To do what I should and not what's so damn tempting.

'Cause, fuck me, the mere thought of Davis Franco, someone I've denied myself for a long fucking time because I *know* thoughts would lead to actions, drives me mad.

The damage the girl could do to me.

The damage *I* could do to her.

I need to keep my mind right, and my dick on the same page.

That's fucking that.

Chapter 16
Davis

My job is a godsend, truly. It's easy enough and keeps me busy for hours upon hours. The last three days, I was able to come in before ten in the morning and didn't leave a minute before seven a single one of them. Don't plan to today either, not when I have no homework or exams to study for. I only have two classes left I have to show up in and both are not until next Thursday, when the semester officially comes to an end.

My college career will also officially come to an end.

What a trip.

I'm two hours into my early shift, this fine Saturday morning, when a familiar voice shouts, a little too loudly, from the entrance.

"Davis 'Middle Name' Franco, your services are requested."

Topping a customer's coffee cup off, I stand and carry the pot back to the station and smile at Xavier and his friend, Neo, I think his name was, as they saunter over.

"Hey, guys. The place is like a graveyard this morning, so sit anywhere you want."

Xavier leans in, hugging me, and Neo says his hello.

"I was coming to steal you, actually. What time you get off?"

"Oh. Why, what did you have in mind?" I wipe my hands on a rag and toss it in the basket beneath the counter.

"We're headed to the water park." Xavier hooks his thumb over his shoulder, and I look out the window to find a handful of people standing outside a couple of jeeps.

As if they were waiting, the group all lifts their hands, or holds them out, their shouts muffled by the closed windows of the building.

Laughing, I look to Xavier. "Looks like you already have quite a few people who can go."

"True, but we want you to go." Neo steps up. "My sister's meeting us there. I think you'll like her. She's obsessed with peach-ring candies."

My smile spreads. "So your sister's favorite snack makes you think we'll get along?"

"One, I'm pretty sure you get along with everyone. Two, Crew says you love all things sweet, which is why you'll probably fall in love with me, but we can worry about that later." Neo's smirk is mischievous.

I can't help the chuckles that escape. "Where is Crew?"

I haven't seen him in three days. I heard him come and go a few times, but our schedules have been opposite. Maybe he's with a woman.

Does he have one of those? A booty call on speed dial?

He's a man made of more testosterone than a teenage training camp, so yeah, I'd bet he does.

A pang hits my chest, and I look off.

I hate the thought of him being with someone, I always have. Watching him with his future wife has been one of my fears for years, the irrational kind you think about, play out in your head, getting gray hairs over when you should simply wait for it to happen rather than make yourself crazy waiting for it.

What happens when he finds the one woman he refuses to let go? Can I handle that?

Will she allow our friendship?

Of course she would, right? What threat am I?

"Who knows, that man stays busy." Xavier's voice draws me out of my head, and he shrugs. "So, what do you say?"

Aw, so he didn't send them here to invite me. They thought of me on their own.

Rachel comes around the corner then and I face the boys once more, surprised by the regret that follows. "Sorry, guys. I can't leave."

"Grab your stuff, Davis. You're fine." Rachel walks over, replacing the tub of wrapped silverware. "You said it yourself, we're dead, and Marla's shift starts in twenty. Go, have some fun for once."

"Yeah, have fun for once." Neo wiggles his brows, swiping his tongue over his lip when he looks at Rachel.

She scoffs, shaking her head. "Honey, please. I would eat you up and spit you out."

"I would be oh so okay with that," he plays along.

Rachel tries to hide her smile, but I catch it as she walks away.

Rachel is gorgeous and has that rockabilly vibe going. Deep-red lipstick and a septum piercing that shines off her golden skin. She always wears a bandanna of sorts and pins her curls perfectly in place. I've never seen her in anything but black pants and bright yellow or red tops. Her ears are stretched, and she has no less than six piercings on each lobe.

She's also got about ten years on Neo, who can't be any older than me.

I turn to Xavier. "I'll need to run home and get a swimsuit."

"So long as it's a bikini."

Rolling my eyes, I grab my keys and follow them out the door.

They introduce me to their friends, we stop for my things, and not fifteen minutes later, we're headed for the water park.

The second we hit the highway, my phone dings in my bag. I find a text from Crew.

Crew: Working today?

I frown. I've been going to work every day this week. Is this the first time he noticed I wasn't home?

Me: Just a short morning shift. You?

Three little dots appear at the bottom of the thread, disappearing twice before another message comes.

Crew: And now?

Way to ignore my question.

Me: I'm off.

My phone rings a second later, and I'm about to ignore it and text him back, since it's far too loud to talk on the phone in here without being rude, but Xavier happens to lean over right then, spotting the image of Crew lighting up my screen.

"Ah, the side shot, got me one of those for someone too." He winks, darts his hand out, grabs my phone, and answers, "Hello." He tries using his best feminine voice, instantly making me laugh.

"That was terrible." I shake my head, ready to pull it to my ear, but then Neo stretches over the back seat and puts the call on speaker.

Suppressing my smile, I lift it a little closer to my lips. "Hey. It's kind of loud, can I—"

"Who was that?"

Xavier grins, leaning closer. "Your second favorite Sanchez brother."

"Fuck are you doing with Davis?"

"Going to the water park con esta bellezza."

I look to him. "I didn't know you spoke Spanish."

"We all do." He winks.

Neo takes the mic. "She's gonna be my tube partner for the day, ain't that right, gorgeous?"

"Sure, why not," I tease, shaking my head as I pull the phone closer. "Can I call you back later?"

The line goes dead, and I frown at my screen, ignoring the laughter of the boys around me.

A little while later, we're pulling into the parking lot of the water park, so while they shotgun a few beers because, college students will do that, I text Crew.

Me: Hey sorry. It was so loud in Jeremy's Jeep I couldn't really talk. Did you need something?

Crew: Who the fuck is Jeremy?

He responds instantly.

Me: Oh, I figured you knew all their friends, sorry. Someone from their baseball team, I think. I'm pretty sure all seven of them are.

The boys are tearing off their shirts and closing the doors, so I quickly try to end the conversation.

Me: I think you'll be at work by the time we get home, but maybe I'll come say hi, let you know how it goes.

Crew: How what goes?

Me: I figured this is the perfect time to try out some of your "lessons."

I press send, assuming that's what he'd suggest anyway, so I make sure to say it before he can, the perfectly prepared student that I am.

Turning my phone off, I toss it in the car with the pile of other phones, and off we go.

Sighing, I smile at the mountain of slides ahead.

Today is going to be a good day.

Three hours in, and we're practically running our way out.

"Dude, I can't believe they called you on the overhead," Neo says, jumping around to try and avoid the burn under his bare feet.

"I told you to wear your slides in, dumbass, and, of fucking course, they did. I'd kick Willie's ass if not." He shakes his head. "Miss my niece's birth. You crazy?"

"I thought she wasn't due for a while?" I ask.

Maybe I heard wrong?

"She's not, but my mom had us early, so I guess it's all right." He shrugs, but then his forehead caves into a frown.

"Hey." I stop his speed walk, placing my hand on his arm, and he jerks to look at me. "I'm sure she's fine. He just wants you there, that's all."

Xavier swallows, nods, and picks up the pace again. "Yeah, I'll feel better when I get my phone out of the car." He peeks at me, the corner of his mouth hiking up. "You know you don't have to leave with us? Our wristbands are good for another four hours. The boys would be happy to have you sit on their laps the ride home."

"Get fucking punched, X."

All our heads snap straight, shock jolting us in place.

Crew stands at the back of Jeremy's jeep, arms crossed over his chest.

It's odd, how potent rage rang dark in his tone; yet, his face is a sheet of nothing.

"Layla's fine," he says, his eyes bolted on mine. "Go back inside if you want, but I need this car unlocked, so Davis can get her shit out."

"Wait." I shake my head, confused. "What?"

I turn to Xavier, but the worry and confusion is wiped from his attractive face, nothing but a sly grin written across it now, his best friends mirroring him, but not Jeremy.

Jeremy appears slightly uneasy as he unclips his key from the pocket of his board shorts, holds it out and up with a long stretch of his arm as if he's afraid to accidentally touch his hand to mine.

I open my palm and he gently drops it inside, saying, "You can hide it by the gas tank when you're done."

Frowning, I accept the key, my gaze flicking from one chuckling man to the next as they spin on their feet and book it back toward the water park entrance.

"I don't . . ."

A large hand wraps around mine, and I'm jolted forward an inch as a hard chest bumps into my back.

Hot breath fans over my ear, then a harsh exhale follows, and the body behind mine rips away, taking the key with it.

All I can do is stare as Crew digs around in the jeep, coming out with my bag and phone in his hands. He pushes past me, tossing my things into the front seat of his car . . . that is parked right across from the one I rode here in.

I blink and then I blink some more.

"What the hell just happened here?"

Finally, Crew faces me, his square jaw clenched closed.

Wait, okay. So Layla is fine. Baby girl is still tucked inside . . ."Why did Willie . . ." I begin to work through this nonsense, my frown pointed at Crew. "*You* called the water park?"

His chin lifts.

"Crew, what the hell! Xavier was scared, worried something was wrong. Why did you—"

Oooh. You dumb, dumb girl.

This is about me and the life he cut me out of.

"You're upset I went with your friends."

Silence.

Crew's chest rises and falls in rapid movements, the angles of his face sharp with anger, even more so when his eyes snap to my bathing suit and stay there.

A nauseating sense of unease settles over me, and I shift on my feet, loosely crossing my arms in an attempt to hide my soft body from his critical eyes.

His lips nearly curl, and he jerks forward, but for whatever reason, he halts, his eyes snapping to the left. He walks around, slips into his seat, and slams his door.

Left with no other option, or maybe it's understanding any other decision likely wouldn't end well, I climb in beside him, swiftly pulling my cover-up over my head.

I don't bother powering on my phone, and I don't look his way the entire forty-five-minute drive home.

The second we pull up, I tear from the car, fly up the walkway and rush into the house.

I race for my room, but Crew is quick, his booming voice echoing in the hall behind me.

"Don't try to fuck my friends or their friends. It will never happen."

My jaw clamps closed, and I grind my teeth to keep from screaming. Or crying. Still, I spin to face him, unwilling to give him the satisfaction of my walking away.

The long, dark look we exchange has my temper rising, burning my airway as it forces its way to the surface, threatening to spill from my lips like fire from a dragon.

"Why not, huh?" Well, okay then, here it comes. "You don't want me to be a part of your new world, we both know I'm only in it now because I bulldozed my way in with a bribe you probably see as blackmail, so why don't you call on a buddy, ask them to do you a solid and debase your pathetic pain in the ass, so you can send her on her way?"

The way Crew's head snaps back is unnatural. "That was a joke, right?"

I lift my left shoulder. "From what I understand, some guys have a thing for being the first one in. Maybe you should call one of them over and be done with it."

Slowly, I'm talking turtle-in-the-mud *slow*, Crew steps forward. "You want me to ask one of my friends to *do me a favor* and fuck you?"

Crossing my arms over my chest, I glare. "Don't make it sound so scandalous. If you want me out of your world so bad, just do it. I'm sure you have friends who have had more one-night stands than they can remember. Hell, some of them probably have babies they don't even know about running around somewhere!"

"And you want one of them to put their dick, that may or may not have been in a hundred others, inside you?"

"I was willing to take yours inside me, was I not?" I fire back.

Crew's face falls, but slowly, his expression grows fierce. "Watch yourself."

I burst forward, anger radiating through my body. "I'd bet someone you know would appreciate the offer and you'd get to be the hero of the story." I make a mockery of myself.

"Pass off a girl they wouldn't have to waste time wining and dining because she's a guaran-freaking-tee. They wouldn't have to butter me up by paying for my dinner or by pretending my ability to recite the periodic table is anything other than nerdy as shit. I don't need to be let down easy afterward, and they won't have to worry about hiding if they saw me on the streets when they don't call. What a blockbuster bargain you can gift over with a grin, don't you think?"

He blinks and blinks again, and then he flies forward, crowding me, driving me backward until my heels hit the wall. I'm forced to drop my head all the way back to look him in the eyes, and he waits for the moment our gazes crash together, his hands flying up, roughly cupping the underside of my breasts.

I gasp, his move so completely unexpected.

"No motherfucker on this planet will have you handed to them like that, do you understand me?" Crew's muscles constrict. "No man deserves this body when he hasn't earned it." His eyes flash, dark and despondent.

He gives a little squeeze and my toes curl into the carpet.

"No man," he nearly whispers, "will slide his cock inside you without earning the warmth you'll wrap him in." His thigh drives forward, pressing against the triangle of my bottoms. "Fucking drench him in." He groans, his cheek sliding along mine. "God, I could—"

"What?" I swallow. "You could what?"

"Did you do what you threatened?"

"Threatened?"

His jaw flexes against mine. "The bullshit you said before you ghosted me today. The lessons."

"I didn't ghost you. I left my phone in the car like everyone else."

"Answer my question. Now." His knee drives farther between my legs and I gulp, giving him more of my weight.

"I . . . no. Don't think so, but my brain cells aren't exactly at full function right now."

"Did you share a tube with Neo? Wrap your legs with his?"

I shake my head, goose bumps breaking across my skin as his stubble skates over the sensitive spot beneath my ear. "I didn't get to go on the double-person slides, but Neo's sister, Nova, I think her name was, was going to be my partner."

"Good. That's good." Suddenly he pulls away, spinning so fast I don't get so much as a glimpse of his face. "I gotta get back to the bar. Behave. I'll know if you don't."

With that, he walks out, and me?

I'm a sad excuse of a woman, melting over a man moodier than the Mona Lisa.

Chapter 17
Davis

Whiplash. That's what Crew Taylor is and has always been.

A severe case of whiplash.

An unexpected bout of turbulence.

Hot and cold.

Cold, cold, cold.

So cold, I have to replay every detail to determine if such a thing as hot exists, and it does, even if only in situations where he's overcome with the need to remind me he's in charge of the Davis show. As if I could forget.

Whatever lesson he was trying to teach me yesterday, I most definitely did not absorb it.

The only thing I learned last night is I'm a little broken.

Twisted even.

Why else would I find his grumpy, bossy, hands-on approach spectacularly stimulating?

If only he'd be willing to stimulate me on purpose.

As I think it, my senses are swarmed by his spicy, masculine scent.

Seconds later, Crew's reaching across me, his hand dipping into my bucket to peep at what's buried inside. "Do you think you have enough Red Hots?"

"What, these?" I tease, revealing the second layer hidden beneath the first. "They should get me through the night. These two." I point to the three triple-pack candy necklaces I couldn't resist, even if I do have a half box left at home.

He scoffs, scooting closer to snag his piece of Bazooka Bubble Gum from the plastic bins in front of me.

Stealing a glance over my shoulder, I meet his gaze, holding it as he peels the wrapper off, tossing the rectangular candy in his mouth. His tongue rolls, flipping the little pink piece over, before his lips close around it, and I wonder what kind of tricks that tongue can do.

Heat fills my chest and a hidden smirk whispers at the corners of his lips. Crew takes the candy bucket from my hand, nodding toward the ice cream and treat bar leading to the register.

I follow a step behind. "You know, considering how you basically played daddy yesterday and painted me the rebel teenage daughter who went out without permission, you're in quite a tranquil mood today."

"I stay calm until you piss me off."

"Ha! False news. You are always pissed off. Pissed at yourself, pissed at me, pissed at a red light. You, Crew Taylor, glare more than you grin. Bummer too, 'cause you've got a good grin."

Crew shoots me a look. "I am not always pissed off. Hurry up and pick your fudge before I tell the nice lady waiting for you to choose that you get none."

"Sounds pretty pissy to me."

My eyes dart up, meeting the eyes of the older woman behind the counter, her small smirk creating deeper wrinkles in her cheeks.

Crew frowns her way as my laughter fills the air.

The silver-haired woman winks teasingly as she slips a pair of clear gloves on her hands. "You take your time, honey. Ain't no one behind you."

I give Crew a full-tooth smile and face the woman. "What's your favorite?"

"The mint Oreo is to die for. Chocolate fudge on the bottom, mint layer with crumbled Oreos mixed in on top. Can't beat it."

"She thinks mint shouldn't exist in candy."

I look to Crew, and he holds my attention as he says, "She'll have the s'mores bar, and a chocolate-covered strawberry."

"Two chocolate-covered strawberries, add a chocolate-covered Twinkie for the grump here, please." I grin, and Crew turns away before his smile slips free. Not quick enough though. I saw it.

"You got it, honey. I'll have it ready for you at the register."

"Thank you." I slip past Crew, but his arm shoots out, snaking around my middle, halting me there.

"I can show you grump, Sweets."

"I'd say you already did, not that I'm not used to it."

"Admit it," he whispers. "You like me bossy."

Little tingles spread through my stomach, and I bite the inside of my cheek to keep from smiling. *I like you every way*, I think, but say, "I don't hate it."

"Mm-hmm." He tips his head, pushing his cheek against mine. "For the record, if I was playin' daddy . . . the last thing you'd be playing is *daughter*."

My, oh, my, my imagination is a wonderful thing.

He releases me, setting our items on the counter and waits to pay, so I move toward the door, double-checking all the bins on the way to ensure I didn't miss anything I want to try.

This morning when I made my way into the kitchen, prepared to whip up some waffles, I was stopped in my tracks by the sight of Crew sitting at the table, finishing off what was left in his coffee cup. He grinned, told me to get dressed, because we were going out for the day. Maybe I should have shunned him, played the silent game in response to his growly grab-and-go crap yesterday. But I didn't.

I've never dressed so fast in my life.

Thankfully, my hair is pencil straight, so all it took was a quick swipe of a brush and voilà. It looked like I tried.

I mastered putting on mascara in a moving car when I was fifteen, so that was a non-issue, and an hour later, we were fighting for a parking spot near a giant red barn. On the front, painted in blue, on a giant white sign above the entrance, it read, Nana and Pop's Sweet Shop.

I might have drooled in anticipation.

Oh, are those fizzes?

"Ready?"

I look over to find Crew at my side, so I link my arm through his, and we walk out the door, but rather than curve left, where his car is parked, we swing right, headed down a short walking path that leads to the harbor.

"Hungry?" Crew asks.

"Starving, but I'm not against a giant block of crispy graham cracker and marshmallowy fudge for breakfast."

"Yeah, I'd bet not, but it's noon, so I'm thinking lunch is the better option."

"I guess," I tease, shifting to the side to avoid getting run over by a toddler on a tricycle.

Crew pulls his arm free of mine, wrapping it around my lower back instead, and when my eyes flick to his, he only stares a moment, before pointing them forward.

"Thought we'd eat here." He nods toward an older-looking building. The structure is paneled, a light, sun-faded blue with white trimming. In the middle is a circle with bold red writing and a small fishing boat in the center. Around it is the name of the restaurant.

Rockin' Baja Coastal Cantina.

"Aw, it's so cute." We walk over to the patio seating, lucky enough to score a corner table with an up-close view of the docks.

Busy roaming over boat after boat, I forget to look at the menu, so when the waiter comes up to take our drink order, I'm unprepared, so I steal a glance at the tables around. "Margarita?"

"Traditional or strawberry?"

"Strawberry, please."

He nods, looking to Crew.

"Water for me."

The man walks away, and I look to Crew.

"What?"

His lips curve up the slightest bit. "Wondering when you started letting yourself have a drink."

Guilt washes over me, and I lower my eyes to my lap, but he quickly leans forward, catching my chin with his knuckles.

My brown gaze locks with his.

"You're an adult. Smart, responsible. No reason you can't enjoy a drink when you feel like it."

I shrug, looking away, and slowly, he releases me, but I don't look at him. "For a long time, I was afraid of drinking, but after a while, the fear turned into this pit of anxiousness every time I was around it or thought about it." I think of how Crew must have felt as a child, seeing his dad drink himself into oblivion day after day. "Finally, last summer I decided I needed to know how I would handle alcohol, if I'd somehow end up—" I cut off, looking at Crew.

I don't have to say it. He knows what I mean, he was there when my brother slowly ended his life one bottle of vodka at a time—he was there for it more than any of us were.

"Anyway, I don't know." I shrug. "It's nice to loosen up sometimes. I still won't keep it in the house. Never. Just . . ."

"Just in case."

Nodding, I meet his gaze.

"That's why you had me throw out that bottle that had . . ." He pauses, thinking. "Twenty-three percent left in it?"

A low laugh leaves me, and I settle farther into the chair. "Yeah, that's why."

Crew grins then but looks away before it can grow any wider.

"Why do you do that?"

His gaze comes right back, confusion tightening his features. "Do what?"

"Stop yourself from smiling or laughing when I know you want to."

Now he's the one who looks guilty, so I offer a small grin.

"You know I'm happy for you, right?" I ask. "Like, I love that you have new friends, a new . . . family, so to speak. I want that for you, *wished* for that for you." Crew swallows. "You deserve all the happiness after everything. I could cry knowing there are people out there who love you like I love you."

Crew's eyes shift between mine, a crease forming along his brows. "No one could love me like you, Sweets."

"Well, yeah, obviously," I joke, and this time, Crew does laugh.

He laughs, and it's low and husky, and his eyes, they're so damn gentle as they cling to mine.

The waiter reappears, who knows how many minutes later, and I clear my throat, thanking him as I look to Crew again.

"You know," I tease. "If I knew about this little adventure today, we could have put it to good use."

Crew arches a brow, taking a slow sip from his glass.

"This could be a solid lesson on first dates. We both know I need one on the subject."

He studies me for a moment, and then he shoots from his seat, walks around the table until he's dropping into the wooden chair on my right.

Crew yanks mine closer, draping his arm around the back of it, until his fingertips are brushing along my bicep.

He looks into my eyes, lowering his lips to the exposed skin of my shoulder, blindly reaching for my margarita. He lifts it until the straw is teasing against my lower lip, so I use my tongue to pull it inside, and his attention snaps to my mouth.

I suck on the cool liquid slowly, avoiding a brain freeze like the pro–Slurpee drinker I am. Of course, as it slips from my mouth, a small glop of margarita dribbles over my lower lip, and I dart a finger up, lapping up the access.

Crew's fingers twitch along my bicep. "Do that on a first date and you'll send a vibe you might not be ready for."

"I'm ready for it all."

His dark gaze lifts to mine, and slowly, his tongue runs along his bottom lip. "You are, aren't you?"

He says it as if he's only just realized, as if he didn't believe me before when I said I was ready.

I am. I want it all. Everything.

I want it with you . . .

We stare at each other a long moment, and I jump when a woman walks over, setting a plate of bacon-wrapped shrimp in front of us.

I don't wait for him to go first, I pick one up and blow on it, touching the tip of my tongue to the end to be sure it's not too hot. I take a small bite, and the bacon uncurls, falling along my chin. Laughing, I tip my head back and push it into my mouth. I reach for a napkin, doing a double take when I catch Crew staring again.

"What?"

His brows jump, and he shakes his head, taking his arm off my chair, so he can eat with me. "Trying to figure out how no one has grabbed you by the neck and kissed the shit out of you yet."

"That's . . . random." I swallow and I force myself to ask, "What makes you say that?"

"'Cause every time you open your mouth, it's all I want to do."

I go to speak, but nothing comes out, and when Crew looks up, it's nothing more than a quick side peek. I don't miss the pleased gleam in his gaze.

He loves rendering me speechless. Always has.

It doesn't take long for us to kill the entire plate of shrimp, and only then, do I realize we haven't ordered our meals yet, but just before I can suggest we order, the chair across from us scratches against the concrete.

"Sorry we're late! I had to pee twice on the drive, and you'd be surprised how many of the gas stations on the way here don't allow you to use their bathrooms." Layla smiles, stealing Crew's water for a quick drink.

"The last one only let her in 'cause she cried and said she was going to piss in the aisle if not." Willie grins, coming over to my side of the table and leaning down for a quick, one-armed hug. "Hey, gorgeous."

I frown, but quickly add a smile when he straightens. "Hey." I look to Crew.

He knows I'm staring; he can see me from the corner of his eye, but he doesn't glance my way. Julius walks in next, with Xavier on his tail.

They both come to me for a hug, snag chairs from the table beside us and wedge themselves in at the end.

"Parking here is a bitch. We're all the way down by the coffee shop."

"Yeah, I left mine in the two-hour slots by the candy shop." Crew reclaims his water from Layla, his arm making its way around the back of my chair once more.

Willie's eyes zone in immediately, and his grin is as wicked as they come as his gaze finds mine. He wiggles his brows, and I play along, wiggling mine right back.

His laughter follows, capturing the attention of the others, so I ditch my straw, quickly burying my smile in my glass.

"What's so funny?" Crew scowls.

"Nothing, man. Dude back there dropped a plate of something. Poor fucker." Willie licks his lips, winking at his wife as she knowingly shakes her head.

Crew cuts his head my way, but I just keep taking small sips.

"Heard I missed the fun at the slides yesterday." Mischief blankets Julius's features as his gaze roams over me. "Heard you had double braids. Woulda loved to see that, Davis the Virgin . . . or did Jess, the *not* female, help you out with—oh shit!" His chair topples over, sending him tumbling to the ground with a crash.

All eyes fly to our table and a waiter rushes over to see if he's okay, but Julius jumps up with a grin.

"I'm good, all's good over here. Nothing but a case of blue-ball denial. Please, go back to enjoying your meals." He bows.

Of course he bows, then Julius quickly jolts toward Crew, knocking the bill of his backward hat and my hand darts out, catching it before it hits the floor.

"Fucker." Julius laughs, taking his seat once more. "Your woman knows I was teasing, ain't that right, gorgeous?"

"You're too much for me, brother number three."

His mouth drops open in mock hurt. "I'm reduced to bro three? I mean, I know Willie is first class, but X is before me?"

I laugh. "Hey, X is—" I squeal as my chair is yanked, the handle of mine now pressed completely against Crew's.

His arm never leaves the back seat, but his fingers begin skating along the curve of my shoulder. His eyes hit mine, narrowing. "X is . . . *what*?"

"Um." I can feel my blush rising and think of something different to say. "X . . . doesn't flirt every five seconds."

"In the spirit of being transparent"—X raises his hand—"I would if I weren't worried about keeping my balls attached."

"Shut up, asshole." Willie gives his brother a little push. "You're obsessed with Neo's sister, and we all know it."

"All of us *but* Neo," Layla adds with a saucy smirk.

"No . . ." I look at him, smiling. "Really, you and Nova?"

Xavier frowns and jumps up. "I'm going to the bathroom."

The table laughs at his expense, and a moment later, everyone grows quiet, silently skimming the menu, but while I do the same, I can't tell you what's on it. The quiet has allowed my mind to catch up, to process the situation.

If Crew were mad about my being with his friends yesterday, why would he invite them here today?

He wouldn't, would he?

Crew turns to me then, and I meet his stare.

"Know what you want?" His tone is deep, raspy, and coated in something unfamiliar. Unease?

Crew uneasy? Impossible . . .

I nod, because I do, but what I want isn't on the menu. He took it off himself, swapping for the role of chef in this scenario. Crew will create the menu, and I'll be forced to choose between flank and skirt steak when what I want is the filet mignon.

When what I want is him.

Keen, dark eyes implore mine, and when I feel his palm span wide against my arm, mine bends upward. The moment my fingers brush his, his chest rises with a full breath, and he closes his hand over mine, linking ours together.

He gives a little squeeze and I shift, slowly easing his hat back onto his head. Backward, and pushed down a tad, just the way I like it.

He tips his head toward me, so I lean in, giving him my ear.

"I wanted to rip their arms off when they hugged you. Know why?"

I shake my head, peeking at Layla under my lashes when she shifts in her seat, but she's looking at the water behind her.

"They touched you."

That's it. That's all he says, and I have sooo many questions, but Crew pulls back. Not to look at me, to face his friends, none of whom are paying us any attention.

"We ready to order?" The waiter smiles.

The others begin reading off their item of choice, but I was too busy fantasizing to look at the menu, so after Crew orders, I simply say "same," and sit back, ignorant to the conversations flowing around me as I formulate an equation in my head.

I attempt to make sense of the million thoughts running through my mind but can't.

Crew's protective and possessive nature taking a turn in the direction I've been dying for, his newfound need to touch and overall alpha ways.

His open and angry denials, repetitive refusals, and offer to find someone to take what I want to be his.

God, but his whispered confession and the way his hands feel on my skin—heavy and strong, greedy. Needy?

Ugh! It's like no matter how many variables I add in, no matter the words that leave his mouth or the ones behind his eyes he chooses not to speak, mean very little when the result remains the same. Regardless of what I may be confused about, I understand the end won't change.

It will still be me virginityless and Crew a non-participant.

The deal is still on, Davis. Don't scare him away with worthless worries.

"So, what's the plan after this?" Willie asks, pulling me from my thoughts.

"I'm taking her to the pier to ride the Ferris wheel." Crew looks my way. "Good way to end our first date, yeah?"

My eyes shoot wide, and around the table, low whistles and quick laughs follow. Pretty sure Layla coos.

All I can do is stare and then Crew shocks the shit out of me.

He leans over, presses his lips just beneath my jaw, and goes right back to his conversation.

Like nothing.

As if it were no big deal and if he didn't say we were on a date . . . when it's pretend.

As if this weren't simply a lesson . . . when it is.

As if he didn't just insinuate he was on the verge of being mine . . . when it couldn't be further from the truth.

As if he didn't willingly press his soft, plush, perfectly rough lips to my skin . . . when we all witnessed it.

It's all part of the agreement, an extension of our deal, this lesson in first dates and what to expect during it, but I'm still a ready and waiting virgin with an epically pounding pulse. To be honest, I might faint if the others weren't here distracting me enough to remember to breathe, especially when the hand on my chair comes back around to rest on my thigh. My bare thigh, where he tortures me with long slow strokes of his thumb.

It's official. Crew Taylor is trying to ruin me and call me a wayward woman, I'm dying to let him.

He said he won't allow me in his bed, but I wonder what it would take to get him to play in mine a bit?

"Oh, babe, there's a live band!" Layla claps, dragging her husband by the hand into the crowd.

Willie cuts a look our way, slicing his finger across his neck as she tugs him farther and farther into the mayhem.

"It's cute how he acts like he's anything other than pleased to give her all the little things she wants." I smile after the couple. It's so obvious how much he loves her.

He's never not touching her when she's in reach, and when she's not, it's not for too long and he normally finds her, kisses her to get his fix and goes on his way.

"Yeah, he's whipped to the core and loves it." Crew chuckles as he takes my hand. He lifts it until my knuckles are pressed to his mouth and he glides his lips across them with a small nip. His eyes flash, and a moment later, we're as lost in the mob as the others.

Crew slips behind me, holding on to my waist and leads, swaying my hips the slightest bit while I stare at the band. It's not a song I've heard or a band I know, likely a local, but it's upbeat and perfect for dancing in the sand. I like it.

I like this.

Having somewhere to go and someone to go with.

Crew presses closer, his hands tightening their hold on my hips, his chest now flush with my back. "Push into me, Sweets. Let me know you like feeling my body against yours."

Heat pools between my legs at his words, and I swallow, doing exactly what he says.

I press my ass into his thighs, and he bends a hint, so the friction of his zipper brushes along the cotton material of my shorts.

It's intoxicating, the way his hands span wider, how his shoulders close in more, building a cocoon around me. Locking me into him and keeping me as far away from anyone else as possible. It feels as if he wants me to himself, the world around us be damned.

I've danced with men before, but never for more than a moment, and not like this.

"Show me you want more." His lips find the opposite ear now, and he glides them across the lobe. "Let me know you like what you're feeling."

My eyes snap closed, my head dropping onto his chest, and suddenly, my breaths grow more labored. My lungs expand past normal, and with every deep inhale, my mind and body are consumed by Crew.

His scent, his heat, his touch.

God, his everything.

My hand comes up, sliding along his neck until I can tether it into his hair, and I do. I wrap my fingers around his locks and tug. The little groan that fans along my skin has me doing it again, and Crew's fingertips dig into me.

I spin in his hold, and his eyes shoot down to mine. Maybe it's the dopamine coursing through my veins, but I'd almost swear they're half-hooded, wanting, and it's only me standing here.

"Crew . . ."

His brows dip low, nearly touching in the center. He lets go, steps back, and nods his head. "Good, that's good. Mastered on your first try."

I blink.

He walks away, but before I can decide to follow, a smiling Layla is there grabbing my arm. She pulls me forward, Willie passing us by on his way to catch up with Crew.

"You have to come to the festival this weekend! It's going to be so fun. X and Neo can't come because they have baseball stuff, but Julius and my friend, Toni, you already met, will be there. You can help pour beer or slave away on the hot grill with the boys."

"So, this is a working festival?" I tease.

"Yes, yes it is." She laughs. "We're trying to get some investors for Willie's beer, see if we can't up our production and get into more bars or restaurants around town."

I look ahead at the boys. "You sure the boss won't mind?"

"Your boss or mine?"

Laughing, I look at her with a scrunched nose. "Both?"

She winks. "Don't worry, sister. You're on the list. But I should probably tell you now, it's sort of a free-spirited thing, we sleep in these cool teepees, and they're all booked up. Crew would be your roomie."

A tiny teepee with the man who makes my vagina vibrate with nothing but a look.

Sounds like torture.

But, then again, what part of being hopelessly attracted to a man you can't have isn't?

Chapter 18
Davis

Every year, I request the week after finals off, and usually, I spend the time doing absolutely nothing productive but stimulating my mind with some serious binge-watching. During the school year, I won't start shows because I know myself and my teenage, angst-loving heart can't simply walk away after an episode or two, and pick up later like a normal person. No. I watch the sucker from episode one to the bittersweet end. It's honestly the best.

But this week is different, my life will now be different.

With the drop of a pencil, that was it.

My final, final. My very last, last day of school.

I am freaking done, and I am so damn excited about it.

Willie's stand at the Brews and Barbeques Festival couldn't have come at a better time. I'm juiced. Beyond so because, holy crap, I have somewhere fun to go and people to go with.

Layla took away any nerves I had seconds after telling me I should come by, shouting that I *was* coming, and she didn't even have to break it to Crew he'd be my partner in sleep for the weekend. He insisted before she could get a word in.

So, this fine Friday afternoon, we're standing behind a make-shift bar under a giant cedarwood tree. Layla explains the process of brewing, sharing the flavor profiles in the hops they use and different ways of approaching the bitterness versus the citrus options. Half the people want to know every detail she's willing to share, my nerdy little science self included, and the other half nod politely, while waiting for me to pour them their liquid fun.

It's not until closer to seven, when the vendors shut down for the night, and the partying begins. Most people start out in their own camping areas, eating and drinking the leftovers of their day's production and listening to music of all kinds coming from every angle based on preference.

Tucked behind our serving and cooking stations is a giant see-through netted tent, the kind meant to keep the bugs away, and inside are two tables arranged in an *L* shape, paper products, utensils and all the goods spread out along them. I grab a plate and start shoveling a little of everything onto it. Unable to help myself, I stick the pad of my finger into the gravy oozing over my meat and bring it to my lips.

"Good?"

Setting my plate on the table before me, I look to Crew, smiling. "So good. You were right. Layla can cook."

Crew begins serving himself, and my phone beeps in my pocket, so I wipe my hands on a napkin quickly and pull it out.

Jess: Put me out of my misery. Come over. It's been too long.

Shaking my head, I text him back.

Me: It's been approximately twenty-seven hours. You'll be fine.

Jess: That was a quickie. Didn't count. Come celebrate with me.

A laugh spurts from me and then my phone is yanked from my hand.

"Hey!" I frown at Crew, reaching for it, but he holds it over my head like a teenager. "What the heck?" I slap my hands on my thighs.

"What the fuck's he talking about, a quickie? And when did you see him yesterday? I was with you all day."

"I had coffee with him in the morning. He has this cool machine and all these sweet syrups and—"

"You were with him while I was asleep?"

"Uh . . . yeah? I'm not much for coffee, but like I said . . . syrups and he always has whipped cream."

Crew scoffs, glaring at the screen when it beeps again. "Bet he fucking does. What's he mean, celebrate? Celebrate what?"

"Graduation."

Crew's head snaps to mine, creases forming along his forehead. "What?"

"Thursday was my last final. I'm done." I smile, dragging my shoulders up in a long shrug.

His eyes hold mine for a long moment, and slowly, the tension in his muscles eases, a shadow flickering over his features as he glances away briefly. "You didn't even tell me."

"Oh, I'm not having a party or anything. I'm not even going to walk across the stage next week."

"Why? Your parents will want you to. I can't believe they're allowing that."

"I'm an adult, and it was my decision," I tell him. "They know walking across the stage isn't something I want to do, all those people staring at me while I try not to trip on the carpet. No way. I'm just happy I did it. There were times I really wanted to go home, but I stuck it out. And they're proud."

Crew's lips form a tight line. "This is fucking dumb. You shouldn't be here working. You should be out partying with friends."

He glares, and I look down.

What friends, I want to say, but don't, instead following with a different truth. "This is how I wanted to spend my weekend, and you're here so . . ." I meet his gaze. "It's a celebration better than I could have expected."

Crew opens his mouth, but Layla slides up.

"Move over, brute. I'm starving again, and turn on the lights on your way by, would you?"

Sliding my phone into my back pocket, he nods, grabs his plate, and off he goes.

Moments later, soft-blue LED lights flick on around us.

My eyes slide toward Crew, and he looks back at the same moment.

"And someone thought you wouldn't come," Layla whispers, drawing my attention.

We share a low laugh and eat our plates of food in silence before making our way to the "pillow pad," as Layal explained it—it's what every camper sets up at the edge of their site come nightfall, helping make the large, open circle more complete.

It's basically a picnic-style setting, blankets and pillows organized however you want, creating a chill spot to people-watch.

The sun is almost set now, the grassy hill area nearly lit by nothing but string lights for those who thought to bring some, and a few standard ones lit up with generators.

I drop down beside Layla, and we watch as camper after camper migrates toward the middle, the four-hundred-yard clearing between all of us becoming one giant-ass party.

I imagine the campus parties this weekend are the exact opposite of this—a lively kind of mellow. Dramaless.

It's the perfect way to celebrate the end of one stage of my life and welcome the next. If the next looks anything like this, I'd have more than I thought possible.

Sneaking a glance at Crew, I find him watching me, and I swear, he can read my mind.

He doesn't look away, and neither do I, but this time, he's the one who smiles first. It's small, one sided, but it's there.

"Man, I wish I could get drunk," Layla pouts, attempting to tug her sweater over her bump, but it won't stretch beyond her belly button. "You guys seem so chill. I want to be chill."

Willie drapes his arms over her, and she grabs on to his forearms. "You are chill, babe, but you're also getting cranky. Let's get my girls to bed, hmm?"

Layla smacks him as she sits up, waiting for him to stand behind her. "Cute. Say something to get you cut off and follow it up without something worthy of a king's chair."

"I will pack this shit up right now, girl. Don't tease." Willie hauls her to her feet with a smile. "Night, guys."

"Start breakfast at seven, so we can prep by eight?" Crew asks, looking up at him.

"Make it nine, my man. Davis brought these little donut rings, a bunch of giant waffles, and those little peanut butter cup things. We're set."

Crew looks my way, a playful groan pushing past his throat. "You brought treats and didn't tell me?"

"You would have eaten them by now."

"Fuck yeah, I would." He grins, and it's a little loose. Adorably so.

Tonight was the first night I've seen Crew have a drink. It was no more than half a cup of chilled whiskey, just enough to relax him and not a drop more.

I hadn't thought to ask him if he still drank, when he asked me about the subject, but I imagine working at a bar is the ultimate example of strength for him. It's good to know he trusts himself enough to do as he pleases. I always wanted that for him, him to find confidence and faith in himself to help him believe he can be whatever kind of man he wishes to.

"By the way, if you have sex, do it in my truck, if you don't want us to listen . . . 'cause we will!" Willie shouts over his shoulder, and Layla laughs at his side. "And Davis, honey, don't make him wrap it up, all right? My poor kid ain't gonna have no friends if you do."

Before I might have blushed or rambled about how I want him to slide in, but he's refusing a trip down the brand-new Slip 'N Slide. That's not what happens, though.

I don't grow bashful at all; in fact, I laugh, and when I roll my neck along the blanket, I catch Crew laughing too.

Seconds later, it's just us.

"He's an ass but that means he likes you." Crew smirks, tossing an ice cube in his mouth. "And *that* means Layla likes you."

"I hope so, considering she's the one who invited me."

"She'd never invite you if she didn't know for sure I'd want you here."

"Is that right?"

Nodding, he folds an arm behind his head.

"And how would she know that?"

"She asked and I told her."

A chuckle pushes past my pursed lips. "Just like that, huh?"

"Asking what you want to know is always the cleanest route."

Twisting my body, so it faces his, I fold my hands beneath my face and lean on them. "So, the dirty route is trickled with muddy assumptions?"

"Exactly." Small creases form along his temple, as he says the word, and I know something's on his mind.

"So, why not take a power washer to the one floating around in your mind tonight, clear that baby up?"

He watches me closely, and I know I'm right, he does have something he's been sitting on. "It's not all that simple."

"Why not?"

"I already know the answer to the question." He speaks surlily. "But it leads to one I can't fucking figure out."

"Oh, this sounds juicy. Do tell, Mr. Taylor."

He studies me, and then he lays it out. "You're not attracted to Jess. Not physically. Not like you are to me. He's attracted to you, but you're thinking, right now, that that's not true. It is. No damn doubt."

Talk about a veer left, when you expect a right.

Oddly, or maybe not so odd, considering Crew's always been able to read me as if he had a crystal ball on his side. He's not wrong, but like he said, he knew that already.

I'm not attracted to Jess, not sexually or emotionally or any other "jump my bones, neighbor" kind of way and I most definitely don't believe he's attracted to me. But . . .

"And this little palm-reading session leads to what unanswered question?"

"Why?" He asks it so simply, as if it truly makes no sense to him.

Why? I mean, it is a good question, I guess, but the answer I would think was an obvious one. Clearly not, though, if the scowl etching its way across Crew's features indicates anything.

"I don't want him and I don't know that there's a reason why. He's my friend. Never once have I looked at him and thought of anything other than that. He's just Jess, my neighbor down the hall. My study buddy, or former study buddy now. That's all."

"That's what I mean. You've never thought of him differently. I know because, if you had, there's no doubt in my mind he'd have jumped on your first hint of interest. Now, though, you're starting to see what you didn't before. Your eyes are opening, Sweets, and pretty soon, you'll look at men a whole lot different than you do now."

"I don't think so."

"I know so."

And I know I'll always seek you out, even in a room of hundreds. Just you.

"Maybe you're right," I admit, and a deep line dents the space between his dark brows. "Maybe I will or do notice the look in a man's eye in ways I didn't before, but when they look back into mine, they won't see the same thing," I promise.

Crew's lips press together, his eyes flicking to my mouth and back, and my stomach swirls, dips, and twists. Vulnerability is common when staring into my favorite hazel eyes, but tonight, it runs a little deeper because I know he can read between the lines.

They won't find in my gaze what he will.

Want. Need. Trust.

"You know we're celebrating graduation, right?" he says suddenly.

My grin splits fast. "This weekend feels like a celebration. I've never done anything like this before." I adjust slightly, looking out at the last of the crowd in the clearing. There's at least a quarter of them left mingling.

"Tell me you didn't plan to do something else before Layla invited you."

See? He knows me well.

"I totally want to be bougie and go to Napa, pretend I can afford it and pay an obscene amount of money for a bottle of wine, internally praying it's a sweet, sugary one I'll actually drink." Smiling, I face Crew. "I've saved all my tips since March."

"Then we'll go."

"We?"

"Am I not invited?"

"Oh please." I roll my eyes. "You'd be the only one invited and you know it."

Crew chuckles then, and when he faces the crowd, I do the same. "We're going on that trip."

Don't cheese too hard, Davis. Play it cool.

"Okay, two o'clock." I steer us away from plans of the future before I embarrass myself. "The pixie-cut brunette and the Leo DiCaprio stunt double."

Crew looks for the pair, falling right back into the game we used to play all the time, but haven't had the chance to in years.

He considers the duo a moment, gaze narrowing in thought. "She's laughing at what he's saying, but she's not reaching out to touch him when she does, and look. His head turns toward the chicks outside the tequila hut every time he takes a drink."

It totally does.

"I say they fuck when they feel like it," he decides. "But their friends don't know it, and they still hook up with other people."

"Sounds fair." I nod. "Oh! Ten o'clock, blonde girl in a baggy hoodie and scruffy-haired skinny guy."

"Got 'em. Your turn."

"Okay." I stare at the two a moment, sneaking a quick look at the others around them. "I think she likes him, and he knows it, but she's softer than what he's used to. She came with her friend, hoping this guy would be here, but now that he is, she has no idea how to act."

"Because she doesn't want to seem forward, but forward is what he likes."

"Exactly." We stare some more, and the poor girl. "Aw, she's just waiting for his attention, and he won't give it to her until she demands it."

Crew laughs, and I flip on my side again, facing him.

"What should she do?"

Crew watches me closely, and after a few seconds, adjusts so he's positioned the same as me. "She should make the first move."

"But what if he doesn't want her?"

"Trust me." His eyes bounce between mine, then he says. "He does."

Crew

A silent beat passes between us, and slowly, the corner of her mouth lifts. She loves this shit, getting the smallest insight into a man's mind.

Into my mind.

Crazy as it might seem to others, the girl legit feels like she's sitting front row in her class of choice, pen and paper ready.

Her eyes damn near dance under the lights. "So how do you know when someone's making the first move? Like what are some signs they want you?"

"You'd know."

"Humor me." Her scowl is far too playful.

Playful Davis is dangerous. Shit, smiling, pissy, *breathing* Davis is dangerous.

I like all her colors, but the sexually intrigued version is a fucking killer.

Call me Sherlock, 'cause I want to catch her. Keep her.

Punish her, oh so fucking good.

"Crew," she prompts.

Okay, Sweets . . .

"Staring into someone's eyes with a long pause. Shifting around so your skin is touching theirs." I slowly and intentionally lower my gaze, so she knows to follow, and witnesses with her own eyes where her knee has lifted on the blanket. It's hiked up high and pressed to mine.

Right now, with her attention held on the spot our bodies are linked, she's thinking about the way she stared into my eyes seconds before asking her question. Even under the midnight sky, nothing but LED string lights a few feet away, I spot the flush working its way up her neck, feel the deep inhale she pulls in—deep in my fucking groin.

"You're a woman, Davis, your body knows what it wants. It will lead you if you let it."

"Can I?"

I frown. "Can you what?"

"Let it lead?" Her tone is so low, so damn husky.

Finally, she looks up, and the motherfucking expression on her face.

Goddamn.

Her lips are parted with need, her eyes low and swimming with hunger, a neediness she can't hide. Not from me.

Not that she's trying.

It's more than that, though. It's the sense of desire radiating off her, and not of the sexual kind. Desire to take control. To be the one leading and discovering where it takes her.

Can she let her body lead, right here, right now?

I don't say yes.

Don't say no either, and slowly, so. Fucking. Slowly, the velvety pads of her fingertips find the exposed skin of my left bicep. They drag lower, back, until she's gripping my muscle firmly, and her lips part when I make no move to stop her.

Without warning, her leg loops over me, and in a single, swift move, she hauls herself on top.

My back flattens on the blanket, and the second my eyes meet hers, hooded and hovering over me, my cock twitches in my jeans.

I want to touch her, tug her, push against her ass.

I don't.

Little Davis, though, she's got ideas of her own, and she's determined to test them out.

She lowers her hips with caution, bringing them flush to mine, right over the zipper strained against me. Her shorts trek a little higher as her legs stretch around me, her knees pressed firm into the blanket at my sides.

"What now?" A soft, sweet shyness wraps her words in a whisper.

"Your body is leading, remember?" I keep my tone as neutral as possible, when I'm using far too much mind power to keep from grinding up into her.

I know she feels me; it's why she froze the second she planted.

My cock is lined at her center. Right where it wants to be.

Anticipation draws through my veins when a sly, naughty smile pulls at her lips, her lashes fanning along her cheeks as she points her attention to my throat. Her knuckles glide along the vein, pressing against it. "Do whatever *it* wants?"

I raise a brow. "Within reason, and without forgetting, there's a gang of people staring at you straddling me."

"Reason is boring."

An unexpected chuckle pushes past my lips, and my dick decides to twitch.

Her eyes snap to mine, widening as my length grows beneath her.

"Our bodies are in control," I remind her, reminding myself to do the exact opposite.

Her nod is almost unnoticeable, and then she dares to move. Her hips, they roll forward. Once. Twice.

My hands shoot to her waist, and she freezes.

"I'm sorry," she rushes.

My teeth clink shut before I can tell her she's got it wrong, that I grabbed her out of need, and how the last thing I want her to do *is stop*, but this is good.

She had to fucking stop.

Can't dance on my dick.

Can't rip the reason from my mind with her deep forward rolls and slow backward ones.

Fuck me, that's how she'd ride.

Again, I need her to stop, so why do my palms play as a guide, my fingertips pressing into her lower back, leading her to lean forward until her hands are forced to plant on my chest?

Because at this angle, her clit will be worked . . .

Davis rolls once more, and when her lips part with a sharp gasp, my teeth clench.

God, she's discovering the simplest of touches, testing them in subtle waves.

The sounds I would earn from you, Sweets . . .

Desire kicking up, I clamp my lids closed, and seconds later, I'm struck with a hot, wet tongue across my neck.

A groan slips free. It's chest deep and any hope I had to stay at half-mass is out the fucking window.

I'm hard as a rock. Aching.

"This is a horrible idea." The huskiness in her tone is almost unbearable, but the words she spoke slap at my sense, shaking me from the haze she's got me in.

Davis is close to dry fucking me right here, where who knows how many can see.

Our gazes lock.

Her hands push down, and I wait for her to climb off before I'm forced to move her, but then she says, "Can I have the tepee alone for a few minutes?"

All the blood in my body rushes to the tip of my dick, swelling, begging for the release she's in need of.

So fucking brazen, my sweet, innocent Sweets.

Only for me, my mind screams, but I cut the bitch at the collar.

"You want me to wait out here, knowing you're making yourself come in there?"

"Considering you said no when I asked you to watch, yes." Her chest rises and falls rapidly. "This whole, first move, let your body lead lesson is sweet, sweet torture. So yeah. I'm fine with torturing you for a minute or two. Or maybe more." She thinks better of it. "I didn't exactly think to bring my toy."

My brows crash. Her toy.

That's right, she took batteries in her room.

Possessiveness prickles along my spine, and my body jerks upright, arms flying around her back to keep her against me, and then she's right fucking there. Eye to eye. Lip to lip.

"You slide a fake cock inside this virgin pussy?" My hands drag down her ass, and I can't stop them, jealousy burning me up from the inside out. "Answer me, Sweets."

Her headshake is slow. "N-no. It's just a little . . . vibrator thing, clit stimulation and all that. My fingers they . . ."

"Aren't enough for you anymore?" I guess.

She nods.

Of course, she needs more.

This is Davis Franco, my sweet little pipe dream.

A queen in her own fucking right.

Only a man who knows what she's worth can satisfy her needs.

"Please?" she whispers, her thighs quivering around me.

"No."

Her face falls, and I stand with her in my lap, holding on before slowly allowing her feet to meet the blanket. Her neck is cranked all the way back, eyes sloped and on me.

"I won't give you the room alone. I won't watch." My knuckles find her chin before it can hide from me, and I hold her there, stepping in closer, my fingers pressing into the sides of her throat. "But I will listen, and if we hurry, there'll be something for you to listen to, too."

She doesn't ask questions, doesn't shy away.

Davis grabs my hand and leads me to the teepee.

To the death of me.

To my ruin, because I know once I hear her come, the need to see it, taste, to be the one to trigger it will eat away at my restraint. And that bitch is already as thin as the paper her little offer was printed on.

It would dissolve between my lips.

Just like she would . . . if I let her.

Chapter 19
Crew

Inside the thick, circular hunk of leather we're calling home for the next two days, Davis pauses, my back bumping hers before I'm all the way through the opening.

Her fingers squeeze around mine, and after a moment, I pick up on what I expected we'd come back to.

Deep, hushed groans and strangled mews cut off by what can only be a kiss.

"They . . ." she whispers.

"They're fucking," I murmur, ushering her farther into the blackness of the space.

The sound of our shoes falling to the ground seems to echo around us.

"How did you know?" she asks so low, as if she's afraid they'll hear, and the air mattress rustles, letting me know she's lowered herself on top of it.

"They only left us about an hour ago." There's not enough space in here to stand without ducking, so lingering isn't an option. I lower into my designated place beside her.

"Yeah, that's a whole hour."

"Not everyone jumps right to it. I'm sure they do when pressed for time, but the lead-up is just as fun. Maybe they spent a while teasing, maybe they started fucking the second they got inside."

"For an hour?"

"An air mattress isn't the best of settings."

She stills, and I hear her shift beside me. "As in, it could go longer?"

It's not a question, and there's no doubt in my mind she's thinking about her little "five minutes of your time" comment from before. Proof is in her next words.

In the way her exhale pushes past her lips, soft and slow. She's intrigued. Curious.

"How long can you go?" Her question is whispered in the dark, and she settles into the pillow more.

She's readying herself, the sweeping moans of the others breaking into her concentration, shattering her ability to pay attention, and cutting off her restraint. Just like that, the questions evade her.

Nothing is left but the pulsing of her pussy.

And it is pulsing, the quake washing through her body at the low, gaspy cry from the tent over.

The blankets rustle, and I pull the hem up to her chest as her hand dips between her thighs. Her legs shift beside me, her right one stretching up until it's met by mine. She pulls in a sharp breath, her shoulders pressing into the pillow behind her head.

It's dark as shit in here, so dark, I couldn't see a thing when we slipped inside, but my eyes are hungry and find a way. Like an owl in the night, my vision grows laser sharp, and Davis Franco is my target. Our heads are level with each other's, her shoulders a little higher than mine, so I've got a straight shot of her body beneath the covers.

We brought our own, but somehow, in the darkness of it all, we ended beneath the same one, so with every twitch of her muscles, the comforter shuffles over me.

Her arm trembles beside me as she reaches for herself, and then a little mound is formed beneath the covers. Her sharp inhale is instant, and I know she's slipped inside her panties now, her soft, delicate fingers slowly grazing over her swollen clit. That inhale whooshes past her lips within seconds.

Heat buds in my chest, knotting its way down. Further and fucking further, until it's spreading through my cock, drawing my balls up and just like that, with her single breath and the images in my mind I'm rodded beneath my boxers.

Goddamn, the fire we could build . . .

Her head presses into the pillow more, her swallow hard. "What-what do you think he's doing to her?"

Her stuttering words, the labored breaths in which she speaks them.

Fuck.

I'm tempted to reach for myself.

To dive beyond my boxers and treat my dick the way she's treating her pussy, but that's bound to lead to more. No fucking way will my hands not wander. My gums will be bleeding by the time she's done tonight.

"What do you think he's doing to her?" I manage to force out.

A closed-lipped moan escapes Davis, one I know she tried to tamper down.

I'd have your ass for that if you were mine.

Layla's moan follows, it's short and quick; Willie's isn't far behind, and Davis shocks me with a husky chuckle.

"I think they're almost there. They sound f-frustrated. Ready to c-come."

Turning my head, I keep my eyes pointed on the slope of her body, wishing I could see the tautness of her nipples, but focused instead on the increasing speed of her hand.

"I think you're right," I whisper slowly, dragging out every word, so the warmth of my breath trickles over the exposed skin of her neck.

She stretches it back, revealing more for me, silently begging for me to reach out and touch it, kiss it. Squeeze it, but just a little.

I want to bite it like I did that day at Willie's, but only so I can lick it after.

My mouth waters with the need to do just that.

The sounds coming from our neighbors are growing desperate, the air mattress beneath squeaking and grating against the leather of their teepee.

"I'd bet he's got her on her knees now," I tell her.

Davis's leg hikes higher, lifting so it's now rested over mine, and before I know what I'm doing, my palm is wrapped around her knee.

I pull it even higher, and her back bows.

"Can she . . . will she . . ." She gets lost in her own pleasure, that little hand of hers growing frantic.

"Will she finish like that?" I guess her question, and when she gives a swift nod, I confirm, "Oh, yeah. She'll spread her legs wider for him when she's close, and he'll push deeper, thrust harder. His balls will slap at her clit, and after a few full strokes . . ." My grip tightens, my body gaining a little more control over my mind as I guide my palm higher, the pads of my fingertips sinking into the soft thickness of her thighs. "His wife will come for him. Hard, fast and best of all?" Davis pants into the air, her body quaking against mine. "With his name on her lips."

"Oh god," Davis whimpers, and her hand isn't the only thing moving now.

She rolls her hips, and the lift of the blanket where her knuckles press against the fabric lowers. She's cupping herself, pressing hard against her most needy spot, and I bet if I weren't here, she'd flip onto her stomach and ride her closed fist.

Her moans grow deeper, needier, until the sounds slipping past her lips are nothing but anxious cries.

Every nerve ending in my body fires up and I start to sweat, the sounds coming from her too fucking much for this man to handle. I need her to stop.

I need her to come.

"Davis."

"Mmm," is the only thing she manages to say, and her sharp intake freezes in her throat, her muscles locking.

"Come, Sweets," I coo. "Pinch your clit, hard, and squeeze those pussy walls, hmm?" My nose brushes along her shoulder, and she gasps, long and loud.

Her body quakes, and then her head lifts, all to slam back into the pillow as she comes.

The sound, the eager, deprived whimper and the tremble that follows. Fuck me. Her other arm shoots up and I fixate on the movement, anticipating what she plans to do with it.

My Sweets hand slips beneath her shirt, into her bra, and this time, the quiet groan that fills the air might be mine.

She tweaks her nipple and with every move of that hand, she jerks.

Is she pinching or pulling? Flicking or squeezing?

I don't know, but what I do is that she's dragging out her orgasm, intensifying it because coming by clit stimulation isn't enough. She needs more.

This is Davis we're talking about.

She *is* more.

It takes several minutes for her breathing to return to normal, and when a soft little sigh floats past her lips, I release her, letting her leg fall limp between us.

My cock rages, weeping for attention, but doesn't so much as flex.

Not two minutes into the silence a muffled whistling sound breaks through, and both of us break out into a laugh at the same exact time.

Willie's putting air back into their mattress.

"You nasty little fuckers!" he teases loudly. "I'll be expecting a standing ovation for my performance tomorrow!"

At that, we all laugh.

Davis's sleepy sigh follows, and she turns onto her side, tucking the blankets up to her neck, the way she's always liked them.

"God, I seriously can't wait," she mumbles sleepily.

Curious, I turn to face her. "For what?"

The shadow casts perfectly over her face, revealing the slight hitch at the corner of her lips as she says, "To be thoroughly ruined by a man."

Thoroughly ruined, that's what she said.

Is she crazy?

Does she not know there are several things you cannot say to a man and that is on the top of the list?

No, she doesn't. That's where you come in.

If my girl—*she could be yours, you dumb fucker*—said something, anything, close to the words Davis left me with last night . . . there would have been no sleeping.

Not that I got any of that, anyway. It felt like the second my eyes closed, the phone alarm went off, waking my ass right back up. Thank fuck, the day was a busy one, but Saturdays at these kinds of things always are. If it weren't for Drew being semi-reliable and Paula bringing her cousin on to bus tables on a trial basis, I never would have gotten away from the bar.

That and convincing Julius to stay behind to keep Drew company.

Yeah, that was for straight selfish reasons.

"What are you smirking about over there, asshole?" Willie shouts as he officially douses the coals on the pit, ending our work for the weekend.

"Remembering how quick you were to shoot last night, that's all."

"Shit." He drags out the word. "Lie to me some more."

"Your wife's moans *don't* turn me on."

Willie whips me with a towel, and a laugh pushes past my lips.

"Always a funny fucker." He grins, glancing toward Davis. "We freak the little virgin out?"

A quick, huffed laugh flies from me and Willie's the one laughing now.

"I knew I heard her!" He tosses the still-wet tongs in the bin, clicking the lid closed. "All airy and soft and shit."

My mouth waters thinking about it.

The short gasps and warm whimpers.

He said it exactly right.

"So, what happened? You remove the ten-foot pole you cemented between you two for a dumbass reason you won't share with her?"

My head snaps his way, and I toss the bag of spices into his chest. "Don't."

Willie grins, catching the Ziplock with ease. "Oh, my boy and that sexual frustration. So you *didn't* come."

"I'm about to *come* over there and shove your head in that dirty-ass bucket of dishwater."

"I will drop to my knees beside it and let you if you go lay one on her right now. I know you're dying to. Shit, I'm dying for you to."

"She wants me to fuck her, Will."

"So do that too."

"She wants me to fuck her, so she can get it over with."

"If you think for a minute, the cute little thing doesn't have your name etched on her organs, you're a bigger ass than I am." Willie frowns, but it's wiped quickly, and he shrugs. Lifting the last of the black tubs, he shoves it into the bed of his truck, slamming the tailgate before leaning against it. "But hey, what the fuck do I know? Looks like she's having a good time with the flower-power boys."

A scowl builds over my forehead, and I follow the smoking fucker's gaze to the clearing. About fifty feet away stands Layla and Davis, the guys who took the Hawaiian theme of their booth far too fucking serious in front of them.

They're saying something, and both girls laugh, but then Layla stretches, whispering something into Davis's ear before she heads to the group across the way.

Willie kicks off the truck. "Layla asked the cinnamon roll girls to save her a box. Better get over there before she tries to buy them out of their leftover stock. Have fun watching your woman get hit on."

"Fuck you."

"I'll make room in my tent, sunshine!"

Shaking my head, I stare at Davis's back.

It's obvious the guy to her left, the one who definitely perms his fucking hair, is into her.

Every time she turns to say something to the other dude, he

uses the moment to look her over, and he likes what he sees.

Who fucking wouldn't?

Jean shorts stretched over wide, thick thighs with tears along the front, hints of silky skin peeking out from between the small shredding, and a light-pink tank top. It's simple, stretchy, no more than the upper swell of her breasts visible. It's modest, but on her, it looks the exact fucking opposite. Her collarbone and neck, her slender, delicate throat, it's all on full display, begging to be brushed along. To be touched and teased.

She loves that shit.

The asshole slowly slipping closer, eager to possess all of her attention, is looking to score, but he's way out of his league.

She's not even blushing, but she will be.

Downing a water in one go, I toss the bottle into the lawn chair and head right for her.

She's saying something about hops and ginger, explaining Willie's beers, maybe, so she doesn't see me coming. Left guy does though. Right too.

Their eyes flick from her to my approaching body and back, the grins on their faces growing forced. Spinning my hat backward, I reach out, slide my middle finger through the loop of those jean shorts of hers and tug.

She locks herself straight, swiftly looking over her shoulder with a frown, but then she sees it's me, and the fucking smile that spreads . . .

A different kind of heat presses at my chest.

I yank her harder, until her back is bumping into my front, and that velvety giggle of hers finds my ears. I bury my face in her neck, just along the hairline, below her ear, as my arms snake around her and she tips her head slightly, pressing her cheek to mine for a short moment.

Righting myself, I look straight into the man on the left's eyes, my face blank. "Nice shirt."

A tight chuckle leaves him. "Yeah, uh, thanks. Goes with the booth so . . . but hey, we should"—he clears his throat—"we should pack some things up, so it's not such a pain in the morning. You guys enjoy your night."

I wait for her to spin in my arms. To point a little glare my way or raise a perfectly shaped brow.

She doesn't do either of those things.

She drops her head against my chest and takes a small sip from her cup. Unfazed. Accepting. Disconnected from the men vying for her attention and willing to give it all to me.

Just like that.

I like it.

The sound of the live band grows louder then, so I turn us toward where they're playing, a few dozen yards away, and after a couple minutes, she begins swaying to the music, her back never once lifting from its place against my chest.

It's not long before the sun falls behind the trees, the rest of the vendors joining in on the entertainment, and those slow sways of hers turn into full hip rolls.

Rolls that flow through her entire body.

I press my lips to her ear. "What are you doing?"

"What you taught me."

I can hear her smile, and it prompts one of my own.

"I taught you to dance like you're fucking? Like you fucked your hand last night?"

"Ask me what I thought about."

Goddamn. A quick, playful response.

"Nice try, Sweets." My words are more a needy groan than anything.

Davis's laughter is low, tender, and I want to hear it again.

I want a lot of fucking things.

My hands press farther into her pockets, discovering they're not pockets at all as I slip beyond the fabric, meeting and molding the slope of her warm thighs, and she doesn't stiffen or slow. The girl keeps dancing like it's the most natural thing, me holding her like this. Close, tight, and tipped at the edge of her panties. If I slide my hands a quarter of an inch over, my pointer fingers would rest on either side of her clit. I could make her come, right here, and no one would know it.

I want to.

I might.

"I had so much fun this weekend," she shares. "People loved Willie's beer. I think we're one of the only beer vendors who sold out."

"That's 'cause he's smart. He knew all these assholes would keep coming if it meant they could talk to the pretty little thing serving it to them."

"Ha ha," she teases, swatting at my arm, but I quickly pull one hand out, catching hers and bringing it to my mouth.

"I'm not playin'. I watched them watch you from the line, like I knew they would. Why do you think I put the tables on both sides of your booth?" I graze my teeth over her knuckles, gliding my lips from the first to the last, and instead of letting her hand fall, I lock it around my neck, grazing my jaw over the spot within reach. I haven't shaved since Friday morning. The goose bumps rising along her skin tell me she's got no complaints. "I did that so they couldn't step any closer to what they want but can't have."

She chuckles, peeking over her shoulder with playful, narrowed eyes. "Are you trying to get fresh?"

The corner of my mouth tips up the slightest bit. "Who me?"

"No, the other man touching me."

"No other man is allowed to touch you, Sweets." I hold her gaze. "Not unless I say."

She faces forward with a smile. "And you love that, don't you?"

"Fuck yeah." My lips hook up, my mouth running dry as I stare at the slope of her neck. The beat of the pulse there. "And now they're watching."

"Who?"

"Those pineapple punks."

"It's the backward hat. And the sleeveless tee. The tattoos. My god, the tattoos," she teases as if I'm the attraction, reaching up to flick my hat.

"Oh, you wanna be cute, hmm?" I press her into me more. "Wrong, but cute."

The band changes tempo, and the motions of our bodies adjust effortlessly.

"It's the pretty-in-pink brunette with big brown eyes and a deadly smile they're staring at, curious if she's with the man holding on to her, or if I'm just a luckier bastard than they are tonight."

Davis laughs, and I cock my head in time to see her tongue slipping out to slide along her lush lips. We're still dancing; she's still facing forward, so she's not doing it for my benefit. She's not being a temptress, trying to capture my attention.

Little does she know, she's got it.

Had it.

Owns it.

I grip the short, sleek strands of her hair. It's shorter than it's ever been, the tips only long enough to graze her collarbone, so I have to hold it in place or let it fall forward again. I want the area clear. I want to see the gleam of her skin.

I'm not sure if she tips her head or if I tug the shiny locks leading her to, but suddenly, her neck is stretched long, exposed and prickling with goose bumps, without so much as a touch.

My body takes over, my head lowering until my mouth meets her satiny skin, but I don't taste. I press it against her, soft at first, and then a little harder, maintaining the same amount of pressure as it rises. Up and up, until my nose is buried in her hair. I kiss the back of her neck, my left hand coming around to slide my knuckles down her throat.

"Now, they're all watching." I spin her, and her arms come up, wrapping around my neck without direction.

She smiles, holding me loosely. "What are you up to?"

"Hypothesizing."

"Oh, talk dirty to me." She's quick to play along.

Chuckling, I tug her closer.

Knew she'd like that, my little science nerd.

Amusement brightens the gold in her eyes as she waits with bleeding curiosity.

My palms slide up her waist, my fingers spreading wide, wrapped around her upper rips.

Cocking my head a bit, I hover there, waiting for hers to lift, and it does.

"What would they do if they thought you were mine?" I draw closer, my eyes snapping to her lips and back. "Would they keep standing there, wondering what kind of panties you have on under your shorts, or will they move on to another? Take the *L*?"

"They're blue with pink popsicles."

Heat floods my chest, a low rumble fighting to get free, and I glide my thumb along her top. "Same pink as this?"

"Exact same." Her smile is wide. "Wanna see?"

My brows snap together, and as if she knew what was coming, knew exactly how I'd react and watch for it, she throws her head back with a laugh.

My eyes fly down, locking on to the creamy skin, now fully and completely bared to me.

The thin thread of sanity still attached to my conscience snaps.

I dive down, swiping my tongue along her throat, and sending mine into a full fucking roar. My mouth waters at the salty, sweet flavor of her skin, and I slide a little to the right. My teeth find her pulse, and I press against it, close my lips around the throbbing beat and suck.

She gasps, tugging me closer, holding me tighter, and I reward her by sucking harder, her little cry sending a shiver down my spine.

Fuck.

Fuck, fuck.

More.

Yanking back, my eyes connect with hers. The air in my lungs grows thick, harsh, each breath pulled in burning fiercer than the last, as if a true inferno is blazing between us, it's raging, and the girl in front of me lit the match. She *is* the match.

There's no doubt in my mind there's a sweet little minx hidden inside her on the verge of discovery.

She's so fucking needy, I can taste it.

I want to taste her.

All of her.

No way I could kiss her and not claim her, but she's not looking to be claimed. She wants to feel, not fall.

So, I'll settle for the sounds she makes, and when I get a minute to myself, I'll replay them over and fucking over, my cock gripped tight in my hand.

"It worked. They're not paying attention to us anymore."

My tone is deep and raspy, and Davis swallows in front of me.

"They know you must be mine now."

Her eyes glow in eager affection, ready for what may or may not come, and a thrill races down my spine.

"Turn around, Sweets."

Davis shivers in my arms, desire deepening the brown of her eyes. "A lesson?"

Lesson. Right.

I don't answer, but she wasn't looking for one.

She rolls her body rather than turning, refusing to allow a single inch of space between us as she faces herself forward. Once her back is flat to my chest, her head follows, and I can't resist dipping mine.

Chin rested along her temple, I'm the first to start dancing this time, and her hips follow instantly.

"I want to make you feel good," I whisper, slowly sliding my hands into her front pockets, my earlier fantasy playing on repeat in my mind.

"I want everything you want."

If fucking only, baby. If only . . .

I graze my stubble along her skin, and she swallows. "So, you won't stop me if I touch you right here, *right* now?"

"Do I look like a crazy person?"

A chuckle slips from me, but I choke on it when her breasts push out with her deep inhale, and she reaches up, gripping the neckline of her top. She presses against her tits, and I wonder if she wishes she could reach inside and tug on her nipples.

"Crew?"

"Hmm?"

"Touch me."

My chest rumbles, and I tip my head, nipping at the skin of her neck, my pulse hammering through my fingertips as my hands dive a little deeper. The teeniest, tiniest bit. My cock threatens to thicken, swelling in size as my pointer finger finds the little puff of her pussy lips hidden behind the thin cotton of her panties.

Davis gasps, her movements pausing for a single second, but she starts dancing as quickly as she stopped. A little slower, a little more out of rhythm, but she's moving.

The crowd around has grown fuller, the music louder, and the night darker. I spotted Willie and Layla a few minutes ago, both leaning on a tree and talking to a few others. I know he'll head this way soon, so I need to get to work.

We're tucked in with the masses and we're not coming out until my fingers are coated in her cum.

I curve straight for her clit, pressing over it with little to no pressure, nothing but a thin layer of cloth keeping me from discovering how silky soft she is.

I'm instantly flooded with heat, hers radiating off my own and sweeping through my body. The hairs on the back of my neck prickle, and my hips jerk the slightest bit, my dick desperate for friction.

As if she knows what I need, she presses her ass into me, a shaky breath breaking beyond her lips. "Want to know something?" she whispers.

I slip past the hem of her panties, her pussy flexing in response, somehow finding the restraint not to dive right in. "Will it drive me mad?"

"Oh, no doubt in my mind."

Fuck. I clench my teeth, so I say nothing and so I don't bite the shit out of her. She takes my silence as her answer.

"I thought it was a poor figure of speech when women would say, 'he made my panties wet,' but I can now testify, it is, in fact, *not*." She squirms. "It's so not."

"You telling me you're wet for me, Sweets?" I groan. "That when I slide a little farther, my fingers will find a puddle of proof waiting for me?"

"Keep talking like that and people will think I pissed myself."

Chuckling, I go for it. I dive into her panties, covering her smooth pussy with my palm, and push lower. My middle fingers press between her lips, and I swipe deeper, dragging her juices up until I'm painting her pussy with her own arousal.

My chest caves, the soft slickness of her too much, but somehow not enough.

My abdomen grows taut, an unnatural need to make her come undone burning along my skin.

I kiss her neck, swiping my tongue in sync with the stroke of my fingers, and soon, she's rolling her hips for an entirely different reason. I pretend the sensitive spot is her full, pouty fucking lips. Sucking it into my mouth like I would her tongue, massaging it with my own, but only after I scrape my teeth along it.

Davis gasps and the fucking sound!

My cock begs for mercy he won't get.

Locking her clit between my fingers, I give a little pinch, but my left hand dips farther, teasing at the edge of her entrance. Rolling her clit with my right, I press the tip of my pointer finger inside her, and she bites down on her lower lip.

I want to bite it back.

I want her to bite me.

She moans, both her hands coming up to dive into my hair. My hat's flipped off and falls to the grass somewhere, but I don't care.

Her hands lock around me, pulling my head down as she tries to stretch higher, and I'm close enough to flick her tit with my tongue.

Davis shakes, turns her head, and nips at my jaw.

My eyes slice to hers and hers widen at the sight.

I can only imagine how wild I look, like a man on the edge of a mountain, dying to dive off it. Head-fucking-first.

I've got a fucking priceless prize in my palms, and I'm not talking about her pussy, though it deserves the same appreciation. Pure and fucking perfect. Dripping.

I can hardly believe she's in my hands. I want to devour her, own her.

I want to ruin her, so all she'll ever crave is me and my touch.

She holds my gaze, sucking her bottom lip into her mouth.

"What is it, Sweets?"

"Say something bad?" she begs.

My hips thrust forward on their own, grinding into her, and her pupils flash.

"You want me to talk dirty to you?" Eyes locked on hers, I push my finger inside her, lips parting with her small nod. Fuck. "You want me to tell you how wet you are? How soft and tight?" I groan as I pick up speed and lower my mouth to her ear. "How fucking hard you make me?"

She whimpers and I add another finger.

Davis winces from the added intrusion, her body stretching wider to allow me inside, but a throaty moan follows, so I press in farther, grinding her into me as I work her over faster.

"How all I can think about is putting you on your back and sliding my cock inside you, filling you until you scream? Until you *cream* all over me because you would." I press harder, and she starts to shake. "Over and over. And over."

I close my lips over her earlobe, grazing my teeth on both sides, and she whimpers. "And then I'd taste you. Lick up your slit until there was nothing left." I moan. "I'd push you to your knees, so you could try the flavor of us, straight off the tip of my throbbing, dripping cock."

She cries, burying her face in my chest.

"I bet we'd be sweet, Sweets. I bet you are."

She comes apart, her thighs clamp together, trapping my hand, so I leave it there, pressing against her, my fingers still inside. Her pussy walls spasm around me, and my chest rumbles, my cock swollen and aching.

As fast as she came, her body grows heavy, so I carefully tug my right hand free, wrapping it around her middle to hold her to me.

I sway us there, waiting until the aftershock ripples fade.

Slowly, and with uneven breaths, Davis lifts her head, half-hooded eyes locking with mine. Her skin is flushed with a blush I earned. Her temples slick with sweat I put there.

And then she fucking says, "There's only one way to know for sure."

For a millisecond, I'm lost, in her words, in her eyes. In the sweet, sexy little smile curving the corner of her lips, but just as quick, a thrill shoots through me, drawing up my balls and sending a shock wave through my dick.

"Taste me, Crew." An impossible pink colors her cheeks. "Taste me while I watch."

Fuuuuck.

I thrust my fingers deep inside her, and she gasps, tensing slightly, but the wicked gleam that flitters across her face is pure pleasure. She fucking wants this.

Wants to see me suck her cum straight off my fingers.

Pulling my hand out, I slowly bring it to my lips, my mouth salivating with each torturous second that passes. I might fucking drool.

My lips part, the smoky scent of her invading my nostrils, and I savor it for a second.

A second too fucking long because just as my finger hovers between my open lips, a hand slaps onto my shoulder and smacks my arm down to my side.

My head jerks left, coming face-to-face with Willie—the motherfucker with the worst timing—grins.

"'Sup, you up for a game of dice before we hit the sack?" He looks from me to Davis, and his head snaps my way so fast, he's forced to double blink. His eyes narrow. "Or maybe not . . ."

"Definitely not."

"Yeah, for sure!"

We answer at the same time, and now my attention swings to Davis.

She attempts to step away, but my arm is an iron rod around her, locking her to me, and that bitch isn't letting go. It's got a mind of its own and wants to keep her there. Right against me.

Mine.

The fog in my head must be denser than I realized, as the next thing I know, she's somehow breaking free, her body having slipped beneath my arm.

Layla's quick to hook her hand through Davis's and off they fucking go, but not before Davis shoots me a sly, little smirk.

Oh, you're gonna get it, Sweets. I'll remember this.

Every.

Fucking.

Second of it.

Chapter 20
Davis

There's no sign of the sun when my eyes slowly open. I blink into the darkness, a sense of warmth washing over me and delivering my dream to the forefront of my mind.

I close my eyes once more, hoping to fall right back into fantasyland, but as I settle into the pillow, soft hairs brush along my bare legs as a knee presses between mine. Everything floods back in my mind like a sweet, sweet tsunami.

Holy shit, last night happened. Like . . . actually happened.

Every touch, every caress, and every sound that slipped from his lips, possibly unintentionally, perhaps subconsciously, was real. He might have been giving me a lesson in true stimulation, but the way his body moved with mine, and the raspy, raw responses my pleasure brought out in him can't be denied. His wayward whispering, good god.

I'd push you to your knees, so you could try the flavor of us, straight off the tip of my throbbing, dripping cock.

A shiver runs down my spine, heat blanketing me, but it isn't in memory of a fierce fantasy turned reality. It radiates off the man behind me. The man I've imagined between my legs, more times than I care to admit, is at my back, his limbs tangled with mine.

Maybe I did the tangling? Played "Baby Got Back" and drove my ass into him in my sleep?

Pulling in a deep breath, I ready to return his space, but before I can so much as inch away, a heavy, warm arm falls over me, a giant hand pressing on my stomach, rough, long fingers spanning over my abdomen.

"Don't even fucking think about it." Crew's voice is thick with sleep, and he tugs me into him, his hold locking tighter around me. His nose is buried in my hair, the heat of his breath fanning over the nape of my neck. "Breathe, Sweets. Breathe and sleep."

A tingle begins at the base of my scalp and spreads from there. I clench my thighs.

"Stop." Crew grunts in disapproval.

"You know I hate that word, right?"

"Davis. Sleep."

"Right, yeah." Sleep.

Is he crazy?!

The come stun was strong. Layla might have been there to distract me, but I couldn't tell you how long I lasted playing dice.

Hell, I can't even tell you how I ended up back in this teepee, the hottest man on the planet wrapped around me like a snake who's scored its next meal.

I didn't drink a drop after that half cup I had while dancing.

Maybe I was come drunk?

Is that a thing?

Oh my god, I was fingered at a festival with a hundred people around!

Oh my god, *I'd go for it again in a heartbeat.*

Never in my life have I been so wet, so turned on.

So shocked he allowed such a lesson when he's so keen on denying me.

And people say fingering is overrated. Clearly, they haven't had Crew Taylor's long, strong, flexible fingers inside them.

My smile couldn't be wider as I pretend to pass out because, lesson or not?

Crew made me come, and he enjoyed every second of it.

Now, to learn how to repay the piper.

Unfortunately for me, there's no time to talk to Crew about what I want him to teach me next. Layla poked her head in at the break of daylight and bargained for my release from Crew's concrete clutches.

It was kind of fun, hearing him refuse to let me loose, as if he wanted to keep me there beside him, but he did trade my presence for Layla's promise of pie.

So yeah, there's that.

Last night after we closed down, we cleaned and packed up all the little things, so all that's left today is deconstructing the booth and loading up the barbecue. Willie, being the swoony, hot husband he is, traded a couple cases of his next batch of beer for a pampering day for his queen after the long weekend, with a plus-one, so she invited me.

After a quick stop for snacks, we headed toward town, and here we are, four hours later, falling in and out of sleep, in side-by-side baths, full of steaming lavender leaves.

"Will is so getting his dick sucked tonight."

My eyes snap open, and I look to Layla, who cracks one eye and smiles.

"If I had my phone, I would record your face right now and send it to Crew."

My brows draw closer. "Why?"

"Because you look so completely curious." She slowly brings her glass of sparkling cider to her lips, grinning over the rim. "Mouth virgin, too?"

The water is warm, mine more so than hers, baby and all, so my body is already flushed, but heat still blooms in my chest.

"It's on the list."

Layla chuckles. "How long is this list?"

"Long." My response is quick and grumpy.

Layla laughs louder. "Well, from what I saw last night, it's getting shorter."

My mouth gapes, and she shrugs playfully.

"Hey, you listened, I watched. We're square now." She holds her fist out.

Flaming cheeks and all, I meet hers with my own.

"We should start getting ready. The band sets up around seven, and the boys will only be able to hold a table for us for so long. That or I'll have to whoop some bar bish ass when they try and take the seat beside my man," she teases, tapping on her belly.

"How are you not completely exhausted?" I look at her belly as she climbs out.

"Oh, I'm getting there, but I figure I won't get to do all this stuff for a while, so until my body tells me to chill, I shall not." She chuckles, nodding her head, and I follow her out of the water. "So, a couple of my friends are coming over this week. They ordered some fancy pasta from a place I could never afford, and we're dedicating the day to floating in the pool."

I look at her, and she smiles.

"You should come. You met Toni already, and Remy gets along with everyone, you'll meet her tonight at the show, but seriously, come."

"Really?" I try not to seem too eager, but I could seriously use some girl time.

Have I ever had *girl time before today?*

"Would I bother to mention it if not?"

Good point. No, she wouldn't.

"You sure Crew won't mind if I crash?"

"Oh, girl. No. Crew would be the one crashing if he showed up. It's vaginas only."

"Then yeah. Count me in."

"Awesome. Now, let's let these ladies doll us up."

I follow Layla into the third, fourth, and final stop of the spa—a full-fledged salon.

Two hours and a bowl of fresh fruit later, we're headed for the bar.

Crew

Pausing at the edge of the counter, I cross my arms with a glare, and not a second later, Drew and Willie join me, both wearing matching expressions.

"How long 'til we can kick everyone out?" Willie grumbles.

"Two hours, eight and a half minutes," Drew complains.

My frown deepens as he stares at the caramel-haired girl who's far too lickable in lavender, the same shade of purple as the candy necklace stretched around her neck. Her hair is sleek and shiny, looking like Queen Cleopatra, but a softer shade. She's got another pin in it today, this one shaped like one of those little twisty hard candies. It's bright blue and doesn't match the light purple of her dress, but if she took it off, I'd pin it right back into place—a few inches back on her left side. It looks good, fits her.

Reminds me she's as sweet on the outside as on the inside.

Why didn't I slide my finger between my lips last night after the cockblockers stole her from me and led her away?

It was *right there*, her cum, her flavor, creamy and wet on my skin, but I wanted her watching, witnessing the second my tongue became coated in her.

But back to the dress.

How easily I could slide inside. If she were to climb on top of me again tonight, what would I find underneath it?

More matching panties? Maybe the ones with the little jewel?

Need to have a look at those . . .

Julius stomps over, throwing his ass in the chair in front of us, spinning around to scowl toward the girls. "Man, watching them is a full-time gig. Every fuckhead in here is trying to slide into their pussy-power powwow."

Davis, Layla, Remy, and Toni are all tucked toward the right side of the stage, dancing in their own little world, clueless and uncaring that they've become the center of a dozen fuckers' attention.

Xavier scoffs, Neo stepping up beside him. "Who the fuck thought it would be a good idea to bring them here?"

Sighing, I lift a finger, and when I face the group, all their frowns deepen, but I beat them to the punch.

"What the fuck was I thinking?"

My boys chuckle, drawing one out of me, and slowly, we get back to our posts. Me and Drew behind the bar, Will helping all around, and the other two on Layla-and-Davis duty. All right, they're watching all the girls, but let's be honest, it's those two they'd get their ass handed to them for losing.

Julius slams a quick shot and rushes back to the dance floor, but Xavier holds back, shooting me a sly grin.

He waits for Neo to walk off then elbows me in the ribs. "Something about the little sisters, right?"

Huffing, I shove his ass back into the crowd. "Get your ass out there before I tell Neo you fucked her."

"Yo!" he hisses, his head jerking in the direction Neo disappears. "Watch it!"

"Watch her." I grin.

"I am, fuckface, but keep it up, and I might just kiss her."

I fly forward, but he's already out of arm's reach, cracking himself up as he weaves through the crowd.

The dick is only messing with me, but I still want to punch him for playing.

The thought of someone's lips on hers brings my blood to a boil, always has.

That reminds me, she said she's kissed two people in her life.

Who the fuck was the second?

Why do I have the sudden need to know?

And why the fuck is the bass player pointing at her?

Davis smiles, lifting her glass, full of nothing but soda and ice, and fuck this.

"Watch the bar."

"Uh-huh." My brother's chuckle is the last thing I hear before I'm weaving through the crowd, and I don't stop until I'm right behind her.

"Stop making the asshole think he's got a chance in hell."

She whips around with a smile and leans in. "Maybe he does."

"Real fucking funny, Sweets."

"Hey, you're the one who said I should let it happen naturally. I feel like a hot night with a musician is a full-fledged fantasy."

I haul her to me, and she grins wider. "It ain't yours."

"Want to know my deepest fantasy?" she teases.

"Sweets." I shake my head, lowering my lips to her ear. "What makes you think I don't already know?"

"What kind of man knows a woman wants to be laid across the bar top and doesn't take pleasure in doing so?"

My eyes snap shut, images of Davis naked and sprawled across the wooden slab, not forty feet from us, her feet planted firmly against it, her pussy bare and at perfect height for me to bend and dive right in . . . with my tongue.

"You're thinking about it now, aren't you?"

My head snaps up, and I glare. "Stop."

She bites into her lip to keep from smiling. "Hey, you came over here. I was minding my own business."

"What business do you have with a shaggy-haired guitar player named Bones?"

Davis laughs, shaking her head. "Got it, Dad. No flirting with the band members."

My eyes narrow, and she crosses her heart like a brat. She knows what I mean.

No flirting with anyone.

"Behave. I mean it."

The little girl salutes me, then spins back to the others. Her new friends.

My friends.

A sense of comfort washes over me, but I push it away.

Comfort does me no good, not when the princess has her own plans, ones I've still got to find a way to fight for a spot in.

The plan was to get my shit straight, and then drag her ass to me, but she came barreling back before that could happen.

Nothing I can do now but keep myself in check. Semi-check, anyway, if at all fucking possible.

I'm thinking it's not.

I've already crossed the line, there's no denying that, but for my own fucking sanity, I've got to remember where we stand, that this is a deal we made. Guiding her in these lessons she wants to learn, that I stupidly agreed to teach, was a fucked-up idea if I've ever heard one.

I wasn't ready for her, yet here she fucking came, killing me when she asked for nothing more than the physical I can give.

She's got a sweet tooth she's looking to satisfy, and in her eyes, I'm candy to be consumed.

Nothing more.

That's all a washed-out punk who mops puke for pennies is good for, right? As Memphis would laugh and joke about if he were here, as if that shit were funny.

It's not, but I can't say it isn't true.

It makes no sense for a girl like her to want more from an asshole like me. I know that.

In the end, Jess is the type of dude she'll choose.

Someone good-looking and going somewhere, successful and set for the future. A model man, the kind that goes to work and comes home in time for dinner, plays catch with his kid.

I eat beer nuts most nights, and some of those same nights, I never make it to bed.

Shit, I didn't even have one of those until a few weeks ago, when she gave me one.

I'm just a fucking squatter under her roof, and eventually, she'll ask me to leave, likely the second I sign off on the stupid fucking deal we made.

But until then, I'm the guy in control of who she gets close to, and right now, the only man I want her near is me.

I'll worry about the problems I'm creating for myself later. For now, I just have to stop touching her.

Stop thinking about her naked and under me.

I need to take us back to before—me ignoring and denying, her playful but poised.

Not telling me she's wet for me or sharing her fucking fantasies.

My chest rumbles, but I swallow past the budding desire.

This girl, swear to God, she's going to kill me.

Or make me kill someone . . .

My eyes snap to the long-haired asshole who hopped off the stage, the band done for the night and the crowd thinning. Thinning and thinning, until I have a straight fucking line of sight to the beauty in the middle.

My beauty, who smiles at the grease ball stepping up to her, growing more comfortable around men by the day, thanks to my dumb ass.

His hand finds her lower back, his lips on her ear, and she squints, listening.

And then she laughs, the length of her neck staring back at me. Mocking me.

The neck I sucked and licked on just last night.

My marks are there, I saw them, searched for them this morning, when she thought I was asleep.

They're faint, hidden by the tips of her hair and a little farther back, so not as easily spotted by the naked eye.

Next time, they'll be square in the center, big and fucking bold.

Wait, no. No next time.

Grease Head's hand lowers, sliding down the back of her dress, and she pulls her head back, meeting his eyes.

He smiles, touches her fucking hair, and Davis . . .

Davis looks to me.

My pulse pounds angrily, eagerly, my gaze locking on her lips, reading her words, but they're not meant for me.

Sorry, she tells him. She's here with someone.

Me. She's here with me, the motherfucker who's signing your paycheck tonight.

Davis steps back, and then she's headed this way, closer and closer, until she's smiling from the seat right across the bar.

She sets her glass down, so I take it, pour it out and serve her a fresh one, not once looking away.

She grins around her straw, and a second later, the girls are joining her.

For the first time all fucking night, we guys can breathe easy.

I might even have a drink.

Maybe if I do, I won't be so tightly wound when I get home, and it's just me and the girl my dick dreams about.

Maybe.

Chapter 21
Crew

Drew talked me into a drink and went for a second being Davis stuck to soda all night. It took us twice as long to get the bar in order after closing, considering my entire staff was buzzed, but it was a small price to pay to enjoy the bar to ourselves.

The girls passed out a couple hours ago, having dragged out our stash of blankets from the back and stuffed them in a clean booth, but we guys made it through sippin' and bullshittin' about nothing. Damn good way to end a long weekend, and thank fuck, the bar's closed on Mondays and Tuesdays, when there're no paid events on the books.

I'm sleeping all fucking day tomorrow.

"I say we head to the diner. Davis, wake up!" he shakes her. "Diner's open all night, yeah?" Drew's drunken grin is sloppy. "Who can't do with some pancakes right now? Crew's treat."

I scoff, but for real. "I could eat some pancakes."

"I can make bomb-ass pancakes." Layla yawns, popping up.

"Yeah, but then we dirty our kitchen, when we can eat and not worry about the dishes." Willie wraps her up, steering her toward the door. "To the diner!"

Laughing, we follow him out and to the restaurant.

Davis gets a little pep back in her tired steps once we arrive, and the sun's peeking through the windows. She pulls out her work perks, and dashes to the back, sweet-talking the chef, I'm sure, and we're overstuffed within an hour, our portions seemingly double the normal.

Six a.m. rolls around, and low and fucking behold, the black hat dude waltzes in with a crowd of clones.

Davis is standing at the counter, getting change for the tip and chatting with her boss, and the dude spots her immediately.

In my peripheral, my brother looks to me, but I don't take my eyes off the guy, and moments later, he's stepping up behind her.

Davis whips around with a chuckle, and the guy says something we can't hear. This time, she doesn't look at me when he reaches out and touches her. Sure, his palm is simply planted on her upper arm, but that's too fucking much. She should know this.

Clearly, she doesn't, because five seconds later, he steps into her more. Pair that with whatever he said, and her cheeks tint the tiniest bit of pink. A blush.

My blush.

He's buzzed, coming off a night of partying and feeling brave. I'd bet on it. Guaran-fucking-tee it, when his hand finds her hip in his next move.

I don't realize I'm headed their way until her wide eyes land on mine, and then so do his . . . a solo second before my fist comes down on his nose.

Blood pours on contact, and he stumbles backward, falling on his ass like a clumsy fucker.

Davis gasps, her hands flying to her mouth.

He shoots to his feet quicker than I expected, and his friends jump up too, rushing this way. Of course, mine make it first, and the lanky frat-looking fuckers freeze at the sight of four tatted-back built bastards.

"What the fuck, bro?!" the dude shouts, touching his nose.

He doesn't step up, but I do. I push closer and closer, forcing him to look up to meet my eyes, the poor, shortish son of a bitch.

"Touch her again, I'll break your fingers, one by fucking one. Got me?"

"Crew!" she shrieks.

The guy's eyes narrow.

"Find a new fucking diner and a new girl to play with. This one's mine."

"Oh. My god." Davis glares.

I'll deal with her ass later.

Two men in one fucking night? What the fuck?

I'm about to lose my damn mind.

She makes me insane.

Always.

Fucking.

Has.

"Yeah, you and your box of Brads should go." Drew puts his hands on his hips. "My brother's known to fuck shit up, and by shit, I mean shitheads. Like you."

"I concur." Julius grins, leaning his elbow on Drew's shoulder. "Been a minute since his fists have been set free, and I think he's itchin'. Don't be the scratch."

The guys stand there, unsure of what move to make.

"Oh, Jesus H. Christ, get the fuck out already!" Layla's no-bullshit shout gets them moving.

Moaning and groaning and holding on to their last bit of pride, the Frat Row fuckheads walk out the door.

My boys laugh as they go, but I'm too busy staring at Davis, doing my best not to yank her to me and freak the fuck out.

The girl pretends she doesn't feel my frown on her and turns to her boss. "I'm so sorry, Rachel. That will never happen again."

"It might."

Davis shoots a quick glare my way, but focuses on Rachel, who waves her off, sipping from a small coffee cup.

"It's fine, girl." She tries to hide a grin. "We were getting bored waiting for the next rush anyway."

"I could entertain you," Julius offers.

She flips him off then off she goes.

I turn to Davis, who narrows her eyes even more.

"What?" I snap.

"Home. Now." She shoves by. "Layla, thanks for everything. See you in a few days."

Purse hanging from her fingers, she charges out the door.

"Uh-oh, Mom and Dad are fighting." Drew grins.

I ignore his ass and hurry after the brat, watching as she yanks her car door open, throwing her purse inside.

"You're seriously mad right now?" She shakes her head, and my eyes narrow. "What the fuck do you have to be mad about?"

Her gaze slices up, meeting mine over the hood. "Is that a joke?"

"Am I laughing?"

She does then, but there's no humor in it as she climbs inside and slams the door closed.

I drop into my seat, glaring at her. "Talk, Davis."

"Oh, no." She whips out of the parking lot. "You don't get to play clueless, Crew. There is no freaking way you don't see why I would be royally pissed off at you right now!"

She skips the yellow light and barrels into the complex parking lot across the street.

"I know why I'm pissed, yeah. Not sure why you would be. In fact, you should be apologizing."

"What?!" she shrieks, speeding into her parking spot and throwing the car into park. "Are you insane?"

Leaning over the center console, I scowl. "Are you incapable of listening?"

"*What* are you talking about?!"

"What did I say to you, Sweets?" My voice is nothing but a rumble. "No one touches you. You heard it, agreed to it, and guess what that little bitch did?" My eyes shoot wide in mockery.

Davis's mouth falls open, and then she growls, jumping from the car.

I tear the keys from the ignition, since she left them behind, and rush after her.

"You are absolutely ridiculous! I can't even believe you right now."

"Don't act like I was out of line. I'll do it again tomorrow if I have to."

She shrieks, whipping around to face me, and I shove the keys in the lock at her side.

She glares. "You are the most frustrating—"

The door down from ours opens, and Jess walks out, garbage bag in hand.

Fucking seriously?

His attention flies this way immediately. "Everything okay?"

Davis clears her throat. "Sorry, yeah, we—"

"Get fucked, pretty boy. This has nothing to do with you, so you can stop pretending like you take your trash out at six in the fucking morning."

Davis gapes, slowly swinging her head my way, but she says nothing.

"Davis?" The dumb fuck dares.

"She's not yours to worry about." My glare hits him quick and he frowns from her to me. "Tell him, Davis."

"Okay, caveman, calm yourself," she hisses in a whisper, before facing the blond dick. "We're fine, Jess. This is not a fight, it's just . . . well, us."

Yeah, fucker. Us.

Me and her.

I turn the lock and use my body to propel her inside, slamming the door behind *us*.

Me and fucking *her*.

Davis

The man has gone mad!

Shaking my head, I hustle into the kitchen, tossing my purse onto the tabletop before facing him. "Okay, what the hell? Is there some sort of apocalyptic shit happening I'm unaware of? Like testosterone falling from the sky, maybe?"

"What?" he snaps, kicking his shoes off with angry movements.

"Well, there's something in the water making you go ham on the male species, I mean, shit! Were you about to go knock out our neighbor too?"

"I didn't knock anyone out, but if I had to, I wouldn't feel bad about it."

A scoffed laugh leaves me, and I nod. "No, of course not. You're a perfectly sane man."

"I would be if people would stop trying to touch you." He glares.

I study him a moment and his eyes only narrow further.

"K. Well, you can't just beat people up. You have to stop doing that."

His head tugs back. "I can control myself just fucking fine when I feel the need to. Do I enjoy fighting? Yeah, I fucking do, done it for fun plenty of times, but I don't go around looking for one."

"Oh?" I charge toward him, flick the bloodstain on his shirt, and he smacks my hand away.

"That was one dirtbag and he had it coming."

"Uh-huh." I nod. "And the blond hottie guy from the bar the other night?"

Crew's jaw tics. "He was twice your age and you'd have known that if your vision wasn't blurred by rosé!"

"What about the guy at the Chinese New Year's parade a few years back, or the one at Great America." I rush on, "Oh, and the skater guy from the pier and that musician on Haight Street who pulled me onto his lap for the encore when I tipped him?"

"Stop."

"Were they all 'too old?'" I mock, crossing my arms.

"Davis."

"Who knew age gap was a trigger for you."

"*You* are a trigger for me!"

"Yeah, me and the four measly years between us, right?"

"No." He jerks forward, gripping my chin. "*You* and your smart-ass mouth," he snaps.

"I—"

"I wasn't done," he cuts me off, tone dark with irritation, but laced in racy roughness. "You're fire. The spark in your eye when you're angry and how it deepens when you fight me. Defy me. Push me, and girl, you *live* to fucking push me. The low pitch of your laugh is triggering, especially when it follows a dirty little word you dared to say. And the way your tongue curls when you swipe it along the corners of your lips?" A quick moan leaves him, the kind that follows the taste of your favorite chocolate bar. "I could go on and fucking on. Want me to?"

Yes, yes, I do, but . . .

Swallowing, I'm forced to look away, but my gaze is called right back to his when I try to make sense of this. "Does that mean you think I invite men to me with my body language?"

He slips into my space with purpose, his nose nearly touching mine. "If that were true, there's no way you'd still be a pretty, pure little thing."

My throat runs dry, but I manage to whisper, "I'm confused."

"I know. That's a trigger for me too." His gaze locks onto my lips, and his teeth sink into his own. "You have no fucking clue what you do to a man, and baby, you do it without a single fucking ounce of effort."

My nerves come to life, an electrifying sense of possibility coursing through me. "You called me baby."

Crew chuckles, but it's hoarse, and his eyes come back to mine. "Had to call me out on that, huh?"

"Just noting it for my mental record book. This one's getting its own page." I swallow, my body buzzing. "Crew?"

He tips his head a bit, his gaze transfixed on my mouth, as if his body is standing before me, but his mind is miles and miles away. Maybe even in fantasy land.

"This would be a perfect time for another lesson."

"What kind of lesson, baby?"

There it is again.

Muscles meet mush.

My heart beats wildly in my chest, but I don't let it stop me from asking for what I want. "A kissing lesson."

His brows furrow in frustration, but his feet shuffle closer. "Kiss you as a lesson?"

I nod.

His frown deepens, leading me to say more.

"It's just, I really want to kiss you right now, so what better time?" I defend so fast, my words run together. "I figure I can get what I want and you can coach me through, tell me what I do wrong and how to make it be—"

My words are cut off when Crew's lips crush mine, but not in a kiss. They hold there, *right* against me. He speaks with an angry rumble, his eyes sharp and depriving my lungs of the oxygen they need. "You *want* to kiss me, that is what you said."

"I did," I whisper. "I do."

Him being pressed to me like this, our lips mingle with our words, it's too much, and by too much, I mean not at all enough. I can't take it.

I taste his tongue, quickly slipping mine past the thin opening of his mouth.

Crew groans, eyes closing, and then he's nudging me backward, his closed fist pressing at the center of my ribs.

Back, back, back, my last breath held hostage by my lungs until I'm met by the cool wall behind me, where it whooshes from my lips in a hasty, shaky exhale.

"You *want* to kiss me," he repeats. "Not as part of our deal. Not as a lesson. Not to learn a damn thing." His palms flatten on the wall on either side of me, completely caging me in.

It's a glorious feeling, to be surrounded by nothing but him.

"Davis."

My eyes snap open—I hadn't realized they closed.

"Hmm?"

Crew presses closer, his body flush with mine, his thumb stretched beneath my chin. "Tell me what you want."

"I told you," I rasp. "I want everything. Anything."

"And then what?" he wonders, his chest rising and falling rapidly against my own.

"And then I'll probably, definitely, want it again." I look into his eyes. "I'm not good with moderation, you know this. I eat all the Halloween candy in a day, buy a dozen donuts and share only when I have to. It's a problem."

"Baby?"

Good *god*, how this man makes the endearment sound like a dirty little prayer.

"Crew."

His eyes pop up, returning to my lips just as fast.

"While your rock-solid restraint is impressive, I have no doubt your self-indulgence is far more to speak about." I grip his wrist, pressing against the hard planes of his chest. "Make a girl's year and kiss me already."

His thumb glides up, pressing on my lower lip and tugging it down until it pops free of his touch. He licks his own then. "Your year, huh?"

"Year, decade, who's counting?"

"Me, Sweets. I'm counting . . . to three."

The hand on my neck slides back, his fingers diving into my hair. "One."

His right hand finds my hip, and he pushes, locking my body to the wall, preventing a possible attempt at escape.

As if I'd dare to move and change his mind.

"Two."

My eyes snap to his, and his brows dive in the center, the hand in my hair shaking in anticipation as he lowers his head, his gaze locked on mine.

Or maybe I'm the one who's shaking.

Vibrating.

Freaking pulsating from the inside out.

"Thr—"

I cut him off, slamming my lips to his.

Crew growls, those fingers in my hair tethering, tightening, and tugging in sweet, sweet punishment.

Good fucking glory, his lips, his flavor.

His existence.

The hand on my hip slides up to my ribs, squeezing, and my body slumps against the wall, held up by nothing but his. I grip his sides, and his muscles flex beneath my touch.

The hold he has on my hair doesn't let up, his other hand rising to join, twisting and turning me at his leisure. He shifts until I'm exactly the way he wants me and I'm so for it.

It's like I said, I want what he wants, how and when he wants it. Always.

But it can't hurt to drive him further, to test his control.

To hope it snaps into teeny tiny pieces.

I grip his shirt, the material bunched between my fingertips as I keep him close, thrusting my tongue beyond the seal of his lips, and he meets my stroke with several of his own, tangling our tongues in tantalizing bliss.

He massages my mouth with masterful precision, the stroke of his thumbs against my neck sending a shiver through me, and when he shifts against me, his erection hard and throbbing along my stomach, I rip away with a gasp.

Crew doesn't allow that. He comes in for more, stealing my breath, and damn, if I'm not dizzy in his arms. Drunk on his kiss. Only when he's good and ready does he offer a small reprieve, but it doesn't exactly count because, as fast as he frees my lips, his are feasting on my throat, neck, and collarbone. He tastes every bit of skin he can reach, without moving his body from mine, and then a sharp, swift pain zips through me as his teeth sink into the base of my neck, just to the right of my hairline. Right where he teased me with his tongue last night.

My eyes roll back, my toes curling into the floor at my feet as I dig my nails into his chest.

His rumbles on contact, and this time, there's no denying it's he who vibrates before me. A tremor runs through him, and my mouth curves in a small smile.

As if sensing it, his head snaps up to catch a glimpse, and he glares, dips down and nips at it, pulling my lower lip into his mouth and sucking. Hard. A whimper escapes me, and he nods, as if he expected the sound to slip from my mouth.

I clench my thighs, desperate for release, so I slide my hands lower, dipping them beneath my dress and lifting it to my hips as I press my fingers over my clit.

I moan into his mouth and his eyes snap open, and then look down to where my fingers have disappeared into my panties.

Trapping my hand between us with his weight, he glares. "What makes you think you can finish what I started?"

"By all means, master. Roll the credits."

Crew's eyes shine with something oh so dirty, and he nips at my chin.

"Make me come, Crew."

He regards me a long moment, and in one swift motion, swoops me into his arms.

I yelp, locking my legs around his big-ass body, and rope my hands around his neck.

My core muscles tighten in anticipation, waiting for him to take me to his room and then *take me in his room*, but he turns the other way. Crew drops into one of the armless kitchen chairs, unlocking my legs from behind him and lowering them until my toes are touching the floor.

I'm straddling him, my dress up to my damn waist, the look on his face is downright despicable in the best of ways.

Eyes on me, he reaches between us, and I watch, mesmerized as his hand disappears into his jeans. The muscles in his forearm flex, and I know he's got his cock in his hand. He squeezes, adjusts, and then slides his hand out, my attention fixated on the long, thick outline, bulging in his boxers, fighting to break through the layer of clothes keeping it in place.

Crew lazily drops his head against the back of the chair, his eyes hooded, tongue trailing over his lips as he huffs in agonizing provocation. His hands come around, gripping and squeezing my ass, and for a split second, his eyes clamp closed.

And then he yanks me up and sets me down . . . right over his erection.

I fall forward on a gasp, clutching the chair with shaky fingers.

My pussy walls flex at the feel of him beneath me, and it cries, soaking the thin layer, keeping me from dirtying up his bottoms.

"Crew, I—"

He grinds my center into him, my breath lodging in my throat, my body shaking.

"Fuck me, baby," he rasps, tucking my hair behind my ear and drawing my lips to his. "Close your eyes and ride me like I'm inside you. Feel the length of me slide over this pussy, press on your clit, and pretend it is." His teeth sink into my bottom lip, and I cry out, sending a deep rumble through him. "Use my body and make yours shake. Come for me, Sweets. Come all over my lap."

"Holy shit," I wheeze, and with the encouragement of his hands on my hips, I slide over him.

Slow and timid at first, and then harder, faster, but not too fast.

Like riding a mechanical bull, I sway forward, right over his hardness, and back, pressing down more and more, searching for that friction, and my god, do I find it.

I do as he said, close my eyes, use the little bit of porn knowledge I can conjure up, and imagine.

I picture his dick, long and thick and silky, at least that's how it feels, glistening as it slides in and out, burying deep between my legs as I grind against him.

A shudder shoots down my spine and his hands come up, pressing at the hollow of my back and drawing me closer until there's no space between us. I bury my face in his neck, and when he tips his head a little, I taste the skin there.

His cock twitches beneath me, and I press into it, dancing over it.

My clit throbs, the friction setting me on fire, and I start to shake.

"There you go, Sweets." His voice is rough, clipped, and I swear his hips lift the slightest bit. "So fucking close."

I roll into him, keeping his length rubbing along my clit. His muscles tense beneath me, and I do as he did, nipping at his neck.

A shallow breath hisses past his lips, and I grin against him, but I'm peaking, so close to coming. On Crew. Over his dick.

Because of his dick.

I thread my hands into his hair and pull, inadvertently pressing his face into my chest as I whimper into the air around us.

His fingers dig into my flesh, and I welcome the sting, welcome the burn as my body heats to an unexplainable level.

It's almost too much, the deep ache building, tightening my muscles to the point of pain. Heat threatens to burn up my insides like never before.

He must sense it, feel it, I don't know, because his head darts up and he delves into my mouth once more. He kisses me fiercely, fucking my mouth with a ferocity that can't be matched.

Could never be rivaled.

"Don't fight it, baby," he murmurs into my mouth, flicking his tongue across it, pressing his hips up into mine. "Come for me."

I whimper, every nerve ending in my body quaking, my lungs denying me the full breath I desperately need. "I can't—"

"You can. You will."

Eyes clamped shut, I reach for his hand, and at first, he holds it still, but when he realizes I'm tugging, he relents and lets go.

Pulling back, with quite possibly literal stars in my eyes, I meet his. They're dark and dilated, and when I lead him to the thin layer of panties at my center, they grow even darker.

"You need my help, Sweets?" he rasps, gliding his nose along mine. "Want me to bury my fingers inside you and make you cry into my mouth?"

My thighs clench around him, and I nod. "Please."

"Okay, baby. I'll give you what you need." His lips part, gaze holding mine as he slips beyond the cotton, and I lift my hips the slightest bit, my clit rebuffing, but then Crew's long, lean finger finds my opening, and slowly, one sinks inside.

Crew groans, his dick impossibly hard beneath me. "So fucking tight."

My body shatters instantly, and he presses in more, slowly moving out an inch, all to press in deeper. I lurch forward, my chest slamming into his, my mouth aligned with his own. "You're squeezing me, over and fucking over." His chin falls to his chest. "Fuck, let's see how well you take one more."

My body stretches for him, the pressure divine, as are the delicate swirls his finger makes moving around a bit, keeping them inside until my walls stop spasming, then slowly, he eases out.

My vagina cries in protest, trying to suck him back in, but he's as good as gone, his hand hovering beside us, pointer finger covered with my cum.

Heat stings my cheeks, my entire body flushing at the sight.

Slowly, he brings it to his lips, but he doesn't slide it between them. He glides it along his mouth, coating every inch until no spec is left dry. His lips shine with my satisfaction. My release.

My cum.

I don't know what possesses me to do so, and if I were in my right mind, I might hesitate, considering it's not something I've ever, well, contemplated wanting to try, but I flick my tongue across the swell of his bottom lip, tasting myself.

Crew's eyes flash, and he has my hands locked behind me in an instant. He dips forward, so I'm leaning unsteadily at his mercy.

He gets in my face and whispers, "Mine."

And then he licks his lips in one full, solid sweep.

His head bows, his chest rising rapidly, but all I can do is repeat his last word while pretending he didn't mean the flavor on his lips as it echoes in my mind with a single question.

Promise?

"Go to bed, Sweets," he pants. "Fuck me, go to bed," he begs.

Wait, what?

"W- what are you going to do?"

Crew huffs a laugh, groaning a moment later. "I'm going to take care of this."

This.

I look at the small space between us.

His erection.

His thick, long erection, hidden beneath his boxers, a darker spot right over the center where I soaked through.

"I . . ." My face flames. "I could take care of it for you."

His attention snaps up, a deep frown etched across his face.

"Or I could try?"

"No."

My head tugs back at his instant response. "Why not? I want to learn."

Anger builds in along his brows. "You want to use my dick as a test dummy?"

"I want to see if I can give you what other girls can."

Crew stares, and my nerves begin to twist.

"I mean, you could wear a blindfold if that will help . . ."

Something softens in Crew's features, and he grips my waist, slowly standing before lowering me to my feet. His left arm snakes around me, holding me still, and he doesn't have to tip my chin up like I know he would. I'm already locked on.

"If your lips were wrapped around my cock, Sweets." He pulls the candy clip from my hair and runs his fingers through it. "Ain't no way my eyes would come off you, and I sure as fuck wouldn't let you hide yours from me. I'd want to see the moment they water when you get too excited and take me too deep, 'cause you would." His gaze roams over me, and he pulls his lips in a moment. "Yeah, you definitely would."

"Only one way to find out . . ."

Something flashes across his features, but it's gone too fast for me to figure out its meaning.

Crew's hands slide down my sides, taking my dress with it, and just like that, I'm fully covered. Boo.

"It's almost eight in the morning. Go. Climb in bed."

We stare at each other for several long moments, and finally, I nod, turning for the hall, but before I can walk into my room, Crew's voice wraps around me like a warm blanket, halting me on the spot.

"*My* bed, Sweets."

I peek at him over my shoulder—I hadn't realized he'd followed me.

He cocks his head, eyes narrowed slightly. "You got a problem with that?"

My smile is slow but wide. "Is that a joke?"

Crew chuckles, a soft and airy sound, and something inside me settles.

It takes him a moment, and then he starts walking backward into the bathroom.

Once he's locked inside, I take a moment to lean against the wall, toying with my necklace as I replay all my recent time with him, wishing—*praying*—for so much more.

But I know better than that, because every time the universe gives, it claims something in return.

Last time, it took my brother.

I won't survive if, this time, it takes Crew.

Chapter 22
Crew

I fucked up.

Bad.

So fucking bad.

I tasted the temptress, and she's sweet like honey, the pure, candy-coated kind. Soft like satin and as silky as shiny silver.

And fuck me, what a bold little thing.

She's quick to blush, always. The conversation will have nothing to do with naughty natures, and still, her cheeks are colored pink, simply from being the focus of someone else's attention. I want to say I didn't expect a brazen side from her, but that would be a lie. I feel like I knew she'd be this way.

It's probably why I kept my distance as she got older. I knew then, what I know now.

Davis Franco is a fucking prize, the kind that drives a man to put shackles around her ankles and cuff them to their own. The invisible kind, sure, but shackles, nonetheless. Big-ass, unbreakable ones.

Memphis knew, it's why he held her so close . . . so he could keep her for himself. He knew when Davis loved and cared for someone, that person trumped all. Always, no matter what, and he wanted to make sure her loyalty lay with him, so he could call on it when he needed.

And he did, one too many times. He was selfish like that.

She didn't know this, but he saw me give her her first kiss. It was the summer before her senior year. She was at the boardwalk with her friends, and she had no one to ride the

Ferris wheel with because her friends had paired up. I said fuck the Ferris wheel and took her into the haunted house cart ride. The night before she'd asked me to kiss her, but I'd laughed it off and left.

Didn't sleep for shit that night, so when she gripped my arm, tucking her little head into my chest, like she's tucked right now, I gripped her chin. Big, fearful brown eyes found mine, and I couldn't help it. I was angrier, lonelier, and more broken down on that visit home, and couldn't hold back any longer, so I pressed my lips to hers.

The girl melted against me, fit right into the curves of my body. I was drunk on Davis, ready to back out of the bullshit waiting for me and force Memphis to find a way to fix his own fucking problems instead of using me to do it for him. I'd stay behind and wait for her to be old enough to be mine, but then we climbed off the ride, and when I glanced back at the carts behind ours, I spotted Memphis in the last one. Alone.

He looked right at me but said nothing. I knew without a word, if I stayed, he would too, we'd be bringing trouble to their doorstep. I wasn't about to allow him to drag her into the dirt like he did me, and he would have.

Memphis never said a word about that day, but I didn't expect him to. He simply wanted me to know he knew, so he could dangle something else over my head when I threatened to walk away. I hated him long before that day, and he knew it, like I knew if their parents found out I kissed Davis, I wouldn't be welcomed back into the house that became my home with the same amount of trust I'd earned in my time there.

I was their foster son, and they loved me, but Davis was their daughter.

Not that it mattered, I never did go back after that.

But that was then, and this is now, and Davis is grown. Grown and in my bed.

I can't stop replaying last night. Over and fucking over.

And over.

How she rode me with our clothes still on, how she did what I told her and let her body lead. The feel of her lips on mine, the sweet sting of her tongue and teeth on my skin. Testing. Tasting.

If I didn't know her to her core, I might call her a liar. Innocent and untouched, the girl who slid my fingers beneath her dress and was eager to pull my cock into her mouth? No fucking way, right?

Wrong.

So fucking wrong.

She's brazen, but I've seen the way she gets with other males' attention, be it the dude from the diner, or even how she was with Julius the first day.

When it comes to men, she's either subconsciously uninterested, anxious, or unsure.

Not with me.

With me, she's eager, excited.

Comfortable?

A small frown builds across my face.

Is that what brought her to me, a sense of comfort?

"Your hand stopped moving."

Her sleepy rasp pulls me from my thoughts, and I look down to where my hand rests on the curvy swell of her hip, frozen in the spot where her sleep shorts meet the skin of her upper thigh.

"How long you been lyin' there awake?" My fingers continue grazing the area, up and down, up and down.

Davis shrugs against me. "Approximately thirty-seven strokes ago, give or take a few."

"Were you hoping I'd slide a little farther, my little number nerd?" I tease, my lips hooked up as I do just that, pressing my fingers into the dip between her thigh and panties.

"No."

My muscles freeze. "No." I push up on one elbow, leaning over a bit to try and get a good view of her face. "No?"

She shakes her head, giggling when I jump up, swing my leg over and pin her to the mattress.

I cock my head, frowning at her. "I'm not seeing what's funny."

Her lips press into a tight line, the little brat's trying to fight a grin.

"Davis."

"Crew . . ."

I glare, and she laughs, her big brown eyes roaming along my features.

"You're cute when you're confused," she whispers with a smile so soft, the tension wrapping around my shoulders eases.

She wiggles her right wrist, so I let her pull it free, and my lungs expand when she brings it to my hair, gliding her fingertips along the faded sides.

"Do it," she says.

"Do what?"

"Exactly what you're thinking about doing. Do it."

Heat swims in my gut, my eyes moving between hers. "What makes you think I'm thinking of doing something?"

One of her shoulders lifts along the pillow, but the brown in her gaze brightens by the second. She knows I want something, and the thing is, I'm not sure she cares what it is.

She wants me to have it regardless.

Until your deal is done . . .

"You told me no."

"You're not thinking now what you were then."

"And if I was?"

Her lips spread into a wide smile. "You're not, but I'm getting hungry, so you better decide before I climb out of your bed and—"

My mouth shuts her up, and she moans against my lips, gasping as they fold over hers, coaxing them apart so my tongue can swipe inside.

Every muscle in her body eases beneath me, and my forearms fall to the comforter, drawing me closer. I kiss her slowly, and she follows my every swipe with one of her own. She presses on my chest, and I flex my pecs against her palms, leading her to dig her nails into me.

I revel in the feeling, wanting to tear my shirt over my head, but not when she's this close and touching.

"I want to make you come."

Her lips curve around mine, and she kisses me back harder. When she nudges me this time, I roll, ready for her to climb back on, to ride me like she did before, my sweats far less restricting than my jeans were last night.

Flat on my back, I'll feel her shape against me, might even get her juices to seep through a little more to coat my skin.

Davis jumps off the bed so fast, I have no chance of catching her.

I fly up on my elbows, glaring at her as she books it for the door, but freezes there with a laugh.

"You running is equivalent to the word no. I don't like either."

"I bet you don't."

"Davis."

"You can do whatever you want to me, Crew," she promises.

My mind fucking sings her sweet, sweet symphony, and I go to stand, but she holds a hand out, freezing me on the spot.

I glare again, and her smile is fucking teasing, her hair a flirty little mess, shirt hanging half off her shoulder.

Too fucking beautiful.

"You're pissing me off, Sweets. *No* isn't allowed anymore." I probably sound like a psychopath, but I'm not sure I care. Scratch that, I *don't* care.

She broke the seal. She should know what follows.

Davis couldn't possibly be having more fucking fun right now. "Say yes to me, and I'll always say yes to you."

"I'm trying to make you dead on your feet. I will give you double. I'll keep going until you can't take it and beg me to stop. Let me."

"I will let you." Her desire seeps into her tone, and my cock is thrilled, twitching, but then she says, "When you let me lower to my knees for you."

My expression snaps so quick, she throws her head back in a loud laugh, and now, all I want to do is bite on her a bit.

My dick grows hard, sticks straight up, begging me to give her what she wants, but if I do, that's one less thing she needs me for.

I want to keep her as long as she'll let me.

I push to my feet and approach her slowly, much to my surprise, she doesn't run.

There must be something in my gaze that screams I need to come and come now, because her eyes fall to the swell in my sweats. Her lips part, and she toys with the necklace around her neck.

My hand disappears beneath my boxers, and I grip myself, groaning instantly, and she quickly looks up.

"Sweets," I moan, dragging my thumb across her lips as I slowly stroke myself.

She begins to pant, opens her mouth to speak, and then I close my door and drop against it.

It takes her a second, but she lets out a little growl.

"Crew Taylor, I swear to God!"

"Keep talking. It will help." I smirk as I continue to pump myself.

Her little stomps follow, and I don't stop.

I lick my lips, tasting hers, and push my sweats beyond my hips. My cock swells and flexes, thoughts of her tight little heat wrapped around it. The vein throbs, and my hips buck.

Her sweet little whispers swirl in my mind, and I don't hit the pause button until I'm slick with sweat.

I come quicker than I should, and when I'm done, I can't help the smirk that follows.

She wants to play keep-away; I'm game.

Let's see who begs first.

Davis

God almighty, why did I think a no-touch zone would be fun when all the touching makes everything so much *more fun?*

Today was pure torment, as was the night when we fell asleep on the couch and woke with me on top of him. Thankfully, we both had laundry to do today, and Crew had a pile of paperwork to work his way through, so we were semi-distracted from the fact that I knew the shape and size of his prize and he'd tasted mine.

I can hardly believe he did that.

I can hardly believe I initiated it.

But right now? Torture!

We're attempting to cook dinner together. A very domestic thing to do when neither of us is gifted with such skills. I mean . . . I can cook, but I stick to box foods and quick desserts, which is why we're listening to the voice clips my mom sent over and over again while we try and make her famous rice meatballs.

Crowding into the small space is bad for my sanity. Every few minutes, his arm touches me, reaches around me, pulls me in.

It's intoxicating.

He is intoxicating.

And addicting.

And he thinks so slick . . .

Crew grips the back of his shirt and tugs it over his head, throwing it to the side somewhere as he steps back up to the counter, leaving him in nothing but a black tank top.

*

My eyes dart to the heavy bulges of his arm, the sharp dips of his muscles flexing as he rubs his palm over his cotton-covered chest. "All right, I think the balls are nice and tight, don't you?" He lazily slides his eyes my way, playing nonchalant when he knows my eyes are growing greedy.

He's being cute, testing me, and yes, his body is ten times more exotic than it used to be, hints of tattoos painted along his skin peeking from under his tank. I've yet to have the chance to explore him bare chested, at least not in years, but where he's new to the art of restraint, I am not. So I flip the script a bit, dipping my finger in the warming marinara—canned, of course, we're not magicians.

As expected, his attention snaps to my lips, and he frowns, throwing out his favorite word. "Stop."

I do it again, drawing it to my tongue. "What?"

He grabs my wrist so fast, I nearly fall, laughing as I'm tugged into his body.

Is this real life? Me and him, flirting and on the edge of tearing each other's clothes off, in the kitchen we share? Alone?

Me and the boy I've always wanted but could never live up to.

Crew closes his lips around my fingers, sucking them slowly and scraping his teeth along the tip on each one.

My core pulses, and he smirks, then steps back and slides the tray of meatballs into the air fryer.

"Says it takes thirteen minutes, if you want to go take a cold shower right quick."

"No, I'm good, maybe I'll lose a couple layers, like you." I start to pull my top up, but then there's a knock at the door and my actions are halted.

Crew looks from the door to me, and I shrug, heading over to open it.

Jess stands on the other side, piping hot pizzas in his hand. He grins, but my expression must give away my confusion because his face falls.

"You forgot," he says.

I totally forgot.

"No, I . . . okay, yes, but we haven't eaten yet, so it's fine, right?" I look toward the kitchen, where Crew stands perfectly still, staring right at me.

My attention is pulled back to Jess when he says, "We?"

"Yeah, uh." I push the door open more, but Jess doesn't move. Neither does Crew. "You met Crew, my roommate."

"Roommate."

I'm not sure who says it first, but the title echoes from both their lips, seconds after leaving mine, and suddenly, my stomach swims with nerves.

"Come in!" My words are too fast, too upbeat, and my hand flings out like a concertmaster at the end of an orchestra.

Slowly, with shuffling feet, Jess makes his way inside. He eyes Crew as he heads for the table to set the double-stacked pizzas down, but Crew's too busy burning a hole through the side of my head to notice.

I look to him and his eyes narrow further.

"I bought another bottle of that wine you liked, but I didn't want to bring it over without asking you first. I know how you get about having alcohol in the house." Jess grins, cutting a quick glance to Crew.

A small frown builds along my brow, but I wipe it away.

Why did he say that and look right at Crew?

Clearing my throat, I close the door, rubbing my hands on my thighs anxiously.

Why am I anxious? Jess is my friend, and Crew is my, well, Crew.

There should be no awkwardness to speak of, yet tension tightens the air in the room.

Surprisingly, it's Crew who steps forward first, bare chest and all.

"We didn't exactly meet." He eyes Jess, offering him his hand.

I have to give it to Jess. He accepts Crew's hand with a smile, but it can't be easy, when you have the body of a bookkeeper, and the man across from you is built like a beast. A bronzed, brilliantly inked, broad-chested one.

To be fair, Jess isn't lacking in physique. He's not too skinny and average in height, but Crew is just . . . a lot. He's deep cuts and curves. The kind of brawn you can't get in a gym, but that solid, working-man muscle. The kind you get from rock climbing and stocking shelves. The kind that comes from manual labor . . . and a few too many fights.

"Don't worry about it, man." Jess nods with a grin. "You were . . . busy."

Busy at the bar the first time, sure. Busy going caveman when he told Jess to get lost only hours ago, absolutely.

"I'm busy now. With my girl."

My head snaps toward Crew.

He heads my way, slips in close, and my cheeks heat when his lips press to my ear. "Pants. Now. Argue, and I'll toss you over my shoulder right here."

He stays standing where he is, right in front of me, and it takes me a moment to move.

"Uh." My face reddens more as I peek around him, spotting the slight frown on Jess's face before he wipes it away. "I'm going to . . ." He doesn't need to know what I'm going to do. "I'll be right back. Want to grab some drinks from the fridge?"

Jess nods, a half smile on his lips. "Yeah, sure—"

"I'll get the drinks," Crew cuts me off.

"You don't want to put a shirt on?"

Crew scowls in response.

Okay then.

Pressing my lips into a tight line, I dash into my room, pulling a pair of sweats over my shorts rather than taking the time to change them.

It's still not fast enough, though. Crew is already speaking again when I hit the hall.

"When did you and her make plans for tonight?" he asks Jess.

"I can't remember exactly, but I work tomorrow night, so we planned for today. She texts me every morning," he tells him.

Do I?

Jess continues, "We make plans then or I'll stop by when I see her car. We usually hang out a lot, but we've been occupied lately."

"Doing what?" Crew grills.

"You know, job searching, résumé building. I'm trying to figure out if I want to stay around here." Jess looks to me as I step up, and a sly smile forms along his lips. "Or if it would be stupid of me to leave."

Oh shit.

Oh no.

Okay, breathe.

Why do I feel the need to rationalize every word he's spoken since walking in?

I mean, we would go through spurts of hanging out, and yeah, I think we did talk most days before, well, before Crew. Okay, maybe we did talk more often than not, but it wasn't—

Wasn't what? A big deal?

It was convenience, really, or maybe more coincidence, being we were on the same campus every day, lived next door to each other, and had relatively the same schedule for two years. So yeah, our paths crossed all the time, but why is he making it sound so . . . intimate?

Personal?

A prickle of awareness washes over me, and I meet Crew's gaze. There's accusation within them, a harrowing glint conveying the words he spoke to me weeks ago.

Men cannot be friends with you, Davis.

But Jess is my friend, isn't he?

Trying to figure out if I should stay around here or if it would be stupid of me to leave . . .

A harsh weight knocks against my chest then, and it's as if a bright light opened up above me, an astonished, revelatory sound echoing in the distance.

I can practically hear Crew's thoughts saying, *now you get it, now you know, now you see.*

The dinger goes off on the air fryer, and I fly toward it, needing something to do, but as I'm pulling the tray out, Jess begins speaking again.

"You know, now that I think about it, it's sort of odd this guy's your new roommate." Jess speaks as if Crew isn't here, metaphorically stabbing him right in his insecurities. "Him being a bartender and you not wanting liquor in the house. Seems like a big sacrifice to simply share in the rent."

My eyes snap to Crew, who grins at the countertop, but I know better than to be fooled by the curve of his lips.

I know him, and there's no doubt in my mind, he's thinking about what Jess has said. How he's "just a bartender," nothing more than a man with a rag behind a slab of sticky wood. How he's cut from the low-class cloth and can't afford much more than the necessities life throws at him.

I don't know exactly what kind of debt he's in, but I know he's working hard to erase it. That's what a good man: a responsible, admirable man does. He works hard to be the best he can be. I know he thinks of himself as Jess hinted too, and I can't say the outside world doesn't see him much differently, but they're wrong.

Unfortunately, when the world looks down on you for your starting point, you're burdened with building from it, and it creates a sort of hardness. A toughness that can't be penetrated and a slick, cunning tongue to go with it.

Slowly, Crew's gaze lifts, pinning my own in place, and I know I'm the punch line before it's delivered.

Crew makes a show of smirking, his head cocked to the side, palms flat on the countertop in front of him as he serves Jess a slab of *go fuck yourself*. "Sharing a lot more than the rent, ain't that right, baby?"

Just like that, my skin is on fire. It must be. I'm burning from head to toe, utterly embarrassed, yet surprisingly, not pissed off. He wants or needs a sense of self-worth? I'll give it to him if I can. If my words or actions can offer him any sort of self-reprieve, I'm here for it.

All I've ever wanted was to be needed by the man masking his shame in a crude comment.

"But sharing is fucking caring, right?" he quickly adds, slipping past me with his discarded shirt in one hand, keys in the other. "Gotta get to work. Enjoy your dinner date."

Dinner date?

Sharing is caring?

What?!

The door slams with his exit, and when I finally bring myself to look at Jess, I find a broad grin across his face.

He pats the space beside him and says, "Let's eat."

I'm not sure why, but a quick, stuttered laugh escapes me, and before I can stop myself, I'm shaking my head. "Yeah, I . . . no."

I spin on my bare feet and run out the door, but by the time I get to the carport, Crew's already gone.

And he doesn't come home.

Chapter 23
Crew

"Sharing is caring. Sharing is fucking caring?" Willie sits forward, beer bottle ready to slip from his fingertips. "Are you fucked? How you gonna say that and leave? What if she does share? What if he makes a move?"

"I think we should go there." Julius crosses his arms.

"We should definitely go there." X glares.

"Fuck no, we ain't going there." Willie shakes his head. "We'll send Layla!"

The boys nod eagerly, but it's Layla's mocking laughter that calls our attention.

"Honey bunnies, you ain't going nowhere. Crew claimed her, and then he passed her on." She looks away from her TV drama to meet my gaze with a glare. "You get to boil in the pot of shit you stirred."

Willie groans. "I can't believe you walked out of that bitch with him still inside."

Julius sits forward. "That's what I'm saying."

"She won't touch him!" Layla swears.

Willie scoffs, and then he scoffs again. "You sure? From what I hear, heard and saw, little Davis discovered she's a fucking—"

"Watch it."

Willie grins but frowns a second later. "Why do we think she won't touch him? She's a girl and Crew's an asshole."

"An asshole she likes." Julius jabs me in the ribs, and I shove his ass off the couch. "What? Am I lyin'?"

I don't fucking know, is he?

She wants me, yes.

Cares about me, sure.

But does she *like* me?

The girl loves me, I know this, but she's loved me since always. She loves me like she loves Memphis, only less. He was first in her eyes, and I was second. It wasn't a bad place to be when it came to her, but her top spot could never be mine. I know this.

I've known this, and eventually, I won't even be in the top five.

Shit sucks, but that's what's real.

"You guys, this is Crew we're talking about." Layla hauls herself up, narrowing her eyes. "There is *no way* you left them there together alone."

Licking my lips, I sit back, picking at the label on my unopened bottle. "I might have moved my car and waited for the prick to go."

"And how long did that take?"

I look around the group. "She followed me out, sent him on his way a beat later."

"Wait. Wait, wait, wait . . ." Willie jumps to his feet. "We're having a fucking pity party when we should be painting pastries?"

"Bro, what?" Julius frowns at his brother.

"That's what she does when I serve her double!" He points toward his wife . . . who officially exits the conversation.

"Okay, back up a minute." X scoots forward. "So, you got pissed, and instead of tossing her over your shoulder and carrying her out like you wanted to, *and should have*, you left . . . but then you parked where she couldn't see and watched until you saw Jess, the guy, leave?"

I nod.

"And he left *right* after?"

I nod again.

"Pffft." He jumps to his feet. "Man, you're dumb. She followed you. Bet she'd take your call right now if you tried getting a hold of her." Anger slips into his tone and he pouts his way to the fridge for another drink.

"Someone not answering your calls, brother?" Julius teases.

X flips him off, and we all know he's right. His best friend's baby sister won't acknowledge him . . . after he fucked up and fucked her at her birthday party.

"I say you call her." Willie sits back with his arms crossed.

"Nah." I press the heel of my palm into my eye. "I need to get my head on straight. Break away from her for a minute so I can think."

"Why? Ain't we keeping her?" Julius wonders.

A scoffed laugh leaves me, and I drop my head back.

That's the problem, isn't it? Keeping her.

Davis came to me looking for a solution to her "problem," that's it. She didn't ask for more, didn't offer more than that fucking truck I don't even need, but know it'd kill her to sell. It would be like breaking the last tie to her brother. But me and her, we're on two different islands, and they don't collide. I don't deserve her. I know this.

I hide shit, do bad shit, *hardly have shit*.

Memphis drilled all this and more into me for years when I was nothing but a sucker surrounded by stony-eyed assholes okay with pissing away their parents' life savings on classes they didn't bother showing up for. He was my friend, and then he was like a brother, but not long later, he was nothing. Didn't change the fact that his words were true and didn't need to be spoken.

I was aware Davis was out of my league and that hasn't changed.

I have no house, no stupid fucking degree.

She's too good for me, but in the end, not even that shit matters. Those things can be worked past, I know that. What can't, are the two simple truths that can't be denied:

I want her.

She wants to feel wanted.

Those are two *very* different things.

I can give her what she's after, no problem, teach her all she could possibly wish to learn, and show her shit she's never thought of, but then what?

Let her go?

Allow someone else to have her?

Touch her?

Love her?

Fuck that and fuck no.

She's mine until this damn deal is done.

After that, I'll be her shadow, scaring away every man who dares to get too close.

I might not be good enough for her, but no one else is either.

And that's fucking that.

"Uh, dumb fuck who left his wannabe woman with another man?" Julius lets the blinds loose, takes a giant bite of his corn dog, talking with a mouthful. "There's an angry little virgin walking up the drive."

My brows snap together, and he yanks the door open.

"For the record, I'd have dragged you to the room and handcuffed you there," he tells her.

Davis completely ignores the man, slipping beneath his extended arm, eyes connecting with mine in an instant, but mine flash to the rag wrapped around her hand, a giant red stain seeping through it.

I jump to my feet, panicked. "What the fuck happened?"

"Sharing is caring?" She ignores me completely, getting right to it, putting me on blast for my stupid fucking comment, without knowing I shared it already.

"Sharing is caring," she repeats, her tone now free of the sass she walked in here with. "At first, 'I thought gee, Davis, that's a strange thing for the man to say when *every other second of every other day* he gets growly when someone so much as smiles near his little problematic project—'"

"Problematic project?" I jerk forward, my eyes slicing from her hand to her face, trying to stay connected to what she's saying, but going fucking crazy knowing she's hurt. "Tell me what happened."

"But then I played some things back." Yet again, she continues as if I hadn't spoken, hadn't moved closer. "And I thought of how you kept reminding me how my virginal status was at your disposal. Your choice, your timing, and all that, as if I wasn't fully freaking aware, but I need—"

"Oh, this is 'bout to get good," Julius whispers.

"Don't say it, girl," Willie warns, leaning forward on his elbows.

"To know why you picked him. Not so I can argue, I won't, I promise. I said you can pick, and I won't fight it, but you know I'm a thinker, so you can't drop a nuclear missile in my lap and just leave like I'm supposed to know what to do with it. I don't. I one thousand percent *do not* know what to do."

My head cocks, and I blink at the brunette before me. It takes a second, but my motherfuckin' mind catches up.

"Excuse fucking me?"

My voice is low and gruff, rough.

Davis blanches, her gaze roaming my face, tension whirling around her more and more by the second as my body brings itself closer to hers.

"You won't fight it." The tips of my shoes touch hers, and she cranks her neck up to keep eye contact. "You won't fucking fight it?"

"She thinks you want her to fuck the Ken doll," Julius adds, as if I didn't figure that shit out on my own, and Layla comes around the corner, propping herself there with a bag of potato chips.

Davis reluctantly pulls her attention from me, flicking it their way, but only for a split second.

"Did you touch him?" Anger pricks at my skin. "Let him touch you?"

She says nothing, her frown deepening by the second.

"I asked you a question, Davis."

"I asked you one first."

A humorless laugh leaves me, and I don't realize I'm walking until her arms bend back, pressing onto the countertop behind her.

"If he touched you—"

My chest vibrates with every word, but she shakes her head, so I cut off.

"You touch him?"

Another shake.

"Why did you pick Jess?" she presses on in a whisper, but her eyes . . .

Goddamn, her big brown eyes are sloped at the edges, a hint of hope flickering just beyond the surface, but it ain't there for him. It's for me.

I grip her hips, lift, and set her on the counter, so we're nearly eye level. "You think I'm done with you?"

Her eyes fall, but I call them right back with a sweep of my knuckle along her jaw.

Gently cupping her left wrist, I bring her bandage to my lips, whispering against it. "You think I've had enough?"

That I'll ever have "enough"?

The uncertainty coloring her cheeks pink about kills me.

"There's still so much for you to learn, Sweets." I draw my thumb along her lower lip, pressing hard against it. "So fucking much."

Tell her you didn't choose him. Say you want her to stay the fuck away from him.

Tell her you were jealous as fuck, how you saw black and wanted to murder the man, so you had to get out before you did exactly that. Explain how you acted like a dick, so she wouldn't know the truth, that you want her even though you're not enough, even though you can't give her the life she wants and deserves. That you know she won't choose you, but how you want her to want to keep you, not fuck you and forget you.

Not regret you.

Resent you.

Release you.

I say none of that.

How could I? This is Davis fucking Franco we're talking about. She's perfection in the shape of an hourglass and I'm the unsteady surface she'll fall from, shattering all she is. All she wants. All she could be.

I'm a weight in the water, bound to hold her down.

The taste of warm metal coats my mouth, and I swallow the droplets of blood seeping from my tongue, forcing my clenched teeth to release it.

"So, we're not done yet?" she dares to ask.

The break in her voice is like a knife to the chest, twisting and tormenting. It's as if the thought of ending whatever it is we're becoming pains her as it does me.

Do you ache for me, baby?

Whether she realizes it or not, I don't know, but her little hand lifts, pressing gently at the center of my ribs.

My forehead finds hers, and she closes her eyes.

"No, Sweets," I murmur. "We're not done."

We're so fucking far *from done.*

It was a quarter to three in the morning by the time we got home from the emergency room.

Turned out, in her rush to get to me, Davis tossed the dishes in the sink, breaking a bowl and slicing along the line of her thumb, deep enough to need three stitches.

A hurricane of guilt swallowed me whole as she sat there, trembling in my lap, eyes squeezed closed with fear, as the ER doctor stuck the needle into her skin to numb the area.

I drew her lips to mine, but the guilt eating at my stomach wouldn't allow me to take them with my own, so I pressed soft kisses to her forehead and held her tight. Thank fucking god, she held me back.

They sent us home with all we'd need to keep it clean, and the minute we walked into the door of the apartment, Davis dropped onto the couch with a blanket, passing out before the hot cocoa she asked for was done. As much as I wanted to drag her to my bed again, I didn't, not after our little fight, if that's what it was, and not after she got hurt because of me, so I covered her up and knocked out on the chair beside her.

I thought for sure today she'd be pissy, playing a little game of ignore, but I'm not sure why. I should have known better than that. The girl doesn't play games, that's why she showed up at Willie's. She needed an answer, so she came for it.

She came for me and thank fuck for that.

Problem now is, I don't want her out of my sight, and to be honest, out of arm's reach sounds pretty fucking shitty to me too.

I want to reach out and touch her, toy with her in all the wicked ways, but mostly, I'm feeling like a needy little bitch—I just want to hold the girl. In my arms, in my lap, however, so long as she's close.

For a split second yesterday, I felt her loss, and it's not something I'm ready for.

I've spent years wanting to be worthy, but knowing I wasn't. It wasn't so bad when she wasn't around, but I've touched her now, tasted her.

I've been the first person she smiles at in the morning and the last she sees before bed. I sleep beside her, wake with her in my arms. You'd think all the time we have together maybe would be enough.

Wrong.

All it did was make me want more.

Crave more.

Need *more.*

Of her, of us. Of all of it.

Like right now, she's walking around the house dusting the photos on the wall, and all I want to do is grab a little fucking wand thing like she's got and follow.

What the fuck is that about?

"Do you have to work tonight?" she asks, wiping her brow.

Closing the drawer to the silverware, I stack a few bowls and lift them into the cupboard. "No events tonight, so the bar's closed, but I've still got a good hour of paperwork, and I need to sign off on payroll sometime today."

She nods, dropping the dusty wand in the garbage can before tying the bag closed and pulling it from the can.

I meet her by it, taking it from her hold, and she smiles up at me.

"Come with me. We can get honey walnut shrimp from that place on the corner on the way home."

"Make it the taco truck and I'm in."

My eyes slide across the creamy skin of her cheeks, and she pulls her bottom lip between her teeth. "Whatever you want, Sweets."

A flush deepens the skin of her chest, and she tucks her hair behind her ear. "Do I have time to shower?"

I nod.

"Do you want to join me?"

My frown comes so fast, and a quick and sharp "fuck yeah," is on the tip of my tongue, but then she busts up, her laughter loud and teasing, washing away the thickness in the air.

When she turns and walks away, I have to dig my nails into my sides to keep from following, but the second the door clicks closed, a grin splits my lips.

We're good, and that's damn good.

Chapter 24
Crew

"Okay, now you can turn around!" Davis smiles, holding her hands out as if she's praising the talent at the end of a show. "It's organized by the letters of the alphabet, and then date order."

I grin, taking in the dozens of files she managed to make sense of, something I've needed to do for months, but figured would take a week I don't have, and this girl did it in less than three hours.

"How's it look?"

"Better than I've ever seen it."

She takes my extended hand, and I tug her to me.

"Thank you." I tuck her hair behind her ear, and she beams, slipping a little farther between my legs. Taking her hand, I run the pad of my finger gently over her stitches. "You okay?"

"Can't even feel it anymore."

"Let me clean it for you when we get home?"

Her lips pull to one side, and she nods.

"Ready to get some food?"

"And snacks for before?"

I raise a brow, grinning at her. "Before, huh?"

"And after, of course." She laughs, tugging on my arm to get me to stand, and she doesn't let go when we exit.

"So, is it your job as the manager here to increase profit margins?"

I eye her on the way out the door, clicking the padlock in place.

Manager, right.

"It is, yeah. Drew's started helping with some of the ordering shit, but he follows whatever instructions I give him."

She nods, pursing her lips as she looks at me over the hood.

"Why?" My eyes narrow.

She climbs in, so I slide in beside her. "So, while I was cleaning, I skimmed over some things, and you know, number brain and all, I couldn't help but notice the variants in the produce invoices."

"You cleaned *and* calculated the cost of lemons at the same time?"

"Better question is when am I *not* calculating?" She waves her hands between us. "We're literally a giant formula I'm forever trying to find the answer to."

If it weren't for the playful glint in her eye, I might be pissed, but she *is* being playful.

"But anyway." She sits back. "Yes, I did, and while I can't say with one-hundred-percent certainty, I can with ninety-eight point nine, that you're overpaying by six percent."

I shrug. "That's just the way it goes. Their fees change based on supply and who they get it from. Sometimes, my fruits come from completely different places than my herbs."

She tsks her tongue, folding her legs in the seat. "That, Crewster, is because you're contracting through larger corps . . . but if say you went straight to the farmers . . ."

"Cut out the middleman."

"Yep." She grins. "It might take a couple goes to find the right one, but with a little homework, I guarantee you'd see that number go back down. And I bet you could save even more if you agreed to a short-term contract. A little security goes a long way."

"I'll have to work on that."

"I could help."

At the red light, I turn to her, and she chews her lip nervously.

"I mean, if it won't get you in trouble with your boss, or I could just point you in the right direction." She hurriedly adds, "The farmers' market might be a good place to start."

Before I realize what I'm doing, I'm leaning over the console, pressing my lips to the corner of hers. Our eyes lock, her cheeks flush, and then the light turns green.

She sits back, looking out her window, and I continue toward her taco truck of choice. We order and are headed back to the apartment to eat within fifteen minutes. Ten after that, we're settled on the couch, a random movie on in the background while we eat.

I couldn't tell you what's on the screen. I haven't watched a second of it. My focus is on her mouth as it closes over her fork, her fingers when she licks the tips, and she keeps licking the fucking tips, the sugar-rolled treat she had to have coating her skin with every touch.

She's sitting in the corner of the couch, legs crossed, body facing mine, but eyes on the TV, savoring her last churro.

"Let me have a bite."

Her attention snaps to me, and she gives a slow little shake of her head, nipping the thing in the center instead of on the end where she's holding it. "I asked if you wanted one and you, *Mr. I Can't Eat That Sugary Shit,* said no."

I reach out, grip her by the thighs and tug her onto my lap.

Davis gasps, surprised, but settles over me in the next second. Her breasts rise with a deep inhale, her chin tucking close to her chest, all sweet and fucking shy-like.

She is sweet. Shy.

Soft.

My thumbs brush the skin of her thighs the slightest bit. "Please, let me taste?"

An instant flush colors her cheeks, and I revel in it. It wasn't my intention to shoot for a double entendre, but I *love* how her mind spun it naughty, likely thinking about how I sucked her cum into my mouth.

I want to do it again.

She inches in, drawing herself closer to my chest, and the look in her eyes . . .

It's . . . different. So fucking kind, gentle.

More?

"You're giving in, Sweets, just like that?"

With the softest of smiles, she nods. "I was only teasing. You could ask me for anything, and I'd give it to you."

My pulse pounds heavy beneath my rib cage, my grip on her thick thighs tightening a bit. "Why?"

She looks down, so I reach up, gliding my knuckles along her jaw until I meet her chin, then gently nudge it, bringing her eyes back to mine.

"Tell me why, Sweets?"

She stares at me a long, *long moment* and then, instead of speaking, she tears a small piece of the candy-coated treat and offers it to me.

I open my mouth, and she drops it inside.

My mouth closes around it, and I suck the dusted sugar from the crisp breading before swallowing. Davis leans forward then, and with the most hesitant of movements, lowers her lips to mine.

It's a slow, soft, simple press of her mouth against my own, and then she pulls back, not looking up to me as she climbs from my body, wordlessly retreating to her bedroom. The soft click of the door snaps me out of my frozen state.

Why I froze, I don't know.

Why I let her go, don't know that either.

Untamable desire builds and fucking builds within me, causing a flare of fire deep in my bones.

I'm on my feet fast, at her door in seconds.

I don't knock.

Her head snaps over her shoulder as I enter, her breath a sharp-inhaled gasp, and she spins to face me as my feet plant before her.

I don't give her time to speak, but dig my hands in her hair, crushing my mouth to hers.

Shock ripples through her, sending a wake through her body. She shakes in my grasp, her hands coming up a second later and latching on to me to keep her steady.

As if I'd let her fall.

I tug her into my chest, and when my tongue presses at the seam of her mouth, she opens, her arms locking around my neck as I nudge her backward.

The back of her legs hit the mattress, and she lowers, taking me with her, onto her.

We haven't been in this position yet, me on top of her, feeling every inch of her curves pressing to every inch of my body. I can feel the shape of her thighs now that I'm sunk between them, and fuck me, if my hips don't align with hers in perfect fucking precision.

My cock presses to the center of her sleep shorts, and she gasps when I lose control, pressing hard against her.

I groan, driving my tongue deep into her mouth as my hands glide down her sides, coming back up to cup and squeeze her tits. Her full, soft tits.

I want to see them, lick them, bite them.

I want to suck her nipples into my mouth and swirl my tongue along the hard peaks.

I want to make her scream, cream, and then I want to do it all over again.

I want to do what she said she wants and thoroughly ruin her.

I want to make her need me.

Crave me.

Love me.

I dip my face into her neck, and she gives me more of it, tipping her head as far back as she can, her timid little hands sneaking under my shirt.

"Tell me why," I repeat.

"Because you're you and I'm me."

The way she says it, so plain and simple, so matter of fact with a sweet, little softness only she can manage, makes me delirious.

She's her, and I'm me, and look at us.

Unable to keep our hands to ourselves.

Unwilling to let go.

Unable to walk away, at least I couldn't if I tried. Time has proven that. I've left her twice, and she's come back to me each time.

I don't want to leave her anymore. "Why'd you walk away just now?"

She'll leave you this time, my mind screams, *you're a detail in a deal she needs done,* the fucking thing torments, but I tell it to fuck off and kiss her some more.

"I . . . didn't want you to deny me. I wasn't sure you'd-you'd ever touch me again," she admits. "The first time you kissed me, you never came back, and I thought it was happening again."

I growl in response, biting at her collarbone for the painful reminder, and she jolts, her thighs clamping down on mine.

"You like when I sting your skin."

I knew she fucking would.

"Isn't . . . is it not a universal thing?" She moans the last word, her fingers gliding along the sides of my face. "'Cause I can't imagine how someone could *not* like it."

I press against her, sucking on the spot beneath her jaw, and she draws in a deep breath. "It's different for every woman. If a man cares about her, he'll learn what she likes, remember it, and work his ass off to perfect it."

She runs her bare foot along my calf and my muscles flex at the feeling, a sudden need to hike it up over my hip taking over. "And for a man?"

"Same thing. Every man is different."

"So, it's up to me to learn what you like?"

My head snaps up, eyes locking with her dilated ones.

She said *me*.

Me.

I brush my lips over hers, my voice coming out quieter than intended. "Yeah, baby. It is."

I can't help myself. I grind my cock over her clit, and her eyes flutter, her lips parting.

"Let me play, Sweets." She's got me begging. "Let me put you to sleep."

"I-I think this would be a great time to remind you of a sweet little statement."

"Go for it," I say, nipping at her chin.

"You can't."

I freeze.

In the last five seconds, her gaze grew even darker.

I lift a brow. "Is that a challenge? 'Cause if it is, you'll never be so happy to lose in your life."

"Not a challenge." Her fingers graze along my happy trail, a slow smile curving her lips. "An extension of our deal, remember?"

"Fuck our deal."

My early thought bursts from my lips, and she gasps; it's tiny, almost unnoticeable, but I catch it. I didn't mean to say it, but I meant it, so I leave it for her to read how she wants. For now.

Davis pushes past whatever thoughts are swimming in her mind, the feel-good fog too thick for her to sift through at the moment and pushes on.

And by pushes on, I mean she *pushes* past the waistband of my sweats, her eyes flicking to the thick elastic of my boxers, and suddenly, it all comes back.

She said she'd let me do whatever I wanted to her *after* I let her lower to her knees for me.

An image of her soft lips wrapped around me flashes in my mind, my cock straining, jolting until it's brushing against her through my sweats, eager to be played with.

Pulling my hand back, I run the tips of my fingers along her neck, down, down, down, until my pinkie is nearly wedged between the swell of her breasts as they strain against her tank top.

"You want my cock between these lips that bad, hmm?" I murmur, my tongue gliding across my lower lip as I focus on hers. "Want to suck me into this warm little mouth?"

She wallows, nodding. "I want to try."

I snap my eyes to hers, tugging her top down a tiny bit, just enough so I can watch her while I flick my tongue along the fullest swell of her left tit. "Try." I glide a hand along her ribs until I'm squeezing the back of her thighs. "So you can learn?"

She nods again, and a quick and sharp pang hits my chest, but then she adds, "So I can learn how you like it."

My chest rumbles.

Good fucking answer, baby.

I dive in, capturing her lips in a drugging kiss that brings heat through my every vein. "I like you, baby," I tell her between kisses, thrusting my tongue in and tangling it with hers until she moans into my mouth.

"Is that a nice way of saying it's okay if I suck at it?"

"No way you could suck at it."

She takes advantage of my attention to her body, presses against my chest, and rolls us so she's above me.

Her hair spills into her face, the ends brushing along her collarbone, and I reach up, pushing it behind her ears, bending my torso to capture her lips once more.

She smiles, and with shaky hands, she pushes me back down. She stares at me a moment, and when she speaks again, her tone is barely a whisper. "Please."

Her single spoken word is my undoing.

All the blood rushes to my dick, and I swipe my tongue along my bottom lip.

And then I jerk up with her in my hands, and she squeals, latching on as I scoot my ass to the edge of the bed, slowly maneuvering her so her feet meet the floor. I catch her around the waist, staring up at her, and she draws herself closer.

"You really want to do this?" I press my thumb into her bottom lip. "You want me in this mouth?"

She nods, nipping at the tip of my finger, and a throaty sound leaves me.

Slowly, I push to my full height, tracing the stretch of her throat as she tips her head back, refusing to break her gaze from mine. My knuckles slide higher, gliding along her cheek, and she closes her eyes for a long, lingering blink. I lower my lips to hers, and she parts them for me instantly, *eagerly*, but just before contact, I dodge that sweet little mouth of hers, dragging mine along her skin until I reach her ear.

"On your knees, baby," I murmur.

Davis shudders against me, and then she does what I ask, staring up at me with long, thick lashes and a hint of fear, but it's the sheer determination in the way she folds her fingers over my waistband that has me dropping my hands to my sides in surrender.

She said she's never seen a man below the waist outside of TV, so I'm not sure what she expects for size, but the subtle way her eyes widen as she drags the fabric lower tells me she's happy with what she finds.

Maybe a little intimidated, too, but she's beginning to understand her body without having ever used it, so I'd say she knows I'm equipped to satisfy her every desire, even the ones she's yet to discover.

My sweats and boxers slide down my knees, and I kick out of them, my dick coming up and slapping at my belly button before pointing up at her.

She swallows, eyeing the long, thick rod, and her palms flatten on my thighs.

She looks up, and I cup her cheek, my pulse pounding out of fucking control.

"You have no idea what seeing you like this does to me."

Her fingers twitch and my muscles flex on instinct.

I'm having one of those out-of-body experiences right now, the kind that can't be real, that's too real to tame. My weak spot, my deepest hidden desire is kneeling before me, primed to pull my cock between her puffy, pouty lips.

"Tell me what to do," she whispers.

"Touch, trace, squeeze. Anything that comes to mind before, during, or after."

Her eyes move back to my length, and she nods, hesitantly lowering her fingertips to the side of my cock.

I flex, my eyes closing, muscles clenching.

Her touch is warm and soft, and when she closes her fist around me, unable to meet the tip of her thumb with the tip of her pointer finger, she does what I said, and squeezes.

The vein in my cock barks back, bulging, begging as the head swells.

I catch a small grin curving the edge of her lips when my eyes open and she slips a little closer, her chest rising as she slowly glides her hand back and forth, testing the feel of me.

"Soft," she breathes. "Like silky frosting, and the vein here." She presses along it, and I flex in her palm, making her smile break free fully. Her eyes snap up in question.

"Whatever comes to mind," I remind her, doing my best not to let the desperation I feel seep into my tone.

Davis tightens her grip around me, and I see the second she's decided what she wants next, and my ass cheeks clench. Swear to God, it's slow fucking motion when her mouth opens, her tongue peeking out for a taste.

The heat of her breath reaches me first, and I suck in a lungful of air, but it's nothing compared to the warmth of her slick tongue.

First, she flicks it along the tip, grinning to herself when I groan, and then she comes in for a swift, solid swipe, lapping at the underside, and up and over the head.

My chest caves, a heavy breath pushing past the *O* my mouth has formed.

Again, she looks to me, and when she gives a little nod, I replant my feet, squaring my shoulders as I drive my hands into the sides of her hair.

She straightens her spine, holding my cock in both hands.

"Open wide, but comfortable."

She does, and I ease my hips forward an inch.

"Take me in but keep that mouth open until I'm as deep as you want me."

With a shaky breath and an excited gleam in her eyes, she listens, leaning forward.

The head of my dick disappears between her lush lips, the edge of the head scraping along her teeth a bit and making me jerk. She slides deeper, the heat of her mouth curling my fucking toes when she's not even really touching me.

Once buried completely in her mouth, she seals her lips around me.

"Suck and slide back, all the way to the tip."

She does, oh so fucking slow, until her lips are lulling over my head, and then she slides forward again, taking me deeper.

My nostrils flare, my hips pressing forward.

I want to fuck her face, grip her cheeks, and hold her there while I pump deep, but I won't. Not until she's ready for it.

"Use your tongue, swirl it like—" I cut off when she rolls it along me, slurping as she sucks, her cheeks hollowing. "That. Fuck, do that . . . whatever that is."

She moans her satisfaction, a wave of confidence washing over her, and she takes me deeper, her knees shuffling in until her thighs are touching my legs.

She tips her head, swiveling back and forth, taking me in and out, shallow and then deep, so fucking deep.

She gags a bit, and I groan, my head dropping back, my hand tangling in her soft brown hair. I hold her loosely, following her bobs, and my grip tightens, my muscles contracting.

She pulls back, releasing me with a pop, but before my eyes can snap to hers, I'm back in the heat of her mouth, her tongue whirling wildly.

"Goddamn, baby. Mmm." A frown builds along my brow. "Your mouth feels so good."

She slides her lips along me, sucking until there's no room for air in her mouth.

"Mmm, the way you suck my cock." My fist tightens, and this time, I give a little tug. "The things you do with that tongue. I'm fucking gone for you, Sweets."

My girl moans, she fucking moans, her eyes closing and my chin hits my chest.

She looks up, a dirty gleam in her gorgeous eyes, and I know she wants more, but she's not quite sure what "more" would be, so I grip her face like I wanted to do before.

I trail my thumb along her upper lip, and around the bottom, and she gently presses her teeth to my skin.

A sharp hiss leaves me, and I bite into my lower lip, groaning as I flex inside her mouth.

"I'm gonna fuck your face now. Nice and slow to start."

Her eyes flare, her chest heaving, and she tries to nod.

I do as I said, thrusting my hips forward, in and out, my cock sliding along her swollen lips, and she knows what to do.

She seals her shit tight, deepening the friction, and the fire in my groin blazes on, heating every ounce of my blood.

A deep groan rips from me and I press in farther, pulling out faster, and her eyes fixate on my face, flash across it, tracing every single inch without blinking, as if she doesn't want to miss any part of what she's doing to me.

Her tongue curls, sliding and gliding along me, right to left, left to right, all the fuck over, and I suck in a sharp breath, holding it.

Her eyes widen, and I know she's got a little taste, my precum warning her I'm almost there.

I'm *right* fucking there.

I start to pant, eyes on hers, as I tangle her hair around my fists.

I want to fucking kiss her.

Touch her.

Rub on her.

I stop pumping when she flies up and down, doing all the work for me.

She sucks hard, soft little mews slipping from her.

She's turned on, dripping wet, I'd bet, and it's all because of this, what she's doing to me.

She brings me to the edge of the cliff, but what she doesn't know is I've already jumped.

I'm just waiting for my baby to leap, so I can catch her.

"I'm about to come, baby," I tell her, looking her straight in the eye. "In your mouth, on your lips, or on your chest. You pick."

She shivers and draws back.

I pump into her a few more times, and then my breath catches and she gasps, our gazes locked as she frees me from her mouth, but holds me against her open lips, my head resting on her swollen bottom one.

My hips buck, the cum spilling from my cock and shooting along her mouth.

It's the hottest shit I've ever seen.

"My cum's dripping down your chin." My tone is gruff, raw.

She nods, her breaths labored, eyes proud, and then she drags her middle finger along her skin, the gleam beaming off the light in the room, but that's not what has the after wave spitting from the tip of my dick.

That happens when she swipes it along her tongue, tasting me.

A curious expression crosses her face, and then she closes her mouth around her fingers, sucking off every last bit.

"It's . . . salty." Her cheeks pinken. "Sort of sweet."

"And my baby loves sweets," I rush out, yanking her to me and kissing the shit out of her.

I drop back as her arms tangle around my neck, locking and tugging me closer and closer, but there is no closer to be spoken of. She's fused to me, our lips smashed together so hard, our teeth click, but we don't stop.

I kiss her and kiss her, at some point, burying us beneath the covers, where I kiss her some more.

I'm not sure how or when we stopped, how late we were up or what had us falling asleep.

All I know is I want to do it all again.

This girl might not be mine forever, but she is for now.

And I plan to take *full* advantage of that.

Might have to look into those chains I talked about . . .

Chapter 25
Davis

I don't know what supreme being I need to kneel before but send them my way, and I'll kiss the man—or woman's—feet.

Why, might one ask?

Because Crew Taylor is quite literally . . . possessed.

Obsessed.

Repressed?

Maybe. We're not having sex, and I know he's not out getting it anywhere else, but he is getting something. And that something is coming from me.

My first go at *going down* must have been more than decent as the man refuses to take his eyes off me. Hell, he can hardly take his hands off, so he makes sure I'm always at his side.

Last night, for example, Crew had to get back to work . . . so he took me with him, parked me in the seat behind the bar and kept one eye on me, the other on the customers across from it.

A couple hours in, he dragged us up the stairs and into the hall leading to the office, then pushed me against the wall and worked me at warp speed.

"A course on quick release," he called it, speaking my language with a smirk.

I love the switch that flipped, but it's dangerous for me as I too am addicted.

To his touch.

To his kiss.

To him.

I've slept in his bed nearly every night since we came home from the festival, felt his skin on mine more times than I can count, be it his legs, his hands, his lips.

Twelve-year-old me would die to know we made it this far.

Will twenty-two-year-old me have to mourn this man?

Only time will tell.

But, right now, we have more, so until the end rears its ugly head, I'll soak up his attention, even if it drowns me in the process.

Crew flips his hat backward, so he can better see the biscuits he's checking on in the oven.

Yeah, worth the looming loss.

He looks up, catching me watching, and the smile he gives me reaches deep, stirring emotions I've worked hard to keep in check. To keep buried.

This man is making it difficult to hide the way he makes me feel, the things he makes me want, and the hope I dare to think we could have.

He walks over then, Neosporin, alcohol bottle, and gauze in hand, dropping to his knees in front of me.

Without a word, he takes my hand in his, gently dabbing at the area below my thumb, taking special care as you would something precious. You wouldn't even know I was cut if it weren't for the three little stitches there, but Crew ignores me every time I tell him it needs no attention.

It's kind of adorable, how a growly, possessive man like him is capable of such a gentle touch.

Spreading the Neosporin over the split, he looks to me, and before I realize it, I'm already leaning forward, my lips meeting his. His smirk is instant and I feel it along my mouth.

My phone rings, and I fully plan to ignore it, but Crew snags it from my side, accepting the call before we're fully untangled.

"You there, honey?" my dad's voice calls.

My mouth gapes, and I slap at Crew's chest.

He grins, his eyes flashing my way briefly as he tilts the phone toward him. "How you doing, Mr. Franco?"

"Come on now, son. Just 'cause you don't come home no more, don't mean I'm mister again."

A flash of guilt threatens to wash Crew's smile away, but he holds it in place for my father's sake. There's a lot of love between them, even if the last handful of years have fractured it a bit.

"Heard you're retiring soon?" Crew changes the subject.

"Heard you're living with my baby girl?" My dad changes it again.

Crew doesn't blanch. He doesn't make excuses or find a way to explain our new housemate status. He smiles, and my stomach flip-flops. "Yes, sir, I am."

"Hope you two are taking care of each other, I know neither of you likes to put much time into yourselves, but it's important."

Crew meets my gaze over the screen, a dirty promise in his grassy eyes. "I think we're doing a real good job of taking care of each other, sir."

"You tell her you love her yet?"

My eyes bulge.

Crew freezes.

My mother giggles, joining the conversation, and swiftly adds, "Kidding! Could you imagine what Memphis would have to say?"

At the mention of my brother, Crew sours, unable to hold his smile longer than a quick, "Good talking to you two, here's Davis."

I offer him a small smile, one he tries to reciprocate, facing the phone at the floor, so he can press his lips to my cheek and hand it over.

I watch him walk into his room and shut the door before bringing the screen up.

My parents sit together on the love seat in my childhood living room, both smiling at the screen, and my heart instantly warms at the sight.

"Hi guys." A small laugh leaves me. "I feel like I haven't talked to you in forever."

My dad's features grow soft as he takes me in. "Been a little over a week now. We been missin' you."

"I miss you guys, too."

"Oh peanut, I just love your hair!" My mom scoots forward. "Every time I see it, I think how you were meant to be brunette. Don't you think, honey?"

She nudges my dad, and my grin grows.

"Thanks, Mom. I think I'll leave it this way a while."

"How's Crew like it, hmm?" She wiggles her brows.

My mouth drops open, and I chastise her with my tone. "Mom. What's gotten into you?"

"Honey, knock it off," my dad follows.

"What?" She shrugs. "Don't tell me you haven't noticed the fine man he's turned into."

"He's been fine since the day he moved in next door," I say coyly.

My dad frowns so fast, we both laugh.

"I feel like I stepped into girl time," he grumbles. "And I'm the one who made the call."

Laughing, I bring my knees up. "I'm teasing, Dad."

Creases deepen the wrinkles along his forehead. "Uh-huh. Now, how's your résumé coming along?"

Crew emerges right then, slipping into the kitchen with our cups from last night.

"It's . . . slow." As in, I haven't touched it.

My dad continues, "I told you, honey, get it done and into Paul ASAP. We'd have you back home before the end of summer."

The glasses Crew was holding clink hard against the sink.

"Oh, and you know Gavin graduated too." My mom smiles wider. "Been home about a week now."

"Your mama and I went to lunch with Susie and Paul last week," my dad says. "Had to sit and listen to a story about you and that boy for thirty minutes."

"Seriously?"

"Oh, yeah, she told us all about the two of you getting cozy at the graduation party before you left for school."

Crew's head snaps up, and I don't have to look up to know he's glaring.

I can feel the heat of his stare.

I roll my eyes. "I don't know what story he told them, but he kissed me for a whole two seconds before I backed away."

"Best two seconds of his life, way he tells it." My mother practically fawns.

"That's sad if so, Mother."

"Or romantic," she singsongs. "Hurry and send your paperwork in. I'm ready for my baby to come home!"

Guilt spreads like warm water, heating my skin. "Mom . . ."

She hears it in my tone, my father, too, and both their faces fold with an ache I imagine only parents with an empty nest could.

"Oh, baby," she says, her voice a little softer. Sadder. "You decided to stick around there a while, then?"

My eyes slide over the screen on their own accord, connecting with Crew's, who happen to be waiting.

His are tight, sloped, and guarded, leaving me to wonder what he's thinking, yet leading me to share what I am.

I swallow, my smile small. "Leaving is the last thing I want."

I should add "right now" or "so soon" or something that alludes to something else, for their sake, for my heart's, but I don't because the way Crew's looking at me right now tells me I said exactly what he hoped I would.

Is that the last thing he wants, too?

"Davis?" my dad calls.

It takes a moment for me to bring my attention back to him, and when I do, there's a question in his gaze, only I'm not sure what it's asking and he doesn't voice it.

He does, however, sit forward, washing my mom out of the shot completely. "You worked hard to get to where you are, Davis. Make sure you're taking the right steps for the future."

"I am, Dad," I tell him, and it's the truth.

I did work my butt off to graduate, to earn a degree they wanted for me in a subject I enjoy. I'll figure out what to do with it, eventually, but right now, the "right steps" are pointed in one direction and one direction only.

Toward the brown-haired, hazel-eyed man before me.

Something in his gaze sharpens, and then he's headed right for me.

"Hey, guys, I have to go—"

The phone is pulled from my hand, hung up, and my lips are met with liquid, lavish ones.

Crew kisses me senseless, and when he pulls away, it's with newfound determination in his gaze.

I just wish I knew what it was he wanted so much.

I wish it was me.

Crew

Growing up in the Franco's house was a confusing, frustrating fucking time, but if I went back, I'd still stand at the front of the courthouse and tell the judge the same thing, that their home is the one I wanted to be in. And it was.

At first, things were simple, and then they weren't.

I never would have thought the love I had for my best friend would hurtle into hate, just like I never expected my best friend's little sister to become the one I wanted.

In the beginning, we were both young, then she was too young, and then suddenly, she wasn't.

I knew the minute I kissed Davis on that fair ride, I'd lose myself in her if I got too close. Willingly. Pathetically.

I'd have stopped chasing the calm I heard so much about, that I saw in her home when I first moved in, and, at the time, I couldn't allow that to happen. Not when I had so much to prove, so much to learn about what being a man worth a damn meant. My dad was shit for a role model, but Garratt Franco was a great one. He taught me more in my four years under his roof than I learned in my fourteen years with my own.

We spent hours in the garage, taking Memphis—or Davis's now—truck apart and putting it back together, weeks learning how the engine worked and what made the wheels spin. How to cook a steak and how long you had to work to afford one.

I learned it took maximum effort to get the things you wanted, was taught what responsibility and respect could do for a man. I began becoming one under his roof, found myself looking back at my life before them, worrying about my brother, after my parents took off with him, and knowing an easy, worthless path wasn't one I wanted, while hoping like hell Drew discovered the same.

I wanted to build a life I could be proud of, like Garratt did. For the first time in my life, I began to believe I could.

The longer I was with the Franco family, the more peace I felt. They were strongly and solidly in my corner, and slowly, that feeling of being an outsider, the one I tried not to feel but couldn't help, faded. The last thing I wanted was to be a burden to another family when I spent all my life before that feeling like one in my own. That was gone too.

I belonged, and they made sure I didn't doubt that, but then things with Memphis started to change. Unfortunately, no amount of fosterly love could change the fact that no matter how much they cared for me, I wasn't their son, and he was.

When shit got dark, those protective parental reflexes—the ones my parents never gained—kicked in without a hint of realization. They didn't mean to look at me and see fault, it was simply natural, and I understood the facts, even as a teen.

Memphis was the son of a correctional sergeant and third grade teacher. He had scouts in his sophomore year and played for the USAA travel baseball team. He loved his sister and his best friend was a poor kid he treated like an equal, who his parents took in for no other reason than they were good-ass people who cared for him, a bastard of a boy who used his fists to speak too often, was decent at ball, but had no real future to speak of—me.

No way would their son be the one to pinch a pint from the neighbor's RV and get the girl down the street so drunk she blacked out. And he definitely wouldn't leave the poor thing alone after, without calling for help to make sure she was okay. And he would never get the idea to break into a vacant house down the road and squat there with a keg for the weekend . . . but me? Seemed more likely, considering I came from a thieving drunk, right? After all, a few good years with a good family doesn't change the stripes you're born with. A zebra's still a zebra when sheltered in a stallion's stall.

I don't blame them for looking at me and seeing what I came from. Like I said, it was natural and unintentional. They're incredible people, and they do have love for me. But again.

Memphis was their son, and the problems he found himself in led to the inevitable.

I became the mistake maker, the bad influence, and eventually . . . the problem. Of course, none of that came without the lies from Memphis.

He got really good at making me the fall guy . . . because I let him.

He never outright said it was me, but he was really good at insinuations that led to me as the culprit.

"*You've got no one to disappoint, man. Think about what this'll do to my mom if she finds out,*" he'd say, as if it didn't pain her to see me fail. It did.

That woman, and her husband both, gave me all they gave to their own blood. They wanted me to succeed, to have a better life, that's why they took me in. But I understood what he meant, and at the end of the day, it was me who didn't want to see the pain a fucked-up son could cause in his loving parents. In his doting sister.

The sister he didn't deserve, who I craved but couldn't have.

Who I'd never be good enough for, by my, and maybe their, standards.

So, yeah. I let them look at me and worry I could only be what I came from rather than standing tall and showing them all their efforts and time weren't wasted on me.

I *was* better because of them.

I *did* grow under their care.

And I wouldn't waste the opportunities they offered me.

Back then, though, what I wanted and what they needed didn't match.

I knew it hurt them to see me make poor choices, but that hurt was nothing compared to the pain they'd have felt if they knew their son was the senseless one.

They would worry themselves sick, and that worry would have trickled down to Davis.

I couldn't stand the thought of that, so I let him lie and looked his father in the eye, saw the disappointment pointed back at me and listened to every lecture with rapt attention, wishing the only man who acted like a father to me knew I wasn't the failure he tried to shelter me from.

Of course, as we became adults, their parents were forced to face his lies, but Davis is a different story. I used to think she simply saw the good in people, when really, she was blind to the bad, at least that was the case where Memphis was concerned.

Running my knuckles along her arm, she stirs in her sleep, her lips curving into a small smile, though her eyes don't open.

I heard the tone in her dad's voice today, the comments her mom made.

What would they say if they knew what we were doing here?

What are *we doing here?*

Faking?

Falling?

Faking like we're not fucking falling?

Who knows.

Who fucking cares?

When it comes to this girl, I'll take what I can get.

Chapter 26
Davis

Call me captivated, or tragically companionless, but it was hard to leave Crew lying in bed today, knowing if I had stayed home, he'd be mine until the evening rolled around and work demanded his devotion.

Had I not confirmed I'd be at Layla's girls-only luncheon days ago, I might have canceled, but I'm glad I didn't—time lost with Crew be damned.

"That was literally the best pasta I've ever eaten."

"Right?" Layla laughs, pushing off the pool's edge and tugging her glasses down over her eyes. "I told you it was killer."

"Yeah, it'll kill our stomachs later!" Toni shouts. "That shit has more cream than ice cream."

"Worth it!" Remy shouts from the patio, where she's refilling her tumbler with Willie's latest creation—mint and cucumber seltzer.

Glancing over, I spot a bag of recycling waiting to be smashed and turn to Layla. "People really loved your beer at the festival."

"They did, didn't they?" She smiles proudly.

"They were so intrigued with the flavor burst that followed each drink."

Her face lights up then. "That was the first time we sold out like that. Willie had to fill a handful of water bottles and put them in the ice chest to make sure he had something for you guys to drink that night because we were selling so fast."

"I really think you guys are going to have a lot of buyers reach out soon."

"We hope so." She glances at the other girls, floating on the opposite side of the pool.

"Have you ever thought about maybe keeping it exclusive and opening up your own small brew house?"

Layla's head snaps my way.

"It's just," I rush, hoping I don't offend her. "Willie has the space rented already, he's all set up and making magic there, right? You could stick the barbecue you had this weekend out there and serve any of the recipes I've tried of yours, or even go taco truck style. If it worked out, maybe you could upgrade to a small food truck a couple years in, but I don't think you'd have to do that if you didn't want to."

I grip the edge to keep my raft from spinning and continue, "With the college so close and the people coming off the beach in swimsuits, an outdoor spot that's relaxed, where maybe they can even have their dogs with them would be a huge highlight."

Layla looks off a moment before bringing her attention back to me.

"I could help if you want. I studied microbiology as a second, so I know all the health code crap, and with science comes so much more. Numbers and finance are my thing." When she says nothing, I quickly add, "I would do it as a friend. Just for fun, but no pressure, of course. I know it's a lot to consider."

Layla studies me a moment. "Did you talk to Crew about this?"

I frown. "No, why?"

"No reason," she says after a second. Layla tips her head. "You know, you're a lot different than I expected you to be."

"Oh." Her comment catches me off guard, and I'm almost afraid to ask, "How so?"

"In a good way," she quickly assures, but it somehow makes me feel even worse. "I guess I thought you'd be kind of hoity-toity and judgy. Sort of good-girl complex, you know?"

No, I don't know.

Why would she think that?

There's only one answer to that question, Davis.

Crew.

So he spoke of me at some point, probably after I bulldozed back into his life. Maybe in warning, before he brought me to their barbeque, and whatever he said made her—maybe all of them—think I was uppity, that I would lift my nose at . . . at what exactly?

Layla is smart and kind, a good wife, and from what I've seen, a good friend. Her husband works his butt off, trying to make a dream work and loves his family more than himself.

Even if they weren't, when have I ever looked down on anyone?

How could I look down on anyone?

I'm a glitch of a girl.

Friendless.

Planless.

Manless.

I've been a miserable mess, and I didn't realize it until recently, until spending time with Crew reminded me of what I was missing.

You'd think lowering yourself to a sexual bribe that begs your foster brother to be your gigolo would have clued me in quicker.

Besides all *that*! It's not who I am. If anything, I'm the opposite of judgmental and deny the flaws of others. Crew should know this, he's seen it firsthand, and it isn't pretty.

Old Crew knew this, and he hated it.

He told me more than once to "open my eyes" to truths around me.

So then why?

What did I do to make him see me so differently?

Is that why he pushes me away time and time again? Why he only lets me in so far? Because he thinks I'm like Jess, a college graduate who views that little fact as the end all be all, meaning Crew is somehow less without a college degree?

Is that why he didn't tell me he was living at his place of employment? Because he thought I would mock him in my mind?

I would never. Worry, yes, want to help, of course, but for no other reason than I care.

Does my kind of caring come off as condescending?

"I'm so glad I was wrong," Layla admits, cutting through my thoughts and allowing the water to whirl her away. "It would suck to hate Crew's girl!"

My pulse jumps.

Crew's girl.

So, his little first date comment at lunch that day, and the events of the last outing we had together, has his friends thinking he's all about me, the bratty, bribing baby sister.

Only a spoiled brat would think she could convince a man who didn't want her to take her, right? Force her way into a life he was trying to create away from her.

Away from me.

I can't believe I backed him into a corner, where he felt obligated to move in and play "defend Davis" as Memphis would force him to when we were young.

Memphis always did whisper to me how Crew didn't want to babysit me, but Memphis had a way of getting him to agree. It's like I said to Crew in the beginning, there always had to be something in it for him, or why bother with "Baby Franco"? I hated when my brother would share the things he'd say about me, yet I'd bait Memphis into sharing them time and time again.

A wave of humiliation settles over me, and I roll off the raft, sinking down into the water.

Crew planned for us girls to come to the bar after our afternoon. He said he'd save us the best seats in the house, and we'd listen to the new band coming to play.

I packed an outfit, and a couple hours from now, we're supposed to get out and get ready.

Now, not so much. I think I need to be alone, wallow in my worth, or lack of it.

I won't be going to the bar tonight.
I'm going home and baking a giant cake.
And then I'm going to eat it. Every last piece.

Chapter 27
Crew

My attention continues to snap toward the door, waiting for the second my favorite girl walks through it. I'm pushing three hours in before the familiar platinum blonde enters, but it takes two seconds to note there's nothing but a purse on her arm where a tiny brunette should be.

Layla slides right up to my end of the bar, and Willie weaves around, dragging a chair up for her.

"Where is she?" I ask instantly, glancing at the door once more.

"Home." She sets her bag on the counter. "Something about an early shift tomorrow."

My frown is instant.

Funny when she doesn't go back to work until Monday.

"What'd she say?"

Layla lifts a brow. "That she had an early shift tomorrow."

I glare at her, and she laughs.

"What? You want me to run down the whole day?" When I don't look away, she shakes her head teasingly. "We went swimming, ate ten pounds of pasta, washed that down with chocolate-covered cherries and virgin margaritas. Then we got back in the pool and tanned for a while. We got out to get ready, and she said she had an early shift, so she decided to skip tonight."

"Anyone call her while she was there?"

Why that question comes out, I don't know.

Layla smirks, leaning forward as much as her pregnant belly allows. "If they did, she didn't see the call until she left. We had a no-phone rule today."

Tossing my towel in the basket beneath the counter, I jerk away. "I'm taking a piss."

Laughter flows in my wake, but none comes from me.

Especially not when I call Davis and get her voice mail.

The little liar can't cancel our plans and then not answer when I call.

I need to know she made it home safely, that she's okay.

Her location says she's at the house and that is the *only* reason I'm not in my car already. Thank fuck, since there's not much I can do right now, not when I've got four more hours here, at least, and not with the traffic this social-media-made band has brought in tonight.

Maybe it's best she didn't come. This place is prick paradise right now.

I'll deal with the little liar when I get home. Even if I have to pry the truth from her perfectly pouty *pillows around my cock* lips.

Yeah, that sounds like a solid plan for later.

I expect Davis to be asleep when I walk in, but the surprise that settles over me when I step into my room to find my bed empty is nothing compared to when I make my way to hers, and hers is too.

I check the bathroom and no Davis.

I hustle into the front of the apartment again, lifting and tossing the blanket on the couch, even though her body would have been visible beneath it. I move to the table near the door, spotting the bright-pink Laffy Taffy key chain attached to her car keys.

"Where the fuck is she?"

My gaze snaps around the room, settling on the kitchen counter, and the sweet treat on top of it. Walking over, I glare at the half-eaten cake, but it's the two forks beside it causing my blood to boil.

Two fucking forks.

Two empty beds.

A dead motherfucker next door.

Throwing the front door open, I charge to the apartment beside ours, pounding heavily on the cheap wood.

"Open the door, you son of a bitch, or I'll kick the motherfucker in." A few beats go by and nothing, so I slam my fist harder. "I swear to fucking God, I'll—"

The door is yanked open, a shirtless blond prick revealed on the other side.

I slam my forehead into his, and he stumbles back, gripping his head as I charge through the house.

"What the fuck are you doing, man?" he shouts.

My chest rumbles, and I swing my left arm out as I pass an empty office, slamming my fist into the wall without pausing my steps. Shoving his bedroom door open until it bounces off the wall, I charge into the room, yanking his blankets off the bed, but she's not beneath them.

I rush back to the bathroom, and Jess charges forward.

"Get the fuck out of my house!" he screams, blood smeared along his brow.

I grip him by the neck, shoving him into the wall as I kick the bathroom door open, but it's empty.

Tearing away from him, I dash back in his room, swinging the closet open, and it's empty.

Chest heaving, I look around the room, footsteps pounding behind me.

"You need to leave before I call the police."

"Call 'em. They know me." My jaw locks, eyes tracking over every inch of the room. "Where the fuck is she?"

"Who . . ."

Swinging around, I get in his face, and after a second, his brows jump.

"*Davis*?" His head tugs back. "I haven't seen her since I came over with the pizzas."

"Don't fucking lie," I force past gritted teeth. "It's been a long fucking time since I've gotten to beat the life out of someone."

"Dude . . . I'm not." He eyes me closely, seeming to settle, and that fucking pisses me off. "She's not here, man."

I'm about to walk out, to leave, when a spot of red flashes in the corner of my eye. My head jerks toward it, and slowly, I make my way over to his bedside table.

Right there on top sits a hair clip, two pink cherries attached to the stem.

The same one I pulled from her hair.

The same one he pulled from her hair?

In what feels like slow motion, I face Jess.

His hands are up, eyes wide as he takes a few backward steps from the room, but the door bounces closed, blocking his escape.

"That's not—"

"It's hers. Be a fucking man and say it."

My limbs begin to tremble with rage.

"It is—"

My fist connects with his jaw, and I grip him by the shirt, flinging him across the room until he's slamming against the sliding glass door leading to the patio.

"I'm not playing, man. I'll have you arrested!"

I get in his face, screaming, "Why the fuck do you have this?"

"I found it outside!" he shouts, speaking so fast his words go together. "I thought it was hers, and I was going to give it to her, but I forgot about it, man, I swear!"

"Bullshit! Where the fuck—"

"Jess, what's going on?"

Davis's voice slices through the air.

We both look toward the sound, out the sliding glass door, where one of Davis's eyes peeks through her patio's privacy wall.

"Oh, my god, *Crew*?" she gasps, her voice thick with sleep. "What the hell's going on?"

My mind reels, confusion surging to the forefront.

"Your boyfriend is a fucking psycho, that's what!" Jess barks.

A hint of clarity slips through, and my arms fall to my sides, my breath coming too fast to calm, my head a fucking muddled mess.

She's . . . home.

She isn't with him.

She didn't pick him. She didn't leave me or let me go.

Jess jerks from my hold, shoving past me, and my shoulder jerks, my muscles dead as my eyes pop up, locking with the one of hers I can spot through the crack.

A door clicks behind me, and I spin, looking at the man holding it open.

"Leave." He glares.

I think I nod, slipping past him, and when I get outside, several others are peeking out their windows. Curving to the left, I head back for our apartment, the door wide open, Davis standing just inside, eyes heavy with . . . a lot of things, sleep being one of them.

Locking it behind me, I step toward her.

"Baby—"

"What the hell's going on, Crew?" she asks. "When did you get home? Why were you over there?" Her gaze snaps up. "Oh my god, why is there blood in your hair?"

My limbs are still numb but shaking.

"Crew?"

"You weren't in my bed."

She opens her mouth but closes it.

"Weren't in yours either . . ."

Her eyes narrow, and she begins shaking her head. "Wait."

I take a step forward, but she throws her hands up.

"You thought I, what?" Hurt washes over her and I want to punch myself. "Stayed the night with Jess?"

"He wants you."

Her stare is incredulous, as is the shrieked "so" that follows.

"You bailed on me, didn't answer, and there're two forks on the counter."

She stares. "One was for you."

"You weren't in your bed, Davis. I didn't know what the fuck was going on, and I lost it, all right?"

"No! Not all right. Not at all!" she yells, wide awake now. "Did you hit him?"

I lick my lips, and her mouth falls open.

"Jesus, Crew! Jess is not a 'handle it in the back alley' kind of guy!"

"What the fuck is that supposed to mean?"

"It means he could call the cops, and when they see your record, they probably—"

"I don't care." I jerk forward, and she stops talking. "I don't care what happens to me. If you paid attention, you'd know I never have. I thought you were with him and all I felt was blind, hot, rage, so yeah, I went after the motherfucker."

"You can't just do that! I told you, you have to stop hitting people because of me!"

"I can't! Probably won't ever. I thought you were there, and my mind caught fire. I had to go get you and bring you back here, back to me. Maybe it's fucked up, maybe I'm fucked up, I don't know, but when it comes to you, I. Don't. Care. That's the truth, so get used to it."

"And what happens when I do?" she throws back. "It's not like you want me around."

"Is that a fucking joke?" I didn't mean to snap the words, but hers instantly draw anger.

How the fuck could she say some shit like that to me after everything?

Is she fucking blind?

She eyes me a moment, then slowly backs away and rounds the kitchen, only meeting my eyes when she's clear across the fucking room. There's a shadow in her gaze, and I don't like it.

"Why did you bail on me tonight, Davis?"

A humorless laugh leaves her. "You don't get to question me now."

"You're looking at me differently. I want to know why."

"You just assaulted our neighbor and basically accused me of cheating, but guess what, Crew?! You can't cheat on someone who doesn't want you and isn't yours!"

"Girl, I will fucking—"

"Why did Layla think I was going to be some bitchy ballerina with a tiara?" she cuts me off, hitting me with some random shit.

"What the fuck?" My eyes narrow. "What are you talking about?"

"Don't do this. Just tell me."

I eye her a minute, noting the disappointment eating her up. "Something happened at Layla's. That's why you didn't come to the bar."

She says nothing, and I creep closer.

"Davis, tell me now."

"It was nothing."

"It was enough to keep you from me, and I'm not okay with that. Not even a fucking little bit, so tell me before I go over there to ask myself and end up boxing in my best friend."

She gasps. "You wouldn't . . ."

"I abso-fucking-lutely would."

"That's insane."

"When it comes to you, that's exactly what I am."

I'm a fucking hothead, and she makes it worse. Unintentionally and truly, unbeknownst to her, but worse, nonetheless. Guarantee we go on like this, there'll be more men I come to blows with. No doubt about it, really. She makes me crazy, overly emotional, and that's a lethal combination when your life is built around drunks.

No matter where I get in life, no matter what I achieve, I'll never *not* be me.

Even if I could offer her a comfortable future in a nice home with nice things, she deserves more. She deserves a good man who can love her without the mess.

I am not that man. I will *never* be that man.

What I feel for her is messy and wild and strong; it's a twister of emotions whirling around me, sucking the air from my lungs and the sanity from my mind.

I can't be good or proper or rational. Not when it comes to her.

Davis

Crew's frown is deep, and I hate that I said anything, but I know he won't let it go, and truth be told, I can't either. The thought alone has my emotions in overdrive, speaking the words out loud and fearing his response is too much for me to handle, especially at five a.m., when I slept maybe a total of two hours.

"She said she thought I would be uppity and judgmental. Why did she think that, Crew? I've never judged you, never looked down on you." I shake my head. "Even right now with the fighting. I don't care what happened to Jess, and maybe I should. Maybe I'm the one who is messed up because I don't, but all I can think about is the police knocking the door down and taking you away. I'll lose you again when I just got you back." Crew's brows clash, and I continue, "And I know I don't have you, have you, and I stooped really, really low to have you back by bribing you into my life again, when you finally washed your hands of me. I know I screwed up your plans, but—"

"Yeah, you did," he cuts me off, stalking toward me.

Tears pool in my eyes, my lower lip quivering.

"You fucked up *all* my plans," he admits.

"I'm sorry."

"You fucked up my world."

"Okay, I get it." Heat streams down my cheeks, and I look away.

"No. You don't." Heavy knuckles press along the underside of my chin, bringing my attention back to him as his dark eyes pierce mine. "You don't get it, at fucking all."

I suck in a shaky breath and wait.

"Everything I do," he begins, crouching down a little. "Everything I've done, for as long as I can fucking remember, has been with you in mind. What will she think? How will she react?"

A small furrow builds across my forehead.

Crew's hand opens, his palm replacing his knuckles on my cheek. "Could she ever want a low-class man like me? Could I ever be enough for the princess who grew to be a queen right before my eyes, when I'll never be more than a hands' man?"

"Don't talk like that."

"It's the truth. I know what I am and I'm not going to stand here and pretend life is different. It's not. I'm not. I can't give you a white picket fence and I'll never be sitting in a church on Sundays, like your parents did when you were little. I'll probably be in the bar, trying to find a way to hide the smell of vomit and vodka. That stable, standard family shit isn't me. It won't be. Not ever."

The sense of worthlessness, of deep-rooted resolve in the words he's speaking, gnaw at me.

Doesn't he know how much he means to me?

Is it not obvious what I feel for him?

My hands come up, latching on to his wrists, and his eyes slope at the edges. "You think I would change a thing about you if I could?" I whisper. "I wouldn't. I like you the way you are. I always have, even when I understood little of what it meant."

"I was the only man around you, Davis, and you knew no different. Now you do. Now you see. Look what I just fucking did." He frowns. "Look what we're doing now."

"We're just talking, Crew," I gently say, trying to ease the tension overwhelming him.

"Exactly." He pulls his hand from my face, freeing himself from my hold. "I acted a fucking fool and now you're standing here feeling like the bad one? That's fucked, Davis, and you know it. You should be screaming at me, fighting with me. You should have told me to leave."

I hear what he's saying, and maybe some parts are true. Maybe I should, but . . .

"I don't want you to leave."

"Because you need me, right?" He throws his hand out. "You know I'm a piece of shit, but you don't care because you need me here until our deal is done."

"No."

"Yes."

"No. If it were up to me, you'd never leave." The words are out before I can stop them, a heavy dose of embarrassment, of vulnerability, sweeping over me and creating a deep ache in my chest.

He stares at me, his features twisted as he searches for the lie, convincing himself there must be one.

"Crew, I-I want you. I've always wanted you and being with you lately has done the opposite of what you're saying it should. I-I want you even more now." I pause a moment, moving toward him. "You said my body will tell me what it needs, and what it needs is you. What *I* need is you." I grip his shirt, staring up at him. "Let me have you."

Crew stares at me a long, pressing moment, and then he tears away, putting a half dozen steps between us.

He glares at me, taut anger on the outside, pain-laced fear within.

"And then what, huh?" His tone is sharp, though thick and unsteady. "You get what you want from me, what your body is telling you it needs, and you go find something better after, holding on to the memory of the asshole who took your virginity? For what, Davis? So you can say you scored the guy you weren't supposed to want? Your brother's fucked-up former friend? Your childhood crush? Your fucking foster brother?"

I shake my head, but he keeps going, crouching as he stabs his finger into his chest.

"I don't want to be the one thing in your life you regret or the guy you roll your eyes at yourself for later, when you're embarrassed by what you did, of how low you stooped." His brows crash, pain flickering across his face. "I can't be the man you fuck and forget, so—"

"I love you."

I suck in a sharp breath once the words leave me, and Crew turns to stone before me, his body frozen in the crouching position.

After a solid seventeen seconds, he straightens, though his expression remains struck. Beaten, but not by pain or discomfort. It's the refusal to believe what I'm saying, a subconscious insecurity . . . or maybe a shred of hope?

"I love you," I say it again so he knows it wasn't a slipped mistake. That I meant it.

"Stop."

I shake my head, inching closer.

"Davis." His chest heaves, his eyes glued to mine. "*Stop.*"

"I can't. I *won't*. I love you, Crew. Every bossy bit of you." I pause a step away from him, our bodies near but not touching. "Psychotic tendencies and all," I softly tease.

His Adam's apple bobs with a thick swallow, his pinkie brushing mine at our sides. Crew says nothing for a long while, and then he steps closer, bringing his chest flush with mine.

"When did you stop listening to me?" he rasps.

I lace my hand with the one grazing mine, drawing it to my lips to kiss along his knuckles. "When did I ever truly listen at all?"

"Fair enough . . ." Slowly, his hand wraps around my lower back, holding me to him as he holds my gaze hostage, something softer swimming in his own. "I think I know why Layla might have thought what she did."

I'm about to say it's okay, that it doesn't matter, and while it doesn't really, I do want to know, so I say nothing.

"Since the minute I met her and Will, I've been busting my ass, trying to reach for shit I had no business reaching for, trying to become something better, trying to be someone worth something . . . someone worth you."

Tears pool in my eyes, and his hold on me tightens.

"It's my fault she took that as you needing more than I was, but I can promise you, Sweets, she sees the truth now." He grips my face. "It's not that you need more. It's how you deserve so fucking much more than I could ever give. It's that my life might not be the one you want to live."

"You're giving me too much credit," I whisper. "I'm just a girl."

"A perfect one."

My ribs constrict. "Perfect for who?"

His eyes move between mine, flicking to my lips as he presses his own tight.

"Me, Sweets." His words are so low, so, dare I say, fearful, it's agonizing. His gaze flies to mine. "Perfect for me."

There's a but in there that stings me to my core, so I wait for it, and it comes quick.

"But I will never be perfect for you."

You already are, I want to whisper, but it's easy to see there will be no convincing him anytime soon.

I glide my hands up his chest, across his shoulders, and his eyes close when my fingers graze his neck, sliding into the sharply faded sides. Pushing onto my tiptoes, I bring my lips as close to his as I can get them, the heat of my breath causing his eyes to snap open.

"So don't be perfect for me," I murmur. "Be good to me."

The hold on my back grows more possessive by the second, and I welcome the sting of his fingertips, waiting for his resolve to snap.

Please snap.

"Take what's yours, Crew . . ."

Take me.

A deep rumble works its way up his chest, and he dips down, catching my bottom lip between his teeth, his eyes squeezed shut. He scrapes along the soft skin, releasing with a slight nip.

Wild and wicked, he looks at me.

"What's mine, Sweets?" His hand lowers on my back, squeezing my ass in his tight grip. "This?" His other hand finds my breast, fisting tight around it and making me gasp. "These?"

He spins us, my back hitting the wall with a soft thud, as his palm glides down, lower and lower, until he's cupping me over my sleep shorts. "This?"

I take the hand he's pressed to the wall beside me, dipping my head to the side as I trail his fingers over my own neck, down my collarbone and across my chest, pausing right over the wild beat of my heart.

This.

I don't say it, but I don't think I have to.

I told him I loved him, and now I want to show him how much, even if I don't really know how.

He swoops down, slamming his mouth to mine, his tongue forcing its way inside before I have a chance to open for him. Gripping him tight, I leap, wrapping my legs around his body and he hoists me higher, my ankles locking above his ass.

He grinds into me, his hardness pressing against my sweet spot and making me whimper with need. I fight for more friction, rolling my hips with pure abandon as I try to climb him like my favorite tree.

He's my favorite everything.

Crew groans, and I tug on the hem of his shirt, lifting it. He hesitates, but only for a split second before allowing me to pull it from his body. My eyes stay on his. The sheer heat of his skin has me shivering as my hands trail and learn each dip of his muscles as they flex beneath my touch. But as I slide them down his pecs, my fingers brush along a patch of raised skin.

His gaze seems to burn a little deeper, and it takes effort to lower mine.

My brows pull, flicking along his collarbone and chest, down to his abs. At least a dozen nicks litter his skin, all different shapes and sizes, some protruding, others flat, but discolored.

One even hidden near the tattoo coloring his left pec.

"Scars . . ." I whisper, tracing one and then another. "From fighting?"

A ghost of a smirk pulls at his lips. "From winning."

An airy chuckle escapes me, and I lean forward, pressing my mouth against the highest one, curved along the lower edge of his collarbone, nearly dead center.

Crew groans, lifting my mouth to his.

He presses against me then, using the strength of his torso to hold me up, so his hands can roam free.

He tugs the small band from my hair, and it falls around us, his fingers immediately diving in and wrapping the short strands around his fist. He yanks, and a sharp breath escapes me, my head flying back as his mouth clamps over my throat. Sucking. Nipping.

"Fuck," he pants, his voice gruff, his hand shaking. "I'm trying to be gentle with you when I want to tear you apart."

"I don't need gentle."

"You deserve—"

Now it's me who yanks his hair, forcing him to look at me.

His eyes flash with wild surprise, the brown swallowing the green completely.

"I said I don't need gentle. I don't want you to hold back because you think I need that. Whatever you feel you need from me, I want you to take."

His dick flexes between us.

"Let me be what you said I am. Let me be perfect for you."

"Perfect for me," he echoes, nearly incoherent because his mind is so far gone. So deep in desire.

Slowly, his eyes find mine.

"Whatever you need, I want to give you. Whatever you want, I want to be." I hoist myself up higher, bringing my eyes above his, my lower lip placed perfectly between his own.

He stares up at me through hooded eyes and my tongue slips out, flicking along the bow of his lips. His fingers dig into the skin of my thighs, his chest rumbling.

"Take what you need from me, Crew."

"What if I say I need everything?"

My smile is slow as I drop my forehead to his. "I'd say it's already yours."

And just like that . . . he snaps.

Finally . . .

Chapter 28
Crew

Mine.

That's what she said.

With moves so fucking swift I get light-headed, I take her to the couch, perching her on the back of it, so I can grip her face and hold it to me.

I need some fucking clarification and I need the shit *now*.

"What are you saying to me, Sweets? You told me you love me. You said 'everything' is mine." I hold her gaze captive. "You telling me you understand now that *you* are mine? No ifs, no buts, no fucking deal. Just mine to have, to hold, to help—"

"To fuck," she whispers without a hint of hesitation, cutting off whatever the hell I would have said next.

Maybe I was an animal in a past life, because the growl that escapes can't possibly be that of a man.

Her words and the fucking blush that comes with them.

I've never been so hard in my life, so honored, but is this shit real? Can she possibly ache like me? Crave like me?

Emotionally overwhelmed, my hold on her face softens, my thumb gently brushing along the hollow of her cheek. She's so damn beautiful. Perfect.

"Baby . . ." My voice trails off into nothing, and Davis closes her eyes, leaning into my palm, her fingers softly landing on my chest and sliding along the marked skin there, having no idea she's represented in the very place she's touching.

"I want to be yours," she confesses.

Fear and uncertainty weigh her whisper, but she has no idea, no fucking clue, I've been waiting for those words for far longer than she can guess. Longer than she might believe.

The muscles in my body seem to freeze, but as quickly as they do, every inch of me eases. Settles. That dark place deep in my mind that never shuts the hell up, demanding I do more, try harder, keep pushing, quiets for the first fucking time in a long-ass time.

The world shifts, shutting down until there's nothing left but me and her.

Me and Davis.

Me and *my* girl.

My sweet little . . . everything.

Tapping her knee, she opens for me instantly, and I shift into the space, my lips coming down to press against the edge of hers, her sigh instantly fanning over my cheek.

"That's real fucking cute, Sweets. Real cute."

Her lashes flutter open, her gaze connecting with mine.

"If you think, after what you said to me tonight, I'll let you go, you've got a lot to learn," I whisper my warning.

A flicker of fulfillment flares in her gaze, settling deep into my core.

This is what she wants. I can see it clear as day.

A playfulness washes over her in the next breath, and her mouth quirks to one side. "Good thing there's still *so* many lessons to be taught."

Heat pulls at my groin, and I smirk. "Oh, fuck yeah. So many." I dip, kissing her neck. "Dozens." I suck on her earlobe. "Maybe even hundreds."

"That sounds more like it," she pants.

I groan, lifting her and carrying us both to the bathroom, planting her ass on the counter.

She frowns in protest, but I shake my head.

"I'm not going to fuck you while I smell like a bar," I tell her, kicking out of my shoes and pushing my pants down my legs, taking my boxers with them.

Her eyes slice to my cock, hard and ready, and I step up to her, kissing her firm and swift, speaking against her lips.

"And I *am* about to fuck you, baby. Minutes from it, in fact."

Her cheeks turn crimson, and she nods, watching as I retreat into the shower for a quick wash. Or that was the plan until the curtain pulled open behind me, and I turned to find Davis completely fucking naked.

My hands freeze where they are, soap slipping down my body, eyes locked wide and unblinking.

My gaze lowers, snapping straight to her bare chest, her breasts hanging free and full against her creamy skin. Her nipples are peaked to perfection and a few shades darker than the rest of her, a soft mauve color I want to compare the darker shade of my thumbs against.

My attention lowers from there, sliding across her body until I find the mound between her legs. Bare, I knew that, but seeing and feeling the shape of her pussy are too very fucking different things. My cock throbs, my mouth watering as I lock my eyes a little lower, to the bit of her that peeks out from her lips.

Her thighs brush together then, and my head flies up, realizing she's simply standing there at the edge of the shower.

"Get your ass over here, Sweets."

A small smile pulls at her lips, her steps a little slow as she works through the bit of nerves she's working hard to ignore.

It's okay, baby. I'll erase all that soon.

I adjust the spray, quickly washing the soapsuds from my body, so I'm fresh and fucking clean the second she reaches me.

No time is wasted. I swoop right in, claiming her lips like I'm about to claim her.

The air is electric, my world spinning, my Sweets the axis.

The center of it all.

I kiss her fiercely, suffocating us both, unable to pull away from her soft, addictive little mouth until she yanks back, gasping for air.

But I give her no reprieve, no time to catch her breath, swooping in with my lips and taking her neck, chest, and lowering, swinging her under the water so fast, she latches on for balance.

My eyes lock with hers briefly as I pull her nipple between my knuckles, tugging.

Her gaze flicks wider, her lips forming a sweet little *O* and I dip down, closing my mouth over the other one. Her head drops back, water spilling over her face and splashing along mine. The droplets roll down over my lips as they play with her, sucking until she pops from my mouth, but right when she thinks she'll get a moment to breathe, I clamp my teeth around her nipple gently, pulling back until she's thoroughly scraped and teased.

Davis moans, her fingertips digging into my shoulder as she slumps against the wall behind the spray. I look up, nothing but the water between us, and when a naughty little smile curves her lips, I eliminate even that.

Skin to naked skin, my eyes hold hers as I adjust, my cock now cocooned between her legs, settled and straining along her pussy lips.

"I want you," she whispers, reaching for my lips with her own.

My grin is as crooked as they come, and she chuckles, a husky, sensual sound.

"Don't look so smug about it," she teases.

"Oh, baby, I am." I hook her left leg behind the knee, lifting it to my hips, and hold it there. "I'm so fucking smug I might even puff my chest out."

Her laughter dies on her lips when I slide along the ones down low, letting her get a good feel of me against her, and as if they were meant for my cock, they slip around it, covering the skin like the softest silk blanket known to man.

Her thighs clench, the leg I've got a hold of hiking higher on her own accord, until her calf is pressed tight at my lower back. Slowly, she starts to ride, and the lax, brief movements are torture. Sweet fucking torture.

My hips follow, gliding in and out, and I pull back a bit, turning a few inches, so the base of me plays along her clit.

She moans, thrusting her tongue into my mouth as her arms latch taut around me, drawing me closer.

"You're gonna come for me, baby," I say between kisses. "And then I'm taking you to the bed, sliding inside this perfect pussy, and you're gonna come *on* me."

She shakes, her body rocking roughly as she chases what she wants. Takes what she wants.

And she fucking wants me.

I groan, my hands flying to her breast to tug and twist on the pebbled nub there, and my eyes snap up right in time.

Davis throws her head back, crying into the moistened air around us, shivering despite the heat we're standing under, and the minx shocks the shit out of me when she grips the showerhead, lifting herself up just enough to cause my cock to slip, the head pressing at her entrance.

Her chest is heaving, her lungs working extra hard as desire overwhelms her, and she presses down, her eager pussy ready to swallow me whole.

My hands fly to her hips, my grip forcing her firmly in place.

"Not a fucking chance." My voice is rough, thick.

She freezes but doesn't grow shy on me. My baby begs, fighting against my hold.

"Please," she rasps, ready.

And she is.

Reaching around her, I turn the water off, lowering her to her feet, her palms sliding along the scars of my stomach, only stopping when I step away to grab towels from the rack. Wrapping her up in one, I make quick work of drying myself, planning to do the same to her, but when I turn, she's already ready for me.

Davis steps out, pushing herself on her tippy-toes, and I haul her higher, allowing her mouth to meet mine.

"Eager," I groan, and she grins against me.

We're a stumbling mess, spinning and tripping and hitting the wall until she's falling back on the bed. Her bed this time.

She crawls up, her towel slipping halfway off on her way and then gone completely by the time her head reaches the pillow. I'm already over her, my knees settled between her open legs.

I kiss her hard, fisting the blanket in an attempt to let out some aggression. I'm so fucking hard, so goddamn desperate, but not to get my dick wet. Not to fuck or come.

To slide inside the woman beneath me.

To claim her as mine.

To claim what *is* mine.

"It all makes sense now," I say against her lips, dodging hers when she fights to press back, and kiss along her jaw.

"What does?" She squirms beneath me.

"You, my Sweets, and all the slickness between your legs. How no man has touched you there but me." I slide my palm along her ribs, grinning when she shivers. "How no man has tasted the sweetest part of you, but me." My hand glides down her hip bone, dipping between her legs until the edge of my pointer finger meets her pussy. I slide up her slit, the touch so faint, so light, she cries in protest, pressing into me for more. "How no man has ever been inside this pussy and how no man ever will . . ." I brace the tip of my finger at her entrance. "No man but me." I dip my finger inside, biting at her earlobe at the same time, and she gasps, arching into me. My grin comes slow. "Ain't that right, baby?"

"Says the man who wanted to find me someone new." Her hands plant on my shoulders, and she wiggles beneath me.

I gently sink my teeth into her neck, and she chuckles, her legs coming up and pressing into my sides. "No man, but me. Say it."

"You're the only man I've ever wanted, so I am fully on board with that statement."

"Mmm. Better be." I shift a bit, so I can kiss down her chest and flick my tongue over her nipple, fixating on it as it pebbles before me. "For the record, that was a bunch of bullshit. My plan was to drive away any man who looked at you too long."

Another flick and her thighs tighten against my ribs. "I think I did a damn good job."

She laughs, her fingers folding into my hair as I lower my lips to the space between her breasts, softly kissing her there, before closing my palm over her left tit.

I squeeze, massaging the sensitive flesh as I close my lips around the other, sucking and clamping over it tighter as I push a second finger inside her.

She whimpers, and then she starts to ride, and my eyes squeeze shut.

"There you go, baby. Ride my hand like you'll ride my cock soon."

She coos, the fingers in my hair sliding higher and tugging on the ends, so I give her what she wants.

I kiss her hard, my fingers pumping in and out, faster with every dip back inside. "I need you to come again. I need you dripping for me, so I can slide in a little easier, cause I am sliding in, Sweets. Tonight. Soon." She moans in my mouth, and I grind my cock into the side of her thigh. "So fucking soon."

"Do it now," she whines.

"No. Not until you—"

She locks over me, squeezing the fuck out of my fingers, and my cock cries in delight, in anticipation. I'm so ready to feel her warm and tight around me.

I don't allow her to come down but pull myself free, quickly dipping my fingers into my mouth. My groan is instant, and when I look up into Davis's eyes, I find them hooded.

She licks her lips, reaching for me as I settle in more, the head of my dick at her entrance.

Her eyes tighten the slightest bit, and I push her hair back, dragging my thumb over her bottom lip as I lean in closer.

"Spread wider for me, baby," I whisper, holding her gaze.

She does, her limbs trembling as I guide my hips forward, the head pushing past her entrance with a bit of force.

She tenses, her hands flying to my pecs, but she doesn't push. Doesn't panic.

I pause, peppering her cheeks with slow, soft kisses and slowly, her touch becomes soft rubbing. Her eyes close, her lungs expanding with a full breath, and just like that, her legs fall open even farther.

"More," she mutters shakily.

"Okay, baby." I do as she asks, moving in another inch, but her pussy isn't satisfied with that, and sucks me deeper.

I gasp, tensing as a shiver runs down my spine.

My girl's eyes snap open at the feeling, me inside her, me trembling over her, I don't know, but she's watching me now with pure fascination, the glow in her eyes as naughty as it is pleased.

I drive deeper, sliding past her tightest point with a gentle nudge, and she gulps, her walls clenching around my cock, but then she kisses me, so I pull back a bit, my nostrils flaring at the silken heat blanketing me.

"Okay?" I rasp, my head dipping into her neck.

She nods, her hands finding my ribs.

I pump in and out slowly, my moans deep and long in her ear. "Your pussy's like hot velvet, baby. So fucking soft." I push in, deeper and deeper until my pelvis is flush with hers. "So damn warm."

Her muscles have eased now, her breathing no longer tight but fanning in long exhales over my skin. "You . . . ."

"Tell me." I rock into her at a torturously steady pace. "Don't hold back."

I lift, looking into her eyes, and a blush, deeper than I've seen from her before, colors her creamy skin.

"Baby, my cock is buried inside you. The taste of your cum is on my tongue, and soon enough, your pussy will be on it too. You love me. Want me. *Got* me." I grind against her, giving her clit some attention, and her lips part. "You got something dirty to share, I want to hear it. Might die if I don't."

Davis chuckles beneath me, but it spins into a moan when I pinch her clit.

"Now I have to think of something better to say," she teases, her palms lowering until they're resting on the curve of my ass, and when she speaks again, her voice is quieter, but thick with a newfound neediness only her man can recognize. "I was going to say you feel good too."

"Mmm." I start pumping again, rolling my hips in a wave-like motion this time—out and down, in and up, over and over. "Love to hear that, Sweets."

"Give me more," she braves quietly. "I know you're holding back. Don't."

"Trust me. We'll get there."

"I said *don't* be gentle."

"You said take what I need, and what I *need* is to *take* my motherfucking time, and you'll be glad I did." She pouts, making me chuckle. "Trust me, Sweets. You want it this way, cause gentle now, means more later. Deeper tonight. Harder tomorrow."

She moans, her hard nipples pressing into my skin.

"Yeah, you like the sound of that, hmm?" I thrust forward. "Me fucking you over and over and over, and I will. I will and you'll learn every inch of me like I will you. And you're gonna ride me, Sweets. You're gonna climb on top and sink down over me. Can't wait for you to feel the difference. So fucking good."

She starts to shake.

"But I'm hearing you, and if you want a little more now, I'll give it to you." I pin her hands over her head with one of mine, and she stretches impossibly long, her neck bared before me, eyes wide with fascination, body shaking in anticipation. "Is that what you want, more?"

She nods fiercely, so I trail my fingers along her left leg until I reach her calf. I give it a little slap and she understands without a word. She lifts and locks it over me.

I shift her hips a bit, then pull back, until nothing but the tip is inside her.

"You'll take me deeper like this. You ready?"

"Please."

I groan, deep and long, and then I push back inside.

Davis

My back flies off the bed, my head thrashing from side to side on the pillow, hair in my face and sweat beading along my brow. Hell, sweat's everywhere.

Crew is everywhere, all over me. His scent, his touch.

His desire, hard and throbbing inside me. Deep, deep inside me.

He was right, the little leg trick . . . so much more.

Yet somehow not enough. It makes no sense. It's like I can't get close enough, can't kiss fast enough. I need more.

My right leg lifts to join my left, my hips tilting as they know just what to do, and suddenly, I'm stretching further, his dick deeper.

Crew moans in approval, and the sound has me desperate for release.

"That's it, baby," he growls, his lips dragging along my chest. "Take my cock. It's fucking yours. Been dying to be yours."

His words are filthy, naughty, but his touch is sweet and tender. So damn gentle.

I didn't think he had it in him, and maybe he didn't.

Maybe it's me who brings this side of him out to the light.

He drives forward, and I cry out, the stretch a sweet sting.

My core clenches. "Crew . . ."

He grunts then, his speed picking up.

"Crew, please."

"Baby, my name on your lips?" His hips buck faster. "Fucking done."

A fire builds in my blood, spreading and bursting through, wrapping around my bones and locking me up tight.

Tight, tight, tight.

And then he jerks. "Fuck, Davis."

My orgasm rips from me, spilling over him as he spills inside me.

"You're choking me so good. Taking me so fucking good," he croaks, his hips jerking as he pins me to the bed with his hips to keep me still. "Feel me twitching?"

"Yeah." I clear my throat and try again. "Yes, and it's . . ." My face flames, but when his head snaps up, his eyes narrowing, I push on. "It's dripping down my . . . it's dripping on the bed."

"Down your ass." His lips hover over mine, his pants harsh and spilling erotically over mine. "My cum, *our cum,* is dripping down your ass?"

I nod, a fresh wave of desire washing over me.

"That's how we'll prep it one day." His pupils seem to grow, his grip on my wrists tightening at the thought. "With your juices. With mine."

My eyes must widen because Crew chuckles then, the sound low and . . . loving?

He softens before me, a tenderness falling over him. "It might sting when I pull out. You ready?"

I nod, leaning into his cheek when it meets mine.

"You're perfection, you know that?" he whispers, mouth coaxing mine into a soft, sweet kiss as he pulls from inside me.

He's right; it does sting a bit, my body rushing to remove him and clenching tight in his absence.

"Wanna take a bath with me?" he wonders sweetly, quietly adding, "Or a shower alone?"

I link my hands in his, my smile slow. "A bath sounds nice."

Crew's eyes light up, and he pulls himself from the bed, quickly leaning over to kiss me once more as he takes my hand and helps me up.

We walk into the bathroom, hand in hand, and I sit, watching as he fills the tub, sliding inside before I settle between his legs.

We're silent a long time, both coming down from the high and settling into where we are now, a feeling of contentment slowly filling in the holes of doubt I dug into my own mind over the years.

The warm, soapy water paired with the soft, heated skin at my back is so relaxing, my eyes begin to flutter closed, right as Crew buries his nose in my neck, nuzzling me from behind.

"Sweets?"

"Hmm?"

He brushes my hair from my neck, his lips feathering along my spine. "You mean what you said? You love me? Like a woman loves a man she won't let go of? Like she loves a man she'll never forget?"

The hint of shyness quieting his tone is so surprising, so completely charming, my stomach flutters with girlish buoyancy, my lips curving into a soft smile, and I nod against him. "Yeah, just like that."

Crew's quiet for several minutes following my response, and I almost think he's fallen asleep, but then his hold on me tightens, his hand finding mine beneath the water. He laces his fingers through mine, shifting my shoulders as he places my palm over his left pec, over the tattoo there.

My eyes fall to the intricate design, to the triquetra hidden in the center, the three interconnecting loops creating a circle at the center, but as I look closer, I spot the veiled spot in the center. Numbers, written as roman numerals, curve the protected center, coveted, and caged in with chains, a small lock at its edge, free of a keyhole.

Forever fused closed.

But the numbers aren't numbers at all. It's a date, one branded in the back of my mind as it's branded on his skin.

The day he gave me my first kiss.

Tears pool in my eyes, my palm shaking against him, fingers pressing at the memory.

Crew speaks in the lowest of timbres. "I loved you when I shouldn't have, and I've loved you every day since."

My throat runs dry, elation and shock entwining together, and sparking a flame deep inside me, warming places I never knew could be reached. The part I buried beneath insecurities and repetitive cycles of losing the one man I was convinced was meant for me, even when the world worked so hard to prove me wrong.

I hoped for a piece of him, but I never believed he'd give me more than the warmth of his worry, or strength of his hands. I never dared to dream he might have always been mine.

"Crew . . ."

His forehead falls to mine, and my eyes close.

This, me and him, and the things we did with the words we whispered, seem surreal.

Unfortunately, when I dream, I always wake before the best part. That's when disappointment sets in.

I can only hope this is different, and Crew won't find another reason to push me away, but I won't spend my moments with him waiting for the last one.

I'm going to enjoy this while I can.

While he's mine.

Just in case someday soon, he isn't.

Chapter 29
Davis

Crew's nose buries in my hair, skating along the base of my neck and drawing goose bumps to its surface. His mouth curves against its place at the tip of my spine, telling me he's pleased, but still, I don't budge, keeping my eyes closed, my body still.

He wasn't lying when he said there would be more to follow, there was.

After the first time, my first time—good-freaking-bye, virginity!—we fell asleep, but the second I shifted in his arms, his hand left mine, and disappeared between my legs. He cupped me, pressing his fingers against my clit until it throbbed, pressing my ass into him. He rolled me onto my back then, and settled between my thighs, taking me slower than before.

It was a sweet suffering I'd welcome any day.

I had slept most of the night, so I had lain awake in his arms for a while before he woke to use the restroom, and when he came back, he was hard. I met him at the foot of the bed, and he effectively put me back to sleep.

Time has evaded me, the curtains drawn closed to keep even a guess from settling in, but for the last five minutes, Crew has been teasing, coaxing me to wake when I secretly have been for the last hour.

His lips press to my bare shoulder, down my arm, and then the bed dips, the heat of his body radiating onto me, telling me he's half hovering above. It's confirmed when his lips find my jaw, his hair tickling my temple.

"I know you're awake, Sweets," he whispers. "Open those eyes and let me fulfill a fantasy of mine."

My lips spread into a full smile instantly, and his chuckle warms my cheek.

"What fantasy?" I ask, keeping my eyes firmly closed.

"Mm, tell me one of yours, and I'll tell you the one I'm talking about . . ."

"In a spa. One with jets."

He moans, kissing my neck briefly. "That's a good one."

"Tell me yours."

He rolls me over, and I grin as I work hard to keep my lids locked shut, my legs falling open for him, but he doesn't climb between them.

The heat of his hand falls to my bare hip, his thumb drawing slow circles beneath the weight of the blanket before sliding up my ribs. He squeezes there, and then cool air prickles my skin, the blanket pulled back until it lies bunched below my navel. He's perched on his elbow above me and holds himself still.

My nipples pebble, and I know he's grinning without looking. I'm about to give in, tension and nervousness tangling within me, but then he speaks, his words far from what I expect.

"I was the last thing you saw before you went to sleep, baby. Let me be the first you see when you wake."

My eyelids flick open instantly, and the smile on Crew's face has my heart jumping in my chest.

"Morning, Sweets."

My cheeks flame, and he laughs, low and lingering.

Slow and steady, the curves of his lips settle into a soft line, his focus shifting from one part of me to the next. His gaze, uncannily intense, is like a warm caress across my skin, melting my muscles into mush against the mattress. It's as if he's massaging me with his eyes, loving on me with his mind.

Desperate for his kiss, I reach up, gliding my fingers along the growing stubble on his chin, and this man, this beastly, beautiful man, leans into my touch, his eyes closing, if only for a second.

The same need fluttering through us both, we seem to arch at the same second, the same pace, until our lips meet in the middle. The kiss is tender, promising, and my lungs demand a full inhale.

Crew pulls back first, pressing his forehead to mine. "Up, Sweets. Get dressed. We got somewhere to be."

Curiosity sharp, I grin. "Where?"

"Somewhere."

"Oh." I crawl off the bed as he does. "I like this."

A large arm wraps around my naked body, the other coming down for a fistful of ass. "I like this."

"I've arrived at that conclusion already."

Crew chuckles, tapping my ass with a swift little slap. "Clothes, my nerd. Now."

As if he might regret his playful demand, he swiftly spins, disappearing into his bedroom.

I pull a yellow sundress out, one with thin straps and a flowy waist, the kind that will blow up and blind me with the wind, so I tug on a pair of spandex shorts beneath it to be safe. Last thing I want is Crew going apeshit if it happens and a man is within, you know, ten miles or so. He's hit enough people because of me this month.

In the bathroom, I part my hair down the middle, smoothing it flat to my head, and slicking it back into a low, crisp bun, adding a Runtz bobby pin to both sides, the banana popping against my dress.

Crew's in the kitchen when I walk out, pulling sandwich stuff out and setting it on the counter. "Ham or turkey?"

"Salami."

He laughs, glancing at me, and he does a double take, a heady sigh leaving him as he glares at the hem of my dress.

"What?"

"Why did I get you out of bed again?"

This time, it's me who laughs, and I slide open the kitchen drawer, tearing into a new pack of candy necklaces. Drawing it over my head, I smirk at the man.

At *my* man.

My girly inner self screams and squeals and stomps her feet in delight.

"Because you want to take me to this ominous place called 'somewhere.'"

He pouts. "Right."

Amused, I move to the counter, putting away ingredients after he uses them to move us along faster. He passes me mine, and I take a large bite, leaning my hip on the counter. "So," I speak around my mouthful, swallowing. "Any chance we can take a small detour on the way?"

He steps in, peeling the crust off his bread with his lips, and I laugh as he pulls it into his mouth with his tongue. "What kind of detour?"

"Mm." I tip my head back and forth as I consider his question. "The exciting kind?"

"A candy store?"

My laugh flies from me, and I shake my head. "No, but I like the way you think."

"I was doing my best 'think like Davis' for that one." He grins, devouring the rest of his lunch with a single bite. "How long will this little detour take?"

"Five minutes tops."

Crew digs into his pocket, holding his keys out for me. "Lead the way, Sweets."

Giddy, I squeal, and then we're off.

Mere minutes down the road, and we're there.

Crew side-eyes me as I switch into the suicide lane, the only place to go, an old mechanic's shop my dad found me last summer. Turning into the parking lot, I'm sure to keep us on the south side of the building, where the inquiring customers pull in.

Killing the engine, I throw my seat belt off, swiftly turning to Crew when he does the same.

"Wait here?"

His frown is instant, but with another glance at the place and a quick read of my gaze, he agrees. "Two minutes."

"Fair enough." I smile, dashing out of the car and into the building.

The man with the mullet—who only now looks hip, when I'm sure he's had his since the first time they were in style—smiles, his coveralls covered in grease and hard labor.

"Last one, huh?" He steps up to the counter, glancing at the two-hundred-and-fifteen-dollar check on the counter.

"Last one." I beam, bouncing on my heels as he does his part, crossing t's and dotting i's, and with a giant thank you, I'm out the door, opposite the one I came in through.

As I come around the building, Crew's head snaps up from where he stands perched at the back of his hood, phone in hand.

At first, he appreciates, and then recognition clicks.

His frown is instant, deep, and then in slow motion, he kicks off, sliding his phone in his pocket.

I come to a stop right behind his car, and his heated eyes flick along the frame, eating up every inch of the fresh polish and settling on the whitewall tires, an unplanned addition I love, the white hood popping because of it.

"Davis." His voice is low and gravelly, on the edge of flip-the-fuck-out mode.

Shoving my door open, I quickly hop out, hands raised. "Okay, I know what you're thinking."

"I will take a crowbar to this fucking thing before you can stop me if you don't speak. Now. Might still if I don't like what you have to say."

Shit. Right.

Here we go . . .

Crew

My body is vibrating from the inside out, my blood hot and threatening to boil over, sending me into a fit of rage I might not be able to contain.

She said she was mine.

That the deal was off. Done.

Didn't fucking matter.

So why the fuck did she bring me to this shop only hours after the terms of the bullshit deal were done?

Her cherry is good and fucking popped. Mine.

And the item she offered me in exchange for the job is shining behind her, mocking me. Mocking us.

"Um," she starts, swallowing nervously. "I'm not—we're not here so I can give it to you, though, I do think it should be yours."

I reach behind me, popping my trunk, and her eyes widen.

"I just made the last payment!" she says quickly.

"Because that makes a fucking difference." I pull at my restraint, connecting with the crowbar lying ready in my peripheral.

She continues. "I've had it here for a year now. My dad found this place, towed it down, and made the first payment to get things going, but I've been making the rest since. It's been ready and waiting for almost three months now, but it took me a bit longer to pay it off since I had the seats redone to match the originals and got new tires. New seat belts and a glove box, too, so no more tape."

My memory flashes to the white cleat tape me and Memphis dug out of our baseball bags to hold the thing up, sometimes using it as a place to hide a joint or something stupid from his parents.

"Why today, Davis?" Even I can hear the weight of rejection in my tone.

Call me pathetic, but this shit stings. I waited to touch her, to have her. I fucking left her for Christ's sake, *twice,* tearing myself in damn two to protect what I hoped we could one day be.

To protect her from the bullshit I was caught up in until shit was normal again.

Legit.

Safe.

Davis smiles, and it's as tender as they come, as is the touch of her hands when they weave around my waist, her chin lifting to press into my chest.

On instinct, my arms do the same, locking and holding her to me, the need to be near her, to be touching her, deep on a subconscious level.

"Monday was payday for me, but life has been the best kind of busy, so I hadn't made it down yet, that's all," she murmurs. "But this wasn't a random thought trip. I've been waiting for this, I—" She blushes. "I wanted you to be the first person to see it. You and Memphis worked so hard on the truck, I wanted you here for its first time back on the road. It's what I thought about the day I dropped it off and the first thing I thought of every time I came to make a payment."

The warmth of her words, the shy, reluctant way she spoke them, thaws the ice in my veins a bit, and as if she senses it, a hopeful glint flits through her brown eyes.

She said I was the first she thought of, the first she wanted to see.

Me, not her brother.

Not her dad.

My forehead falls to hers.

"This past year, while we weren't speaking, I would come up with conversations in my head on the way home from here," she shares.

"What kind of conversations?"

"The kind that would convince you to go on a drive with me the day it was ready."

She doesn't have to say the in-between; we're both thinking it.

I would have told her no and she wouldn't have understood why.

Last year, and the one before, were ten times harder than this one's been, and this one is no cakewalk, so that's saying something, but she has no idea the shit I've struggled with. Because I didn't allow her the chance to find out.

She did what I hoped she would and poured all her focus into school, herself and her future. I told myself she wasn't missing me, that if I crossed her mind at all, it didn't hurt her the way it did me to miss and think of her, to worry about her or secretly check up on her, like I had so many times.

It doesn't take a genius to know I was wrong. She wasn't the only one blind to things around her. Clearly, I was too.

She wanted, maybe even needed, me all along.

"Don't be mad at me," she whispers, her eyes closed. "Promise, I'm not giving it to you. It's too pretty for that now."

An unexpected chuckle leaves me, and Davis grins, her lids slowly opening.

"You saying I'm not pretty, Sweets?"

"You are so far from pretty, you're like . . . Atomic Fireballs hot."

My head falls back with a laugh, and then I'm pushing forward, her back against the sleek ride, in one swift move.

Davis's eyes flash wide, desire quick to darken her pupils. "Okay, this is a whole new level of fantasies. I feel like if I knew what I was doing, I'd have dreamed of this when I was young, when I would stick around and wait for you to strip out of your shirt after an hour of being under the hood."

"You watched me, Sweets?"

"Straight perved. It was all part of my routine."

"What if I said there were times I watched you, too?"

"I'd say I'm going to need a list. Chronological order, please."

I grin, and a groan quickly follows.

Fuck, this girl, she kills me.

Her big brown eyes implore mine, but she doesn't wait, knows she doesn't have to.

That I'm hers.

She takes what she wants, pressing her lips to mine for what I thought might be a sweet, soft, *please forgive me* kiss, but that's not what I get at all.

Davis crashes her mouth to mine, fists my shirt to drag me closer and dives right inside my mouth, hungry for me. Starved to know I'm not angry with her, and, oddly enough, I realize I'm not. Her explanation was sincere, her words far more powerful than she realizes.

The girl has no fucking clue how long I've wanted to be the first thing on her mind.

It's like I told her this morning, I wanted to be the lucky motherfucker who coaxed her eyes open in the morning after satisfying her all night.

In a way, these things mean more than being the first inside her body, though that was a gift I'll forever feel a need to repay her for. Preferably in bed. *Naked.*

A horn sounds, and I tear away, glaring at the tow truck across the lot when the dude behind the wheel holds his hand out the window. "I tried to be patient, but let's go," he shouts.

My jaw clenches, and I take a step toward him before I realize it, and Davis grips my wrist.

My head snaps her way, and she grins.

"Down, boy." She dangles the keys in front of me. "What do you say, Crewster?"

I wrap my hands around hers, bringing my lips flush with hers. "I have to say, I'm a little disappointed you're wearing shorts under this thing." I squeeze her waist. "I'd have loved to set you on my lap, where no one would know I was buried deep inside you."

I yank the door open, and it doesn't creak as it used to, bringing a grin to my lips. "Inside the truck, baby. We've got places to be."

Davis smiles and climbs inside.

If there wasn't a bald dude behind us, waiting to get out of the parking lot we're blocking, I would do this slow, slide the key in and listen to the baby purr, glide my palms along the steering wheel and fist the stick good and tight. But there is a bald guy behind me, so the moment I turn the key, I kick the thing into gear and roll forward, out onto the main road.

I can't help the laugh that leaves me as I hit the gas, the truck jerking a bit with the quick speed it gains.

"You like it," she says softly.

"You know I do, it's why you used it as bait."

"I'd do it again if for no other reason than the bite that follows."

My eyes snap her way, finding she's fighting a laugh, the little tease.

"Baby, you like when I bite?"

Her eyes narrow playfully, and she throws my words right back at me. "You know I do."

"You know I'm a man, right? And remember when I said men were dumb?"

She nods.

"Well, men need to hear all about the shit you like, even when we already know, and it's exactly why we do it in the first place."

At that, she does laugh. "Noted. I'll compile a list."

"Chronological order."

Davis drops her head back with an airy giggle. "Anything for you, Crew Taylor."

Grinning, I focus on the road, telling myself she means that literally, and is prepared to do whatever it takes to keep it that way.

Chapter 30
Davis

"Shut up." I scoot to the edge of the seat, smiling at the long row of pop-up canopies and bike cops. My head yanks toward Crew, whose smirk is pointed out the front window. "Are we about to save some money?"

Chuckling, he reaches over, squeezing my knee. "We're just checking shit out, seeing if your idea about cutting out the big chains will pan out."

"That's a start."

He cuts a quick grin my way, pulling through the parking lot and choosing the very last spot in the farthest back corner.

"You did see, you know, the other hundred spots, right? Pretty sure I spotted one in the front row."

"Oh, I saw, but you don't park a carriage beside a saddled horse. Space, Sweets. This baby needs space."

Fireflies. I'd swear my stomach was full of them.

I pictured him behind the wheel of this for so long, imagined his reaction to seeing the project that meant so much to him, when it was more a pain in the ass for my brother—even if he too loved it, his drive was to show it off. For Crew, it was different.

It was the first time he had direct, positive attention from a man, the first time anyone put real effort into teaching him something he didn't know, first time he experienced patience and realized not all mistakes are unfixable and not all men used their hands negatively when those mistakes were made. Lessons could be learned without fear or fights.

I don't think Crew was ever physically beaten by his dad; I know his mother was, but when it came to his kids, Crew's father used words—a mental attack that never stopped, bound by impossible expectations. But his dad somehow thrived on their fear. He would break things, punch holes in the walls and throw glasses across the room. One time, I overheard him telling my parents his dad had flipped the dinner table . . . in the middle of their meal—a rarity that was ruined when Drew, only nine at the time, spilled his juice.

Both the boys slept over that night.

Crew might not understand, at the deepest level, why the mere thought of this truck is accompanied by thoughts of him, and that's okay. I planned to try and find a way to gift it to him down the road, but maybe I don't have to.

Maybe it can simply be *ours*.

His and mine.

Mine and his.

"You've got a faraway look in your eyes."

Crew's words snap me out of my head, and I smile his way, more fireflies fluttering around when he glides his hand over the handle in appreciation before tugging on it. "What are you thinking about?"

"You."

His eyes narrow, but there's a smile within them and he climbs out with a hint of a grin on his lips. "Come here."

I take his outstretched hand, but before I can climb out, he wedges himself between my legs, swooping down like a crow starved for its next meal. His mouth takes mine in a searing kiss, his hands burning my skin when he wraps his long fingers around my upper torso, sliding down until one is disappearing beneath my dress.

He cups me, pressing my center firmly with a low growl. "I hate these shorts."

"You're going to love them when the breeze hits and the hem of this dress floats up to my waist."

I feel his frown against my face and peek an eye open and chuckle.

"I want you," he rasps, pressing his hard-on against my knee.

"I want . . ." I trail off, gripping his face to deepen the kiss, his hat falling over my shoulder and tumbling to the floorboard. "To see a man about some lemons."

"Fine." He pouts and with a reluctant groan, helps me from the truck, gently closing the door behind me. "But only because this place closes in an hour. Know you're mine the second we get . . . anywhere alone."

"Deal."

I grin as he lifts his shirt up, exposing his strong stomach, so he can softly glide the material over the handle to erase all traces of his touch. Just like that, it shines back, not a single smudge to be seen. Hand threading through mine, he leads us toward the farmers' market.

"So, what's the plan, Stan?"

"This is your show, Sweets. You tell me."

I squeal, toying with the ice cream cone on my hanging necklace, making sure it's not tangled with the candy one settled above it. "Okay, let me feel some of them out, ask questions, and you fill in any blanks I don't know the answer to . . . and you know what, it's sad because there's a lot. If I had known about today, I would have studied your books. A couple hours and I'd blow your mind in a way you never knew numbers could."

I look to Crew, who stares at me with lowered lids. "What?"

"You're fucking sexy, you know that?"

My frown is instant, and Crew laughs, tugging me into him, his arm going around my shoulder. He kisses my temple and keeps walking, eyeing a bulk nuts vendor as we pass.

"Crew Taylor, I can feel those wheels spinning, and it's awesome."

He taps his forehead to mine. "Think bulk nuts from someone out here could save a penny too?"

"Maybe even ten pennies," I tease.

He squeezes my shoulder in response, and I love that he's discovering something he never thought of, realizing he has options and figuring out where to find them.

"Okay, three tents down. They have lemons and oranges, but I'm not seeing limes. Looks like maybe a mix of fresh herbs, too. Ideally, you'd find someone you could get all the citrus from at once, that would make your order larger, and make it more likely to lower the cost because of that, but don't count them out."

"Wouldn't dream of it," he jokes.

I smack his chest, melting when he catches my hand.

"What about over there?" He jerks his chin.

On the right, one vendor has two pop-ups, all the citrus you could ask for and fresh fruits to make it even better.

"Jackpot."

Crew's shoulders shake in amusement, but I ignore him, heading straight for the young men manning the station.

They can't be more than sixteen, their skin tan from hours of hard work on what I'm betting is a family business, by the lax way they lounge in the shade, counting this as a break from their summer job duties. I'm sure it is, their typical work likely ten times harder.

As I walk beneath their tent, one of the boys nudges the other's leg, keeping his face in his phone while the other head pops up.

Must be his turn to wait on a customer.

The young man looks at me. "Hi."

"Hi."

He leans on his forearms over a stack of mason jars full of canned peaches, a crooked grin on his face. He lifts a small green basket of black cherries. "Try one?"

"Sure," I accept, but before I can pop it in my mouth, Crew is bumping my back, and my hand jostles. I look up over my shoulder, and the brute is staring at the young boy, his face blank.

"You gonna offer me one, too?" He messes with the kid, gaining the attention of the other one.

"Uh, yeah, sure . . ."

Nudging him backward, I round the white-linen-covered table. "Do you guys work for the Kellpa family?" I read the name on the logo.

"It's my grandpa's farm or, well, our farm, too."

Bingo.

"Do you know if they offer wholesale, or do you only keep to town events like these?"

"No way." The other boy laughs. "We'd be throwing away hundreds of pounds of product if we did that."

Perfect.

"Do you guys allow visitors at the farm?"

"I don't think so, but we have a little shop you could come to. Gift baskets and treats and stuff."

"What kind of treats?"

"Woman, stay focused."

The boys laugh as I blush, and they seem to perk up when Crew grins their way.

"You got a number for someone we can call to talk to about order and fulfillment needs?" he asks.

"It's on the back of the receipt." The kid smirks.

Fighting a smile, I look to Crew, who hides a grin just the same.

"Let me get a bag of cherries and a basket of strawberries." He fishes out his wallet.

Proud of himself, the kid rings him up, and I step out, peeking at the next booth—also full of bright, colorful fruits. I turn back to see if Crew is done, bumping into someone as I do.

Their hands lock on my arms to steady me as I rush to apologize.

"Oh my gosh, I'm so—" My eyes snap up, colliding with familiar ones.

"Jess . . ."

He offers a tight smile, his hands lowering to his sides. "Hey. How's it going?"

"Good." I nod, a pang of guilt in my chest.

I enjoyed hanging out with him, it was fun and easy, but I would be lying if I said I was missing it. It's like with my job. I would look forward to going, ready to chat with Rachel and the cooks, pass the time and make money while doing it.

I hated being home because that meant I was alone, and all I had to do then was study, so I did. All the time.

Now? The thought of going back to work tomorrow sucks.

I want to fall asleep with Crew at seven in the morning and wake at one in the afternoon, with the understanding that it's perfectly acceptable to eat Cinnamon Toast Crunch at that time. Or pancakes.

Anyway, I don't want to go to work and lose time with him.

Maybe he needs time to himself, Davis? You've been in his face for days now.

Jess clears his throat, and I shake my head, looking up at him.

"How about you? Any leads on work or . . .?"

Jess nods. "Yeah, I uh . . ." He pauses when a shadow falls over me.

Crew is at my back, silent, and likely blank faced.

"I decided to go for my master's, so it's back to school for me," he shares.

"Oh my god, that's amazing. Congrats."

"Yeah." He smiles but then quickly clears his throat again, erasing it. His frown flicks over my head a moment and back. "I'm headed back home in a couple weeks, there's a program I'm joining at the college nearby. Half the price and close to my sister, so . . ."

He has a sister?

I didn't know that.

Crew presses closer, his hand possessively landing on my hip and pulling me into him.

Tension claws at my skin, waiting for him to snap something, but he surprises me.

Shocks me, really.

"Why don't you come by the bar before you go," Crew offers. "I owe you a round."

Sure, his tone is flat and hollow, maybe a little forced and not at all excited about the possibility of Jess accepting, but it's the words that matter, right?

"A round?" Jess scoffs, but not in anger. "You owe me a night."

I look up and over my shoulder at Crew.

"Yeah, all right." He nods slowly. "You plus one."

Jess nods, looks to me and a small smile forms on his lips. "Later, Davis."

I lift my hand in a wave, but he's already turned to walk away, so I spin, wrapping my arms around Crew's middle.

"What?" He glares.

"You know what. That was nice."

He groans, leaning down, and pecks my lips. "Fuck that guy."

A laugh flies from me as he grins.

"Come on, Sweets. We got people to meet."

And on we go.

By the end of the long rows, we've collected six numbers, two of the vendors sending us home with a giant box of mixed citrus for "testing" purposes.

"Potentially saving some money *and* getting free stuff." I grin as I open the tailgate, hopping up on the edge as Crew sets the wheelbarrow down in front of me.

"I'd say that's a solid afternoon." He grins, quickly unloading all the goods from the day.

He pushes the box of fresh-baked monkey bread to the side, but I swiftly lean over, snatching it up.

"I'll take that."

"I bet you will."

Digging in, I tear a piece off the edge, my whole body melting when I get the first taste of the candy pecans coating the top.

"Baby, don't be making sounds like that out here."

My eyes open, my legs following when he slips closer.

"It might make me snap."

"Snap, crackle, pop, babe. Please. I'm so ready for it." I take another bite, tearing at the thick breading with my teeth, and Crew dips forward, biting off the excess hanging from my mouth.

His frown of surprise is epic, instant, and now he's the one moaning.

I laugh, licking the glaze from my fingers.

"You weren't playing. That shit's good. You need to make that. Naked."

"Challenge accepted."

"Don't move. I gotta put this wheelbarrow back along the fence."

"Oh, I am perfectly fine where I stand, but don't be shocked if this baby is gone by the time you get back." I tear off another piece.

"Trust me, Sweets. There would be no shock there."

I watch his shoulders flex as he walks away, the veins in his arms begging to be licked on like my favorite lollipop.

"Sweet ride."

My head snaps left, and I offer a close-lipped smile at the man walking by, swallowing the mouthful of sugar before I can speak. "Thanks."

"A 1939 and with the original framework?" He lets out a low whistle of appreciation.

"Mirrors and all."

The man smiles, nodding as he rounds for a better look, but leaves the five feet of distance between us. "Original color?"

"Original color, but fresh paint. Obviously." I laugh and the man follows.

He's tall, his hair dark and with grays sprinkled near his ears. His face is a bit weathered, but he's in great shape for his age. I'd guess he's no more than early forties, handsome enough, but in that hard, greased-up kind of way.

"Car connoisseur?" I guess.

The man shrugs, but a smirk follows. "I'm a lover of pretty things."

"In the truck."

My head snaps right to find Crew's body stretched tall and wide, his face set hard and blank, his steps swift.

I open my mouth to tell him the guy was only admiring the truck, but Crew doesn't even have to look at me to know I was about to speak.

He simply adds, "Now."

There's something about his approach, about the way he's completely shifted when he was laughing and teasing two minutes ago, leading me to do exactly as he asked. I climb down without a word, bag in hand, and climb into the cab.

After a few moments, I dare a peek into the side mirror.

Crew has stepped up to the man, his hands clenched at his sides, jaw set tight, but the other man is grinning, his body relaxed, as if he has not a care in the world and is used to testosterone-driven young men. And maybe he is. He's wearing biker boots, after all.

But then Crew gets in his face, and just like that, the man's features shift, his eyes suddenly beady and dry.

He says something, holding out what looks like a business card in front of Crew, and the muscle in Crew's neck bulges.

Lipreading is not a strength of mine, so my attempt is a full-on fail, and then the man's gaze finds mine in the mirror.

I jerk away, anxious, but not ten seconds later, Crew is sliding into the seat at my side.

His hand shakes in anger as he slips the key in the ignition, and this time, he's not gentle on the pedal.

Crew spins the tires, smoke barreling behind the truck, burying the man in it before peeling out onto the road.

Several minutes pass before he lets out a harsh breath.

"Everything okay?" I ask tentatively.

"Fine, just . . . give me a minute." His tone is familiar, the dark and deranged one he uses when fighting for control . . . and trying his best not to tear off the heads of those around him. He was always notorious for picking fights, but he was smart about his choices. By that, I mean he would pick someone who deserved it . . . but also making sure they were larger than him because an easy knockout did nothing for his need to release the rage.

Unease settles in my gut, and I rack my brain for an idea of how to calm him when it hits me.

"Let's take the long way home."

"We're headed for the bar. Best to take this stuff there." His response is clipped and short, and he regrets it instantly, reaching over to smooth a hand down my thigh. "But, yeah, we can take the long way."

I love how he doesn't question what I want, just gives because he's able. And if he weren't, he'd work to find a way.

Crew rolls the windows down, turns the audio up, though not too loud, and after a few minutes, his exhales smooth out.

He's so simple to please. Nothing but the breeze or the stars, a quiet night in or out, is all it takes to level him, but I know his mind continues to run regardless, which is why I plan to take it over.

The moment we hit the back roads, I unbuckle my seat belt, gliding along the seat until I'm at his side.

As I knew he would, Crew drapes an arm over the back of the seat, making more room for me to settle beside him, the road clear of stop signs, so the gears needed no more shifting for several miles.

First, I lean in, gently kissing his neck, and I swear the man purrs.

Next, my hand finds his thigh, rubbing up and down, before my palm presses firmly over the growing bulge of his light jeans.

"Baby . . ." he rasps, his frustration swiftly morphing into desperation.

"I know," I whisper, unsure if he can hear me over the radio, and then I'm flicking open his jeans.

He groans, shifting his hips so he's at a more maneuverable angle on the seat.

So eager. Zero fight.

I love it.

Love him.

I pull him free, wrapping my fist tightly around him, and he presses his head against the back window, both his hands coming to lock onto the wheel.

"Now, Sweets, I need that mouth now."

My smile is slow, and I dip, sliding along the seat until my stomach is flat, my knees pressed to the warm leather, legs crossed in the air.

I dip my head, pulling his swollen dick into my mouth, and a long, low groan rumbles from his chest.

I suck him hard and fast, knowing he needs a harsh, hard release, not a softly built one.

I hold his base, bobbing up and down, using my tongue to swirl around him the way he said he liked it last time. My toes curl in my sandals when he swells, his hand fisting and destroying my slicked hair.

My core throbs, and I wish I had a pillow to ride to ease the pressure while I swallow him as deep as I can.

His hips buck up, and he shifts again, nothing but his ass and shoulder blades touching the leather, allowing his length to grow longer.

I gag on him, but I don't stop, taking him deep and sucking on his head so hard, I'm surprised it doesn't hurt him, before sliding back down. My hand is soaked with spit, his cock rock hard, the large vein along the shaft thumping against my cheeks.

Suddenly, the tires screech, and I tense, my head snapping up to look out the window, my hand flying out to catch the dash, but in the next blink, Crew's crashing his mouth with mine.

He's unbuckled, and I'm on his lap, his hands roughly tearing at my shorts until a sharp rip fills the cab.

I gasp into his mouth as his fingers thrust inside me without warning.

He growls. "I fucking knew it." He kisses my cheek, jaw, neck. "So fucking wet for me." He smacks my ass. "Lift, Sweets, you're about to drop down on my cock. I need inside you."

I moan, doing as he said while also throwing my head back, inviting him to suck on my chest.

He doesn't disappoint, yanking my dress down and pulling my nipple into his mouth for a hard sucking.

I whimper, and then he's hard at my entrance, so I don't hesitate. I drop down, gasping and clutching his shoulders tightly when he fills me in an entirely different way.

Slicker.

Deeper.

More curved.

"God, *damn*," he moans. "I'm in your fucking stomach."

I nod, hips rocking, and Crew encourages me, his hands on my hips, swaying me back and forth.

"Yeah, baby, like that." He buries his head in my neck, licking along my candy necklace and taking a bite out of it. "So. Fucking. Sweet."

My body is overcome by this new intrusion. He wasn't playing. I swear I can feel him in my stomach. Every inch of me is stretched, and it's glorious.

My hands latch on to his shoulders, my hips swinging in deep grinding motions.

"This is—" I gasp, grinding harder, faster, my deep breath stuck in my throat. "Good, it's—"

"Good. You take me so good, baby." His last word is a deep growl.

My eyes clamp shut, my pussy squeezing him.

This position is insane. I can feel everything. Everywhere, and oh my god, the clit stimulation with the stretch of him inside me?

So. Fucking. Good.

I shatter, shaking like never before, muscles aching they're so tight as I come over his cock.

"Mmm," he moans. "This pussy was made for me."

Crew licks up my neck until he's taking my lips again as he thrusts in deep. I cry out, the waves crashing through me doubling in intensity.

I squeeze my thighs tightly over his, the feeling too much, but he doesn't relent, his hips dive up, his palms pressing me down, and then he's falling over me, burying his face in my hair, fists tangled in it as he jerks, his cock twitching inside me.

Several minutes go by, my fingers combing up and down his spine, dead weight in his lap.

And then he laughs, lifts his head, and kisses the top of my nose, his forehead falling to mine.

"You're mine. I hope you realize that."

"What does that mean, exactly?" I test the waters, running my hands up his chest.

"It means if you try and leave me, I'll bring you right back, cuff you to my bed and keep you there."

"That sounds like a good time. Maybe I should test it."

Crew nips at me, and I grin, folding my hands around his neck and tugging him to me.

"I hope you know," I whisper. "That's exactly what I want. To be yours."

His hands skim down my back, his kiss slow this time around, and a few moments later, his hips begin to press up again, my own answering with a lulling rock.

We fuck each other slow, steady, jumping when there's a harsh knock on the window.

Both our heads snap over to find two farmers, somehow missing the sound of their tractor as it stopped beside us.

"Oh my god." I drop my head into his neck.

Crew only chuckles, making sure my dress is covering all it needs to be as he rolls the window down, I didn't even realize he had rolled up.

"There's a crew of fifty dudes with tractors out here shaking lime trees, and this is where they're headed next, so you might wanna get moving."

My head snaps up, and I look to the men, a smile spreading across my face. "Did you say limes?"

Crew laughs loudly, the men blush, and I'm ready to talk shop . . . after I free my vagina of the half-cocked cock.

Chapter 31
Crew

As we pull up to the bar, Drew, Paula, and her cousin, Kenli, my official new hire, are all waiting outside the door.

Drew's mouth drops open, and I grin, climbing out right as he steps up.

"Bro, what the fuck?" He reaches out to touch the paint, but I slap his hand away.

"Remember this?" Davis asks with a smile, climbing out my door rather than her own.

I tug her to me, wrapping my arms over her shoulders from behind and posting my chin on her head.

"Oh, fuck yeah, I—" he cuts off when he looks to us. "Do." He lifts a brow my way.

"We just picked it up today." Davis steps away, admiring the shine against the beating sun. "It was its first time on the road in thirty years."

"Can I drive it?" my brother asks.

"Fuck no."

"Sure."

She and I say at the same time, looking at each other.

"Fuck no," I repeat, and she shrugs, looking away, but not before I catch the smile she tries to hide.

"Dude, what's with all this?" Paula frowns at the bed of the truck. "We got a shipment two days ago."

"These"—Davis opens the tailgate, smiling at the bed *full* of freshly picked limes—"were free."

"What?!" Paula gapes, looking to me. "How?"

"Davis embarrassed them."

Her mouth drops open, cheeks growing crimson. "I did . . . not."

"Baby, you so did, and you know it."

In my peripheral, I catch both Paula and Drew's heads snapping my way, and I have to keep myself from puffing my damn chest out like an egotistical motherfucker, especially when Davis shares a secret smirk with only me.

Truth, I want everyone to know she's mine, an irrational, twisted part of me needing my brother to know she can't and won't ever be his, even when I know their relationship is no more than friendly teasing.

Drew starts the unloading, lifting a box and reaching in for a second while balancing the first on his thigh.

"Here, let me." I take the second, setting it on top.

My brother frowns, his lips pinched to keep from grinning. "You want to help with the shit you asked all of us to be here an hour early to carry in?"

I shrug, stacking two for myself. "Why not? We'll be done quicker."

"Uh-huh." He side-eyes me, and I follow him into the bar. "Someone's finally getting his d—"

I slap him upside the head, and he laughs, disappearing inside the bar.

My brother and I might not be as close as we were when we were little, me moving in with the family next door and leaving him behind will do that, even if it was his choice to stay, but the wall between us isn't so solid now that he's here with me. He came home for me, after all. When I needed someone to have my back, he came.

I owe him for that.

I'll have to sneak away to talk to him today when Davis isn't paying attention.

Paula grunts, shifting the boxes to the edge of the bed, and I turn back to the task at hand.

"Let's prep a box of these for tonight. Test 'em out, and

then tomorrow, we'll go back to what we have, so we don't end up with rotten shit we're forced to toss," I tell her.

"Sounds good, boss." Paula passes a box to Kenli, and they too head inside.

I call my girl to me with nothing but a look, and just like that, she's standing before me.

"You up for some fun?"

She sways playfully, her dress brushing along the thighs of my jeans and testing my patience. "What did you have in mind?"

"Oh, it's good. Your kind of foreplay."

Her tongue pokes between her teeth as she smiles. "Is there candy involved?"

"There will be as quick as I can get DoorDash here . . ."

She waves a hand. "Meh, my purse is stacked with sour gummies and my last pack of Red Hots."

"Oh no." I tug her to me. "Guess we gotta take a trip back to the candy store."

"*Such* an inconvenience." She plays along, her arms looping around my waist.

"I'm about to give you something you've been dying for, baby." I wiggle my brows. "Head up to my office."

Her eyes light up. "No . . ."

"Oh, yeah. Books are all yours."

"Archives and dates and numbers, oh my." She grins, already tearing away.

I hold her back a second longer, my knuckles pressing at her chin.

"Don't overwhelm yourself and don't stress over it," I tell her. "It's a shit show I've been trying to work through for a year now."

Davis pushes up on her toes, so I bend, giving her my lips, but she only speaks against mine.

"Challenge accepted."

And then the girl straight skips into the place, leaving me here to do nothing but stare after her, my brother reappearing as she disappears.

"Could be a permanent thing, you know," he says, tipping his head toward the door when I frown. "Her being here, helping with shit . . . if you'd buck up and tell her you bought the fucking place already."

My eyes slide to the entryway. "When I'm ready, I will."

"Dude, you're living with her, doing a fuckton more than that now, apparently, and I've seen nothing from her to make me think she ain't cool with you working here. Fuck's the difference?"

The difference is huge, and this asshole knows it. Right now, I work as a manager at a bar, a job she might assume is temporary and can get behind. But tell her I own the place? I don't know about that.

Davis might have forced herself to *trust* herself by finding a healthy relationship with alcohol, but for it to be part of the foundation her future would be built on with me as a partner and this place my livelihood and focus?

Not so sure she would want that. Not sure it would be right to ask her to, knowing there would forever be a fear in the back of her mind, a worry she might lose me, herself, or someone else to the shit she lost her brother to. She must want a family one day, right?

What woman wants to raise her kids around a bar?

"Crew."

I turn toward my brother, my eyes following him as he steps up to grab the last two boxes of limes.

"You worked your ass off to make something happen for yourself." He holds my gaze. "Take a second to be proud of yourself, instead of kicking your own ass over the things you can't or should do."

Pressure falls on my chest, and I eye my brother.

How he turned out as decent as he did, I don't know. He doesn't talk about the years he was alone with our fucked-up parents—a choice I think he made simply because he was only ten when the Franco's asked for legal guardianship over me. That, or my dad got in his head when I wasn't around, which is very fucking likely. He doesn't want to talk about it though, and I've tried a time or two.

I don't know the shit he saw or what he went through, but I know it was no cakewalk. The day he turned seventeen, he had one foot out the door, waiting for eighteen to get there, but just before his birthday, our dad went to prison—finally—and my mom convinced him to stay. He lasted a while before shit went south yet again.

He took off, lived in solitude in Yosemite before I called him and begged him to come here.

I nod, and he squeezes my shoulder before lifting the last box.

"Hold up, I have to tell you something."

Drew looks back with a frown, but one glance in my direction, his features smooth and then he's standing front and center. "Talk to me."

Crossing my arms, I lean against the door, staring at Davis. She's sitting on the floor, the cot folded up, desk pushed to the side, and papers strewn out all around her in a chaotic mess that likely makes perfect sense to her. Her staple candy necklace is still strung around her neck, but now stretched across her jaw and face, allowing a few tiny pieces to settle along her lips, just enough to give her a hint of sweetness with each move of her mouth.

It takes her a second, but she finally looks up, the stretchy choker rolling down her chin and leaving a streak of white. She frowns. "What time is it?"

"A little after four."

Her eyes widen. "We were supposed to be at Layla's."

"I know."

She opens her mouth, but I lift my hand.

"This can wait. Come on. Let's go eat."

"But—"

"A pregnant woman spent the last hour getting a meal ready for you, you really want to ditch her for this?"

"If by 'this,' you mean increasing this place's ROI by no less than eleven percent and counting, yes, yes, I would."

"Wait, for real?" My ears perk up.

Increase the return over investment?

I step into the room. "How?"

Davis is damn near giddy to nerd out for me, jumping up with a notebook in her hand. "I'll tell you all about it on the drive."

And she does, breaking down things I never even thought to think of, shit that should be obvious but wasn't. At all.

The way she explains things, though, makes it easy to understand.

"That's crazy," I say, killing the engine in front of the house. "I didn't even realize I was paying that tax."

"That's because it's presented as a 'flat fee,' which it is, but when you don't see the tax amount, your brain automatically assumes you're getting a deal, when in reality—"

"They're charging at a higher percentage and hiding that under the simple price mark."

"Exactly." She grins. "And all this, Crew, is only based on changes that are right there to be seen, and solely on the liquor side. Wait until I look at the beer and draft drinks. Plus, we still don't know what can be saved using local farmers."

"Damn." A long exhale leaves me. Maybe I can pay down the loan on this place sooner than I thought.

"I haven't even told you the best part." She pushes her door open, meeting me by the hood. "The ROI increase is based on last year's sales alone, and with one quick peek at this quarter's? I think that number will be even higher. The bar has really picked up compared to a year ago."

Pride blooms in my chest, but I lick my lips to keep from grinning.

I had thought we were bringing in more revenue, but using more product means ordering more, so I guess my mind focuses on the checks I cut versus what came in to make the move necessary.

"If you're up for it, there are a lot of other ways to add a little more into the registers."

We step into Willie's living room. "Like?"

"Like charging a small fee at the door when you have a live band?" My face must give away my unease, because she rushes to say. "You're the only bar in town with live music, Crew. That's big. Even if you keep it low, like three bucks a pop, it would, at the least, cover the band's pay for the night, if not more."

"I don't know. I don't think our customers would like that."

"So include a drink ticket, and bump entry to five." She shrugs. "There's a seventy-six percent chance that every person who steps into the door will purchase a second drink, and fifty-three percent of those will go for a third. You could keep it to draft beer only or choice of bottom-shelf white or gold."

"Damn, she's good." Layla walks up grinning. "That's a solid idea."

"Yeah." I stare at Davis, my chest growing tight, images of a future flashing through my mind. "It is."

Davis smiles and spins, pointing at Layla. "Speaking of ideas, we went to the farmers' market today."

I look between the girls, my eyes narrowing as I follow behind.

"Davis . . ."

"Hear me out. You know those killer stuffed mushrooms you make? I was talking to this woman—"

"Leave them."

I jerk to a stop, glaring at my best friend leaning over the kitchen counter. I swiftly look back, and Davis already has Layla on the back patio, and Layla's thrusting a parfait into her empty hands.

"What was that about?"

Willie smirks, sipping slow as fuck from his beer like an asshole, before popping one and passing it to me. "Try this."

Sighing, I step toward him, taking a small sip from the bottle. My eyes widen, and I look at the glass, swirling it around. "Damn, that's good shit, Wil."

"Your girl gave me the idea."

My brows jump.

"Little less yeast, longer brew time and a couple scoops of caramel malt. That shit's gonna hit. I can feel it."

"Bro, I think you're right."

Willie nods, pulling a tray of barbecued chicken from the oven and dropping it in front of me.

I grab it while he loads his hands with watermelon and potato salad then follow him onto the patio.

Layla laughs, catching my attention, and I look as Davis's hands flail all around as she explains whatever the hell it is she's talking about.

"She gave Layla an idea, said use the slab of concrete on the side of the brew house as an outdoor seating spot, serve street food and bring in beach walkers. Use Layla's recipes and serve my beers with 'em. Offered to be a part of it, excited to see my beer do well and confident in mine and Layla's ability to make it work . . . according to my wife."

My pulse jumps, and my head slowly turns toward him, eyes waiting 'til the last second to leave the stunning woman in yellow.

I meet Willie's gaze, and he smiles, but it's softer this time, his hand on my shoulder firm and reassuring.

He slips by, clapping his hands and saying something to the women, but my feet stay planted where they are, my mind whirling.

She's settled right into my world, carving out a place of her own within it, like I hoped she one day would. Doing good things for my friends as she is me, helping find and navigate avenues they never knew they had. Because she's kind and good, accepting and understanding.

Because she's Davis.

"I'd give you anything you wanted."

"Why?"

"Because you're you, and I'm me."

It really is that simple for us, isn't it?

Davis smiles from across the pool, waving me over.

I don't make her wait, but I sure as fuck cut dinner short. The second she swallows her last bite, I catch her by the wrist, hauling her from the seat.

"What the hell? I thought you didn't have to be at the bar 'til seven?" Willie pouts from where we left them at the patio table, plate lifted high in one hand, fork in the other.

"I don't, but we've got homework."

Davis and Willie both frown.

"Homework?" She cocks her head, entwining her fingers with mine.

"Math homework." I speak her language, tugging her along.

"Math?" She scowls, confused. "Should we go back to the bar and grab the invoices?"

"Nope."

"You sure?"

"Yep." I yank her into the house, pushing her against the wall, and take her lips with mine while blindly unlocking the front door, and then we're at the truck, climbing inside. "It's a real simple equation."

"Simple equation . . ."

"Oh yeah." I tug her lower lip into my mouth. "Seventy minus one, baby."

Davis throws her head back with a laugh.

And just like that, the worries of the day are drowned out by the pure perfection that is Davis fucking Franco.

Chapter 32
Davis

If there's one thing I've learned in the last several days, it's that Crew Taylor is completely insatiable . . . and a little more paranoid than I remember.

His need to watch over me, be near me, be *inside* me is marvelously exhausting, yet somehow, I still wake in the middle of the night unable to keep my hands to myself, but I should have expected as much, considering how long I've waited for this.

Truth be told, I had given up on a chance to go from him and me to "us," especially once we made that stupid deal. I thought for sure his rejection confirmed I was out of my league, and in many ways, I am. Crew's this tall, strong, walking enigma—tanned and toned and primed in inky art, where I'm so standard across the board, I can hardly find pants or shoes I want, my size so . . . average. So common.

I mean, I'm not even a real brunette, but a basic and boring blonde, no pretty waves or deep ringlets to speak of.

But what the hell do I care if Crew chooses to have me on his arm, under his body?

It never really bothered me to be the unspectacular girl next door in comparison to others, but I would be lying if I said I didn't want to be prettier or sexier or any other ideal I assumed Crew preferred over what I was. Is that a little pitiful? Maybe, but it's honest. What young girl doesn't look in the mirror at least once, wishing to magically morph into exactly what the boy she likes would like? Not many, I'd bet.

To know Crew wants me as I am settles me in a way I can't explain, in a way I didn't know I needed. His tentative, one might call *obsessive*, ways make it that much harder to be away from him. It sucked worse than I thought it would to go back to work this week, but that's life.

If only I could figure out what the hell to do with mine. According to my parents, I'm suddenly supposed to know exactly where to go from here.

What a load of crap.

So I graduated college with a degree in both mathematics and microbiology, cool. And?

I'm as clueless now as I was when I enrolled.

I wonder if Xavier feels the same? I think as I spot him pulling up outside—Crew insisted I have an escort to the bar, rather than driving myself there. I guess he wants me to ride home with him after closing.

Clocking out, I say bye to the girls and meet X at his truck.

"What's up, girl?"

"Hey." I smile, spotting not one but *two* 7-Eleven cups in the holders.

I meet his gaze with pleading eyes, and he laughs.

"Yes, girl, one's for you, and while I would love to take credit, I won't." He smirks. "This time."

Chuckling, I go right for it, settling against the seat with a sigh as he pulls onto the road. I decompress a moment before I turn to X.

"What do you want to do when you graduate?"

His head snaps toward mine at the unexpected question before focusing on the road again.

"I mean, I've still got a year of school left, and while I'm a badass on the baseball field." The man literally pauses to grin my way and I shove his shoulder. "I have no unrealistic notion of going further, and while I can't say if someone came to me today and offered me a spot on a roster, that I wouldn't accept it, but . . ."

"But?"

"But I'm simple folk." He laughs at himself. "I kind of want to rise with the sun and be home before dark. Maybe have some kind of farm, but nothing fancy. Shit, I can manage with a buddy or two."

"Aw, that's so cute."

"Aye, Mommy, don't say that." He shakes his head with amusement. "Sounds like a good life though, don't it?"

"Yeah, it does." I take another long, slow drink, letting the cold linger on my tongue until my teeth grow sensitive. "So, what are you majoring in, then?"

"Bullshit that keeps my grades decent enough to play. My coach helped me figure it out, but turns out, he's a prick who only cares about himself, fucked my buddy, Tobias, over pretty good, so I should probably go see a counselor."

I almost spit out my Slurpee, laughing at him. "Ah, fuck it."

Xavier's grin widens, and he too grabs his ICEE, but he's not skilled like me, and not ten seconds later, he's gripping his head with a grunt.

Boys, such crybabies.

"All right, I had strict instructions to deliver you to the back door, however, that tow truck looks like he's got his work cut out for him."

I look to find the truck attempting to wedge between two buildings, a broken-down van, hidden in the dark. "Oh, that looks sketch."

"Girl, it's eleven p.m., not much isn't." He shrugs, reversing and pulling around the side. "Front entrance, it is. I'll just be sure to walk you in."

"Good save," I tease.

Climbing from the truck, I wait in front of it for Xavier to lock up, and a car comes down the street. The black El Camino rolls slowly by, and a small frown builds along my brow when a flash of silvery-black hair catches my eye.

"Hey, X . . ."

The car speeds off, burning out before shredding from the parking lot.

"Whoa, that thing's got some power." Xavier steps up, concern drawing his brows in when he spots me. "You good?"

"Yeah. Let's go inside."

Just as we make it through the door, I spot Crew disappearing around the corner, so I stay beside X until we're close, and then break off, heading up to the office.

My feet lock in place, eyes bulging as I reach the room's threshold.

It's free of Crew, so I have no clue where he went, but right now, I don't even care.

This is the space I was in not three days ago; yet it looks nothing like the stuffy, broke down place it did before. Not in the slightest.

A sudden tsunami whirls in my stomach, my hand shooting out to catch the frame of the door, my knees literally threatening to grow too weak to hold my body up. My blood runs warm, yet a shiver runs down my spine.

The dusty cream walls have been painted a soft gray, the window free of the ancient, split blinds, and in their place, dark-blue curtains, sheer enough to allow the sun in before dark.

The rickety bookshelf is nowhere to be found, a larger one in its place, the color a perfect match to the curtains, everything placed exactly as I had it on the other—a little messy, a lot left to do, but on its way to being organized.

The cot in the corner is still there, but it sits nearly twice as high, a fluffy gray comforter draped over it and hiding the bottom, blue pillows perched against the wall to make it look like a cozy couch or perfect reading nook.

There's a whiteboard on the wall above it, a giant crisscross square in the center, ready and waiting for a game of tic-tac-toe.

My eyes grow cloudy, my fingers shaking as they rise to press at my lips.

This is . . .

"You were supposed to wait so I could see your face when you walked in."

Crew's gravelly tone wraps around me from behind, and my chest inflates with a deep inhale.

"I'm pretty sure my face has yet to leave the state of *holy shiznit, he did not, he so did, this is . . . yeah.*"

Crew laughs loudly and comes around to step in front of me because I can't seem to make my feet shift or head turn to face him.

He calls my eyes to his, bending and getting into my direct line of sight.

My lips press firmly together to keep from crying like a baby, but I don't think I'm doing a good job. Crew's face transforms, the amusement fading into something deeper, softer, and I want to bottle the expression and keep it forever. The vulnerability, dipped and wrapped in pride, is a good look on him.

"Baby, you like it?" His voice is so low, my chest aches.

"Are you joking?" I whisper.

Crew chuckles, reaching for me, but I'm frozen, my eyes snapping to the left corner, where a three-tier rolling cart sits, stacked to the nines with all the things my nerdy heart loves—paper, pens, folders, labels, sticky notes, and on top . . . snacks.

His hand finds my cheek, tucking my hair behind my ear as he eases my eyes to his. "Is it too much?"

"Is that another joke?"

Crew smirks, but his gaze is a little tense, so I press my hands to his chest, and his muscles settle beneath my touch.

"You did this for me?" My voice cracks. "Changed your office, got all this . . . for me?"

His nod is slow, eyes pinned to mine.

"But . . . why?"

"Isn't it obvious, Sweets?"

I shake my head, and his soft laughter wafts over my skin, causing my eyes to close for a few brief moments.

"Baby, I want you to have a comfortable place to be when you come here, and on the chance you want to keep working your way through my mess, I wanted to do what I could to make that easier on you."

My lids open and his lips curve to one side.

"I'm shit at all the things you're good at, but I want to be good at giving you all the things you need."

"I just need you."

"So you don't want the bag of Cheetos over there?"

"Hey now, don't get crazy."

Crew skims his tongue over his lower lip, grinning, and I wrap my arms around his neck, pulling him down for a long, slow kiss. His forehead falls to mine once he breaks away.

"Being what you need is all I want, Sweets, so to hear you say that has me all twisted."

"How about we twist up the sheets over there?"

Crew smirks. "Love to, baby, but I've got a twenty-first birthday party in the reserved section downstairs who booked for fifteen people and showed with twenty-five. Shit's getting wild. I've got to get back down there before Drew beats someone."

Laughing, I pull back, but Crew hesitates.

"What?"

"I don't want you to feel like you have to touch any of that shit." He jerks his head to the bookshelf. "That's not why I like you here, and that's not why I did this. My hours are fucked up and unfair, so I wanted you to have a spot to sleep on the nights you come to me."

"Thank you, but this is good for me. I'm bored at home. Without school, I need to keep my mind moving or I'll go crazy, but the way this room was, was okay with me. I didn't need any of this, Crew, but the fact that you did all this just for me . . . I kind of feel the need to bow to a king right now."

"Wait until you open the drawers."

Excitement blooms, my grin stretching.

Crew steps closer, pressing another quick kiss to my lips, smacks my ass and heads out the door. "Love you, Sweets." My insides turn to mush and I nod. "Be back up to check on you in a bit."

He walks out, and I rush right over to the desk, smiling down at the drawers.

I tug the first drawer open, laughing at the perfect rows of Pixy Stix, then pull open the second to find it full of mini boxes of Red Hots and Lemonheads.

Last, I pull the large bottom drawer out, practically stomping my feet at the dozens of individually wrapped candy necklaces.

A deep, happy sigh leaves me, and I shake my head. "I fucking love this man."

"Oh, yeah?" Layla's voice has me whipping around. She smiles at the room, laughing as she meets my gaze. "He should so get his dick sucked tonight."

A laugh bursts from me, and she smiles wider, her hands folding over her growing bump.

"I'm headed home. I just wanted to say bye, and . . . thanks."

"For?"

She shrugs coyly, her eyes flicking to the ceiling. "I might have made an appointment with a friend to talk loans and permits."

"What?!" I gape, running to her. "Oh my god, that's amazing! But don't pay a fee. I can help with the permits part, or the filing, anyway, and figuring out what kind you would need. You'd just have to pay the filing fees, assuming there are some."

"Davis, no. I don't want to take advantage."

"What? No. Oh my god, Layla, my mind is so bored. You have no idea how much I used to study. I basically need this." I laugh.

She chuckles and then says, "What if I hired you?"

My face falls. "What?"

"I pay you what I planned to pay them. It's fair."

"But I want to help, not take."

"You are helping, Davis. Don't make me feel like a snaky broke bitch and take my money or I'll find someone else."

Okay, I understand where she's coming from, but. "Okay, I get it. What if . . . what if we make a deal?"

"What is with you and deals?" she teases but adds, "I'm listening."

"I help you get everything in motion, and you can give me whatever you were going to pay them when we celebrate *after* a successful grand opening."

Layla purses her lips, eyes narrowing, but then her smile spreads wide, and she flails her hands up. "Holy shit, I'm opening a business!"

We squeal, jumping up and down like girls will do.

Willie comes around the corner just then, stealing his wife from me with a quick tug of her top. "What did I walk into?"

"None of your business." Layla winks my way.

"That means she'll tell me *after* I spread—"

"Okay, time to go!" She waves, leading her man out the door.

I drop back onto the cot turned fluffy dream nook and fold my hands beneath my head with a smile.

God, my life.

A few weeks ago, I was alone, mentally and physically, and now?

I have friends, a boyfriend, and something real to look forward to.

Something more.

I may not know where I'll be professionally a year from now, but I hope to hell, on nights like this one, I'll be lucky enough to be in this exact spot . . . waiting for my man to take me home.

Chapter 33
Davis

I'm not sure what time it is when I wake to the warmth of Crew's lips trailing over my skin, but I don't open my eyes until he tells me to, finding him bent beside the bed with a grin. His room was the one of choice last night. By some miracle, we were able to sneak out of the bar by three this morning, and we fully intend to take advantage of his one day off this week, the same one I, somehow, scored off as well.

"Time to get up, Sweets. Your bath's getting cold."

I quirk a brow, my face still smashed against the pillow. "Bath, you say?"

"Oh, yeah. All the bubbles and shit, too."

I fight a smile. "I didn't have any bubble bath stuff."

"Shampoo, Sweets. Even I know that."

Chuckling, I push up, stretching my arms over my head.

"Shouldn't you be sleeping still?" I follow him into the bathroom, smiling when he undresses me.

Crew smacks my ass hard enough for it to sting, and I frown playfully at him. "Don't worry about me. Get in the water. Relax. I'll be back in a minute."

"You're not getting in with me?"

"Don't tempt me." His gaze tracks my skin inch by inch as it disappears beneath the water.

Only when he's satisfied I'm settled does he walk out.

Dropping back, I let out a small sigh, weaving my open palms through the water.

I don't even have words for how incredibly shocking my new world is.

When the boys left home, I didn't know what to do with myself, but I held on to the fact that I'd see them every break and have them home all summer long. It lasted the first couple years, but then Crew kissed me and never came back.

That's when I turned my thoughts of following them here into an actual plan, one my parents were thrilled about, until they realized, Memphis or not, this was still where I wanted to be. Deep down, I think they knew what Crew was to me, but like me, I doubt they ever imagined we would be more, and then I got here, Crew not but a few blocks away at the time, yet somehow, he felt farther than before, until eventually, there was no denying he was.

The distance between us was Grand Canyon wide, and I saw no chance of crossing it, not when he grew so angry at the world for reasons I never knew.

When I called him to try and make my deal, I had secretly hoped it would take a while to get to the endgame, allowing me time with him, but when he denied me, yet again, I was a mess of emotions. Sad he couldn't seem to stomach the thought of touching me, but thrilled he was willing to find time to be around me, even if it was just to help me find another man—something I now know he never had any intention of doing.

He said he wanted to put a pause on my rush to rid myself of my virginity, and he'd figure out what to do about it later, but his possessiveness, his inability to hide how he hated other men anywhere near me, was too potent for the man he grew into.

He was a boy before who fought an onslaught of temptation, as all boys must at some point, but Crew was no longer a boy when I came to him, and while some learn patience with age, he was not one of them. My man has little self-control when it comes to me, and I swear I could choke on the flutters knowing so gives me.

My man.

What a wild fact.

What a wild ride this has been. So fast, so easy, as if we were meant to endure the distance between us, so we could end up right here, right now.

Each of us stronger and ready for what the world offers with age, because really, what could seventeen-year-old me do for twenty-one-year-old him?

The bathroom door creaks open, and Crew walks in, a tray of deliciousness in his hands.

"What did you do?" I eye him suspiciously, stretching my neck as he bends. "Pancakes?" I squeal.

"With strawberries and whipped cream."

I sit up, opening my mouth instantly, and Crew laughs, sliding a forkful past my lips. Moaning around the fork, I close my eyes a brief moment. "So good."

Crew grins, seemingly proud of himself, and I reach out, skating my wet fingertips over the sides of his freshly cut hair.

"You know you don't have to do all this kind of stuff for me." When creases form along his forehead, I lift a single shoulder in a small shrug. "The office at the bar, the fresh stack of my favorite frozen pizzas in the freezer, all this, this morning."

He scowls down at me. "Let me spoil you."

A soft chuckle leaves me, and I shift in the water, leaning my arms on the edge of the tub, and accept another bite. Swallowing, I add, "I just want you to know you don't have to."

"I avoided you for years because I was afraid of what I might do, but I'm pretty sure it would have looked a lot like the night I dragged you from the bar. You tossed over my shoulder, me going fucking crazy with your pussy so close to my face, I was tempted to take it right then. Now that I can, now that you're mine, I want to do all the things I didn't get to think of because I was too busy trying *not* to claim you for myself." He dips close, glaring. "So let me."

My skin heats, an entirely different kind of excitement flittering through me, but amusement is trickled in with it. "You're cute when you go caveman."

"I want to fuck you like a caveman, so hurry up and eat, so I can."

I open my mouth, and he chuckles, obliging me with a mouthful.

We chat about the data I've found in all the old files thus far, and I share with him the next step in my and Layla's plan to get the ball rolling on her and Willie's new adventure—we're supposed to go to their house tomorrow afternoon. He also tells me how his crew is happy with the produce they've been sampling each night from the three merchants we narrowed our search down to.

We make plans to take a trip to the cabins my parents used to take us to before summer is over, and I convince him that the Chevy needs to be driven at least twice a week to keep the engine healthy, which he literally knows is a load of crap, but he relents easy enough, eager to drive it, but unwilling to admit as much, considering I pimped him out and used it as payment.

In time, I tell myself with a grin.

It's not long after that the plate is wiped clean, Crew sharing the sweet, both literally and figuratively, meal with me, but when I climb out, stepping into my room, he doesn't allow me to open my dresser drawer, but slides up behind me, cupping my bare breasts in his large, calloused hands.

My head falls back onto his shoulder, and he kisses my temple.

"Is it playtime now?"

His lips curve against their place on my skin. "It is. And later, I want to take you to dinner."

"Mm, that sounds nice."

He palms me a little rougher, spreading his fingers wider, so he can wedge my nipples between his knuckles for a long, tight squeeze. "Is there anything new you want to try?"

"Yes."

Crew freezes, slowly shifting his upper body until his gaze can possess mine. "That was quick," he accuses, eyes narrowing. "You've thought of something you want to do and held it back?"

"I wasn't sure—"

"No," he cuts me off with his sharp word and the shake of his head. "Consider me your guinea pig, test dummy, personal fucking blow-up doll. Robot, even. You want, you don't wait, don't hesitate, don't ask. You take, and believe I'll be ready to give."

Heat whirls in my core, and I nod.

My submission is all he wanted, as the grin that follows is far too mischievous. He jerks forward, nudging my legs open in the same motion, and I'm forced to lean, catching myself with my palms on the top of my dresser.

His hand is between my legs from behind in an instant, his fingers teasing at my opening. "What is this . . . naughty thought my baby had, hmm?"

I try to push back into him, but he holds me steady, refusing my body with his torturous curiosity, but I think I'll give him something better than the control he lives for.

"Sorry, but I heard you loud and clear."

My voice is raspy with need, my nipples sharp with desire, my body humming with anticipation. My muscles relax, and like I knew he would, he presses softly against me, waiting for the wetness to flood between my legs, as he knows it will, but I spin before he can, nudging him in the chest.

"I'm afraid this is my show now."

Crew's pupils double in size, his teeth sinking into his lower lip as I guide him backward. "Baby, what are you after?"

"Does it matter?"

"Not a fucking *bit,*" he groans, ready for what comes next when he has no idea what it is.

His knees meet the mattress, and he drops down, his hands coming up to grip my waist, his head quickly dipping to kiss my stomach.

Sighing blissfully, I run my hands through his hair, my fingers tangling into the thick waves on top before nudging him until he's flat, and he takes my cue, sliding back on the bed. Olive gaze unblinking, he tracks me on my way to him, glued to me as I climb up, my knees pressed to either side of him. I then crab walk my way past his hips.

The hint of embarrassment I expected to creep in doesn't come, and while my chest does flush, there's something empowering about the way Crew's looking up at me, perched on the pillow at the head of the bed.

One knee at a time, I climb higher and higher, Crew's chest rumbling with realization as my bare ass slides along his skin until I'm straddling his shoulders, my sex inches from his chin.

His mouth must water as he swallows good and hard, his jaw flexing with anticipation. "Baby, you about to ride my face?"

"Don't make me shy," I whisper, yelping when Crew goes Crew and demands a little control, grabbing me around the ass and hauling me the last few inches, my clit now pressed to his warm lips.

I suck in a sharp breath, my hands latching on to the headboard behind him, and his smirk is half-hidden beneath my body, waiting for me to do the work. He doesn't have to wait long.

Eyes on his, I let my knees slide a little farther on the pillow, and suddenly, my lips are fully pressed to his. I clench instantly, the feeling of my skin to his enough to send a shiver of desire through me, but it's not enough. He knows it, his gaze wicked and playful as he does no more than part his lips, his tongue teasing, rested at the seam of my entrance.

Slowly, I begin to make forward-rolling motions as Crew's eyes take on an entirely new shade. They're low and liquid, dazed in pleasure at the sheer sight of my own.

His hands come up and around my thighs from behind, and he palms my inner legs, massaging them as his tongue takes center stage. *Finally*.

He licks across my clit, swirling around while slowly sucking me into his mouth. I press firmer, grinding down onto him, and he groans, shifting slightly, and then his thumb meets my ass crack. He glides it lower as I lift myself to tease my own body, so he's *barely there*, but in the exact spot I need him most. My muscles grow taut, my body shaking, and I cry out, my head dropping back, hands growing sore from fisting the frame so hard. I try to move, to ease the heat that's threatening to tip me over the edge too soon, but he doesn't let up.

He holds me there, showering my pussy with sloppy, wet kisses and swift, sharp sucks.

I gasp, my lungs starved. "I can't . . . it's too much, I can't—"

"You can. You will," he growls, his words muffled and cut at the end by my hips grinding down onto his face.

His thumb finds my hole then, rubbing small circles and making a new part of me clench. He applies pressure right as his teeth close over my swollen clit, and my body surges forward.

Uncontrollable shakes bound through me, the sounds leaving my mouth downright dirty. Sinfully loud.

Begging.

"Crew, please. I need . . . God, I need . . ."

"Fuck my face, baby. Almost there."

My muscles lock, every inch of me trembling, my eyes clenched shut as I clamp my legs around his head, likely cutting off his hearing, though he doesn't seem to mind.

He growls against me, his thumb pushing a little harder . . . or maybe it's me who's pushing back into it. I freeze, shuddering, and Crew begins to roll my hips for me, not letting up, giving me no time to prepare for the break that's coming.

Suddenly, a hard pinch comes down on my nipple, a quick sting of pressure on my hole at the same time, and I cry out, my neck rolling until my chin is dropped to my chest, my limbs twitching.

I come so hard I can't breathe, desperately seeking air I can't seem to find, until finally, my gasp breaks through the knot in my throat, and I gasp.

"Oh f-fuuuck." I twitch again.

I don't know how long I stay hunched like that, but when my hair is pushed from my face, Crew's warm hand holding it in place, I peel my eyes open and look at him.

His eyes shine brighter than normal, like a candy apple sucker, the caramel kind, so full of hunger and satisfaction.

Appreciation.

Love.

I slide down his chest, and he rolls me so he's half on top, his forehead coming down to mine for a brief moment.

"I want you," he rasps.

My legs fall open with no guidance from me.

A smugness falls over him then. "Not that you seem to mind but let me wash my face first."

Warmth floods my cheeks when he dramatically laps his tongue in a giant circle around his lips.

With a low laugh, I hit his chest, and he grins, slipping off the mattress and into the bathroom, while I pull on the discarded T-shirt and step into the sleep shorts on the floor in case we left windows open in the living room.

"I'm dying of thirst."

"I think I drank all I can drink for now," he shouts back. "I might even burp, I'm so full."

I roll my eyes, though my smile is wide as I pull the fridge open, debating between a Squirt and a Squeezit, but before I can decide, there's a knock on the door. Frowning, I go for the Squirt, popping it open as I close the fridge and make my way to answer.

"Expecting anyone?" I shout, but my voice is likely drowned out by the water, so I unlock the dead bolt, leaving the small security chain Crew recently added in place.

My entire body freezes, my face falling, cool liquid splashing all over my legs as the can slips between my fingers.

"Davis?" Crew calls from somewhere behind me.

I don't answer, frozen in place as I stare at the man on my porch.

Blue eyes lock with mine, and my lip begins to tremble.

"Sweets, who is it?"

My lips part, but it takes me a moment to speak. "It's—"

Crew's chest meets my back, and we speak his name at the same exact moment.

"Memphis."

Chapter 34
Crew

No.

Fuck no.

Hell fucking no.

My chest pounds with heavy thumps, my heart threatening to rip free of my chest, a deep-rooted compulsion taking over, telling me not to hesitate, not to wait, but to beat on the fucker in front of me and send him on his way before a trail of terror follows him to this very doorstep.

He cannot be here; he should not be here.

Not ever, my mind screams before whispering back, *you should have seen this coming.*

He always did have a knack for "wrong place, wrong time," or so he'd claim when problems fell at his feet, and with an ease a real man wouldn't possess, kicked it toward mine.

Forever the victim, yet always the fuck-up.

"Surprise." Memphis smiles, but there's tension in his form, and it transforms into something a lot fucking deeper, the second his gaze finds mine. "You gonna let me in, or is my buddy the only one allowed?"

Real fucking subtle, asshole.

"Oh!" Davis shouts, hustling to step back.

She's shaking, completely overcome with the sight of her brother. Her hand flies to the chain lock, and before I know what I'm doing, mine covers hers, halting the movement.

Her eyes snap up, the shock-infused happiness filling the

room only moments ago morphing into confusion, creating creases along her temple.

Don't let him in here, my conscience screams, *only pain and problems will follow.*

"Crew . . ." She frowns.

There's no fucking way I can get rid of him, not now, not when she's set eyes on the man she's missed. Biting into my cheek, I gently nudge her, so I can close the door fully, as it's the only way to dislodge the lock, my hand briefly skimming over her back, a heavy need to hold on to the invisible tie between us.

Davis yanks it open, wrapping her arms around her brother in a hug so tight, a pang of jealousy heats my skin, as ridiculous as it might seem.

It's not though, not really.

Memphis meets my gaze over his sister's shoulder, his expression fixed with a pinched smile.

"Come in, come in." Davis jerks out of the way, allowing him to step by.

Teeth clenched tight, I track the man's movements as he steps farther into the apartment with an ease he shouldn't feel. This is his sister's house, yes, but she doesn't even know him anymore.

Not that she understands that. In her eyes, he's still her protective big brother.

Davis's smile is wide as she locks the door, but before she can pass me to get to him, I block her path, holding her gaze and searching for something deeper than the bright shine of happiness in her eyes, but that's all I find.

Lifting my hand, I swipe the tears that slipped free, offering her a small smile she returns, even if she does move out of my grasp so fast that my arm stays suspended in the air a moment after her escape.

Memphis is frowning at the two of us when I spin, but he quickly settles his features, focusing on his sister. "Man, look at you. It's been a minute."

It's been four years.

"Yeah," she says anxiously, tucking her hair behind her ear as she moves closer to him. "God, I can't believe you're here." She shakes her head.

"I can't believe he's here."

Memphis looks to me, and Davis follows, her eyes flaring wide, mouth frozen open as if she's not quite sure how to respond.

Of course, that's the first shit he says. Prick.

Standing tall, I move in behind her, wrapping my arm around her waist and tugging her into me. "A lot's happened since you've been gone."

Davis's hand instantly settles over mine, her touch tender as she curls her thumb around mine.

His eyes narrow slightly. "Looks like it."

I hope it fucking does.

Davis laughs nervously, maneuvering herself from my hold, but not before squeezing my arm reassuringly.

The twitch of Memphis's lips as she does has my chest flexing.

"I'm so happy you're here, I . . . where did you come from?" She moves toward him, her hands fiddling in front of her. "Are you okay? I mean, you know, are you—"

"Are you clean?"

Her head snaps my way, eyes widening as if to say *what the hell,* worried the question might trigger him, I'm sure.

"I am, yeah. I'm done with it." He nods, pushing up the sleeves of his shirt, only to pull them back down. "No desire whatsoever. I'm good."

Liar.

Maybe he's been off the bottle a few days, possibly a week or two, though not likely, but the "no desire" part? That's a load of shit. It's not easy, I know this, but denying I hear is worse.

Davis begins crying again, and he nearly stumbles when she goes in for another hug.

I want to tear her away, shield her, but when it comes to Memphis, that's never quite been possible. She's always been blind when it comes to her big brother.

The man is as toxic as the poison he pours into his body.

"That's amazing!" She looks to me. "Crew, did you hear? How awesome." She whips around again. "We should call Mom and Dad and tell them! They'll be so—"

"Whoa, whoa." Memphis's laugh is tight, and he nudges her off him as he steps back. "Not yet, but maybe soon. I want to visit with you first." His eyes snap to mine. "Maybe alone."

"I live here."

Memphis's head yanks back toward me. "What?" He looks to his sister, the same chastising expression he used to give her when she chose the seat in the middle, beside me. I want to slap it off his pale face. "Dad's allowing him to bunk with you?"

"She's not a child anymore, Memphis. She doesn't need anyone's permission for anything."

He scowls, unease clawing at my skin when Davis looks to me, and I steel myself so I don't react when she brushes off the topic, to avoid a possible argument when the asshole only arrived, but my girl doesn't do that.

"Mom and Dad are happy I'm not living alone anymore, but even if they weren't, it wouldn't matter. This is my place, and Crew isn't just a roommate." Davis smiles my way, unable to hold it in. "We're together now."

I want to beat my chest like the caveman she calls me.

I should have known she'd have my back, that she'd be proud to be mine as I am to be hers. I don't know why I doubted her just then.

Because it's always been Memphis's feelings first, the world's second.

Memphis clears his throat, looking away as he nods. "Wow, I uh . . . didn't expect this, but I guess I'm cool with it."

Cool with it.

Cool with it?

Like I fucking care.

Like we need his blessing or approval.

My glare is instant, and I take a step toward him, but Davis spins to him then, smiling, completely missing what I did fucking not.

"Are you, I don't know . . . hungry? We were going to go to dinner later, but we can stay in. I could order something, or we have frozen pizza?"

He nods, looking around. "Yeah, that works. Think I can use the shower while you make us something?"

"Yeah. Yes!" She jolts forward, eager to cater to his every need, just like she used to. "It's the middle door there"—she points—"the towels are in there."

"Cool." He starts down the hall, pausing a few steps in and facing her again. "I don't have anything else to put on." His eyes lift to mine.

Prick.

As expected, she turns to me, a hopeful look in her eyes.

"Yeah." I grind my teeth, my footsteps heavy as I slip inside my room, grabbing a scrubby pair of sweats and a T-shirt I don't care for. I stop in front of him, dropping them into his hands.

"Thanks." He studies me a moment before closing himself in the bathroom.

Davis dashes into the kitchen, yanks the freezer open, and grabs the frozen pizzas. She tears at the box, dumping the frozen things onto a cookie sheet, pulling flour and sugar down as well as if to create a dessert to go with it, her mind running a mile a minute.

I have to talk to her before Memphis is out of the shower.

"Baby—"

"I can't believe this!" she says, scooping a cup full of flour into a pan, laughing seconds later, before setting it all down and gripping the counter.

She hangs her head, and when she looks up, tears shine back at me, but it's her smile that creates the ache in my chest. It's damn near blinding.

I hold my arms open, attempting to lodge the sigh threatening to escape my throat, and like I knew exactly what she needed, she barrels into me, curling into my chest, my arms tight around her.

"He's clean, Crew. And he's here? Like what? I can't believe it."

"Yeah, it's a surprise, Sweets." I kiss her head, bending when she raises hers, and press my lips to hers. "Why don't you go get dressed? I'll take care of this."

"I know you guys aren't on the best of terms, but—"

"Hey," I call her eyes to mine. "Don't worry about me, okay? Go. I got the pizzas."

"K." She settles, a soft exhale leaving her. "I love you."

"Love you, too, baby."

I watch her walk away, dragging my hands down my face, my eyes closing a moment.

Fuck me, my muscles are stiff with unease, the inevitable clusterfuck looming over me like a fucking hurricane.

People can change, I know this. I know alcoholism is a disease that can be overcome, but this is Memphis, and while I'd love to be proven wrong, I know I won't be.

It has to start at the core of the person consumed by it, and I have zero faith he's ready to ride the wicked wave of recovery.

If only Davis would allow herself to consider the possibility. She won't, and it's part of the reason I love her. She's incredibly selfless and somehow holds on to hope when experience should have dimmed the light in her eyes that still shines for him. I don't want or expect her to give up on him, but I don't want her to hurt because of him. Hurt for him, of course, we all have at one point, and she's his sister, how could she not? But *because* of him?

Absolutely fucking not.

No part of me believes his sudden arrival is random. I just have to figure out what it is that brought him here, so I can attempt to prepare for what comes next.

Knowing my old, fucked-up friend, it's nothing good.

How hours go by so fast after Memphis's arrival, I don't know. I'm pretty sure I spent it staring at the side of his head while he kept his focus on his sister, his jerky movements every few minutes letting me know it was no easy task.

Now, it's after midnight, the show Memphis and Davis put on over, but I don't realize this until ending credits make a loud exit, a preview for something else popping onto the screen.

Davis finally allowed herself to close her eyes, her body settled into the left side of the couch, Memphis on the right.

The two talked for hours, mostly about old memories I was around for, and while she tried to pull me into the conversation, I answered as soft and as short as I could, preferring to take the silent chair for the evening.

"She's asleep," Memphis announces.

As if I didn't know.

Wordless, I push to my feet, stopping at the edge of the couch, prepared to scoop her into my arms.

"I can carry—"

"She's mine, Memphis," I tell him plainly, and I don't bother saying more.

One swift move and she's in my arms, my knees bending to gently lower her to the bed, not a minute later.

Hair falls into her face, and I use my knuckles to glide it back, tucking it around her ear.

Davis smiles in her sleep, burying her mouth beneath the covers with a soft sigh, the second I fold them over her.

Back in the kitchen, I ignore the man whose eyes are tracking my every step and grab both sets of car keys from the counter, Davis's purse on the back of the chair, and double-check that the locks are clicked into place.

"I guess I can take the couch," Memphis says as I pass him, almost huffing the words.

"Then my bed would be empty." I stop, locking my gaze with his.

He stares back for a long beat. "Right. You're actually *with* my sister."

I don't acknowledge him but start moving again.

It's not until I'm seconds away from closing myself in the room with my girl that he speaks again.

"Think that's smart?" he quips, a hint of objection in his tone.

My head snaps over my shoulder, glare sharp and instant.

Memphis stands at the end of the hall, glaring right back, so I meet the motherfucker where he's at. Chest to fucking chest, but my eyes are two inches higher.

"In a perfect world, you never would have knocked on this door."

"Oh, I don't doubt it." He smirks. "Too bad she's *really* happy to have me."

I want to wrap my hands around his neck and squeeze until his face is as blue as the circles beneath his eyes, as the bruises he thinks I didn't see on his arm.

"Don't fuck with me, Memphis. Nothing is like it was four years ago when you tucked your tail between your legs and ran. *Nothing*."

He stares, face blank, but eyes searching, and then suddenly, he laughs, tapping my arm with his hand. "I'm playing, Crew, damn. I'm just happy to be here, see her and find you."

Find me . . .

My eyes narrow, but he's oblivious.

"Anyway, I'm gonna hit the sack. I haven't slept in a bed for far too long."

His hand comes up, clasping onto my shoulder for a split second before he steps away.

I stand frozen long after the door clicks in place . . . and just like that, everything else does too.

I watched the sun creep through the patio doors, having tossed and turned all night, but I must have managed to knock out right after because the next thing I know, I'm reaching across the bed, finding nothing but a pillow.

She left me in bed.

Pushing to my feet, I drag my hands down my face and glance at my phone.

My brows jump. Damn. It's almost one.

Not bothering with a shirt, I step out of the room, headed to find my girl, and I must have been anxious, but too tired to realize it, as the second I see her, a heavy exhale pushes past my lips.

She's balanced on the couch, laughing at something Memphis says, and as I round the corner, slipping into full view, his words die in his throat, my girl peeking over her shoulder in the same second.

The irritation threatening to show itself disappears when she hits me with a wide and warm smile, instantly pushing to her feet and padding across the floor to meet me halfway.

"Hey," she whispers, an apology in her tone.

I know why it's there. Do I hate that he was the first person who got to see her smile this morning, fuck yeah, but it's not like she snuck out of bed for a private conversation she wanted to hide from me, and even if she did, I shouldn't be pissed. I would be, but that's the irrational, jealous side of me. The hint of sanity I somehow have when it comes to her manages to understand she needs quiet time with her brother, but I know her. She doesn't want me to feel like I'm being left out or cast aside. She's too sweet like that. Maybe the younger me would feel exactly that, but I'm not a punk kid anymore and Davis is no longer the untouchable girl across the hall.

Yet, you're tripping like a little bitch, too many thoughts and possibilities racing through your mind . . .

Still, she has nothing to apologize for, so I force a smile, wrap her up, and lower my lips to her forehead. "Morning, baby," I whisper.

"Morning." She melts into me, hugging what looks like a cup of cocoa in her hands. "I was going to make breakfast, but we're out of milk, and apparently, everything I have requires it."

"You mean you only wanted pancakes or waffles or French toast?"

Her grin is instant, and it's her who pushes on her toes, bringing her mouth to mine.

Fuck yes.

"That's exactly what I mean." She laughs, her lips meeting mine, on a slow sigh.

"I told her we could go get it right quick," Memphis pipes up.

My muscles tense before I can stop them, and Davis lowers to her feet.

"I didn't want you to wake up, and us be gone." She shrugs one shoulder.

I press my thumb to her chin, sliding it along her jaw. "Thank you for that."

"Man, forget the milk," Memphis breaks in again. "I'm shocked she owns a coffeepot."

"She didn't." Without saying it, I tell him it's mine.

She's mine.

He pretends he didn't hear me.

Reluctantly, I release Davis, whispering for only her to hear, "I'm going to take a shower if you want to join me."

I know when I offer what the answer will be. While she might have kissed me without thought, the need to feel the connection between us as strong for her as it is me, she's not going to be comfortable with her big brother knowing she's naked under the water with me.

Her smile is rueful, but I wink for her sake, and then she turns my blood to lead.

"They didn't allow Memphis to have any of his things in the program he was in, and he came straight here after earning his token. I offered to take him to get a few things today."

My jaw clenches, but I nod, running my fingertips up and down her left arm. Program. Right.

"Okay." I nod again. No big deal. I'll be right there to watch his every fucking move. "What time are we going to Layla's again?"

"I texted her a little bit ago, and she was happy to reschedule to Thursday."

It's already starting.

I run my tongue along the inside of my teeth. "You sure? You were excited to get things started, Layla too, from what I heard."

"No, yeah, I am." She nods swiftly. "And we will, soon, but Layla honestly seemed relieved, something about bandannas and chaps?"

"Oh, shit, that's right." I chuckle, despite the strain in my stomach. "It's her birthday Saturday, and Wil promised her a tribute to Magic Mike."

Davis's eyes bulge, a small blush settling in when I raise a brow.

"What? Every girl has seen that movie."

I log this shit for later. I want to know what it was in that movie that has her turning redder by the second.

"Don't worry about Davis, Crew. I'll watch out for her, and we won't be gone long, but she said you have somewhere to be at four. We definitely won't be back by then."

My eyes slice to Memphis, holding, but before I say something I shouldn't before I lift my woman and carry her to the room to seduce some sense into her, I kiss her forehead and walk straight into the bathroom, closing the door behind me.

Is he fucking joking me? He knew good and well what he was doing, making sure I was out of the picture for the afternoon, and for what? To lie to her some more?

Program.

Yeah, fucking right.

His parents took out a second mortgage on their house to put him through one for the third and final time. He had sworn he was ready to get clean that last time, willingly putting his parents in deeper debt when they'd already pulled thousands from their savings in an attempt to help him over the years. What he didn't tell them that last time was he had no choice, if he didn't go into a program "willingly," as his public defender put it, the courts here in San Diego County planned to throw his sorry ass in jail. One too many drunken arrests will do that.

There's no way his parents would step in again, and by the way he acted when Davis excitedly suggested they call them, I know I'm right—not that he called them to ask.

Not that he called them at all.

When he bailed on the program and didn't show for court, his dad cut him out, unwilling to watch the way his son hurt his mom with every move he made. Or didn't make, depending on how you look at it.

Combine that and the fact that I would bet my life Memphis has not a dollar to his name, there was no fucking program. No reset in his life.

Once a liar, always a liar.

Davis doesn't know this, and I hope she never has to learn, but liquor is not the only problem Memphis has, gambling is too.

The guy gets drunk and spends what he doesn't have, tripling his trouble when bookies come knocking.

He said he "found me."

Wonder who the fuck came looking first?

Davis can't go out alone with him.

Guinness World Records would be impressed with the length of my shower—I'm in my room, angrily tearing clothes from my closet before the stupid fucking song playing in the living room loops into the next.

The door opens behind me, and I whip around, lip curled and ready to tell the motherfucker to slow his roll, to back the fuck up and get the fuck out. He might have my bed for the time being, but that's only because I don't need it. I have hers.

I have her.

But my eyes crash with whiskey-colored ones, and just like that, my mood shifts. Lifts.

She comes to me, her hands planting on my still damp neck and sliding up until her fingers are flitting across the short hairs near my ears.

My fingers follow suit, threading through her hair and tugging until her head is tipped back, giving me control.

My tongue plunges into her mouth, and she kisses me just as hungrily, her breaths growing short and quick, so when she asks without words, pulling her lips free, I give her what she wants, closing my lips around the hollow of her throat, and sucking her skin until I meet her earlobe.

"Baby, you need me?"

"Yes." Her fingers find my towel, tugging, and then it's pooled around our feet. "Can you be fast?"

"Oh, I can be supersonic when I want to be—"

"Ready when you are, sis," Memphis interrupts, a heavy knock on the fucking door.

Motherfucker.

Davis's eyes fly to mine, low and dilated, but I know we're done here. For now.

Sensing my concern, her frown settles in. "What's wrong?"

"I don't like you out alone."

She grins, loving my protectiveness, but she's missing the point. "I'll be with Memphis."

That's the problem, Sweets. He is the problem.

As much as I hate it, this is a good opportunity to figure out what he's up to. I might not be mixed in the life he dragged me into anymore, but many men have stumbled into my bar over the years, some from the years I want to forget, some joining it after I was free of the life they lived. Either way, I have people I can ask without drawing attention.

Sighing, I kiss her lips, squeeze her ass, and make a promise. "Tonight."

"Tonight." She beams.

"Keep your phone charged and in your back pocket, not in your bag."

She smiles, not requiring an explanation. "Yes, caveman."

She walks out the door, and I'm right behind her, my phone on my dash, tracking her location with every mile driven.

Thank fuck she took Willie's offer to park the Chevy in the empty lot behind his brewhouse until her apartment had a second parking space added to the lease. The last thing she needs is the guilt that would follow if Memphis saw it and realized it really was hers now.

Will she tell him about the truck anyway?

Does he even know she graduated college?

Does he even remember the contingency in place in their grandfather's will? That the truck would go to the first Franco grandchild to graduate college.

Sure, her dad sent it to the shop before she was done, let her pay for the parts and labor, if needed, just as he did Memphis. And, like Memphis, if she couldn't keep her end of the deal, he would honor his dad's wishes and take it back.

He knew his daughter would never drop out of college, like his son did and never get kicked out like his foster son did.

Knowing the man, he likely put the title in her name the day he realized Memphis was lost and didn't want to be found.

Davis never did catch on to that. On one hand, I hope she won't have to, but on the other, I wish she'd figure it out now to save herself the hurt of his backslide.

I try to focus on the paperwork in front of me, but it's no use. The words and numbers and bullshit are all running together, and I can't fucking sit here anymore, so I head down to the bar, my mind reeling.

I want to know what time they woke up and what they talked about this morning. Did they have hours to speak about a lot? Did she ask him where he's been and what he's been doing?

Is she asking him now?

Will he lie to her face?

Does he have reason to lie?

Are you being a paranoid prick?

Groaning, I shake my head.

I hate that I have to worry like this. I should be able to trust the man she's loved longer and deeper than anyone else in her life, the one she'd give anything for, always, without question, but I can't. For her sake, and for mine, I fucking can't because I refuse to watch him destroy her.

Closing myself inside the bar, I start on the main floor, putting some music on and get busy. One by one, I remove all the bottles from the shelves along the back wall, cleaning the mirror behind them even though Paula did four nights ago. Digging out the LED strips I bought a while back, but never took the time to put on, I tear them open and roll them out, sticking them to the underside of each shelf to keep the strips hidden and to allow the bright colors to beam against the bottles that'll be beneath it.

Once it's all back in place, I polish the bar top, the tables, and the frame of the stage. I shine the silver of the stools and swap the VIP tables around a bit.

I'm knee-deep in bleach when Drew's shoes come into view. "Damn, brother. Fuck up so soon?"

Huffing, I drop back on my ass, glaring up at him.

He offers me a hand, so I slap my palm in his, letting him tug me up.

Eye to eye, my brother looks deeper, a frown building across his brow. "What happened? Where is she?"

"Memphis is back."

My brother's face falls flat. "Oh fuck."

"Yeah." Oh fuck is right.

Chapter 35
Davis

I couldn't wipe the smile off my face if I tried, but really, why would I, when my life is literally all I ever wanted it to be?

Crew Taylor is mine, and my brother is back, clean, and staying with us.

Us!

Me, Crew, and Memphis under the same roof again after all these years.

There is a little tension, understandably so, since Memphis fell into a world of addiction, and all it entails, while Crew steered clear of that lifestyle, having lived through what his father had become. But Memphis is clean now, and they were best friends once.

Maybe they can find a soft place in the middle again, in time.

I haven't gotten to see Crew much since our time together on Monday, if you don't count Memphis's arrival Tuesday afternoon. With work and my brother being here, I've avoided going to the bar in the evenings, feeling as if home is where I needed to be as much as possible. Plus, I haven't exactly mentioned where Crew works in front of Memphis, not that he's asked, but I'm not sure what to say or how to say it. As far as I know, the mere mention of a bar or anything alcohol related could have a painful triggering effect, forcing him to have to check himself back into another program.

Those are concerns for another day, though.

Tonight, I need some time with Crew. I miss him, miss us, and I know if I'm feeling a little out of it, he must be too.

Luckily, Memphis went to bed early, tired from a long day of online applications, so I wrote a note, just in case he wakes, and am on my way to see Crew.

Layla and I had rescheduled our meeting for Friday, but then she called to cancel, saying she wasn't feeling well, and her cold lasted long after the weekend. I hate that for her, but I can't pretend I wasn't happy she was the one who canceled, so I didn't have to let her down again, and I think that would have happened. Leaving Memphis when I don't absolutely have to makes me uneasy. But she called me today, finally back to her old self, and Willie, the godsend he is, offered to step in at the bar tonight if I needed him to—with events at the bar both Monday and Tuesday this week, Crew is set to work twelve days straight. Clearly, Willie is worried about his friend and aware my time has been spread thin lately, Crew on the lowest receiving end, so I took him up on his offer.

He's meeting me at the bar to help finish off the night, on the condition I don't get out and walk in alone, and like he said he would be, he's waiting at the edge of the parking lot for me to pull in.

We waste no time heading inside, but I pause, frowning at the bouncer who nods our way, counting back cash to the group of girls waiting to be let in.

"What—"

My voice is drowned out by the loud bass of the band, Willie not pausing his steps with mine, but continuing to drag me along, headed straight for the dark-haired man behind the counter.

The moment he spots us in the cluster of customers, the flat expression on Crew's face morphs to confusion, to worry, and then glee.

It's adorably endearing.

He stops mid-pour, passing a bottle of something off to Paula, and all but runs around the side of the bar, his big-ass body nearly colliding with mine and lifting me off my feet.

My arms go around him, and I laugh, burying my face in his neck as he nuzzles mine.

"You come to eat all your snacks and bury yourself in fluffy pillows?"

"I came to steal you away, so I can hold you tonight."

Crew's head pops up, and he shakes it. "Baby, I can't leave, this place is—"

"Swamped? Packed?" I play with the tips of his hair. "Charging for entry?"

Crew tucks my hair behind my ear. "Some little genius told me how to increase revenue. Seems people love the idea of a free drink."

I smile as he sets me to my feet, a teeny, tiny hint of something sour in the back of my throat. Disappointment with a little longing maybe. "Why didn't you tell me?"

"I didn't want you to stress over it if it didn't work out," he says.

Guilt mixed with a touch of rejection rolls through me, and I get the feeling it's a little more than that but shake it off. I came to enjoy time with him, not worry about other things.

Hugging me to him, he leads me toward the bar, but I dig my heels into the ground, and he faces me.

"Sweets . . ."

"Just look over there."

Willie is already in Crew's vacated spot, keeping up like a champ, Drew on his right, Paula his left. Kenli snatches a tray from Drew, and weaves in and out of the seating zones, setting two drinks here, three there, and pausing for orders on her circle back.

"He's staying to help with closing. Layla's sister is in town, so she's covered. Nothing to worry about."

Crew stares a moment, and then he whips around, diving into my neck and biting softly. "Wrong, Sweets, so much to worry about, starting with finding a way to keep you quiet when I fuck you tonight."

"Yes, please," I moan. "It's been too long."

Crew chuckles as I yank him toward the door, but before we make it, he pulls me back, his hands looping around my waist and then he starts to sway.

"Babe, bed."

Crew's lips curve against my temple, but instead of leading us out the door, he leads me where we stand. "Soon, baby, but right now, I wanna dance with my woman a while."

My eyes close, my stomach fluttering at the softness in his voice, at the patience in his touch and his need—his desire—to do nothing but hold me close.

My arms wrap around him, and I melt into his frame. "Yes, please."

My mind whispers to me then, something I'm pretty sure I've always known, but this moment makes sure to trigger a necessary reminder.

I need nothing in my life like I need Crew.

Not even Memphis.

Crew

She's putty in my palms, every inch of her molded perfectly to every inch of me. The little minx had plans for me when she came here tonight, coaxing me into the passenger seat after exiting the bar, pulling over in the same orchard we were caught in on the way home, and climbing over to settle herself in my lap, her back to my chest.

And I'm about to reward her for it.

Gliding my hands along her waist, I continue down until I'm dipping between her legs and guiding them open, so her knees can hook over my thighs. Pulling down the sun visor, I adjust it until her pink panties are in view in the mirror.

"Are you putting on a show for me?" She drops her head back, turning it to kiss my jaw.

"Sorry, Sweets." I nudge her with my nose, clamping my lips over her neck for a quick taste. "That's purely for me."

A soft mewl leaves her, and she presses her ass into me, her voice low and thick with need. "Liar."

"Liar?" I tease, nipping at her skin.

"Everything you do is for me, if not both of us."

My chest rumbles, and I take her mouth.

She sees it, understands. Believes.

I must be doing something right.

While I have her distracted, I hike her dress up, reaching between her legs to wrap the material of her panties around both my pointer fingers. One good tug, and they shred, my eyes flying to the mirror. My cock twitches beneath her at the sight of her bare pussy staring back at me from above.

Davis turns her head to look, her muscles contracting. I

click the AC on, angling the vent low, and her back bows the second the chilled air hits her most sensitive spot.

"Crew, please," she pants, her hand sneaking behind her in an attempt to squeeze me through my jeans.

"Up."

She's quick to perch on her toes, holding herself on the suicide bar above the door as I hastily shove my pants down my legs, my boxers with them.

My cock bounces free, straining when I grip it tight, and Davis needs no direction. She finds me, holds me at the edge of her entrance and drops down, her legs instantly flying back into the position I had her, a sharp gasp filling the air.

"Finally," she breathes, her hips rolling instantly.

I drop my seat back a bit and grab hold, leading her to do the work while I watch from the mirror.

Her pussy is slick and soaked, my cock thanking her for it, swelling thicker, growing longer, and filling her completely.

Davis's head finds my shoulder as she dances on my dick, and I tug her dress beneath her breasts, freeing them and watching as her nipples sharpen, begging for attention.

"Love the way you feel, baby," I rasp, touching no other part of her tits but the nipples.

I tug, stretching them as far as they allow and she clenches over me, her speed picking up.

My smirk spreads along her cheek. "You like a bit of rough play."

"I like everything you do." She moans, then picks up speed, her hips grinding, breaths sharpening.

My mouth drops open, my head falls back, eyes closing as I focus on the feel of her.

The warmth of her heat.

The rhythm of her hips.

Her.

It's not long before she's pulsing, begging, as if she has no clue she's bringing herself to the edge, grinding and angling as she pleases, seeking out her orgasm and demanding it on her terms. It's sexy as hell, but I'm a jealous motherfucker, as is my cock.

He wants to own her cum, so I take over.

My palm presses on her spine, and as if she was waiting for this, for me to take control, she hums in answer, willingly falling forward.

Gripping her hair, I hold it tight, my hips thrusting into her with force, nothing but heavy breathing and sweet, sloppy slaps filling the car.

She moans, long and deep, and then she shatters, clenching, pulsing, and squeezing around my cock.

"There we go, baby."

"Don't st-stop," she stutters, her forearms folded on the dash, body slick with sweat but desperate for more.

My groan is deep, and I lift her ass up, staring in the mirror as I drive in and out of her, her body limp, but refusing to let me go. I pick up speed, and she whimpers, squirming, and with one final slam into her, she throws herself back, hitting my chest.

I clamp her nipples firmly between my fingers, sucking the slope of her neck even harder, enough to leave a mark. A big one and she cries into the car, her every muscle quaking with a second, longer, stronger release.

"I can't . . . mmm." Her hips keep rolling slowly. Painfully.

My brows snap together, my breaths short and ragged.

Minutes go by and she's still riding me with barely there movements. She doesn't stop until her limbs refuse to listen, and then she's deadweight in my arms.

I free my dick, carefully maneuvering her, so she's cradled in my lap, and I hold her there until her breathing settles. Her eyes begin to close, so I ease her into the seat as I slip from the car, grinning when she tugs me by the collar, desperate to keep me close.

"I'm just gonna get us home, baby."

"I love you," she whispers.

"Love you, too."

"Take me home, tuck me in, and hold me until morning?"

"It's cute you think you have to ask."

An exhausted chuckle escapes her, and then her eyes close, so I quickly run around and slip into the driver's seat.

And I take my baby home.

The room is still dark when a loud crash sounds in the hall, and I fly up in bed, Davis slowly stirring beside me. My pulse pounds as I quickly rush to the door, tearing it open, but I jerk to a stop at the sight of Memphis, picking up a chair he clearly knocked over.

He laughs lightly, lifting and scooting it back into place.

"My bad," he whispers, headed back into his temporary room.

My blood heats, my teeth clenching as I stalk forward, but Davis's voice wraps around me from behind.

"Everything okay?" she rasps.

Freezing, I swallow. "Go back to sleep, Sweets."

I head for the kitchen, pull the trash out, and, sure enough, there's a pile of unused paper towels on top. Shoving them aside, I find the empty bottle.

My frown doubles as I stare at it. Fucking seriously? He went hunting under the bathroom fucking sink?

"How could you?"

My head snaps up, eyes narrowing on Davis, who stands with her arms crossed over her chest, eyes pinched.

"What?"

"You . . ." She shakes her head, tears welling in her eyes. "You brought that here. From the hospital. I told you, no alcohol here. How could you be so careless?"

"You had a cut that had to be cleaned."

"Why didn't you throw it out after?"

My head tugs back. "This is my fault? He drank *rubbing alcohol* to get smashed, and this is my fault?"

"You know I don't keep it in the house, and this is why!" she whisper-shouts. "In case one day, he came home, and he *came* home, Crew. *Sober.* I can't have alcohol anywhere near here, not while he's trying to get better."

I feel like I've been punched in the gut, unsure of what to say to the one person in the world I hate to disappoint over anyone else. She doesn't realize what she's saying, and that might be the hardest fucking part.

The bedroom door opens and Memphis steps into the hall, a small scowl on his face, but this time, it's pointed at his sister.

Instinctively, I move to shelter her from his bullshit, but she quickly moves toward him.

"Memph—"

"I didn't drink it," he tells her, lifting his shirt to show a large bandage over his left side.

Davis gasps, shooting forward. "What happened?"

Memphis drops his shirt, taking a few backward steps, and she halts her advance.

"I went with you to several stores the other day, Davis." He avoids her question. "Have been by myself all week while you were at work. I could have gone for a bottle, but it's like I said, it's under control."

"Memphis, I'm so sorry," she whispers.

I eye him, but he doesn't even glance my way.

"It's okay, I get it. You're the one who found me on the bathroom floor last time I touched that shit in a desperate moment."

Her tears fall, and she nods, watching as he backs into the room, closing the door behind him.

Her hand flies up to cover her mouth to muffle her cries, and she turns into my chest.

Limbs numb to her warmth, I wrap them around her, guiding us back to her room.

She drops onto the edge of her bed, face falling into her palms as she cries softly, but I can't bring myself to sit.

I can't.

I'm . . . fucking terrified, because when it comes to Davis, I've never been able to snag the number one spot. I think I was close, real close, but now? With him back?

Never.

She will always choose him over me, and she already has, whether she realizes it or not, whether she means to or not. Hell, he's her family, maybe she's supposed to.

Maybe I'm being a little bitch.

Maybe this is what I deserve for hiding all the shit he put me through, for covering up everything he's done and being his fall guy. For shielding her from the truths I didn't want her to have to bear the weight of. I thought that was what you did for someone you love, protect them, no matter the lies told along the way.

Maybe none of that was right.

"Davis . . ."

Slowly, her head lifts, her face streaked with tears, brows furrowing. The crestfallen expression on her face has me wanting to drop to my knees before her, but my feet hold still.

"Why are you looking at me like that?" she says so low, I almost miss it.

Honesty is the best and *worst* fucking way to go, even when she knows the answer before I say it.

"Because I came home tonight reeking of too many liquors to count, like I do every night. Like I will every day that follows." My world is built on what she's trying so hard to protect her brother from.

The small frown along her forehead deepens, her mind trying to work through the meaning behind my words. No more than seconds pass and her lips begin to tremble.

My chest stings, temples pounding as I wait for her to say something.

Her inhale is sharp and piercing, straight into my fucking gut.

This time, I do drop in front of her, her cries tearing me apart, piece by pathetic piece.

Her hands come up, cupping my cheeks as she stares into my eyes, her thumbs stroking the sharp edge of my jaw that I can't seem to relax, and I lean into the touch.

Her tears fall over her cheeks faster now, and I catch a few, swiping them away, but they just keep coming, her breaths now shaky, soft sobs.

"I don't know what to do, Crew. He needs someone's help. He needs me." *I need you.* "I've waited years for him to be ready to get clean."

I've waited years for you.

My teeth clench, and I offer her a tight smile.

Davis throws herself at me, knocking me on my ass, and curling into my lap. Her hands tether around me and mine do the same, holding her close to my chest.

I press my cheek to her temple, eyes closing. This is fucking rough.

I hate Memphis more than I hate my own fucking dad, and that's saying something, but I can't tell her this. She loves him more than anyone in the world.

She loves him more than she loves me.

She'll choose him, if it came to that, but I would never make her face the question or say the words. I would never force her into a position of guilt that would only lead to resentment.

"Don't leave me, Crew. Please don't leave me."

Every muscle in my body stiffens, and slowly, I pull back, needing to meet her gaze.

The moment her tear-stained face finds mine, her features pull tight with confusion, and even tighter as realization sets in.

"Crew . . ." Her voice cracks.

I'd almost swear my ribs did too.

She shifts suddenly, so she's straddling me, but only so she can possess my full attention.

"Crew, this is . . . this is real for me," she whispers, her palms falling to my chest, pressing over the date marked on me. "At first, I didn't know if I fit in your new world because I was, well, me, but I've never felt more like myself than I do when I'm a part of it. I want to be a part of it. I want you to want me forever because I know now that I have you, I can't go back to before us. I don't want to. Having Memphis here this past week has been amazing, a prayer answered, if I'm honest. We can figure out how to be us with him around because I do want him here, but Crew, I *need* you here. I need you like I need nothing else. Not for now, not for a while, for always."

My heart is beating out of control, a knot forming in my throat as too many thoughts, hopes and damn dreams overwhelm me all at once.

My limbs begin to shake, and she brings herself closer, forcing me to confess, "I own the bar."

She stills. "What?"

"Sideways Sippin'. It's mine. I'm still paying off the last owner, but it's mine, Sweets."

Her tear-streaked face furrows. "What . . . since when?"

"Last year. I didn't plan on it, I only started working there because it was the only job I could get at the time, but then the opportunity came, and I realized I was interested. I needed to build a life I could be proud of, have something worth a damn."

Something to offer you, a way to take care of you, like a good man would, like your dad did for your mom and your grandpa for your grandma.

The deflated expression on her face has me wanting to set her on the pedestal she deserves, all so I can drop to my knees before her and beg her to stay, but Davis never ceases to amaze me.

She draws me closer. Her hands come up, pressing into my cheeks as she stares into my eyes. "I hate you felt like you had to hide such an accomplishment from me, but I am so proud of you, Crew." She strokes my lips with her thumb. "So proud," she whispers, tears brimming her brown eyes.

It only takes a moment for her to realize what I thought the revelation would lead to, considering it was a valid fear. I don't have many things I fear, and all are wrapped around the woman in front of me.

"Baby," she breathes. "I love you. Don't leave me."

My forehead falls to hers, her words her way of telling me, no matter the situation, she's choosing me for me.

One hand slides up her back, the other easing into her hair, drawing her lips to mine. "The only way I would ever leave you is if you told me to go." I close my eyes, pressing my mouth to hers. "But not before I put up one hell of a fight to stay."

She sighs into my mouth, and then she claims it as her own, kissing me until exhaustion sets in and her head falls to my shoulder.

I lift us, lowering back into the bed.

Davis doesn't stir once, staying in a deep sleep, but I can't say the same for me.

Her words mean more than I know how to express, and I believe each one spoken, but that's not what keeps me up the rest of the night.

It's knowing I have to be back at work tomorrow, haven't told my best friend what's going on, and the fact I have to keep Davis away from the place I want her.

It's the look in Memphis's eyes tonight, the yellow hue surrounding the irises, and the laugh that left him before he walked back into the room. It's the fact that that bottle was more than three-fourths full and hidden beneath napkins.

It's how he wouldn't let her get too close and the wrap on his stomach.

It's the chatty fucker outside of the farmers' market and the "interest" he had in what kind of work I did that required boxes of fresh fruits.

It's the fact that following that day, a beady-eyed bastard's been posted in the farthest corner of my bar each night, ordering a beer he doesn't touch.

This is how it started our freshman year at Avix.

Big fuckers in steel-toe boots—that hurt like a bitch when connecting to the gut—sat in the stands at our games.

Parked in our spots at our dorms and slowly, somehow slipped into our classes, sat right behind us, and literally breathed down our necks.

Because Memphis has little self-control, and when it slips?

We all fucking fall.

Chapter 36
Davis

The harsh crash has my eyes flying open, the dark room around me spinning a moment, my limbs locked from being startled awake.

My senses begin to stir, and while time seems to stretch for an eternity, it's only a split second, the rattle of hinges jarring me upright.

I knew I heard the door.

The blanket falls to my stomach, and I swiftly climb to my feet, snagging my phone off the bedside table to check the time.

It's nearly three in the morning—I was asleep for no more than an hour, lying awake with worry, waiting for my brother to come back home.

Blasting from my bed, I step out into the hall, alarm freezing me in place as I round the corner. Memphis leans over the counter, his head in his hands, blood dripping down his forearms.

"Oh my god, Memphis!"

I rush forward as his head snaps up and my eyes widen at the gash along his brow. "Holy shit, what happened?!" I'm in front of him in an instant. "Are you okay?"

"We flipped. Rolled down into an empty canal." He coughs.

Confusion whirls in my mind, and I follow his gaze when it lifts over my head, my spine shooting straight at the sight.

Red rimmed and shifty, dark eyes narrow on mine, and my breath lodges in my throat as I stare at the stranger in my house.

The man is tall, broad, and also bleeding. The dingy white shirt under his leather vest is streaked with dirt and deep crimson, but it's shards of glass sticking out of his arm that makes him look far scarier. I'm not even sure if he knows they're there.

"You said no one would be here," the man barks at my brother, his lip curling when his words make me jump.

Seconds later, a third man appears, having stepped out of my bathroom and my eyes shoot wide, shock and confusion coiling my muscles.

"You . . ." I breathe, my gut twisting.

"Hello again, Davis." The man comes closer, the familiar black hat, the one he wore each and every time he came into the diner, hanging from his hand, bloodied and bent. His blue eyes are locked with mine, hazed over, yet wide with adrenaline.

Everything in me screams to run, that something is off and to take myself as far away from it as possible.

Trying to appear calm while unease stabs at my every nerve isn't easy, but I manage to keep my steps slow and steady as I round the counter, putting distance between myself and the men, my brother included.

My mouth opens, but I'm not sure what I planned to say, and then Memphis's groan has my head snapping back.

"I didn't think she'd be home." He pants, his breathing labored as he grips his side, the color draining from his face. "Ignore her, she's no one."

A pang hits my chest, but I ignore it.

"Memphis, we have to get you to the hospital. I can drive, I—" My hand reaches into the bottom of the bowl, my attention snapping to it. "Where are my keys . . ." It's not really a question, more my way of trying to retrace my steps, but my brother answers.

"I told you." He kicks off the counter, and I reach out as he stumbles back, but it's no use. He falls into the chair behind him, nearly tumbling to the floor. "We flipped."

I stare at my brother, at the wounds on his hands and the gash on his head, at the dirt covering his jeans and his laces soaked a cherry red . . . to the wristband on his left arm.

Gone when I got home, stumbling in after the two-in-the-morning last call.

The single-shot bottles in the gutter near the curb that could have been anyone's . . . but likely are not.

Tears prick my eyes, and I clench my jaw to keep them at bay. "You're drunk."

The lanky man, *Black Hat Guy,* laughs, and I jolt, shifting right as he moves left on the other side of the countertop.

"Relax, Davis." Black Hat Guy demands, my name leaving him in three incoherent syllables.

"Yeah, *Davis,* relax."

My head snaps toward the big guy, and I clutch my phone tighter, my limbs beginning to shake. Using my thumb to unlock the screen, I quickly lift it, hit number one, and draw it to my ear. "You need help."

The line rings once and then the phone is torn from my hand, a large palm wrapping around my bicep. I gasp, whipping around to come face-to-face with wild, dark eyes.

"No cops!" the man shouts, his words so harsh and booming, so close, speckles of spit wet my face.

I nearly whimper as he crowds me even more.

"I . . . I—"

The man's arm flies up, and I flinch when he chucks my phone across the room, a small squeal leaving me as it smashes against the wall. His gaze is hard on mine, slowly snapping up over my head.

"Handle your bitch, Memphis."

Yes, please, Memphis! Do something!

My heart sinks, my pulse threatening to knock me out as I dare a look at my brother.

My brother's eyes are half-closed, his body slumped against the chair. "Go to bed, all right? We gotta lie low."

He keeps talking, his words a mess of things I can't make out, but my body is shaking so badly, I can hardly stand. The man in front of me stares at me impatiently, and I realize Memphis told me to do something and I'm clearly expected to do as I'm told.

My steps are so slow and thought out, I'm sure I look off, stiff and robot-like, but it feels like a safer bet than running and slamming the door behind me like the terrified woman I am. With restraint I didn't know I had, I gently close my door, having to try twice to turn the lock into place, I'm trembling so badly.

The second I'm locked inside, my hands fly to my mouth, my tears overflowing as silent sobs rack my body. I allow myself no more than seconds of panic, as it threatens to swallow me whole. I try to take a deep breath and lower myself onto the edge of my bed.

My leg begins to bounce, and I count quietly to myself in sequences of ten.

No more than a minute passes and then there's a harsh knock on my door.

"Open up!" *Black Hat Guy*. "You better not be on the phone in there!"

Tears spring into my eyes, and I look to the patio. Even if I could climb up to the top, I can't squeeze through the wooden slats.

Why is he here?

How does he know Memphis?

God, what do I do?

A few minutes go by before the shadow of feet beneath my door disappear, and I pull in a deep breath, but the reprieve only lasts a few moments as shouting begins, the rattle of my doorknob following.

Saying nothing, I quickly dig for the bat my dad always taught me to keep hidden at my bedside. I've only reached the tip of the barrel when my door is forced open and a body shoves through.

I scream, my eyes slicing upward, widening instantly.

"Jess!" My heart rate spikes.

"Davis! Are you okay? Are you hurt?" His eyes fly across me, and when he reaches out, I stumble into his open arms.

My head shakes, his eyes holding mine as he blindly yanks a blanket from my bed and drapes it over my shoulders.

"Come on." He guides me into the living room, my brother now seemingly passed out in the same spot I left him, his head hanging to his chest.

"Where you think you're goin'?" Black Hat Guy shouts, and footsteps stomp behind us.

"Hey!"

I go to look, but Jess traps my head, so I can't, his steps picking up.

It's no use though, the big guy is faster, even in his state, and then our exit is halted.

The man puffs his chest out, his hands in fists at his sides, blood dried in long strips down his cheek and neck. His lips curled. "The fuck you think you're doing, huh?"

My heart ceases, my nails digging into Jess's skin, making him flex.

"Just move out of the way, man." Jess lifts his left hand into the air. "We don't want any trouble."

A dry chuckle leaves the guy, and he inches closer. "I can't let you walk out of here and send the cops."

"It's not the cops you have to worry about."

My head snaps up, relief flooding me instantly, but it only lasts a moment, because when I look up and over the shoulder of the man blocking Crew from me, the look in Crew's eyes is animalistic.

Truly.

His pupils are hiding the hazel completely, his body radiating with rage and taking my breath away.

"C—"

"Get her out of here." My plea is silenced before being freed.

Jess doesn't have to be told twice, but he *does* have to pick me up and carry me as my feet refuse to leave the man I love with these men my brother brought home.

My home.

Mine and Crew's home.

Jess carries me all the way back to a bedroom—his or a spare, I don't know—and closes us inside, slowly lowering me onto an armchair in the corner.

He crouches down in front of me. "Davis—"

"Don't let him kill him." My head snaps to Jess.

His eyes bulge instantly, worry weighted in his words. "Will he?"

"He might."

Somehow, his gaze seems to grow even wider, and I lift a shoulder.

"Fuck." Jess runs his hands through his hair. "Do I call the cops?"

"No cops."

Jess shoots to his feet, both our heads flying toward the door to find Julius.

I jump up, running to him, and he wraps me in his arms.

"Oh my god!" I cry. "Willie?"

"Yeah, mama, he's in there." He squeezes me. "He'll stop him just before it's too late."

He doesn't have to say the rest, we both know what he means. *He'll stop him only seconds before it's "too late" and not a one before then.*

"That guy, the skinny one, it's the guy from the diner. He's been coming in for weeks and asking for me. He . . . he's asked about Crew, I—" I start shaking harder.

Julius cuts me off with a shush, whispering words I can't focus on in my ear as he rubs his hand up and down my back.

Time seems to slow, Julius keeping my body folded into his chest. With every shout and crash reaching us, he adjusts a bit, attempting to conceal the sound with the rustle of his shirt against my ear, or the clearing of his throat.

Each second passing has my body growing heavier, and just before my feet give way, heat warms me from behind, the gentle palm pressed there, the one that belongs to the man who belongs to me.

My body falls into him, and I'm scooped up in an instant, tucked into his embrace, my face burying into his chest. His chest rises and falls rapidly, his muscles rigid, but as my palm falls to his left pec, my lips meeting his neck as I breathe him in, dragging him into my senses, my eyes close at the same moment his entire being seems to settle.

"I've got you, baby. I've got you."

That's the last thing I remember before my adrenaline crashes, and exhaustion wins out.

I couldn't wager on the time if my life depended on it, and the closely drawn curtains of the foreign room are no help. Slowly, I attempt to lift onto an elbow, but Crew's soft voice envelops me from behind.

"Lie back down, baby," he whispers.

His tone is so low and heavy, I'm flooded with a need to look into his eyes, but he senses it, and nuzzles closer, further hiding himself. "Baby, breathe, and let me love on you a little. Can you do that?"

The heaviness settling over me is nearly drowning, but Crew's strong arms are the only place I want to be. "Yes."

"Can you tell me you're okay?"

I nod against him, flashes of last night and his decision to bring us to a hotel not too far from the bar, rather than the bar itself.

"Say it for me, baby. I need to hear it."

"I'm okay. I wasn't hurt."

There's a pause, and then. "There's a bruise on your arm." His tone is gruff, tense. "Tell me who put it there?"

Oh.

The man left a bruise?

"Davis." The sharp edge of his tone is doused with fear, and I realize then what he is considering.

Crew tried to warn me before that time changes people, that distance changes things, and that pain blankets the truth. He thinks he knows the answer to his question, that the mark on my skin was put there by one of the two men Memphis brought home last night, but he can't ignore the fact that there's a chance he could be wrong. He doesn't want to ask but he has to know if my brother has changed so much that he's as capable of manhandling me as he was willing to bring someone who is into my home.

I like to think the answer is no, but maybe the blinders I thought I'd thrown away long ago didn't make it all that far.

"The big guy took my phone from me. That's all."

Crew's heavy inhale stays lodged in his throat for far too long before filling the dark room around us. Several minutes tick by, and his hold tightens, as he buries his lips in my hair.

The sheer relief radiating from him is painful.

Crew truly has no trust in my brother, and for the first time, I think I understand how deep the problem runs. If Memphis could put me in the position he did last night, conscious of it or not, I can't imagine what Crew has been dragged through by staying at my brother's side.

This time, when I press onto my elbow, Crew allows it, his grip loosening, but only enough to allow me to move without removing his arm from me completely. I turn, facing him, a dim shadow marring his face and hiding half of it from me, but the cut above his left brow stares back, so I lift my hand, gently gliding it just above it.

Crew's eyes search mine in the dark, and slowly, I lower my lips to his for a gentle kiss, the slight split there rough against my mouth.

But Crew presses more firmly into mine, his exhale long and soothing. "Baby, that man's been at your work. We will talk about what that means later, but right now, I need you to agree to quit your job and come work with me. I need you with me, always."

I shouldn't want to smile; I should want to claim my independence and demand I retain it, but he's not trying to take *from* me. He's trying to take care *of* me. He *needs* to take care of me.

My lips curve up, and I whisper, "I've been waiting a couple weeks to hear that."

Crew's chuckle is instant but too short, a weighted breath following.

"What?"

"We should stay here a few days. I can go get you some things from the house, have Drew come sit with you."

Shaking my head, I cling to him. "I don't want to be away from you."

"I don't want to take you back into that house just yet."

"Please. I just need to be with you. I'll stay in the car if I have to."

Crew stares a long moment and with a resigned nod, agrees. "Okay, baby. Get dressed. We'll get this over with."

He tries to sit up, but I shake my head, pressing on his chest.

"Not yet. We'll go soon, but first, it's my turn to take care of you a little bit. Let me fill the bath." In case he decides to object, I add, "This way, we feel better in the clean clothes Willie dropped off last night."

He's hesitant to release me but slowly nods, rolling onto his back.

The tub's in the corner of the room, not quite separated from the space altogether, but semi-blocked by a short extension of the wall. It's large though, and when I turn it on, I spot the jets at the head and feet.

"Warm or hot?"

"Whatever you want, baby."

My lips quirk. I figured he'd say that. I've yet to inspect him for injuries outside of the few cuts and scrapes along his face, and while hot water will sting a second, it will be better for his stressed muscles in the next. Crew *is* tense, there's no doubt about that, but there's a type of resilience that comes from loving an addict. You resign yourself to the bad for the few moments of good you know will come, and they do. Sometimes fewer and further between, but they come, and you revel in the feeling, in the familiarity and comfort.

You soak in the presence of the person you love as you don't get to experience them often, because no matter how much one tries to deny it, when their demons win over, the person you know and care for is buried beneath the surface. Not quite reachable, yet not quite gone.

A faint shadow in the fiery sun.

That's always been the hardest part for me, staring into the familiar eyes of the brother I love endlessly, but hitting a metaphorical barrier, keeping me from truly "seeing" him.

Sober, Memphis is all the things I've claimed. He's kind and selfless and willing to give you the shirt off his back, no question, no concern, but under the influence? You just never know.

At least this has been my experience. I imagine it's different for everyone.

I know it is for Crew.

Footsteps sound behind me, my eyes closing when he dips down, kissing my temple as he pulls me to my feet, holding my hand, so I can step inside, both of us having slept naked, being we had no clothes but the dirty, bloody ones from last night, mine filthy from him cradling me to his chest. I stay at the back of the tub, leading him in front of me.

Together, we lower, my legs wrapping around him from behind, and he settles into my chest, his head pressed right between my breasts.

He doesn't so much as wince from the sting the water must provide, his eyes closing as if he's soothed simply by the touch of my skin to his. I wet his chest with a rag, taking careful care to dab at his face, gently washing along his scalp, in case I come across an injury, but from where I am, he has no others. No black eye and outside of the small bruise on his shoulder blade, the two cuts on his brow and lip, he has no other visible damage.

I lift his hands, inspecting his knuckles. The middle and ring finger are both split open and threatening to scab over.

"It doesn't hurt, baby. I can't even feel it," he murmurs gently, his eyes closing, hands drawing small, soothing circles along my thighs.

Tears pool in my eyes, and I nod, though he can't see me.

We sit submerged, the silence somehow a heavy form of comfort, or maybe it's simply us, safe in each other's arms.

It's not until the water is no more than lukewarm that Crew stands, drying himself before pulling me up with him, and drying my body for me, his hands lingering in places longer than necessary, but his need to feel me in all ways essential.

He pulls me into his arms, pushing my damp hair from my cheeks, and drops his forehead to mine, exhaustion clear along his face.

"You didn't sleep."

He shakes his head, lifting his hand and sinking it into my hair. "I will."

Just not yet . . .

His eyes, heavy with the need for sleep, shine with something deeper, the honey hue of the hazel appearing more golden than normal. They cling to mine, and his hold on me tightens with purpose.

"What?" I whisper.

"You called me."

My brows pull, and he continues, a tenderness blanketing his hard features in an instant.

"Last night. You called me when you needed help. When you felt unsafe. You called me. Not the police. Not your dad."

My palms come up, latching over his wrists. "You're the first person I thought of. You're always the first person I think of. Happy, sad, mad. Scared. Since forever."

His eyes close, only to open a few seconds later. "I don't deserve you, but I won't let that stop me from keeping you."

Silence falls over us, understanding settling into our bones, one we've felt long before today, but last night drove the need to speak the words out loud.

My emotions seem to settle in, and I blink rapidly, attempting to calm myself.

"Davis," he murmurs, his hold tightening. "Baby, don't cry. I can't fucking take it."

"I'm sorry, I just—" I swallow. "I can't believe last night was real."

I meet the hazel eyes I used to dream about, and the sheer

sadness within them breaks the dam. "He stole my car, brought those men to my house. How could he?" I weep, collapsing into Crew's chest.

His arms come around me, and he barricades me in his strong embrace, but he remains silent, allowing me to whisper to myself what I wish, without sharing what's on his mind.

I imagine it's not a lot of good, which is exactly why he keeps it in.

He loves me and the last thing he wants to do is be the reason for the weight settling over me with each passing second. I know he's thinking about the man from the diner, how he pushed me to talk to him for my benefit, blaming himself for not seeing something deeper. And there is something deeper.

I have a feeling Crew knows what that might be, and I trust he'll tell me, but I don't want to think about that right now.

A stuttered breath bushes past my lips and I hold him tighter.

My parents warned me against seeking out my brother when he first disappeared without a word, only days after being released after the hit-and-run that almost killed him as well as the family he spun into.

Maybe I should have listened . . .

Chapter 37
Crew

The control it takes to walk into this fucking house with a calm bravado, something I don't feel in the slightest, is damn near impossible to maintain. All I want to do is kick the door down, if only to make the bastard inside it piss himself in fear, but I don't want to worry my girl, who is sitting in the passenger seat of my car, her eyes on my back, Drew's resting on the hood of it, just in case—a bullshit task I shouldn't have to fucking ask of him, not that he minds. He loves the girl like a sister, always has. He'd insist, but that's beside the point.

There should be nothing to fucking ask.

Nothing to worry about.

Nothing threatening the safety of the woman I love.

But her brother's name is Memphis Franco, and that in itself, is a threat.

His name is known in all the small cities around here, and not for anything worthwhile.

For his ability to charm his way into circles he doesn't belong, and then proceeding to fuck shit up.

He robs Peter to pay Paul, and then he does it all over again until there's no one else to screw, which is when he comes crawling to me.

I let the door slam with a little added force, but it doesn't matter.

The asshole doesn't even twitch.

He's still out cold, slumped in the armchair, his chin dropped to his chest, clothes the same dirty ones he wore last night.

He's bloody and bruised, his face shiny with sweat, eyes sunk in, his body dehydrated and in need of water.

I take a cold bottle from the fridge and walk over until I'm standing two feet from him.

Looking at him makes me sick, and that's a damn shame. The man had potential; he was smart with endless support, even long after addiction took him by the throat.

The problem? Support wasn't what he was looking for. I knew at a young age what his family had to discover the hard way, what Davis may only now be on the verge of understanding.

You can only help someone who *wants* to be helped, and the only kind of help this man has ever been willing to accept is the kind that feeds his habit.

A lift to the liquor store.

A six-pack of seltzers.

A few bucks for a bottle.

Alcoholism is no joke. It's a disease, a chronic sickness, a deadly poison, and when it works its way into the veins of those you love, all you can do is pray it doesn't kill them. Them, or someone else.

I won't allow Davis to become the "someone else."

I hate this for her.

I hate him.

Uncapping the water bottle, I pour it over his head.

Memphis jerks, flying forward on instinct, but I shove his ass right back into the chair, my shoe coming up to stop it from rocking back and forth.

Disoriented, he looks around, his attention settling in on me.

The night comes back to him in a flash, or pieces of it, depending on how fucked up he was, or got after we left—wouldn't put it past him to keep the binger going when no one was around to tell him to stop.

"Crew—" he begins.

"What happened last night?" I cut him off.

"Listen—"

"*Why* did it happen?" I fire again. "Who were those men?"

His silence says it all; he's in fucking trouble. Again.

Things are different this time though.

He didn't only bring problems to my door.

He walked them right through hers.

My blood boils beneath my skin.

"You're just going to sit there silent, like a little bitch, after putting Davis in danger? Your own fucking sister?!" I'm screaming now, close to losing it and pummeling him until he passes out again.

Finally, he opens his mouth, but his words are pathetic. "I didn't plan that!"

"They were with you, were they not?!"

"They found me and jumped in the car!"

"That you stole from your sister, who gave you a free fucking place to stay!"

"I only meant to borrow it!" He sits forward. "That's it."

"You drove it drunk and fucking crashed, Memphis. How you could do that when you almost fucking killed someone's entire family doing the same damn thing, in *my car* you stole, I don't fucking know!"

"I wouldn't have crashed if they hadn't gotten in the car."

"You're fucking pathetic." I scoff, my fists clenching at my sides. "Who were they, Memphis?"

He shakes his head, throwing himself back in the chair and looking away.

"What, man enough to do and take as you please, even at the risk of the one and only person left in the world who still loves your sorry ass, but not man enough to admit what you did out loud?"

"You already know." His eyes come back to mine. "You just want me to say it, so you can look at me like I'm a piece of shit."

"Would a good man bring thugs into his sister's home, knowing she was here alone? Knowing what they're capable of? What they will do to women they want without a fucking care?!"

"I wouldn't have let anyone hurt her!"

"You did, motherfucker! And you hurt her just the same! If I didn't call her friend next door to help her, someone else might have broken into her room. They tried to open her bedroom door! Did you know that?" Rage prickles across my skin, tempting me to shred it from my body. "You were so trashed, you had no idea what was going on by the time I got here. I could have taken her and left, and you wouldn't have even been able to protect yourself, let alone your innocent sister."

He shoots to his feet, a fretful look in his blue eyes, a pathetic lie he can't possibly believe rolling off his tongue. "I could have protected her!"

"She should need no fucking protecting!" I get in his face. "That's the *fucking* point!"

"I didn't mean to bring them here! They jumped into the car, put a knife to my throat and told me to drive. We wrecked and a ton of people saw, they called the cops, Crew. I had to run."

"You didn't have to run here," I force past clenched teeth. "You came to town knowing someone was after you. Last night, or last fucking week, it doesn't matter. You put her in danger coming home."

"I didn't plan this!"

"No, you just came back, knowing someone was after you!"

"I had no choice! I had to come back, and you were nowhere to be found," he tries to reason. "If I knew where you had moved, I never would have come to her—"

"Yes, you fucking did!" I scream, my ears vibrating from the echo around us as I push into his face. "You had a fucking choice, you're just a weak son of a bitch who pushes your problems onto other people. I won't let you ruin my life again, Memphis. You—"

"I don't understand . . ."

Davis's worrisome words reach us and both our heads snap her way.

She steps into the door, and my eyes flick to Drew over her shoulder.

He holds my gaze, and I know she refused to sit still any longer.

She frowns, stepping in even farther, gasping slightly at the sight of the rooms around us.

The couch is broken, the chairs in the kitchen knocked over. Blood stains the floor, glass shards are scattered along the back wall, and if you look close enough, you might spot a couple teeth that belonged to the big fucker who scared my girl, who *touched* my girl.

I should have cut off his trigger finger.

Davis steps beside me, her gaze on her brother, who cowers into his seat.

"What do you mean you had to come back? Had to come to me? Did you not *want* to see me? You just . . . what? Had nowhere else to go, so I was the last resort, and not even the happy kind?"

"Davis . . ." he begins, reaching for her.

I can't stop myself; I block his path before I realize I'm doing it, and I'm glad for it. He doesn't get to go near her.

He glares at me, but his features soften some as he looks at her.

"Did you not miss me at all?" Her eyes cloud, and I have to dig my nails into my palms to keep from laying him out for causing it. But then she looks to me. "And why did you need Crew?" Her eyes narrow, anger washing away some of the torment.

My pulse beats widely with each passing second.

"What did you do to him?" she accuses, her tone harsh yet low, eyes on me, but her words are not. She's speaking to him.

The world spins a little, leveling out the slightest bit.

"Nothing!" he tosses quickly, jumping up and stepping around me.

This time, I let him, because she keeps her attention trained on me, waiting for him to continue but needing to judge my reaction to his words before deciding how to feel about them.

"I didn't do anything." Memphis lies through his rotting teeth. "I just needed his help. That's all. We have it under control, sister, I—"

"Stop," she whispers, and I want to wrap my arms around her, hold the weight he's tossing at her on my own shoulders. Moisture pooling in her eyes, she looks to him. "Stop lying to me, Memphis. Tell me what I don't know."

She isn't angry, her tone bleeding a sadness I don't see how he can't feel, yet still, faced with the task of telling the truth, Memphis clamps his lips closed, scrubbing a hand through his hair. I wait, hoping for once he'll do right by her, knowing it's too much of an ask for him. And it is.

Memphis says nothing, and rather than drill him some more, Davis looks to me.

"Your brother is the real reason I was kicked out of college," I offer instantly. "He blamed me and I let him."

"Crew, what the fuck?!" Memphis barks.

Davis gasps.

I keep talking, my eyes holding hers as I give her brutal honesty, something I should have done a long-ass time ago but thought I had to protect her from. "He's not only a struggling alcoholic, but a gambling addict. A broke one." I glare at him, hating to do this, but refusing to hide it from her when she's asking me to paint his true colors for her to see.

She looks to her brother, shocked, yet a trace of something more in her eyes, almost like she wondered if there was more to the troubles he faced, but never took it a step further to consider what it might be. But then she shakes her head, looking to me. "I don't understand. What's that have to do with the school?" she wonders.

"The day the people he fucked over decided they were done waiting, a couple thugs came looking for him, he just so happened to bail on class, one we had together." A sickening sense of betrayal I've refused to allow myself to feel claws at me. "Three of them found their way into the class, attacked me in front of everyone. It was complete fucking chaos, but I walked out with a few cuts and bruises, and a gash on my chin. They couldn't even stand. Cops showed up, they were put in the back of an ambulance. I was expelled because, supposedly, I was running a betting ring I didn't even know existed, and they were my unhappy customers. They said I posed a threat to the school, and that was that."

Memphis sat back, watched me pack my shit with campus security breathing down my back, and fucking thanked me. I glance at Memphis, who won't even face me like a man, but stares at my shoes on his feet. "Your brother fucked over the wrong club and sent them to me when he couldn't pay." I'd already hated him by then, but that was the moment I was done, ready to let them do whatever they wanted to him. But it wasn't so simple, especially after what I did to their "punishers" as they called the three goons who came after me.

"After seeing me fight, they used it to their advantage." Something I could never prove Memphis planted in their head, and the attack was simply them testing the information, but if I were a piece of shit like him, I'd bet on it.

Creases build along her forehead as she processes what I'm saying, her hand subconsciously pressing a palm to her stomach as she remembers what she saw on mine.

I nod.

Yes, baby. The scars.

"They forced me to take fights to pay off what he owed while he was off getting shit-faced and fucking over the next dumbass," I continue.

Davis presses her lips together, her question low. "How long did you have to work for them?"

I didn't work for them, I was controlled by them, but I don't say that.

Masking my expression, I do my best to keep any emotion from my tone, knowing she'll hurt for me once I tell her.

"Three years."

A mix between a cry and a gasp escapes her, and she reaches for me, gripping onto my arm to offer her strength, in case I need it.

I don't, I'm good ,and over the bullshit that came before her, but the gesture is purehearted, and I fucking love her for it. For wanting to take my pain, should I have some, and offer her support.

"Why did you do it?" she wonders quietly.

The answer is simple. "Because they threatened to go after his family if he couldn't pay, and I couldn't allow that. The main dude gave his word he wouldn't go searching for you, if I didn't give him a reason to, so I didn't. I did everything I was told until the money was paid in full."

She stares at me, both our gazes softening as understanding slips over her.

"That's why you never came back home," she whispers. "That's why you stayed away from me."

Yeah, baby. That's why.

I hold her eyes for a minute, before looking back to him. "How much, Memphis?"

"Twenty-five."

I wait, and his head lifts, his stare connecting with mine.

"Thousand," he finishes.

A humorless laugh leaves me, and I step away, shaking my head. That's a lifetime's worth.

"Crew, please." He darts toward me, and in my peripheral, Drew slips closer. I'd almost forgotten he was here. "These guys aren't like the last ones."

"That's your problem, Memphis. Not mine."

"How can you just say no? What about Davis?!"

I'm in his face so fast, he loses his balance and falls into the chair. "I sacrificed everything, let dirtbags control my life for three fucking years because of you with a *fraction* of that number owed, and you have the nerve to come back here and ask for my help?! After you brought them to your sister's front fucking door, the one person I did all that for, that I let go of to protect?!" I jerk forward, gripping him around the collar and yanking him off his feet, speaking through clenched teeth. "I could have lost the only fucking thing that has ever mattered to me because of you! If I died, she never would have known what she meant to me!"

"They'll kill me, Crew!"

"I should fucking kill you!" My body shakes in rage. This is Davis. No one hurts her. No one.

Davis wraps her hand around my arm, gently tugging.

It takes a moment, but I let him go, his eyes shining with tears, but I'd bet they're for himself. He looks to his sister, his throat bobbing with his swallow.

Something in the pit of my stomach stirs, and when he opens his mouth, but closes it a moment later, I realize, like a fucking fool, the churning sensation was hope.

Despite knowing better, I hoped for a single fucking second, he'd speak up, say something, anything to the girl hurting at my side.

I know her mind must be reeling, and as her brother, as a fucking decent man, he should be driven by a need to settle her some. To ease the pain, I don't have to look at her to know what is written all over her face. I sense it in the air, feel it in her weighted touch.

But he isn't a decent man.

He's a weak and selfish one.

It's one thing to be a slave to the disease that owns you, but it's another to stand here silent when sober enough to have the conversation, staring at your little sister, who was once your whole world, and she was. Memphis loved her, protected her to no end. I'm sure he still does to some extent, but the years and distance between them have affected him differently than they did her.

She spent the time missing and worrying about him, waiting for him to come home.

He spent it so lost in his own demons, that if he ever did think of her, he likely drowned out the memories in a bottle of booze. I don't fault him for that, but I do for this.

For right now.

Davis gently steers me toward the door, releasing me as she steps out onto the porch, Drew places a hand on her lower back in support as he guides her out, a bag he must have packed for us hanging from his hands.

With heavy steps, I follow, but Memphis snaps out of the internal war his mind is likely waging.

"Crew, I wasn't lying. These guys, they're dangerous," he rushes out desperately, his voice growing closer, letting me know he's taken several steps toward me. "They'll kill me, man."

"Maybe you should have thought about that before you chose to fuck them over." My words are low and tired, and I glance back, my gaze connecting with his. "Fix your own fucking problems, Memphis. I'm done doing it for you."

With that, I walk out, hoping like hell the shitstorm surrounding him won't follow.

Knowing in the back of my mind, it will.

It always fucking does.

Chapter 38
Davis

We haven't spoken much since arriving back at the hotel yesterday afternoon, a nice place only blocks from the bar and Willie and Layla's house—the only way Willie was willing to go home the night he had to drag Crew—literally from what I heard—from my apartment and off the man he had brutally beaten, if the shredding of his knuckles tells me anything.

They must be sore, but every time I try to inspect them further, he kisses me, his way of attempting to clear my mind. It's sweet, but it doesn't quite work, and he knows it.

We came back here, showered, even though we took a bath before leaving, and after having lain there for hours, simply holding one another, his eyes finally closed, mine following.

I've been awake for a little over an hour now, the red-lit alarm clock reading two-fifteen in the afternoon. We slept nearly twelve hours, and still, I'm exhausted. I'm in that state where you can't tell if you slept too long and now your entire day is ruined, or you didn't sleep enough.

Snuggling into Crew, his arms tighten around me, his nose burying in my hair.

"How long you been awake, baby?" he rasps.

"Not long."

His lips press to my neck, and he rolls me, so I'm facing him, his eyes half-closed and heavy, a weight within them I can't even begin to comprehend.

If my soul is heavy, his must be suffocating.

Before I realize it's happening, my eyes cloud over and Crew's face softens, sorrow slipping over him, though he tries to hide it.

"We gonna talk now, Sweets?" he murmurs.

I nod, swallowing beyond the lump in my throat.

Crew's hand pushes into my hair, moving it from my face, and I catch it in both of mine before it can drop to the mattress. I kiss his knuckles one by one, pressure falling on my chest as his lungs expand with a deep inhale.

"I love you, you know," he tells me. "Some might say too much. I'd do anything for you. Always."

"I know." I scoot closer, our foreheads nearly touching. I don't know where to start, so I go with the question that keeps popping into my mind. "Where did you go when you left school?"

He threads his fingers with mine. "I was broke when I was kicked out of school, had about five hundred bucks to my name that I'd saved from working at the car wash downtown, no car 'cause Memphis had already totaled it. I got a small storage unit for my shit, slept in it the first few nights, but the manager was tipped off by someone and made me leave. Turned out those thugs were watching me around the clock. I had no privacy, and if I did something they didn't like, they let me know."

The way he says it with a light sharpness and crease of his brows has me thinking they didn't use their voices.

"I started staying at some charge-by-the-hour hotel; it was disgusting but cheap. Every time I'd find work, they'd fuck it up and get me fired. Force me to leave mid shift for a quick alley fight or drive us a few counties over to another crew's stomping grounds, put me in the ring with dudes three times my size, and I couldn't say no." He considers something a moment, tracing my lips with his eyes before meeting mine. "I was hospitalized once. Just for a few days, but all it did was leave me with another bill, and then the school decided I had to pay them back for the damages. That was another bill

I couldn't pay. The main dude found out and paid off both as a show of 'good faith,' as he called it. Psycho motherfucker," he mumbles the last part.

My heart aches, literally, the pain sharp and constant.

All this time, I was heartbroken, assuming he didn't need me anymore, that he never cared the way I was so sure he had, that I was so easy to leave, being both my brother and his best friend, my foster brother, the boy next door could simply forget me when I didn't wake a day without thoughts of them. None of it was true.

He not only needed me, he loved me, and with that love came the largest act of selflessness I've ever heard of.

Crew gave years of his life away for me. To keep me safe.

His silent pledge of love and loyalty.

"When did it get better?" I ask.

"When I met Willie." A small smile forms on his lips and he tugs his hand free, wrapping it around me and tugging me closer, sitting up slightly, so his back is pressed against the headboard, my body slightly cradled in his. "A year of shitty hotels and no money, they finally trusted me not to run and let me get a real job. I went to the bar, met Will, and I don't know. He understood me, without me having to share shit, and convinced the manager at the time to give me a job. Then he gave me a room. I still had the Mazda Memph crashed to pay off, so I took a few fights to help with that for fun, but with some guys I met at the bar, not the gang who made me. I was good at it and enjoyed it, so being able to *choose* to fight instead of being forced felt good.

"Eventually, the debts were all paid, and my life was mine again. I saved enough to get my apartment, worked up the nerve to call my brother and ask him to come here. I needed to rebuild all I broke, so I started with Drew, and then I worked my ass into the ground, both at the bar and a fight or two here and there, just trying to find a way to look myself in the mirror and not hate what I saw. Will and Layla helped with that too."

Crew grips my chin, tipping my head to his. "You'd just gotten here, and I was dying to go to you. I did once. Watched you from across the street, but there was still so much for me to accomplish, and I didn't know how to do that. Buying and keeping the bar going cost a lot more than I expected and I had to let go of my apartment to keep above water. I didn't tell you because I was embarrassed. Felt like I was lacking all over again."

My lips pull into a small smile, despite the sorrow threatening to drown me, and I stretch my neck, pressing my mouth to his. "I would have been honored to have you at your lowest, Crew Taylor. I didn't need anything from you, just you."

"I know, baby." His lips glide across mine, his hands tightening around me. "But I needed to be more for me, to believe I was worthy of you."

"You are."

"Show me . . ."

I don't hesitate. I seal our lips together, kissing him softly, slowly, but it quickly grows hungry, desperate, and I shift in his hold, straddling him on the bed.

He stays where he is, half sitting as I roll my hips over his naked body, his dick already hard and ready between us. Without a word needed, he lifts me, sliding me back down until he's filling me.

Heavy moans leave us both, and I lean forward, right as he presses me closer, the need to be fused together heavy for us both.

The room is silent, nothing but our heavy, sensual breaths filling the space.

We fuck slow, steady, drowning in one another's touch. In the searing, slow kisses.

Crew's hands bury themselves in my hair as mine find his face, and we hold each other close. His tongue flicks over my lips, dipping at my neck until he's nipping at my collarbone.

My head falls back, my hands moving to the nape of his neck as I roll my hips forward, and he meets me with a full thrust.

It's like we're living in slow motion, the ache building both mentally and physically.

We need the release as much as we need to stay just like this, pieced together forever and ever.

But the pressure is too much for us both, our bodies slick with sweat and shaking in need.

Crew captures my lips with his, kissing me hard.

Claiming me with his mouth, and it's as if an invisible string tethers us in that moment, binding us together deeper than before.

Stronger than ever.

I feel it in my bones. Feel him in my soul.

"No matter the situation, I love you, Crew Taylor," I whisper along his lips. "I want you always."

He kisses me once more, his eyes closed, and it's as if he's only now allowed himself to believe when he whispers with a tone so sure, "I know."

My forehead falls to his and we stay like that for several minutes before he finally lifts his head.

"I love you, baby."

I smile, pushing his sweat-slick hair from where it curls over his forehead. "I know." I take his words as mine, making him chuckle.

The moment passes too soon though, the silence stealing the peace of moments ago.

Crew's gaze is tender as he pulls me forward, so I'm leaning against his chest. "Say it, Sweets," he encourages.

"Do you think these people will really try to kill him?" I whisper.

Crew's face falls, even though I suspect he knew what I was about to ask, though maybe not as the first question.

He looks to the side briefly. "They can't allow someone to screw them over."

That's a yes.

A shiver runs through me and I chew at my lips, looking away.

Crew brings my gaze right back with a press of his knuckles to my chin. His eyes narrow, though I'm not sure he realizes it. "Promise me you'll stay out of this. I can't allow this to touch you. Promise me."

I must hesitate too long, because he sits up farther, tugging my head back with a soft grip to my hair.

"Promise. Me."

"Okay," I whisper.

His eyes roam mine, his mouth opening, but he's cut off by a soft double tap against the door.

I jump, and Crew's grip tightens, his eyes flashing to the clock.

"It's Will. He said he'd bring you some of Layla's pancakes for breakfast. Looks like he got tired of waiting for me to call."

My smile is small, and I only let go once he's too far for me to hold and quickly slip the T-shirt he tosses me over my head, covering my lower half with the blanket.

Crew winks, pulling open the door, but the smell of warm butter doesn't waft inside.

The suffocating scent of ash and alcohol does.

Willie stands in the hall, Drew at his side, and I shoot to my feet, Crew subconsciously shifting to block me, but not from their eyes, from whatever it is twisting their handsome faces with agony and anger.

Sadness and fury.

The very things that fill my veins when Drew speaks.

"The bar . . . it's . . . bad."

No . . .

When they said the bar was "bad," I must have assumed they meant it was vandalized, that the windows were busted and the walls were spray-painted, maybe even the sign shattered and hanging from its place above the door.

I never expected the sight before me.

The windows are busted, yes, the bars barricading them bent a bit, but the giant steel door, swinging wide open in the daylight, the giant chain lock cut and hanging to the ground should have been my first clue it was much, much worse.

It is.

Glass crunches beneath my feet as I follow Crew inside the building, and my eyes shoot wide, my nostrils instantly brimming with the overpowering stench of alcohol.

Gone are the tables that created the lounge, each one having been chopped into nothing but piles of wood, the splintered pieces perfectly arranged as you would a campfire, pointed to a tip, rags and napkins stuffed between them. There are small char marks staining the ends as if they planned to burn it down but didn't . . . or wanted the threat of the capability of doing so to be clear. Possibly a twisted gift to light it up and put it out, showing mercy by leaving it standing.

The back wall, where the bar once was . . . gone. Chopped and added to the piles, perhaps?

Busted bottles are splayed along each and every wall, deep puddles of their contents pooled at the edges. The mirror, nothing but shattered pieces, the new shelves and lights Crew put up nowhere to be found. Electrical cords hang from wide-open gaps in the ceiling, revealing the chipped and dented foundation behind it, a large pipe sticking down where the largest fan used to be.

The walls are no longer walls, but a mess of drywall hanging from the frame, a sledgehammer or worse having torn them to shreds. Water drips from the stairs along the back wall, slowly seeping into the mess surrounding us.

I can't even bring myself to look at Crew, so when something crashes to the floor near us, and Julius grips my arm, I allow him to lead me out the door, on Crew's silent demand, I'm sure.

Outside, I pull in a deep breath, walking a few feet away, my hands folding over my head, only to slide down my face.

My palms shake, or maybe it's my body that's shaking, but when Julius tries to offer support with a hand to my back, I step away from it, posing a tight smile.

There's only one man who can comfort me right now, but he's the one who will be in need of said comfort after this.

What happened here?

Was it the man—men—from last night?

Someone else?

Is this Memphis's fault?

Don't allow the blinders to go back up, Davis . . .

I run my hands through my hair, flipping it to the side.

How—

My eyes catch a hint of color, and I jerk left, bending to pick a small card off the curb. A business card. My head snaps up to find another, and then another.

I pick up twenty in total, all piled high, dirty, and wet in my palm, but it's the car on the front that flashes in my memory—a black El Camino, candy-painted and shining off the thick paper.

The same one from the parking lot the night X dropped me off, but that's not all.

This card, it's the one the man at the market gave Crew, the "lover of pretty things" man. The same man who sat behind the wheel of said black car.

Crew bounds from the door right then, his head whipping right to left, until his eyes meet mine. While his body visibly releases some of the tension it holds once he's found me safe and sound and near his friends, it's nowhere near enough to erase the rage building within him.

His eyes are wild, his body seeming to vibrate as he yanks me to him, only seconds after I stuff the cards in my back pocket.

I don't want him to get hurt by hunting the man they belong to, but something tells me he won't have to.

Crew

Numb.

Enraged.

Accepting.

If someone claimed a person could experience all three of those things at once, I'd call them a liar. But I'd be wrong.

Pathetically wrong.

I'm fucking consumed by all three, my muscles weightless and airy, my heart and head steady, my skin hot and prickly.

Part of me wants to laugh at what I'll do to the fucker who did this to me, and another wants to run and hide, knowing it won't be easy to stomach. An ugly fucking sight I might savor.

My jaw aches from clenching it so tightly, my palms slick with sweat from my clenched fists. I'm trying to keep some semblance of calm, so I don't scare the silent and still woman in the back seat, but it's easier said than done.

The air in the car is charged, Willie, Drew, and me all trapped inside the small space with tempers tipped at the edge of sanity.

All I've worked for, all we worked for . . . gone.

I have nothing now.

As if angered by the weak thought, a sharp pain hits my chest, my eyes flicking up to the rearview mirror and landing on Davis.

I have all I need.

It's true, but it's fucking sad. I wanted to give her a life I could feel a sense of pride from.

Now all I have to give, is me.

The loan on the bar is high, the sacrifice to be able to afford it being the added insurance offered. I have none, and if I spend what's in the business account, I won't be able to stock the bar or pay the employees, let alone keep the lights on.

I'm fucked.

And I'm five seconds from fucking up worse.

That's my last thought as I tear from the passenger seat of Willie's car, taking two steps at a time toward mine and Davis's apartment.

The door vibrates on its hinges as I throw it open, anger doubling when I find it completely unlocked.

Drew yanks Davis back as he realizes, and she shouts after me as Willie and I dart inside to sweep the place. It doesn't take long to figure out it's empty, which should make me happy.

It doesn't.

We're coming out of the back room when Drew and Davis finally move inside, but she doesn't look at me, her steps are slow as she glances around the space.

There's no more glass littering the floor, no liquid splayed on the wall, and the broken and busted couch is gone. Everything is back to how it should be, minus the missing piece of furniture.

It's like nothing ever happened.

It's like Memphis was never here, a fact she realizes right away.

She tries to hide the sorrow sweeping over her, and I hate that. She's doing it for my benefit, so I temper the anger within me and go to her, cupping her face in my cheek.

Her hand comes up to wrap around my wrist, a single tear rolling down her face as she smiles sadly at me. "He's gone."

I say nothing, just hold her, and when she gasps slightly, nodding as if to say it's okay, I drop my forehead to hers, kissing it briefly. The last thing I want to do is let her go, so I tug her even closer and tuck her head into my chest, so she can't look at the expression I can't seem to wipe away, my teeth grinding together to keep the growl from tearing from my throat.

Everything is fucked, and what's worse, I have no fucking clue if I can fix it.

Chapter 39
Davis

Much to my surprise, we never left the apartment after returning in search of Memphis. I thought Crew would be far too paranoid to be here considering, but he insisted, and I think it's because he knew I needed the comfort of my own space to try and deal with all the things happening around us. The problem is . . . I have no idea what *is* actually happening around us.

Everyone remained silent, nothing but long sideways stares and pacing. Two days of it.

How Drew, who hasn't left the apartment for a single minute since arriving—likely why Crew is comfortable staying here—hasn't worn out the soles of his shoes, I don't know.

He seems the most on edge, and I wonder if it's because he came back into his brother's life amid his last struggle, and now worries how Crew will get through a second one.

Or maybe he thinks someone's going to bust through the door at any second and he doesn't want to be caught off guard.

The moment I think it, there's a knock on the other side, and Drew's head jolts up, brows furrowing as he charges to it without thought. He's kind of scary when he's mad, a side of him I've never quite noticed before, as if his silly and playful side is nothing but a mirror meant to bounce back on you, hiding the darkness beneath it. The pain.

He's struggling to keep it together, and I don't know how to console him.

"It's all right, Drew." Crew appears from the bedroom, having stepped inside to change out of his sweats.

Drew's expression is tense as he waits for his brother to pass him and becomes the shadow at his back.

"Thanks for coming," Crew says, slowly opening the door all the way and stepping back.

Jess stands in the doorway, his expression slightly guarded as he nods. "Yeah, of course."

He finds me curled up on the new-to-me couch Willie surprised me with yesterday and a small smile pulls at his lips. "Hey."

"Hey . . ." I push up, my gaze sliding to Crew in question.

I don't like this.

Why is Crew taking so long to look at me?

"Jess is here for pizza night," he says as Drew peeks out the door before locking it behind our visitor.

Panic builds in my chest, my heart pounding as I wait for Crew to tell me he's leaving, that he has an "errand" to run while pretending Jess isn't here to distract me from God knows what he'll be off doing.

But then Jess moves into the kitchen as Crew settles beside me on the couch, then takes the remote and starts searching for something to put on the TV.

My mind eases the slightest bit as I rise to my feet, joining Jess.

I go to turn on the oven, but he shakes his head, a small, slightly forced smile on his lips.

"Figured we earned the good shit this time around, so I ordered about a half hour ago. It'll be here anytime."

"Pineapples?"

"What do I look like, an amateur?"

His tease comes easy, and we both laugh a little.

"Thank you for the other night. I know it was a lot to walk into."

Jess nods, not denying he was out of his element, but adds, "I'm just glad I was home when he called me."

My brows furrow, and Jess tips his head slightly. "You didn't know he called?" He cuts a quick glance toward Crew, who is likely pretending he isn't listening to our conversation.

"I guess I didn't think about it. How did you get by those guys?"

"The door was unlocked, I just let myself in. One guy shouted something, but stumbled, so I kept walking, and I didn't see the others until they came out of one of the rooms, but I already had you with me by then. I wasn't sure which one was your brother so I did my best to ignore them all."

I nod. "Well, I appreciate it and you not calling the police."

He eyes me a moment, a forced smile following.

He wants to ask who they were and what they wanted, how I'm involved, but I don't think he knew my brother was here, so I'm sure he already assumes Crew brought the trouble here. He helped regardless, and he's here now, so it doesn't really matter. He's moving back home anyway, so there's no reason to go into too much detail.

The doorbell rings and Jess claps his hands, happy to end the awkward conversation and busy our mouths with food.

Crew's phone rings and I look at him as he picks it up, Drew heading for the door, but before he can open it, Crew's head snaps that way. Drew freezes instantly.

Crew looks to me, concern in his gaze. "Lock yourself in your room."

When I don't move, he barks, "Now, Davis."

"Pizza's here!" Someone chuckles from outside. "Hurry up before it gets cold!"

My muscles lock, and Crew's glare doubles.

He charges me, grips my face firmly, his voice stiff and harsh, his eyes soft and begging. "Go. Now. And do not come out. DO you understand me?"

Tears prick my eyes, and I nod, heading for my room.

"Go with her."

I don't look to see who he's talking about, but I know it's not Drew, because the person actually listens.

Jess and I lock ourselves inside my room, tears stinging my eyes.

There's some shouting followed by a loud thud, and I jolt, dashing for the door, but Jess throws himself in front of it, shaking his head.

"Jess, you don't understand, I—"

"Maybe not, but I can't let you go out there. He said stay, that means he thinks you're safer in here. So stay, Davis." He frowns, quickly adding, "Please."

A small growl leaves me, and I drop my head back, trying to keep my tears at bay.

"Fuck you!" Drew's shout booms from the living room, something crashing to the wall with a hard crash. "Tell your boss my brother is off-limits!"

Another crash, one that rattles the door on its frame.

I meet Jess's eyes, and his tighten, his hand wrapping around the door, conflicted.

"Touch him again, you're dead." Crew's voice is loud yet somehow low. It makes no sense but hearing him has my lungs expanding. He's okay.

A third crash, too many shouts to count, and then, "You shut the fuck up! You *back* the fuck up before I stick this fucking pipe up your ass!"

Willie. Willie's here.

I nod to myself. This is good.

Maybe.

"Tell this *Kaleb*, he can suck my fucking dick. We're not interested in what he has to say."

My ears perk.

Kaleb . . .

Dashing to my side of the bed, I dig my pants from beneath it, tearing into the back pocket, where I saved a single card left outside the bar and read the service listed.

Kaleb's Car Service.

It was him.

My head snaps up, my eye meeting Jess's, his narrowing as I fish my phone from where I left it on the nightstand.

I dial the number, heart pounding as I bring it to my ear.

"Davis . . ." Jess studies me. "What are you doing?"

It rings twice before it's answered.

"Kaleb's Car Service." The humor in the man's voice makes my stomach turn. "What can I do for you . . . *Sweets*?"

My gasp is unavoidable, and the chuckle that fills my ear coils my insides, but I steady my quivering jaw, backing away from Jess as he steps closer.

"Is it you?" I try to keep my tone steady. "The bar, my brother, the men—"

"Inside your house? I take it you ruined my not-so-subtle hints?"

"I picked up the cards, yes."

I swallow, and silence follows for a long moment, my body shaking.

I'm about to check to see if he hung up when his voice reaches me again.

"If you didn't call to tell me good news, hang up now, princess. Let men handle men things."

"You're a bastard."

"You have no idea. And you don't have twenty-five racks."

Looking to the card once more, it's as if all my tangled thoughts tie together, my promise to stay out of things evaporating with my next breath. My shoulders seem to square, and I meet Jess's gaze. "No, but I have a Classic worth twice as much."

Crew

My muscles strain, my ligaments threatening to snap, they're so tense, so tight.

As pathetic as it might be, I had to consider the bullshit with Memphis had nothing to do with the bullshit happening to me, but now I know for sure it does.

The men who paid off a pizza driver to step up to our door are connected to the ones I beat the shit out of, and the man who fucked up, bringing this shit down on us, is my old best friend.

The piece of shit who bailed without a parting word, his problems, once again, falling right into my lap.

"You're not fucking going! Fuck that!" Drew gets in my face. "They got a call and left. Must not be that big of a deal if they didn't come in here with guns and shit, dragging you out."

I look to Willie, who glares at me.

He's pissed I didn't confide in him the second shit started to stir around me—I'd sworn I always would, after he witnessed the shit I went through the first time. But Layla's pregnant, he's about to be a dad, and his wife needs him. I didn't feel right having him out or up all night, stressing about me and my problems, and we haven't had the time to sit back and talk this shit out yet.

"I don't have a choice here."

"Yes, you fucking do, Crew! Yes, you do!" Drew frowns, rushes out the front door and looks around, only to come right back to glare at me some more.

"I have to meet him, see what he has to say."

"We know what he's going to say. He wants the money Memphis owes him. You can't afford that shit!"

"I'm not going to stand here and allow this."

"You don't have a say."

"I won't let them ruin your life. What are you going to do if they just keep coming? What happens if they show up when Davis is here alone, because eventually, she will be!"

"I won't let anyone near her!"

"Fuck with these guys and you might not be around to protect her!"

"Then I will die trying!"

"It's done!"

All eyes snap to the end of the hall, where Davis slowly steps from the room, a stiff, frowning Jess at her back.

My pulse beats out of control, my breaths deep and shallow, but I attempt to calm myself as she approaches.

Wait . . .

"What's done?"

She looks to Jess, who drops his eyes to the floor, slipping past her and positioning himself near Drew. Closer to me.

My eyes narrow. "Sweets . . ."

"I paid them off," Davis says in a rush.

My muscles lock, everyone's attention is honed on her.

In what feels like slow motion, I turn so my body is facing hers.

"You . . . what?"

Davis wrings her hands in front of her, her gaze flicking to Jess, who's glaring at the floor.

"What the fuck is going on?"

Jess looks to me, clears his throat, and nods toward her, forcing her to say it.

Davis flicks her gaze over the four of us, wetting her lips before speaking. "They left cards at the bar, in the gutter, and I . . . picked one up. I didn't really know why or what to do with it, but I heard you say Kaleb and that was the name on the front. I called, and he answered. I . . . the men from the house came around the back. I passed the keys through the gaps of the privacy walls."

"Keys, what . . ." My brows snap together, realization dawning.

No . . .

She nods.

"Davis."

"It's done."

An angry growl tears from me and pushes toward her. "You went behind my back when you promised not to touch this? Called the people who fucked up our livelihood? Brought the people who hurt you *to* you?"

"Crew—"

"Everyone out."

"Crew, man—" Jess begins.

"I said OUT!" I scream, and seconds later, Willie's shoving them all out the door.

The door echoes with a loud thud as it closes, and then it's just Davis and me.

"You could have been—"

"I wasn't." She's quick to cut me off, an anxiousness in her tone, but she doesn't cower away from me.

She knows she has no reason to. I'd never hurt her, but I've got this sudden desire to punish her a bit, to consume her, to feel her, overpowering every other thing attempting to fry my brain. As if sensing the charge in the air, Davis's lips part, her palms planting on her thighs.

We come together in a clash of teeth, hers scratching along the cut of my mouth and making me growl, which she takes full advantage of, thrusting her tongue inside my mouth. I've got her dress hiked up and her body against the wall in seconds, my chest slamming into her back as I flick open my jeans. She whimpers, dropping her head back, ass poking my way for attention.

My cock is free and pushing inside her in the next breath. She cries out, and I pump into her, closing my eyes and getting lost in her tight heat.

I need this.

Her.

Us.

Just for a fucking minute, before the world buries me beneath the dirt, when I just shoveled the final scoop from the last time I was fucked over.

I thrust into her again, her body jutting with mine, her palm slapping onto the wall beside us, rattling the photos on the wall.

She whimpers, seeking my lips, but I tip her head, attacking her neck with my mouth instead, and sucking hard enough to burn.

"God, yes," she pants.

"This how you imagined it?" I lick up her throat. "Yeah, it is, isn't it? Your pussy's clamping over me, baby. This is exactly what I did to you when you thought of being pinned to the wall."

Her response is a heady moan, one that sizzles down my spine, raising the hairs on the back of my neck.

I pull back, gripping her hips, and she folds her arms in front of her, leaning her head on her clenched fists.

I drive into her with swift motions, tugging her back to meet my every move, and she cries around my cock, walls quivering. She's about to come, but she's going to have to wait.

Pushing in again, I hold still when I'm as deep as the position allows, and she gasps from the stretch of her walls.

"Crew, please."

"No." I hold still, clenching my ass and smacking hers, all to squeeze it a second later.

She whimpers, and I groan, dipping forward to nip at her jaw. "Don't *ever* put yourself in danger like that again, you hear me?"

She nods frantically, pushing into me, but I hold her still.

"Promise?"

"Y-yes."

Tipping her head to mine, her wild, half-closed eyes find mine.

I slam my mouth to hers, pressing in farther, and she cries between my lips.

"I believe you, Sweets." My tongue traces her lips. "You can come now."

I pull back, swiftly bucking forward once more, and she explodes, every part of her trembling until she's nothing but loose limbs in my arms.

Lowering us onto the couch, I fold her into my arms, closing my eyes, so I can get lost in her a little longer, but as the minutes pass, the sex haze clears, and everything else grows foggier, for both her and me.

"It's okay now, right?" she whispers hopefully, looking up at me, but that hope doesn't quite reach her eyes. "I fixed it. Paid him. The truck is worth twice what Memphis owes."

Tucking her hair behind her ear, I offer a small smile. "It's too late for that, baby."

Confusion and unease create creases along her eyes, and I wish I could wipe the worry away. "I don't understand. Why?"

"These people didn't come to my bar and destroy it to collect a measly twenty-five *K*. That's chump change to them."

"Then why?"

I stare at her a moment. "He did what he did to make five times that."

It only takes her a moment to understand, fear, shock, and hurt flicking across her face all at once. "He wants you to fight for him."

I don't have to nod, and neither of us has to say what we're both thinking.

It's the only fucking answer there is.

This motherfucker saw what I was willing to do for her, what I am capable of, period, and plans to use it to his advantage, but that's not the worst of it.

It's the simple fact that the only way the man could possibly know about any of this—her, me, my past—is if someone told him.

Her brother, my foster brother, my best fucking friend, turned enemy, sold me out to save his own ass.

Again.

Chapter 40
Crew

Growing up, Memphis was strong.

I watched the guy bench nearly double the rest of our baseball team for years, despite his leaner build. His swinging power was unmatched, to the point that the university he chose wanted him so badly, they allowed the little ultimatum disguised as a request he tossed their way—bring my "brother" on too, who has speed and build, but needs fine-tuning in mechanics, and I'm in.

It worked, got me a foot in the door at Avix U, after two years of busting my ass with Mrs. Franco, and when I was lucky, Davis, as my own personal tutors. Even years younger, she knew her shit well enough to guide me through mine.

We headed off to school together.

There were always little things he had that I wished for, but not to the point of hate or envy, simply ideals and dreams living in his world made me want to strive for.

His family pushed me to be better. Still do when I feel helpless and think back to what they taught me.

It wasn't until Memphis started getting into deeper trouble out here that I witnessed for the first time something he had I didn't want any part of, fear.

He was afraid his family would hate him for what he was doing and hiding.

Afraid he'd lose them.

Afraid he'd get kicked off the team, dropped from school, and have nothing and no one and so on and so forth.

His addiction preyed on his insecurities, and eventually, on his conscience.

It was a downhill battle there, and I was the rickety wheel on the front of the barrel, doing all I could to keep him from tumbling the rest of the way down.

That is, until he removed the screws himself and I was crashing to the ground on my own, no hand to lift me up, no shovel to dig me out.

Then I met Willie. His relationship with his brothers is what gave me the courage to call my own. Time and age might have pulled us apart—what ten-year-old would willingly walk away from their mom? Especially said mom paired with a manipulative son of a bitch called dad, a decision I know he regrets, but neither of us can change it. I know I would if I could, I sure as hell would.

Now I have a gang of guys, of family, at my side. People who will stand with me, not behind me.

People at risk of being hurt, if I don't do what I've always been dangerously good at.

If I don't fight.

But what will it cost me this time?

Another three years?

My girl?

My life?

"You owe me a free shot after this, but you already know this," Willie snaps, his face blank, eyes facing forward.

The man isn't talking about liquor. He's more than mad, which means he might even knock me out when I give him that free shot.

If I told him I held back because Layla has been sick, and getting closer to delivery, he wouldn't wait until after all this to swing. He'd whoop my ass right now.

Or I'd have to let him, I mean.

"You can get me on my good side."

He frowns at the window but says nothing.

"Ready?"

He nods, and together, we step out, lifting our hands into the air to let the no-neck dipshits search us.

Across the empty lot, standing against a black El Camino is the bastard I beat unconscious on Davis's living room floor. Did I say standing?

I meant balancing on a crutch, his right arm in a sling, a thick white brace wrapped around his neck, black-and-blue bruises coloring most of his skin. Mix that with the thick stitches laced across his face, and he looks like the redheaded doll from *The Nightmare Before Christmas*. A fucked-up version.

"That's right." A familiar voice speaks, and I face forward to find the silver-haired prick from the farmers' market. The asshole responsible for destroying my bar. He smirks, waving a hand toward the guy glaring at me. "You met my brother. Doc says his hand might not be the same after this. Nephew ain't looking too hot either, but he's young, dumb, and needed a scar or two to dirty him up."

He glances left and I follow his gaze to find the prick from the diner, his face still puffed and bruised—lucky he can stand. Willie pounced on me the minute I had the fucker by the throat, knowing I'd do worse to him for damaging the sense of safety Davis felt within herself. I only got a few hits in on him, lucky punk.

I say nothing, and the silver-haired asshole tips his head.

Picking his teeth with a knife he casually pulls out, he stares at me. "Don't waste my time, son."

"Then say what you want, so I can tell you to fuck off."

A big dude with a fist tattooed on his neck steps closer, and I keep my head held high, my eyes locked with his. Big dudes fall fast, if you know where to start.

The silver-haired man laughs, flicking his blade closed and pushing to his feet with a grin. "One fight, that's all I'm asking. This ain't my territory, so I can't stay long, but there's a card coming up in a few days, about fifty miles from here, so we'll be on common ground with two other clans, but see, I'm the only one without a fighter on this card. That's a problem." He steps closer, and Willie's hands flex at his side. "The prize is too mighty for me not to have a hand in. That's where you come in." He grins. "You can thank your girl's rat of a brother for that, if the little bitch ever comes out of hiding again."

I survey him.

His being run out by who the fuck knows which gang is better than I could expect, not that dudes like this are always honest with the "help." But he got what he came for in double with Davis's truck, and he's right, Memphis cut the second he had the chance, leaving no sign of him behind, other than a sad sister I'll continue to comfort. That's shit for another time, though.

"I know a lot of people, kid. Big people in big places. You're good, son, one of the best I've come across and you can't tell me you don't love the rush." He watches me closely. "Do this, help me walk away with what I want, and I'll make a call."

My eyes narrow, his words lost on me and probably complete fucking bullshit. Do I like to fight? Yeah, I do, but not at someone else's command.

None of that matters right now, though, so I ask what does. "How much?"

Willie stiffens.

"You win, I give you the three hundred grand you need to rebuild the damage someone caused on your little bar." His lips tip higher. "And I skip into the sunset without batting a lash at the loss of fifteen percent."

"Absolutely not!"

We whip around to find Julius battling Davis to keep the window closed.

"Ah, the princess is here."

I dart forward, pushing into the man's face, but two men with their hands under their shirts block my path. I pretend they aren't there, guns ready at their hips. "Do *not* look at her."

The man's grin grows, and I want to carve it from his cheeks, Joker style.

"Davis," I snap, not looking back. "*Now*."

I don't have to say more, the girl *knows* what I mean.

Get your ass back in the window and roll the shit up.

"Okay, okay, but if three hundred grand is only fifteen percent, which holy crap, that's insane—"

"Davis!"

"Sorry, but that means he's still getting one point seven million! Just so you know."

Willie jerks away, and seconds later, a door slams shut and then he's back.

Thank you, my little math nerd, but your ass is grass later.

Licking my lips, I lift my chin.

This guy isn't in this for the money. He mentioned other plans and a price he can't miss out on. What that could be, I don't fucking care.

He's looking for a win, and knows I can give it to him, which is why I say, "That's not gonna work for me."

His glare is sharp and instant.

I make him sweat a second before adding, "But I'll tell you what will."

The crew leader—Kaleb, according to Davis, when I'm pretty sure it's nothing but the preppiest, prep-boy name they could think of as a cover for their "car service"—wasn't joking when he said the fight was in days, the plural of that barely squeezing fucking by.

If she hadn't hidden the cards from me, I'd have found them, and likely called him up just as he wanted, falling into his hands and securing his crews' name on the fight card a few days sooner.

Fuck him. I'm glad he had to sweat a couple more days, if a man like him is capable of worry. If that would have happened, my girl wouldn't have been there to drop math bombs on me, making this fight the biggest opportunity of my life—as twisted and fucked up as it might seem, since I don't have a choice, even if the asshole pretended to give me one.

We both knew he could have threatened my friends and family, and I'd have agreed for nothing. But he also knew the fire it would light to know how going in and giving my all would benefit me as well, not just him.

I win tonight, I walk away with half a million dollars, untaxed . . . and my girl gets her truck back.

That's three hundred K for the bar.

One to help get my best friend's business off the ground—he doesn't know this yet.

And one I'll anonymously deposit into my parents'—the Francos—savings account, paying back all they put into their son's failed recovery, and allowing them to settle into retirement without worry, just like they deserve.

I spoke to Garratt last night on FaceTime, and for the first time since I was nothing but a boy, when he asked how I was, I told him the truth.

I was tired, anxious.

In love with his daughter.

The way my muscles coiled at the confession was pointless.

The man actually choked up, and I felt the relief wash over him as if he projected it all on me. The creases along his eyes seemed to disappear, making him look younger in a single second. It was like he knew I would love her the way she deserves, and then some. That I would protect and care for her, the way he hoped a man one day would. By the end of the conversation, I almost wondered if he'd always quietly hoped that man would be me.

He didn't resent me.

Never thought less of me.

"My children have done many things over the years that brought pride to my family, but son, I need you to know, I have never been prouder of anyone than I am of you, for all you've overcome and what you've accomplished along the way. You're a strong man, Crew Taylor. A good man."

The man loved me and my faults, and that's an honor I'll never take for granted.

Would he kick my ass for what I'm about to do? Yes. But that's why kids don't tell their parents everything, at least not until after it's done. He'll only do his best to talk me out of it and worry when it doesn't work.

I'll be the first to admit, it's not ideal to have two lousy days to mentally prepare for a fight that will either give back all that was stolen from me and more, or leave me high and dry, like the punk kid I was at fourteen when my neighbors took me in—worthless, penniless.

Hopeless.

But even if I did lose, which I won't, the rabbit hole won't swallow me whole this time around because, no matter what happens tonight, tomorrow, or the day after, I'll still have the one thing that means more than any damn dollar could bring.

I have the girl.

The girl who "refused" to stay in the suite we've been "guests" in—pretty sure guests don't get locked in from the outside—the last forty-eight hours. Davis wrote, practiced, and delivered a three-minute—absolutely fucking adorable—presentation on why she should be with me tonight.

I didn't have the heart to tell her there was no fucking way she was staying behind if she wanted to. No way in *hell* am I ready to leave her somewhere I'm not.

Maybe in six months or so, I'll allow her out without me.

Maybe not.

From what we saw pulling in, in the RV they moved us to in the middle of the night, the fight is being held in the middle of nowhere, in a makeshift boxing ring set up behind an old broken-down mill. The floor is nothing but dirt, the rope, something you'd use for power conditioning, is woven through metal loops, welded to stakes likely hammered into the ground.

The lights run on generators, nothing but motorcycles and giant-ass trucks lining the yard, people piled all around them, yet a few feet of space between each large group, slightly segregating each club from the next. Weed, cigarettes, and cheap cigar smoke billowing all around.

We've been waiting around for hours now, Willie pacing anxiously as Davis chews her nails down to nothing. My fight is the last of the night, the best and worst spot to be. Best, because it means highest paid; worst, because every fucker around will be a six-pack past drunk by the time it begins.

The chaos of the crowd as we step out of the giant fifth wheel proves my thoughts correct. The place is drowning in drunks.

My hold on Davis's hand tightens, and she grips my upper arm, standing tall and strong and facing forward, just like I told her. *Kaleb* walks us to the back corner, where a few of his guard dogs stand in a half-square near the wall, and we step behind them.

"No backing out now, kid," he says, a grin splitting his lips, but a sharp warning in his beady eyes. "Ready to roll in two minutes. Do your job, and I'll change your life."

I lift my chin but don't respond, tracing his steps as he moves to the camper across the circle. Me, Davis, Willie, and Julius stare as the dude I'm about to fight is let out.

The guy's tall, broad in the chest, but no more than me. His body is covered in colorful ink, his bald head included. The dude doesn't even have eyebrows. He's greased up, roided up too, if I had to guess based on the unnatural bulge of his biceps. His arms are twice the size of mine, something Davis must assume is bad, if the way her grip tightens tells me anything.

All it says to me is my reach is better, maybe by a full two inches, and I'd like to see him try and choke a motherfucker with those balloons in the way—he could never sink it airtight.

Kaleb smirks my way, and my gaze instantly finds *the man* at his side.

The one I'd have happily ended if not for Willie's decision to let him breathe another day. Kaleb called him his brother the other day, whether he meant that literally, I don't know. Don't fucking care.

It's like I knew he put his hands on her before actually knowing—I cracked his fingers and busted the bones of his hand, before popping his shoulder from its joints.

Let's see him try to ride a bike like that.

The man glares, and I stare at the hack job someone, likely someone in this crowd, did on his stitches.

Good.

He'll have the scars to remember me by.

I turn to my girl.

Worry draws her brows in close, and my attention lowers to her arm, where the asshole's fingerprints still torment me.

I've touched, kissed, and run my tongue over each small spot, more times than I could count, trying to erase the memory of how they got there . . . and convince myself not to go fucking mad and do something stupid, like kill the guy before I beat the other fucker's ass and get my money.

Davis looks to me, and I step into her.

This will be the last time she's in a position like this.

That's a deal I'm making with my damn self.

Davis

Crew might not notice, but it isn't my grip tightening on his, over and over again, tonight; it's the opposite. He's anxious, but not for himself, for my presence among this mob, but we're going to run a bar together when all this is done, so really, there's no better time to get used to a rowdy crowd.

Yes, these are our typical customers turned up to eleven, but still.

Crew releases my hand, facing me, his beaten expression immediately zoning in on the bruise on my upper arm.

Hazel eyes slice up to mine, fury swimming behind them. I sink into his embrace, and he tips my chin up, his thumb stretched along my throat.

"No one will ever hurt you again. *Never*, and no one can hurt me but you." His promise is fierce and soul searing. A reminder any blow he may take, or blood he may lose, is only surface-deep. It will heal like the mark on my skin, like the scars on his. Only I have the power to make him ache, and it's one I'll relish yet never release.

Willie shifts beside me, and I know it's time, so I press my palms to Crew's chest, rise on my toes, and meet his lips with my own. "Kick his fucking ass, baby." I move to his ear. "And come kiss mine once you do."

Pulling back, I meet his gaze, darkened by my words and something far more sinister.

Crew's lips twitch, but it's quick, and only once I nod does the mask slip over his face.

In that second, he becomes a blanket of nothingness. He grows a foot taller, his dominance dripping from his very being.

He's the picture of power. May someone, somewhere, watch over the man across the mat tonight. After mine takes him out, of course.

One wordless glance at Willie, and his best friend loops his arm through mine, leading me to the edge of the circle where Drew waits. He takes my hand and tugs, locking my back against the wall behind him. Julius joins us, both bodies creating one in front of me, allowing nothing but my eyes to peek through the slight curve between where their shoulders press to one another's as Willie rushes ringside.

Poor Layla. She's likely pacing a hole into the carpet, waiting for the second this is over, so she can hear her husband's voice as he promised. If she weren't pregnant, she'd be here, she swore it, but I didn't need her to say it. I already knew.

It's what friends are for.

It's what *family* is for.

A sense of guilt-laced sorrow washes over me at the word, but I don't shy away from it.

I realize now why I didn't have any relationships in my life that truly mattered. I didn't allow people in for fear of filling the spots left empty by the two most important people in my life when they left home, left me, and I don't regret keeping them open until those people returned. Even if only one of them truly did.

How many years will go by before I meet my brother's blue eyes this time?

My thoughts are immediately drowned out by the man with a megaphone.

"Ready for the rules?" the giant of a guy shouts, the crowd quieting instantly. His hollow laugh follows, and he lifts the heavy plastic to his mouth once more. "Well, baby, there ain't none. Balls to the walls, and hold your bitches on your britches, boys. It's go time."

Just like that, the entire crowd shuffles backward.

A shiver runs down my spine as Crew bends, slipping under the thick rope, the man he's set to fight doing the same.

His bald, tattooed opponent hops from foot to foot, rolling and cracking his neck, swinging out his right arm, followed by the left, stretching each one behind his shoulder blades.

Crew does none of this.

He stands perfectly still, straight, *scary*. He's a stone statue, fierce and flawless, completely lax, unfazed in the middle of a boisterous crowd, who wants to see him busted and bleeding.

He's breathing easy, the energy leaving him almost that of a bored man. If I wasn't so terrified, it might be hilarious, how adorably cliché the complete coolness the bad boy from the bar has when faced with a fight.

Any thoughts of laughter disappear when the speaker man leaves the circle; Crew and "Snake" as they chant around me, shifting toward the center.

My heart pounds wildly in my chest, and I reach up, gripping both Julius and Drew's forearms. Both flex the moment my fingers close around them, letting me know they've got me, that it's going to be okay.

That Crew will be okay.

He has to be.

My heart is in my throat the minute the gun goes off, Snake having jumped a second early, his fists swinging at Crew before the smoke has left the barrel.

Crew doesn't move his feet, his torso simply twists, the upper half leaning back and to the side, like some *Mortal Kombat* shit. Snake's momentum is so strong, he stumbles into the rope. Crew capitalizes on the position, swiftly spinning and wrapping his arms around the man's neck, tipping him back and kicking his feet out from under him, but the guy reaches backward, jabbing his fingers into Crew's left eye.

Crew jerks, tossing Snake to the floor, and clamps the watering eye closed, but only for a second.

People shout as the fighters round each other, and heat brims along my skin, fear and anxiety warming the blood in my veins.

Snake swings over and over again, clipping Crew in the jaw, but it almost looks purposeful, as if Crew allowed it, because in the next second, Crew is dipping to the right, the exact way his head snapped, his dominant fist connecting with Snake's kidney. His left follows, right against his opponent's lung.

Snake's chest caves and he jerks back, seeking the ropes for a moment of reprieve, which Crew doesn't allow.

He attacks, his body moving swift and smooth, as if he's the king of salsa and this pit in the dark, dirty clearing is his dance floor. I've never seen anything like it. Swing, swing, dip. Roll, spin, swing.

Swing, swing, swing.

My lips part, Julius's body jerking in my hold, and I realize my nails are piercing his skin, but I can't let go. I push closer, and they push back, smashing me between them and the wall completely, my nose buried between their biceps.

Blood pours from Snake's nose and brow, from his temple and—

I jolt when Crew's elbow slams into the side of Snake's face, and a loud crack is heard, followed by a sharp scream, charging the air around us.

Blood gushes from Snake's mouth now, and he chokes, coughing and spraying red into the air as he turns, the crowd jumping back with shouts to avoid the splatter. He trips into the rope, fumbling around it, and attempts to steady his feet.

I push onto my toes, my pulse bounding wildly in my chest as something changes.

Drew and Julius stand taller, both growing rigid.

Willie darts right, attempting to squeeze along the ropes.

To get a better view?

To get to Crew?

Why?

I try to shout, to ask what's going on, but my voice is drowned out by the roar of the crowd.

That's when I see them, two men shoving their way to the front of the spectators. They reach the ring's edge, lean forward, and grab hold of Crew's arms, pulling them back, his chest bowing forward.

Crew's mouth opens with a loud shout, the veins in his neck bulging as he fights against the hold.

Panic flares in my chest, and I try to push through the boys, but they only push back harder, each chancing the quickest of flicks of their gazes toward one another.

"We have to help him! We have to help him!" My fearful screams fall on deaf ears but pulsate through my own.

Snake wipes his face along his arm, slowly coming at Crew, and Crew kicks out, nearly tripping him, but Snake catches himself, a sinister smile turning up his face.

That's when I see it, when we all see it, if the jolt of Drew's body tells me anything.

The hint of silver hidden in Snake's palm flashes against the light, a single second before it's thrust into Crew's side.

I scream, shoving at the bodies in front of me, and in their moment of shock and worry, in the middle of Drew's mind, torn between rushing to help his brother and doing the one thing his brother made him promise, keeping me safe, I dip down, squeezing between their legs and dart forward, freezing as the knife is yanked out and shoved into Crew's other side.

"No!" I cry, my shout blending with Crew's battle cry.

I run, but I'm caught around the waist and yanked backward, hard enough to knock the wind out of me.

I briefly register the sound of Julius's voice in my ear, but I don't hear a thing he says.

"Let me go!" I gasp, kicking and clawing. "Please! Someone, please!" I scream, but no one can hear me.

The crowd is cheering as they watch Crew's head drop to his chest, his muscles stretched, body thrashing as he fights to get free.

Willie is shoved away, barricaded by a brigade of bikers, but continues to try and bully his way to his best friend.

That's when I see him.

On the left side of the ring, a bottle of bourbon in his hand, he creeps closer, busting it along the cement post holding the rope in place, ducking underneath it and into the ring.

He's noticed on entry.

Snake spins so fast, he can't brace, but he doesn't attempt to do so either.

Air whooshes from my lungs, my temple pounding as I stare, horrified.

Memphis shoves the broken bottle into the man's neck . . . but not before Snake's knife thrusts deep into my brother's chest.

Time slows, then stops.

"No!" A tremor racks through me, and my muscles give, my scream loud and piercing. Deafening, yet, somehow, the slamming of Memphis's body as he collapses to the ground reverberates around me. Choking me.

Snake falls next.

I look to Crew, now free of the bounds holding him back.

Struggling in the arms keeping me still, I try to yell, to shout, but somehow, no sound slips from my lips.

Dead silence falls over the crowd, but not a split second later, cheers erupt, and then they scurry like mice, bike after bike firing up, the motors rumbling through the air.

I manage to tear free, flying forward and falling to my knees, pain shooting through my legs as I crawl under the rope.

"Memphis! Fuck!" Crew is on his knees beside his old best friend, staring down at Memphis with wide eyes, blood seeping from his own wounds. He dips down, pressing hard against my brother's chest. "Why the fuck did you do this?!" he shouts. "I'm the one who fights, Memph. Me. Not you!"

Snapping out of his unconscious state, Memphis's head jerks toward Crew, and it's as if he's preparing for a second attack, because his hand flies out, bracing to shove the person coming near away. But then his barren eyes find mine, and the dread filling them has me trembling.

"Davis," he croaks.

I scramble closer, gripping Crew's arm for support, but then my eyes fall to my brother, pale and sweating, blood pooled all around him, and my hand flies up, trembling as I go to touch him but fear to.

"Oh my god . . ." Tears blur my vision as I stare at him, my eyes quickly locking on Crew's torso. "Crew, you're—"

He shakes his head as if to say he's fine.

Slowly, Memphis's hand lifts off the dirty ground. "Davis—"

I jolt, taking his fingers in mine, my lips quivering as I try to smile.

"Shh, I'm here." I push his hair back, holding his cheek. "It's okay, you're going to be okay." I nod, fear heavy in the pit of my stomach.

"I'm sorry," he rasps, trying to swallow. "For everything I-I did and didn't."

"Stop, it's okay. You're okay. You're going to be okay."

A small, sad smile curves his lips. "I love you, baby sister."

A cry escapes before I can bury it, and I shake my head. This can't happen.

It can't.

I just got him back.

I thought everything was better.

Memphis's eyes begin to close, and I gulp. "Memphis!" I scoot in, squeezing his hand tighter. "Memphis, please. Help! Someone help!" I shout. "Please help!"

Familiar keys are tossed in the dirt at my brother's feet, and my head jerks left to find Kaleb. His face is blank, eyes on Crew, but my brother's coughs draw my attention back, his entire body jerking, and I scream, gripping his shirt.

"We have to do something! Someone, please!"

Feet shuffle closer, and I look up into Julius's wide eyes, at Drew, who drops his chin to his chest, Crew's warm hands wrapping around my biceps in the next second, his body cocooning me from behind.

"No." I shake my head, refusing to believe. "No, no, no," I croak, looking down at my brother.

"It's okay," he rasps, a faraway look in his light eyes as they flutter half open. "Davis . . ."

"I'm here," I sob, tears soaking into the blood on his shirt.

His smile returns, his grip on my fingers fading. "Nothing hurts anymore."

"Fuck," Crew curses, one hand gripping me tighter, the other leaving my arm and pressing into his old best friend's cheek, gaining his attention.

Memphis looks to him, his chest deflating as a single tear slips from the edge of his eye. "I love you, brother. Forgive me."

My hand slaps over my mouth, my breath lodged in my throat as the man at my side gives a single jerky nod. "Always, my man. Always," Crew breathes, his body shaking.

My brother's eyes flutter closed, a slight jolt racking through him.

"Memphis." I push up on my knees. "Memphis!" I shout, shaking him. "Memphis, wake up!" I cry, my head falling to his chest as I tug on him. "Please—"

"Get her out of here."

I jerk up, gripping the hem of my brother's shirt, tearing the soaked cotton as I'm lifted off the ground. "No, I can't leave him, please! I can't . . ." I go limp with silent cries. "I can't leave him . . ."

Please.

Memphis, please.

Don't go . . .

Chapter 41
Crew

One year later

If someone would have asked me three hundred and sixty-five days ago where I'd be a year from then, I have no fucking idea what I would have said.

I might have knocked the person out in a fit of rage because that's all I felt that night.

White-hot rage from the bottom of my shoes to the hairs on top of my head. Some might say that night, in a busted-ass, makeshift ring in the middle of nowhere, late at night, changed my life, and they wouldn't be wrong.

My life did change, thanks to a twisted fucking promise from a thug I wish I never met, but if the option to go back in time to change it all existed, I'd hit the reset button in a heartbeat, even if it meant I wouldn't be standing where I am today.

The life I lived before that night may have been one of simplicity and struggle, but I never needed easy, and I worked my ass off for the little I did have.

The girl included.

Davis was the drive behind the dreams. She was the reason I kept pushing for more, for better, for bigger.

Was, is, always will be.

My Sweets, my girl, my future wife—if she says yes to me tonight, and she will.

Young or not, it's been hard to wait when I'm damn near desperate to claim her completely, but I found a way to be patient for her, the need to paint today's memory a different shade deeper than any desire I might have.

No matter what I do, pain will always settle into her bones when this date rolls around, especially as the memories weaken with time, but I'll be here to love her through it. It'll be my privilege to patch up the pieces as they wear. That's what she's done for me my whole life, dry up the tears, glue the gaps, while trying to convince me I could hold my head high on my own, so long as I believed it.

I didn't, but I do now.

I see now.

I'm *proud* now.

Of me.

Of her.

Of us.

But most of all *of him*.

Davis

The sun shines down on the balcony, warming my skin as I point my chin to the sky, eyes closed.

I always did like to soak in the sun. I'll admit, I'd prefer a soft patch of grass beneath my back to a four-inch pair of heels planted on a cement slab fifty floors high, but the latter is pretty damn awesome too.

Crew picked them out, a glittery, bright baby blue.

A familiar blue, like the sky at noon when it opens up above the ocean, or the blue rings on my candy necklaces.

The blue of my brother's eyes.

My hand subconsciously lifts, touching the sugared jewelry around my neck.

It was Memphis who bought me my first one.

We were at the party store, getting things for his eleventh birthday party that I wasn't invited to. It was his first boys-only event, and every item we got that day was a girly girl's nightmare, and I may or may not have pouted the entire time, and the entire week leading up to that moment at the store.

But the second we got home, Memphis told me to close my eyes, and when I opened them, my wrists and neck were covered in candy jewelry, they were *the girliest thing he could find,* he teased.

How he convinced my mom to buy me a dang thing, I don't know. She wasn't one to cave to fit throwing.

Now that I think about it, Memphis might have stolen them.

"What are you laughing about over there, girl?"

My eyes open and I turn to Layla, ignoring the fact that I'm totally giving her a quick crotch shot when I bend down, opening my arms and calling my favorite little human to them.

Evie's little palms slap along the hardwood floor as she crawls to me, pulling herself up on my hands. Swooping her in my arms, I lift her, kissing her chubby little cheeks, but she's stolen from my arms as fast as she's in them.

"Nope. Nu-uh." Julius shakes his head. "I am on 'don't fuck with Davis' duty, and even pretty little baby puke doesn't make the list of 'Davis dos.'"

"Baby puke isn't cute." Remy steals the baby, stolen from me, and doesn't look back.

"Hey, you don't get dibs. I'm her uncle!" he shouts after her.

"And I'm her favorite!"

I gape at her, my frown meeting Layla's the moment Julius's does.

My friend laughs but doesn't clear up for me or for J who Evie's favorite actually is. She simply loops her arm in mine and drags me to the door.

She looks at me, pulls my glasses over my face and gives a curt nod.

"Ready?"

Shaking my hands out, I nod. "Ready."

Julius tugs the door open and out we go.

Flash after flash threatens to blind all of us—thank God for Julius's genius idea of full-face lenses, the side of the sunglasses work as blinders to the lights.

Microphones are shoved in our faces, too many questions to make out a single one shouted into the air, as we work our way to the double doors at the end, where the men in bright-yellow shirts that read *Security* will keep all the crazy on this side.

We step into the event center seconds before the overhead glow fades out, leaving nothing but a bright-white light pointed at the sealed doors in the center of the wall.

The music starts low, slowly growing louder as the bass climbs. The crowd begins to cheer, and the beat of my pulse hums with pride at the sound.

Just like that, the doors are thrown open, a hyped-up Willie and Drew flying through, whipping towels over their heads in a helicopter motion, as they lead the main event contender toward the center.

Several seconds go by before he comes into view, and when he does, my smile spreads. I cup my mouth and shout, but I don't need to.

He looks right at me.

Right where he knew I'd be waiting, front row center.

He winks, his lips twitching into a small curve as he steps forward, goes through a quick check, and then he's in the ring—his first fight as a number-one contender.

He wins tonight, he gets a title, something he should have had to work years for, yet earned in less than one. Sure, the originally planned fighter didn't make weight, and they asked him sort of last minute, but who cares! It's a million-dollar contract, win or lose, and if he wins?!

I couldn't even fathom the thought, so I made him promise not to tell me.

At first, we couldn't believe the title holder agreed to put his belt on the line, but he did what everyone has done to Crew Taylor since he was a boy.

He underestimated him, and so the current champ took the fight.

Now, my man will prove to him, as he has all others, what a mistake that is.

He's about to brawl with a beast, and he *will* lose.

Plugging in my earbuds to drown out the crowd, I smile at the nonchalance of the man I get to call mine, wait for the two to touch gloves, and close my eyes to make a wish.

Crew floats around the ring, circling, taking small jabs and waiting for his opportunity to strike. One punch is all he needs, and after taking a few himself, he finds it, sooner than even I expected, an impressive thirty seconds left in the first round.

Julius pulls out my earbuds with a wink, and Drew shows up at my left, tugging on my hand until I'm at the cage.

I curl my fingers into the chain-link fence coated in black vinyl, grinning up at Crew as Willie wipes his chest with a towel and tugs a *Sanchez Sangria and Brews* T-shirt and hat over his head—of course the friend plug is a must in an opportunity like this, millions of people watch these pay-per-view fights. It's a shock Willie still makes time to be Crew's main man with how his and Layla's business is booming. But he did hire a team to help him run the place.

The TV personality climbs inside the ring for questions, but Crew steals the mic, taking a few steps away from him, and looks out over the roaring arena—knowing his upbringing and the hardships of life he faced, Crew was an overnight favorite for those in love with the sport. Everyone loves to see a man they can relate to accomplish more than they dare to dream about achieving.

"This night means a lot to my family and me," he begins, the crowd going wild, and I bounce on my feet. "And as much as a fight, let alone a win, against a badass motherfucker like Delacruz is, it has nothing to do with what just happened here."

His eyes find mine through the gaps of the cage, and a long exhale whooshes into the mic.

"See, one year ago today, my family faced something I couldn't protect them from, and we lost someone we loved." Crew licks his lips, facing the crowd again. "He was a special man, a brother to me when I couldn't even be one for my own blood." He looks to Drew for a moment. "His name was Memphis Franco and he—" Crew drops the mic, looking off a moment before bringing it right back. "He was my best friend, but I, uh, I let a lot of things go unsaid for a long time, and when he died in my arms, regret like you wouldn't believe hit me like a fucking truck. I didn't get the chance to tell Memphis what he meant to me and now I never will."

Tears slip from my eyes, my gaze soft on the man in front of me.

This year has been hard for all of us, but together, we've pushed through, letting go of the bad and remembering the good alongside my parents, who moved closer to us after Memphis was laid to rest. There weren't a whole lot of people who came out to celebrate my brother's life, but everyone he loved was there and that's all that mattered.

Nothing hurts anymore, he had whispered that night, and I hold on to that when the grief gets too great, as it does. Usually when we least expect it, but I find comfort in his last words.

My brother is in a place where darkness can no longer find him, and peace can hold his hand.

Crew clears his throat. "I think about how things were left a lot, about time and how we waste it. Thoughts and feelings and how we hide them for some fucked-up reason we're convinced matters but probably makes no sense." Crew allows the mic to lower a bit, and when it comes back to his lips, gone is the sadness that weighed his words, a smirk and teasing fire now replacing it. "That's a mistake I'll never make again, so baby, my Sweets . . ." He makes a show of looking at me. "Get that ass in here."

Suddenly, I'm lifted off the ground, a sharp squeal leaving me as I lock onto the bodies beneath me—Julius and Willie, who I hadn't even seen leave the ring.

They carry me like a queen on a throne up the four short stairs and lower my heels to the floor until I'm standing right in front of Crew, in the center of the octagon.

Screams and shouts and cheers surround us, drowning out my own thoughts and confusion as I laugh nervously, leaning into Crew's chest.

"What are you doing?" I mouth, but he only winks.

Layla appears at his left side, Evie in her arms, Willie joining her, Drew and Julius on his right.

Crew's arms are wrapped around me, and I stare up at his handsome face.

"This girl right here," he begins again. "She knows I love her, that I'd do any damn thing she asks me to, but what she doesn't know is that she's going to marry me, soon."

My body goes stiff, and while he doesn't look at me, his smile grows. Crew speaks louder this time.

"Wanna know what else she don't know?" he teases, and the crowd booms. He chuckles again, licking his lips. "She's got the ring on right now, but she won't find it until her sweet tooth kicks in and she tries to eat her favorite piece of jewelry."

My brows snap together with confusion, my mind racing as Crew steps back and looks down at me. It clicks then and I gasp, my hands flying to my candy necklace and I swiftly pull it over my head.

Crew laughs loudly as I bring it to my face, but I don't have to search.

It hangs longer than the rest, shining in the light of the ring.

A white gold band, a single, simple sapphire in the center.

A blue sapphire to match my blue shoes.

To match my new office at the bar.

To match my brother's eyes.

To match the date added to Crew's chest.

The month and day etched on the inside of the ring shaking in my grasp, a second date beside it.

My eyes find his, blurry and leaking.

Crew's gaze is soft, and right on time, Willie's got the wraps cut from around Crew's wrists, and he takes my face in his hands.

"You made me an offer that day," he whispers for only me. "Today, I make you one." The mic is held in front of him by his brother. "I want to keep you, Davis Franco. Let me." Crew's eyes pierce mine. "Deal?"

I bite into the candy necklace, tearing the stretchy string and sending little candy rings all over, the one I wanted falling right into my palm. I press it to his chest, right over the first date that changed our lives forever, linking the three together.

Stretching up as tall as I can get, I meet his lips with mine, smiling as I say, "Deal."

Epilogue
Five Years Later

Davis

Winding my hair up, I loop a hair band around it, high-fiving Layla as she slides up beside me, having done the same.

Julius walks backward toward the entrance, grinning as he shouts, "Doors are opening in three, two . . ."

Excited shouts and shrieks instantly fill the space, my smile spreading impossibly wider.

It takes a few seconds for our entry team to get things moving, and then duos and trios, and more are rushing through the short hall to get the first glimpses of the dance floor, a thick plexiglass over a layer of blue and purple glitters, the shimmers reflecting along the deep-navy walls.

Within minutes, the club is full, my dad's eyes widening as he comes around the corner, his tool belt still hanging around his waist.

"Wow." He looks at us with a grin. "Looks like it's an overnight hit."

"Having mega hot, famous husbands will do that." Layla winks, passing him his keys from beneath the bar.

"I guess so." He chuckles, his keen eyes moving from Julius to Drew, and every other male employee we have in here tonight. "You girls sure you'll be okay? I can stay until the boys' plane gets in, no problem."

"Problem." I laugh. "Mom called twice already, and said Evie is asking when Grandpa G. will be home."

Layla smiles, shaking her head as she starts pouring shots for a group of girls. Her daughter has claimed my dad as her best friend, thank goodness for that since his own grandson has chosen his grandma as his. Crew says as Max gets older, he'll make the swap from grandma to grandpa, and it's adorable he felt he had to explain all the reasons why it would happen, as if my dad was worried or sad because of it. He constantly reminds him how he'll need his grandpa to help teach him to play ball and change a tire, and all the other things my dad taught Crew, that Crew wants my dad to carry on and teach our son.

My dad only smiles, knowingly watching the love the little guy has for his gram. Not to say he doesn't pout. He does, especially when we go over for Sunday dinners and Max reaches for my mom first, but my two-year-old takes after his mom, as my dad's learned—his attention can be bought with treats.

My phone vibrates in my pocket, and I pull it out, glancing at the screen, showing it to him. "There she is again." I smile.

"All right, I better get out of here before this place is too packed for me to move. Let me know if that door jams again, and I'll be back to fix it."

"I will, thanks, Dad."

"Love you. Good luck, girls." He begins to walk away. "Stay behind the bar!"

"We know!" we sing-song.

Minutes later, we're left with no room to talk. The DJ is slaying, and the crowd is swaying.

It wasn't ideal—for Crew and Willie, that is—that the grand opening of our new club was set for the same night as their newest fighter's debut fight.

But us girls took over operations on both the bar and brewery three years ago, combining both businesses under one umbrella and becoming fifty-fifty partners in both, while the men worked their asses off getting their new MMA training gym off the ground. They now have seven fighters signed, and dozens of others attending an array of classes they offer.

Life is busy, full, and more than I could have ever dreamed it would be.

The night blows by, me and Layla using our bartender school skills to make a show out of serving our customers.

When an entirely new type of ruckus reaches our ears, Layla and I meet each other's smirks.

Boys are home.

Crew

There's something carnal about walking into a place created, designed, and run by the woman you love that makes you want to puff your chest out in honor of being hers.

And I'm nothing less than honored to be the man behind the brilliant fucking woman who does more in a day than I could in a week.

My gorgeous glowing woman, tucked behind a bar, flipping bottles into the air and spinning with a laugh as she does it.

And I thought she wouldn't want to be a part of this world. The girl fucking doubled down on it and created something better, dove in headfirst and swam deep. Her ideas are endless, and while I've tried to convince her to revamp Sideways Sippin', even back during the rebuild six years ago that took us five fucking months, she refused to make any changes to what I had created outside of ones that increase profit. She wanted the place to remain the reminder, should I ever need one, that I can do whatever I put my mind to, even when it feels fucking impossible.

Still don't think I deserve the woman who's now my wife, but I sure as fuck love how deeply she disagrees, and there's no doubt in my mind she knows what she means to me.

I remind her every chance I get. With words . . . and in plenty of other wicked ways.

Thank fuck for grandparents and babysitters.

Speaking of babysitters.

My Sweets thinks she's slick, that I'm oblivious to what she's trying to hide.

She couldn't be more wrong.

I know my girl, I know her body, and *I know* there's a tiny little human growing inside it again.

A sibling for Max.

Another friend for Evie.

A second niece or nephew for Drew to look out for.

For Memphis to watch over.

Sidling up to the bar, I lean against it, Willie having already hopped over to wrap himself around his wife, but I play stranger, and Davis bites her lip, desire building in her pretty brown eyes.

"What's good here?" I cock my head.

"Depends." She plays along, coyly shrugging and refusing to give me her full attention but winking at the girl she passes a Mango Micha to—Willie's newest creation come to life. "What do you like?"

My smirk is slow. "Something real . . . *sweet*."

My girl's eyes dilate, her tongue sliding along her bottom lip. "I think I've got just the thing."

She looks left, jerking her head and Jess appears with a grin, sliding right in as my wife slips off.

She doesn't look back, so I listen like a good fucking boy, and follow her through the slim hallway, past the employee bathroom and up the half flight of stairs leading to the large flat consisting of the entire top floor—an identical addition the girls also added on at the bar and brewery.

A mini apartment of sorts, one corner set up with a dual-sized desk and file cabinets, the rest bright and blinding with every color of the rainbow, games, and toys, and snacks and anything else our littles might need on any given day.

But it's the cabinet in the front corner my girl walks straight to, opens, and tugs at.

A twin-size bed comes down from inside and she wastes no time, spinning and falling back onto it, her brown eyes on mine.

"Come here, husband."

"On my way, wife." I've already got my shoes off, my shirt gone in the next second, pants following and then I'm settled between the softest of thighs.

She wraps her legs around my body, tugging me closer until my cock is testing at her panties, her skirt allowing the easiest of access.

"You wear this for me?" I fist the pink suede, pushing it higher.

"You know I did."

"My baby knew I'd fuck her the second I stepped inside, didn't she?" I lick her tits, pressed tight against her tank top, but hidden beneath the stretchy material. "Knew I'd need inside this pussy." I slide my cock inside in a slow, painful push. "That I missed it. Missed the way it squeezes my cock." I bite at her collarbone, and she moans into the air. "Squeeze my cock, baby," I whisper, and she listens.

Doing exactly what I say when I say it.

"Good, baby. Just like that."

Later I'll take her over the bar, fuck her while she stares at our slick bodies in the mirror behind it, but for now . . .

My mouth finds hers, and I kiss her hard, my fingers pressing along her sides until I reach her neck.

I slowly pull the candy necklace from her skin, taking her wrists in mine and holding them over her head. I wrap the stretchy thing around her wrists, smirking as her lips part, her hips pressing up into mine, begging me to move.

My eyes flick to hers, narrowing. "Leave them there."

"Yes, boss."

My groan is deep and I pull back, slamming into her until the bed shakes, her body bouncing, so I tear her top down, her left tit popping free.

My teeth close around the pebbled peak and her back bows, her moans growing to whimpers, her legs stretching out straight into the fucking air as she wills me deeper and deeper.

Bringing my knees up under me, I hike her hips up, holding them in the air as I pound into her.

My head falls back, my growls filling the air. "Fuck, Sweets, this pussy's so good. Missed it. Missed you."

"Yes," she pants. "Missed you."

"You missed my cock. Say it."

She whimpers, her walls clamping over my dick and making it flex on command. "I missed your perfect cock."

I grin, dipping down to claim her lips and she sinks her teeth into my bottom one, refusing to let me go, yanking her hands free and sending tiny candies flying around the room. She's adjusting our position, her ass now in my lap, legs still in the air behind us, hands tugging on my hair as she cries out, over and fucking over.

This position allows me deeper, and with every thrust, her G-spot is poked and prodded. Teased, so I take one of her hands and place it over her clit. Instantly she starts to rub, her body grinding along mine, desperate.

"Come for me, baby. Milk my cock. Take what's yours and give me what I own."

She nearly screams, her teeth biting into my chest, right over my left pec and I swear she draws blood.

She pulses around me, her pussy convulsing, her body going limp, so I dip her back, lay her flat and pull out, swiftly bringing my dick to her lips.

I run the head across the bottom one and her eyes flutter open, hunger darkening the brown before me. "Suck me dry, mama."

My voice is gruff, rough. My cum *right there* waiting to be claimed.

My baby doesn't make me wait.

She opens, lures me between her lips and sucks herself off me while drawing the cum from my cock until I'm dripping down her chin. Her tongue slips out, lapping me up and I slide back down her body, pressing into her once more.

"God," she croaks. "Again. Now."

"Don't be greedy, bitch!" Layla's voice reaches us and we freeze. "It's our turn!"

The two of us lock eyes, laughing and slowly force ourselves from the bed.

Davis makes swift work of fixing her outfit while I pull mine back on, and then I take her in my arms.

"I love you, Sweets."

"I love you, too, my handsome husband."

I kiss her, dropping to my knees in front of her, and her eyes twinkle knowingly. "And I love the shit out of you, little one." I kiss her belly, slowly rising to my feet.

Tears pool in her eyes and she leans into me. "Are you happy?" she whispers with a smile, already knowing the answer.

Fixing the cherry clips in her hair, I lift her chin, bringing her lips to mine. "I never knew life could be so good, mama, and I promise, it only gets better from here."

Her smile is radiant, and she wraps her arms around my neck, kissing me fiercely.

My hands tether around her body, squeezing and she jumps up, grinding her—

"Do not even think about it, asshole!" Willie laughs through the door. "Our. Turn."

Chuckling, we pull away, and I smack her ass. "Come on, Sweets. Let's go rock the night, so we can get home before our little man wakes up in the morning."

Davis slides her hand in mine, and we head downstairs.

What started as love let go turned into a deal gone rogue and here we are.

Me and the girl of my dreams.

Us and our boy.

A growing family.

A tight unit.

A complete and total fucking honor I'll spend my life fighting for, protecting. Loving.

Davis changed my life the day she passed me her little essay from across the cheap iron table at that café.

It wasn't long after that I made a deal with my own damn self.

Davis would spend her life cherished, loved . . . and thoroughly fucked.

And my girl? She gives as good as she gets.

Tonight, we'll work side by side.

Early morning, we'll make our way home to our son.

And every day after, I'll continue to honor the deal I made with myself years ago.

I'll make sure my family knows they're my entire world.

All I need.

All I ever wanted.

My dreams—the ones I didn't dare to have—come true.

I'll spend eternity changing the way the Taylor name is spoken of.

My kids will be loved.

My wife worshiped.

And my life?

More than any man could ever ask for.

They say no family is perfect.

I beg to fucking differ, but tonight, once the club closes, it'll be my wife who begs, her banging body bent over the bar.

Yeah, life is fucking good, and its lessons only get better . . .

Thank you so much for reading Davis and Crew's story!

Don't you love the badass growly man who falls for the sweet, quirky woman?!

This one was a lot of fun for me. You guys know I never write the same style books. Mine always vary in angst, grit, and emotional damage LOL.

But this came to me during a time of loss in my life and allowed me the escape I needed to get through.

Pain comes to us all in many different ways, and with this book, I was able to infuse some of mine in a way that helped me refocus. I hope you loved this story as much as I loved telling it.

Xoxo,
Meagan.

Are you or someone you know struggling with addiction?

Call the free, confidential *Substance Abuse and mental Health Services Administration* hotline @ 1-800-662-4357

Stay in touch with Meagan Brandy:
@MeaganBrandyAuthor
@MeaganBrandy
@MeaganBrandyAuthor
@MeaganBrandyBooks
www.meaganbrandy.com

Acknowledgements

To my papa, who wanted to read my books, but was successfully scared away by my aunt Lisa with words that made me hide my face in my hands! Thank you for showing us what being a good man means and for loving us endlessly. I'll forever miss you.

Rebecca, as always, your hard work and dedication to helping me reach the point of pride in my stories. I don't know how I would do it without your help and support.

Melissa! My personal ass-whooper-into-shaper! Never leave me and I'll do my best not to release on your birthday anymore LOL.

Ellie and team at My Brother's Editor, thank you so much for always working with me on such tight deadlines. Maybe one day my shit will be together.

Lisa! Thank you for jumping on as a beta last minute and working so fast! Your ideas helped tie the story together even more seamlessly. I'm super grateful you're awesome like that.

Bloggers and early readers!! You guys are so such an invaluable part of the process! Thank you so much for taking time out of your busy schedules to meet my newest couple and help spread the word. I hope their journey was as satisfying to you as it was me.

And lastly, to my readers!!!! YOU GUYS MAKE THIS POSSIBLE!

Thank you so much for sticking with me and allowing me to change my style of stories with each release and being here for everything that comes next. THANK YOU so much for taking this ride with me.